DAVE HOLLISTER
HEARD THE BURST OF AK FIRE
IN THE ALLEY.

Aware that the private was armed with an M14, he shouted to Hassen, "Sounds like the Maggit ran into trouble. Cover the wall!" His words were lost in the explosion of a grenade thrown from the corner of the billet. Bleeding from dozens of needlelike shrapnel punctures in his arms and shoulders, Dave grabbed a grenade and hurled it at the corner. The grenade ricocheted off the billet and exploded harmlessly. A VC sapper cradling a homemade bomb in his arms leaped around the corner and charged.

The VC's intent was clear. Scrambling out of the pit Dave dove in the hole with Hassen, who was already taking aim. "Cut the bastard down, Hassen! Shoot or we'll go up with him!" Hassen froze. Pounding the giant mess sergeant in the kidney Dave screamed, "Shoot! Shoot, you fat son of a bitch!" At the very last second, Hassen squeezed off a long burst. The high velocity rounds took the VC in the stomach. His guts spilled out on the bomb and he stopped in his tracks. Hugging the wall Dave covered his ears with both hands. When the ten-pound charge exploded, it gouged a deep crater and the VC disintegrated.

Before the dirt and debris stopped falling, Dave was out of the hole. Halfway to the mortar pit . . .

THE
PAWNS

FORREST EARL TODD

POCKET BOOKS

New York   London   Toronto   Sydney   Tokyo

An *Original* Publication of POCKET BOOKS

POCKET BOOKS, a division of Simon & Schuster Inc.
1230 Avenue of the Americas, New York, NY 10020

ISBN: 0-671-66815-3

First Pocket Books printing December 1989

10 9 8 7 6 5 4 3 2 1

POCKET and colophon are registered trademarks of
Simon & Schuster Inc.

Printed in the U.S.A.

In memory of Samuel Donald McClary and all the others who died in Vietnam whether they believed in the cause or not.

Acknowledgment

The author thanks Betty Todd and Nancy Davis without whose encouragement and assistance the writing of *The Pawns* would not have occurred.

Chapter I

AMBUSH

In a gloomy, sandbagged bunker near the center of a central South Vietnam border camp two American Special Forces sergeants sat at a makeshift table playing gin. Both men were stripped to the waist, their skin deeply bronzed from long hours under the hot Vietnamese sun. The smaller of the two was Sergeant First Class David Hollister, the detachment engineer. His thick yellow hair was long, covering his ears, and together with his gunmetal gray eyes and smooth leathery skin, it was difficult to determine his age. He could have been forty or, just as easily, thirty. Even with boots on he stood only five feet ten, yet his deceptively slender frame carried a full one hundred and eighty pounds.

The other man was Master Sergeant John C. Rictor, the detachment intelligence sergeant. A slightly crooked nose and thin scars above dark piercing eyes hinted at some long-forgotten violence. In his early thirties, Rictor's black hair was already streaked with gray. He had the shoulders of a fighter, and his six-foot frame carried its two hundred pounds with ease.

The payday stakes gin game was a never-ending pastime. For more than ten minutes neither Rictor nor Dave had spoken. Only half-concentrating, Rictor drew and discarded mechanically. His mind had drifted back to Fort Bragg, North Carolina, and stateside duty following the Korean War. God, had he been bored with that day-to-day, spit-and-polish soldiering. When his enlistment was up, he'd taken a discharge and gone back to school. He had been determined to stick it out, but the Korean experience had left him with very little in common with his fellow students. By the time he was twenty-one, he'd met a girl, gotten married and fathered a son. He tried to fit into civilian harness but it had not worked. He began spending most of his time, when not in school, carousing, drinking and raising hell. He took up boxing and developed good hands. Those quick hands, combined with a low tolerance for assholes, made him well-known to the local police and judges. He woke up one morning and realized leaving the army had been a mistake. He reenlisted that same day and volunteered for Europe.

During the ensuing six years, he completed Special Forces training and served two short tours of duty in Vietnam. When his enlistment expired, his wife argued that they had a young son to raise and she wanted him home. No one would fault him for leaving the service. Yet she had not understood that he had to reenlist. He genuinely cared for her and loved his son. He couldn't have cared less what other people thought but had expected her to understand. He was a combat soldier. That's what he did best. If there was a war, he needed to be there. Aware that the decision would cost him his marriage, he reenlisted and volunteered for Vietnam.

His attention once more back on the game, Rictor drew a card and discarded. Nodding with satisfaction he spread his cards on the table. "Gin."

Dave grunted his disgust and tossed in his cards. "I've had it!" He cast a glance at the score book and asked, "How much you figure I owe you?"

Rictor busied himself collecting the cards. "You mean this game or all-total?"

"Everything I've lost since we left the 'B' Detachment."

Rictor yawned and reached for his canteen. "I'd need an adding machine to figure that out." After a long drink he set the canteen on the table and toyed with the cap. "How would you like to get off the hook?"

Dave was curious but cautious. "I feel a screwing coming. What's your proposition?"

A grin tugged at the corners of Rictor's mouth. "I'm willing to call it even for that Swedish-K you picked up on our last operation."

Dave shook his head with disbelief. "Rictor, you're a no-good bastard! You know damn well how I got that gun. If that fuckin' Charlie (Viet Cong) hadn't run out of ammo when he did, I'd be dead and roasting in hell."

Rictor shrugged and picked up the canteen. "Just thought I'd ask. Seems like a fair offer to me."

Dave held up his right hand and made a gesture with the middle finger. "This is all I've got for you. Before I give up that gun, I'll put on a wig and give you a hand job with the whole damn team watching."

Unable to keep a straight face, Rictor turned his head. "I'll wait. It's just a matter of time. I wonder how you're going to look in a wig."

"Well, you can wait till hell freezes over!" Dave growled.

Rictor cocked his head toward a framed doorway in the sandbag wall which led to the radio room and held up his hand for silence. The broken beep of a wireless radio signal was faint but unmistakable. Rictor got up from the table and headed for the radio room. "I'll give Terry a hand decoding the message. You get Biggerstaff."

Dave nodded. "I hope that's the goddamn order to move. After three days of fuckin' around and waiting, I'm ready to get the hell out of here."

The wireless message was lengthy. Rictor watched as Terry quickly and effortlessly transposed the rapid flow of dots and dashes into letters and numerals. The radio signal ended abruptly. Terry rested his pencil, touched the signal key and tapped out an acknowledgment that the message had been received. Finally he hit the radio off switch, removed the headset and reached for the codebook. Rictor stepped forward. "I'll give you a hand decoding."

Terry made no effort to hide his irritation. "You figure I can't handle it?"

"As a matter of fact you're great, but I'm in a hurry. Slide over."

Terry cursed and moved to make room.

Ten minutes later Rictor was studying the message when the murmur of voices announced the arrival of Dave and Captain Biggerstaff, the team commander.

Terry snorted. "Here comes Biggerstaff. I'll bet that fat ass has got a ration of crap for all of us."

Terry's reference to the captain brought a grin to Rictor's face. Biggerstaff was a huge hulk of a man, three inches taller than Rictor and overweight. A former enlisted man, he was boisterous, authoritative and inflexible. Generally no amount of reasoning would alter his thinking. Rictor had learned that the best way to deal with the captain was to suggest an idea in a manner that made him think it was his own.

Biggerstaff stalked into the room with his hand out-stretched. "Let's see the message."

Rictor handed the message to Biggerstaff and turned to Dave who had stopped at the door. "Where's Zung?"

Dave touched a match to the unlit cigarette dangling from his lips. "He's over at the Vietnamese Special Forces CP (command post). Seems like the Vietnamese commander got a message that there's a strong Viet Cong buildup along route nineteen east of here. The captain left Zung over there to find out what's up."

Rictor grunted. "The Vietnamese are not likely to share any intelligence with us."

Dave was annoyed. "Fuck that! Are we moving to Qui Nhon in the morning or not?"

Rictor nodded but before he could respond Biggerstaff said, "Listen up, we've got orders to move. We depart here in the morning at ten hundred hours with that resupply convoy Shay told us about. We'll stop off in Qui Nhon just long enough for an intelligence briefing then head for Binh Hue District head-quarters." Biggerstaff lowered his voice, "The raid has taken on a higher priority. Group headquarters has unconfirmed re-ports that Charlie is moving enough troops and supplies into the Highlands to cut the whole fuckin' country from east to west along route nineteen."

The canvas door flap rustled and a slender Vietnamese in his midtwenties appeared. Biggerstaff bellowed, "Zung, I told you to stay at the Vietnamese CP and see what you could find out!"

The young interpreter was not intimidated. "Captain, you also told me if I learned anything to come and report to you. Do you want my report or do you want me to go back to the command post."

Biggerstaff cursed. "Don't get smart!"

Suppressing a grin Rictor said, "Spit it out, Zung. What did you learn?"

Zung turned to Rictor. "The Vietnamese commander is very excited. He has reliable information that a large Viet Cong main force unit is moving into the Mang Yang Pass east of here."

Biggerstaff nodded with satisfaction. "That's consistent with group headquarter's report. If we don't get out of here tomorrow, the goddamn road will probably be cut and we could be stalled here for . . ."

The door canvas rustled again and a short, almost petite, form appeared in the doorway. It was Shay, the camp's weapon sergeant. He addressed himself to Dave, "Hey, Hollister, I hear you people are moving with my supply convoy in the morning."

Dave nodded. "And not a minute too soon to suit me."

Shay faked a hurt expression. "Well, ain't that a fine fuckin' howdy do. I came over here to show a little hospitality by inviting you people up to the team house to get drunk tonight, and you act like you're anxious to leave our little piece of paradise. You got no class, Dave, no fuckin' class."

Dave laughed. "Yeah, and I heard you were being assigned to the Pentagon as protocol officer. The only good news I've heard since we got here is that we're leaving, and you've got some drinking whiskey." Dave stepped toward the door. "As a matter of fact I'll walk over to the team house with you and see if I can get a sample."

In no mood to be drawn into a bullshit session with Biggerstaff, Rictor decided to escape. He caught Terry's eye. "You and Zung come on. Let's go with Dave." So as not to be too obvious he turned to Biggerstaff. "You coming, Captain?"

Biggerstaff shook his head. "I'm going to sack out for a while then go over to the CP."

As Rictor stepped outside Biggerstaff called after him, "You people get as drunk as you want to but in the morning I expect you to be clearheaded and ready to move on time."

Rictor waved that he had heard and kept moving.

Shortly before 1000 hours the next morning, Rictor eased the three-quarter-ton truck in behind the last of ten convoy trucks lined up bumper to bumper near the camp's main gate. He shut the engine down, stretched and reached for a cigarette. Standing in the truck's open cargo compartment, Dave shaded his eyes from the bright midmorning sun. "My old buddy Shay is right on time," he said. "I see his Irish ass up front by the lead vehicle. He looks like he's got one helluva hangover, but apparently he's ready to move out."

Rictor shook his head. "Considering the amount of bourbon he drank last night and the number of songs he murdered, I'm amazed that he can walk or talk."

Leaning on the truck's pedestal-mounted machine gun for support and clutching his fiery red head with both hands, Terry said, "If he don't feel any better than I do, this convoy may not get moving today."

Biggerstaff, seated next to Rictor in the passenger seat, shifted his massive body and climbed down from the truck. "Rictor, you come with me to coordinate. The rest of you people wait here." He started forward, stopped and looked back. "Don't anybody go wandering off looking for the hair of the dog. That means you, too, Zung." Checking his watch he said, "This show was supposed to be on the road two minutes ago."

Terry grinned but his obvious dislike for the captain crept into his voice. "I think Biggerstaff's forgotten that we're just tagging along with the convoy until we get to Qui Nhon and he ain't running the fuckin' show."

Sergeant Shay and a young lieutenant were studying a map

spread on the hood of the lead truck and apparently did not hear Biggerstaff and Rictor approaching. Shay said, "I don't give a good fuck what command wants. I agree with you. When we get to the mouth of the Pass we had better dismount and walk through. If we get hit bunched up on these trucks, we've had the course."

The lieutenant looked up and spotted Biggerstaff. "Good morning, Captain, glad to have you along."

Biggerstaff made the necessary introductions and got right to the point. "When are we moving out?"

The lieutenant picked up his map. "We're ready now. Just as soon as I get you briefed, we're outta here."

Biggerstaff nodded and reached for the map. Shay moved close to Rictor and lowered his voice. "Partner, I feel like shit. I must be getting too old for these all-night stands."

Rictor grinned. "You don't look any worse than Dave or Terry. As a matter of fact I wouldn't want to look in a mirror myself. Not changing the subject but yesterday I was under the impression that we were straphanging with a supply convoy headed for Qui Nhon. You must have a couple hundred troops on these trucks. What's up?"

Shay nodded. "They changed my orders. There's a VC (Viet Cong) buildup around the 'A' Detachment camp at the east end of the Pass. The two companies I've got on the trucks are going over to reinforce."

Rictor was mildly surprised. "That camp is under operational control of my 'B' Detachment. Wonder why they're bringing you folks in?"

Shay shrugged. "Beats the hell outta me. Apparently the senior MAC-V (Military Advisory Command Vietnam) advisor at II Corps recommended it, and the 'C' Detachment commander agreed. There might be a problem though if Charlie plans to attack the 'A' camp. You can bet your beer ration he's got the Pass ambushed. Our orders are to convoy through, but the lieutenant and I think the loaded trucks are death traps. We're gonna dismount at the mouth of the Pass and make the next ten miles on foot with the trucks following."

Rictor nodded. "Makes good sense to me."

Shay scribbled some numbers on a piece of paper. "I'm

glad you guys are coming along. With you bringing up the rear, it gives us a little security we hadn't counted on. The lieutenant and I will be in the second truck from the front." Holding out the paper he said, "Put your radio on this frequency and we'll stay in touch."

Biggerstaff barked, "Let's go, Rictor. We're moving out."

Once outside the camp the convoy picked up route #19 and headed east. Very rapidly the terrain changed from flatlands to rolling hills. The convoy wound like a snake through the foothills and twisted its way into a jagged mountain range. The grade became steeper by the moment. Rictor had geared the truck down but was having a tough time maintaining the fifty-yard convoy interval. He rounded a sharp curve and stood on the brake pedal to avoid crashing into the rear of the next truck which had stopped and was off-loading troops.

As Rictor silently cursed the Montagnard driver for the abrupt stop, he let his eyes scan the horizon and the gaping twisting trench that slashed its way through the mountain range. They had reached the Mang Yang Pass. Dave let out a low whistle. "I've flown over this son of a bitch a bunch of times. From the air it looks tough but from down here it's awesome."

Terry said, "I read somewhere that back in the fifties the French lost a ten-thousand-man force to the Viet Minh in this Pass."

The radio crackled and Dave held up his hand for silence. "Knock it off!"

Shay's voice came through loud and clear. "This is where we start earning our money, boys. We're going to hump it from here. You guys in the back ride herd on the trucks. Don't let them straggle."

Dave picked up the radio handset and pushed the talk button. "Roger that, Shay. You guys keep your heads down."

Biggerstaff was already dismounting. "Rictor, you drive. Terry, you man the machine gun. Dave, you take the left flank. Zung can carry the radio and stay over here to the right with me."

"If someone else wants to drive, I'll walk," said Rictor. There were no volunteers. Rictor slipped the truck into gear and for the next hour the convoy moved at a snail's pace up the steep grade and around hairpin curves. The Montagnard foot troops and trucks became strung out for more than a half mile. Concerned that the truck's clutch would not last, Rictor concentrated on his driving. His concentration was broken by the distant drone of chopper engines.

Looking back toward the camp Dave pointed at four helicopter gunships armed with rockets and machine guns overhead. "Looks like we're getting some overhead air cover."

Terry pointed farther west at an unarmed transport helicopter. "Here comes a slick, too. Wonder what that dude's doing out here?"

The radio came alive and the convoy ground to a halt. Zung passed the handset to Biggerstaff, who monitored a lengthy transmission. The slick joined formation with the gunships, all orbiting over the convoy at a thousand feet. Biggerstaff took the handset from his ear. "The MAC-V colonel that cranked up this operation is in that slick. He's the new deputy corps advisor and this is his first operation. He just told that young lieutenant up front to mount these troops on the trucks and get his ass moving. The lieutenant's putting up a helluva argument." Biggerstaff put the handset back to his ear. A moment later he said, "That brown bar lieutenant's got balls. He's still trying to make his case."

After another lengthy transmission Biggerstaff shook his head. "The lieutenant just lost the argument. The colonel has taken direct command and given him an order to mount the troops. The lieutenant's gonna do it but he refuses to take the responsibility. I'd hate to be in his shoes when we get clear of this Pass."

Dave snorted. "How would you like to be in his shoes at the front of this convoy?"

Biggerstaff blushed. "I don't need any crap out of you, Sergeant Hollister."

Rictor said, "Knock it off, Dave! Everybody get mounted."

Within five minutes the convoy was moving again. As the truck strained to reach the summit the walls of the Pass became steeper and more threatening. From behind the machine gun Terry broke the strained silence. "Man, you could hide a division in this goddamned elephant grass."

Rictor studied the head-high, weedlike grass that lined both sides of the road and mentally speculated as to how effective the gunships would be if the convoy was hit. In the event of an ambush he felt certain that Charlie would have support weapons on the high ridge line. He noted the lack of room to maneuver in the narrow Pass and concluded that if they were hit, the gunships would be useless and might just as well be on the flight strip at Qui Nhon. He also saw that the slick carrying the MAC-V colonel had departed the area.

At the Pass summit, Rictor shifted to low gear to make the thousand-yard downhill run that lay ahead. Halfway down the mountain he saw a civilian bus as it rounded a curve and approached the convoy from the east. Biggerstaff let out a sigh. "The Pass must be clear if civilian traffic is getting through."

Rictor nodded. "Maybe, but something's got to give. That bus can't get by these trucks unless somebody leaves the road." He watched the bus draw within fifty yards of the lead truck. The driver gave no indication of giving way. Realization of what was about to happen flashed through Rictor's mind. He yelled to Biggerstaff, "Ambush!" His warning was masked by an explosion as the bus disintegrated in a ball of orange flame. Screaming civilians, some of them burning, were thrown in all directions. The smoking remains of the bus completely blocked the road. The Montagnard drivers had been caught by surprise, too, and the troop trucks closed on each other, the convoy slowly stalling. The lead truck took a rocket hit in the side and exploded. Troops pouring off the trapped trucks were caught in a withering hail of automatic fire, most cut down as they touched the ground. A line of Viet Cong sappers charged out of the elephant grass, throwing grenades and sachel charges under the trucks.

Rictor's reaction was swift. The instant the bus exploded he shifted to reverse and attempted to back out of the killing zone. Terry was working the machine gun and laid a steady stream of fire along the flank of the helpless trucks. Dave and

Zung fired point-blank into the elephant grass but their fire was masked by small arms rounds ricocheting off the truck.

Biggerstaff yelled, "I've got Shay on the radio. He's hit and the lieutenant's dead. He wants us to get clear and work the air support." Keeping low, Rictor moved the truck backward at a rapid clip. He had put two hundred yards between the truck and the burning convoy when a rocket ripped off the front wheels and flipped the truck on its side. Rictor was thrown clear. Landing on his back in the elephant grass he groaned and rolled over. Nothing seemed to be broken. Using the overturned truck as a shield, he crawled back to the road. Cut and bruised but otherwise unhurt, Terry and Dave were attempting to free Biggerstaff, who was pinned in the truck. The obese captain cursed with every breath as he struggled to get free.

Dazed and bleeding from facial lacerations, Zung staggered out of the elephant grass and made his way back to the truck. Clutching his broken left arm, he kneeled down next to Rictor. Biggerstaff broke free from the truck and tumbled headlong into the grass. Small arms fire grew more intense, and movement on the far side of the road told Rictor that Charlie was moving in for the kill.

Terry and Dave had taken up positions near the front of the truck and were returning fire. Having lost his rifle, Rictor used the truck for cover as he fired his pistol point-blank at the VC on the other side of the road.

Biggerstaff crawled out of the grass and located the radio. Aware that their position was untenable he yelled, "This is suicide! Follow me. I'm going to try for the high ground." He eased off the road and was immediately swallowed up by the elephant grass. Rictor grabbed Zung by the belt and dragged him along. As they clawed their way toward the ridge overlooking the killing zone, Dave and Terry laid down a base of fire to discourage the pursuing VC.

The radio had been damaged in the rocket attack. At a covered position on the ridge Biggerstaff stopped to attempt to repair it. Rictor crawled out on a ledge next to Dave and lay belly down watching the slaughter taking place below.

Viet Cong swarmed over the trucks, policing up equipment

and stripping the dead. Resistance had dwindled to sporadic bursts of fire as the VC found wounded Montagnards hiding in the grass. Dave snapped, "When are them goddamn gunships going to get involved?"

Rictor shifted his attention to the gunships. They were returning fire on VC support positions along the top of the cliffs. "My guess is they don't know where to attack and they're not going to strike close to those trucks without orders."

Terry eased up next to Rictor. Pointing he said, "Look at that bunch of Charlies surrounding the second truck. I think they may have found Shay and the lieutenant."

Rictor crawled over to Biggerstaff. "Any luck with the radio?"

Biggerstaff shook his head. "Get Terry over here, I need help."

Rictor said, "Let me use your field glasses. I lost mine." He returned to the ledge and sent Terry to assist Biggerstaff with the radio. Rictor focused the glasses on the second truck and confirmed Terry's suspicion. The lieutenant's nude body lay next to the burning truck and the VC were in the process of stripping Shay.

Rictor made a quick scan of the area looking for friendly survivors. He detected none and decided that if there were any, they were hiding in the grass. He shifted the glasses back to Shay. Cursing softly he spat and handed the glasses to Dave. As soon as Dave focused the field glasses on Shay, his jaw muscles tightened then went slack. He turned to Rictor with tears in his eyes. "The motherfuckers are taking Shay's head! I'm going down there!"

Rictor put out a restraining hand. "Dave, we've got a pistol, two rifles and less than twenty rounds of ammo between the five of us. It won't help Shay for us to commit suicide." After a long moment he felt Dave's shoulder relax.

Dave relented. "Okay, but let's get them goddamn gunships down here and make Charlie pay the price."

Terry called out to Rictor, "The radio's working. Biggerstaff's got the gunships on the horn but they won't strike the kill zone. They're afraid of hitting friendlies."

Rictor crawled across to Biggerstaff. "There ain't no friendlies and Charlie's mutilating the dead. Tell them to strike the fuckin' trucks!"

Biggerstaff shook his head. "I don't have the authority. I'm not in command."

Dave had crawled up next to Rictor. He caught Biggerstaff's eye and held it. His words were half-plea and half-threat. "Captain, there is no command and the bastards took Shay's head. Order the fucking strike!"

Biggerstaff hesitated. He shifted his eyes to Terry then to Rictor. Seeing their expressions of determination he nodded. "I guess I'm the ranking survivor so that oughta put me in command. I wish that MAC-V colonel was still up there. This was his show."

While Biggerstaff was ordering the strike, Rictor and Dave crawled back out on the ledge. The VC were confident the gunships would not strike. They milled around in the open methodically stripping then hacking up the bodies. Rictor watched the four gunships break formation and come in low over the killing zone. Their rockets and machine gun fire chewed up the area around the burning trucks. The VC were caught in the open and took heavy casualties. As the gunships circled for another run the surviving VC scrambled into the grass on both sides of the road.

Dave pointed skyward. "We've got a FAC (Forward Air Controller)."

Rictor glanced up and immediately spotted the small plane above. He knew that with a FAC on station, attack aircraft were on the way. He nudged Dave. "If Charlie stays in that grass, he's gonna get his ass scorched."

Dave nodded. "I hope the Air Force barbecues every son of a bitch in the valley."

Biggerstaff called out, "I've got the FAC on the horn. He's bringing in napalm and wants us to mark our position."

Before Rictor could answer, Dave's frustration spilled out. "Captain, that damn FAC is out of his mind. You mark this position, and every fuckin' Charlie on that ridge will be pouring fire down on us."

Rictor snapped, "Tell the FAC to stay off the north ridge

and we'll take our chances. We don't have anything to mark with anyway."

While Biggerstaff was coordinating, Rictor turned his attention back to the killing zone. The gunships were making another run, and the VC were concentrating their fire from hidden positions in the grass. The third ship in trail was hit by a barrage of small arms fire and veered off to the left. The people on board never had a chance. The chopper hit the canyon wall and exploded in a ball of fire. Rictor cursed. The fourth gunship was hit but managed to clear the Pass. Trailing smoke, it turned east headed back toward Qui Nhon. The two remaining ships broke off the attack and gained altitude.

Biggerstaff called out, "Get your heads down. Here comes the Air Force." Approaching from the west, a flight of three Skyraiders—World War II vintage fighter bombers—broke formation and peeled off in trail. The lead pilot entered the Pass with all guns blazing and held his dive until he was less than five hundred feet off the deck. Breaking upward, he released napalm canisters and slingshotted out of the Pass. Rictor had the glasses trained on what had been the lead truck. The jellied gasoline hit fifty yards in front of the truck and skip splashed over the first four vehicles. The entire area around the trucks was ablaze and the VC that ran out of the grass looked like human torches. There was no escape. The second and third Skyraiders dropped their napalm to overlap the first strike, and the entire killing zone was engulfed in flame.

Dave's face was flushed from anger and the intense heat that rose from the killing zone. He nodded satisfaction. "Fuck you, Charlie. You got yours. Hell won't be big enough for you and Shay!"

Rictor studied Dave's expression. He had never seen his friend so intense. He started to speak but realized there was nothing he could say.

Biggerstaff said, "The FAC's going to work the gunships and Skyraiders along the south ridge. Apparently that's where Charlie's concentrated his support weapons. They're not going to strike this side of the Pass. We're supposed to work our way to the top so we can be spotted. A slick is on the way to pick us up."

Terry said, "Zung's gonna need help. His arm's broke."

Rictor had momentarily forgotten about Zung. He looked around and spotted the young interpreter leaning against a rock clutching his left elbow with his right hand. His dazed expression had been replaced by one of pain. Rictor said, "I'll help Zung. Terry, you take the point. Dave, you bring up the rear."

Biggerstaff stood up. "Let's get moving. Terry, I'll be behind you with the radio and you take it easy. There's a lot of VC on this mountain."

Terry grinned as he said, "No shit, Captain," and then started to climb.

Rictor motioned for Zung. "C'mon, stay behind the captain. If you run into anything you can't handle, I'll give you a boost."

Bruised and cut, Terry's five-foot-ten, hundred-and-eighty-pound frame seemed smaller as he snaked his way up the mountainside. He made trail where there wasn't any and climbed at a steady pace. In an hour he had clawed his way to a covered spot very near the top. Biggerstaff signaled a halt. During the climb several VC who appeared to be withdrawing had been seen near the top of the ridge. Biggerstaff sent Dave and Terry forward to scout the area while he tried to contact the FAC. Rictor's bruised ribs were giving him a fit. He sat down next to Zung and studied the south side of the Pass where six Skyraiders were pounding the ridge line with bombs and rockets. He spotted a high-flying slick approaching the Pass from the west. When it began to orbit at two thousand feet he figured it was their ride to Qui Nhon.

Dave scrambled back down the hill and reported to Biggerstaff. "We didn't spot any Charlies but we did find a fairly flat clearing big enough for a chopper to set down. Terry stayed back as security."

Biggerstaff spoke into the radio mike. "We'll be on top of the ridge in zero five minutes. I'm going to set the grass on fire to mark. You send that slick in upwind of the smoke and don't bullshit around. When we fire up that grass, our asses will really be hanging out." Satisfied that the FAC understood, Biggerstaff followed Dave up the hill. Zung and Rictor brought up the rear.

At the clearing Rictor crawled up next to Terry. "You see anything?"

Terry shook his head. "I think the hill's clean, but I'm not sure."

Rictor was concerned; the fire wasn't such a hot idea. He glanced skyward and saw that the FAC had broken off the attack on the south ridge and was forming the aircraft in a tight circle directly overhead. Biggerstaff struck a match to a handful of dry grass and within seconds the wind had whipped up a spreading blaze.

The slick pilot made no effort to avoid ground fire. He came in through a hail of small arms fire on a low-level direct run. He hovered the chopper three feet from the ground in the small clearing and it shuttered from the impact of bullets as the VC gunners found the range. The crew chief waved and screamed frantically as Biggerstaff led the charge across the clearing.

When the others were aboard Rictor boosted Zung up to the door and scrambled in behind him. The slick took off the same way it had come, low and fast.

Chapter II

A DEVIOUS PLAN

Binh Hue District headquarters was a postage stamp size camp perched on a bare hilltop in a wide valley surrounded by rice paddies in coastal Binh Dinh Province. The camp was commanded by an ARVN captain who also carried the title of district chief—the civilian administrator for the district. The camp was well fortified with automatic weapons bunkers and barbed wire entanglements interwoven with barrier-type mine fields, backed up by two 155 mm. artillery pieces.

The camp defense force consisted of two hundred undisciplined, half-trained, regional force troops, the Vietnamese Provincial National Guard, who, for the most part, were unwilling participants in the war. The troops were supported by an eighty-man reconnaissance company which occasionally displayed some discipline and a limited degree of military proficiency.

In a run-down, two-room stucco building near the western perimeter of the camp, separated from the district headquarters building by several hundred yards, Rictor sat on the dirt floor leaning back on his rucksack. Biggerstaff had just hurried into the room and sat at a field table studying a lengthy radio message which Rictor had already read. While waiting somewhat impatiently for Biggerstaff to finish reading, Rictor reflected on the events of the month since the Mang Yang Pass ambush.

From the time the rescue slick dropped the detachment off at the Qui Nhon airstrip there had been one screwup after the other. The MAC-V detachment in Qui Nhon had been either unable or unwilling, Rictor wasn't sure which, but he suspected the latter, to provide any logistical support for the Binh Hue District mission. With route #19 cut, it had taken a week to get a three-quarter-ton truck and other replacement equipment flown in from the parent Special Forces *"B"* Detachment at Kontum.

The only bright spot in the ten-day stay in Qui Nhon was that Zung, after a two-day stint in the hospital, had been able to spend a week with his wife and young son who lived there.

When the support equipment arrived from Kontum, Biggerstaff was opposed to Zung continuing on to Bien Hue with the detachment. Zung was persistent and had enlisted Rictor's support. Rictor argued that broken arm and all, the mission needed Zung, and Biggerstaff finally relented.

The trip up the Binh Dinh coast had been made tagging along with an ARVN convoy. After two days of start and stop they had finally arrived at an ARVN base camp in northern Binh Dinh Province. There, the MAC-V detachment commander assigned to the ARVN camp advised Biggerstaff that all roads leading north and west had been cut by the Viet Cong and that farther travel by vehicle was impossible.

Leaving the truck and all but essential equipment in the care of the MAC-V commander, the detachment had hitched a ride on two slicks and flown to Binh Hue District headquarters.

The ensuing two weeks had been frustrating to the point of insanity. Three times, using the district's Recon Company as a strike force, a raid on the Viet Cong–controlled village of Bien Me had been planned. And three times the raid had been compromised and aborted before it could be executed. Rictor suspected the district chief was deliberately compromising the raid.

Dave entered the room cursing, flopped down next to Rictor and let out a sigh. "Where's Zung? I've been trying to negotiate for some duck eggs with the camp food peddler more than a half hour. Either the bastard don't understand or he's fuckin' crazy."

Rictor grinned. "He probably understands you, and we're probably better off without them damn stinking eggs. Zung's over at the district headquarters building. The district chief got a message that there's a Vietnamese Paratroop Battalion on its way here. Biggerstaff left Zung over there to find out why but I doubt if he'll learn much. Even the Paratroop Battalion commander doesn't know what his real mission is."

Dave lowered his voice. "Okay, smart Sergeant! How do you know so damn much about it?"

Rictor pointed to the paper Biggerstaff was reading. "It's in the message. The paratroops are coming in to support the Bien Me raid."

Dave laughed. "You don't really think the Vietnamese paratroop commander is going to take orders from Biggerstaff, do you?"

"No, but because of previous security leaks the paratroop commander was given a simple road-clearing mission just to get him here. Two MAC-V people attached to the battalion are bringing a written order signed by the Vietnamese high command in Saigon. That order gives Biggerstaff authority to use the battalion as he sees fit. You can bet he'll delay issuing the order until it's too late for a security leak."

Biggerstaff finished reading the message and said, "Looks like the raid is on. When the MAC-V people with the ARVN paratroops arrive, we'll work out the details. In the meantime, keep quiet. I don't even want Zung to know what we're planning."

For once Biggerstaff's reasoning was clear to Rictor but Terry, who had been standing in the radio room doorway, felt called on to question it. "Jesus, Captain! If we can't trust Zung, who can we trust?"

Biggerstaff barked, "Nobody!" and stomped out of the room.

Terry opened his mouth to reply, thought better of it and cursed under his breath.

Rictor said, "Forget it. It's not that he doesn't trust Zung, it's just that Zung doesn't have a need to know right now. He'll find out what's going on when the time's right."

Dave stood looking out the window. "Speaking of the devil, here he comes!"

Seconds later Zung came running into the room. Gasping for breath he said, "ARVN paratroops are entering the camp."

"From the way you were running I figured a company of Charlies was dead on your ass," scoffed Dave.

Zung ignored Dave and directed his comments to Rictor. "The paratroops are carrying wounded and a dead American. They also have VC prisoners."

Rictor picked up his rifle and headed for the door, and Dave hastily followed, catching up with Rictor near the camp gate. "I guess you know that if the MAC-V man carrying the high command's new order was left behind or captured, the Bien Me raid's compromised again," he said. But Rictor had spotted Biggerstaff talking with an American who looked familiar. He grunted and kept moving. As they drew near the gate Dave exclaimed, "Well, I'll be damned!"

Rictor smiled. "Yup. Looks like Burt Gardner. I haven't seen him in a while. Last I heard he was on Okinawa."

Dave said, chuckling, "I bumped into him down there four years ago. We really laid one on. I must've been hung over for a week. I heard he was somewhere in Nam. Come to think of it, he's been here about three years."

As Rictor approached his old friend, he noticed deep stress lines on Burt's face but chalked it up to Burt's recent combat experience. "Hey, Burt, you look like a fugitive from Uncle Ho's firing squad! What brings you to god's country?"

As Burt clasped Rictor's outstretched hand he said, "I heard some Special Forces people had their asses in a sling up here, so I came up with a battalion of paratroops to bail them out." Reaching for Dave's hand he said, "If I had known it was you two guys, I probably would have stayed in Saigon."

Dave laughed. "Looks like you're the one that needs help. You're skinny as an out of work road whore." Indicating a nearby squad of paratroops he continued, "You been sick or don't these zipperheads feed you?"

Rictor spotted a bulky object wrapped in a blood-spattered

20

poncho lying just inside the gate. "Is that the other American advisor?"

Burt's mouth tightened as he nodded. "He was just a green kid fresh from the States. He wanted to be a hero. I guess he made it."

Biggerstaff had grown impatient. He said, "Get on with it, Gardner! Let's hear what happened out there."

Annoyed by Biggerstaff's abruptness, Burt lit a cigarette before he responded. "Four days ago my battalion outloaded from Saigon, flew to Qui Nhon, then moved by slick transport to an abandoned airstrip fifteen miles east of here to conduct a road-clearing operation over to this camp. Late yesterday afternoon we finally arrived at the airstrip and at first light this morning headed here. Less than three miles from the airstrip we ran into about a hundred VC. From all indications they were as surprised as we were. It was a helluva mess. Boggs, the kid in the poncho, charged down the trail firing his M16 from the hip. He wasted a bunch of them but a couple he didn't see stepped out from behind the bushes and cut him to ribbons. Twenty minutes after the shooting started it was over. The VC pulled back leaving eighteen dead and twelve wounded. We had fourteen dead and twenty-five wounded. The paratroop commander sent most of his casualties back to the airstrip for evacuation. He wanted to send Boggs but I insisted that we bring the body with us."

Biggerstaff grunted. "You carrying a written order from the ARVN high command?"

Burt reached inside his shirt and took out a crumpled waterproof envelope. "I was told to give this to you."

Biggerstaff crammed the envelope into his pocket without opening it. Turning to Rictor he said, "I'm going to see the district chief. You get a message out to the 'B' detachment commander in Kontum. Inform him that one of the MAC-V advisors was killed and ask for a chopper to pick up the body. I'll see you back at the team house."

Burt watched Biggerstaff leave, then turned to Dave and said, "Friendly bastard, ain't he?"

Dave grinned. "You think you dislike him now, wait until

you get to know him better. Then you'll see what a real ass-hole he is."

"C'mon, Burt, it'll take a while to get a Medevac chopper. We'll wait at the team house. It's not much, but at least we can get out of the sun," said Rictor.

Burt nodded and headed toward the gate. "I'll be right with you." A squat, thick-chested Chinese armed with a sawed-off shotgun and machete stepped through the gate and Burt spoke to him in Vietnamese.

When Burt returned, Dave asked, "Who's the Chink?"

Burt answered, "His name's Wong but I just call him the Chinaman. He keeps an eye on my back while I watch the VC."

Dave eyed the sawed-off shotgun. "That smoke-pole looks wicked but it couldn't have much range."

Burt grinned. "He uses the shotgun because he likes to work real close. I told him to keep an eye on the body. Let's go see about getting the chopper."

As they walked toward the team house Rictor asked, "How many prisoners did you people take and where are they now? I'm curious about their mission."

Burt took a final draw on his cigarette and flipped it away. "We captured twelve VC but four of them were shot up too bad to walk so the paratroops put them out of their misery. We brought the remaining eight in with us. They should be under-going interrogation by now. Having seen the paratroop inter-rogators work, my guess is the prisoners will spill everything."

Rictor said, "I doubt if that will help us, still I want to see the interrogation report. We know that a VC battalion moved into this district last week but I'm surprised you made contact with a company-size unit on the open road in broad daylight."

Burt shrugged. "Like I said, I think they were as surprised as we were. Judging from the shovels they were carrying, I figure they were fixing to dig in and set up an ambush. We just ran into them before they were ready."

"If they had a lot of digging tools, maybe they were headed to a supply cache," Dave suggested.

Burt shook his head. "Maybe, but I don't think so. They

were in full combat gear and carried extra ammo and mines. If they were on their way to dig up supplies, I figure they would've been lightly armed and had a civilian carrying party with them." Rictor agreed, his sixth sense telling him that the unexpected paratroop encounter with the VC had a direct bearing on the planned raid.

When they arrived at the team house, Rictor sent Zung to find out what the interrogators had learned from the prisoners, then helped Terry prepare a message for the *"B"* detachment commander.

Terry had just finished sending the message requesting a chopper to come for Boggs's body when Zung came flying into the radio room. Dave barked, "Jesus, Zung, if you don't stop running in this fuckin' heat, you're gonna have a stroke to go with that broken arm."

As usual, Zung ignored Dave and addressed himself directly to Rictor. "I think you should come to the interrogation building! There's something you should see."

His curiosity aroused, Rictor asked, "What's important enough to bring you over here on the run?"

Zung hedged. "You must come and see firsthand."

Rictor attempted to read Zung's expression but found it impossible. Certain that whatever it was Zung wanted him to see was important he said, "Okay, let's take a look." Glancing at Burt he said, "C'mon."

Burt shook his head. "No thanks. You go ahead. I've seen enough interrogations to last me a lifetime."

Rictor shrugged. "Suit yourself. Let's go, Dave."

Terry stood up. "If you're not going, Burt, how about keeping an eye on the radio gear. I think I'll tag along with Rictor and Dave."

Burt glanced around the room. "You got any drinking whiskey?" Terry pointed to a rucksack in the corner and headed for the door. Burt called after him, "Take as much time as you like. I ain't going nowhere."

When Rictor reached the interrogation building on the far side of the camp, he saw thirty or forty curious paratroops pressed against the outside of the wire fence which enclosed it. He caught up with Zung and said, "What the hell's going on?"

Zung remained silent but motioned for Rictor to follow as he pushed his way through the crowd of paratroops. At the fence Zung stopped short. "I had hoped you could prevent an unnecessary killing but I see we're too late."

Rictor scanned the enclosure. All he could see was a decaying building, two wooden posts and an interrogator cleaning his machete. Rictor barked, "Damnit, Zung, what the hell's going on?"

Zung pointed to a burlap bag covering the top of one of the wooden posts. Rictor said, irritated, "What about it?"

Before Zung could answer the back door of the interrogation building burst open and two paratroopers came out dragging a prisoner whose hands and feet were bound. The prisoner was forced into a kneeling position in front of the wooden post. The interrogator with the machete stepped forward and screamed out a question in Vietnamese which Rictor didn't understand.

The prisoner was defiant. He spat at the interrogator and remained silent. Infuriated, the interrogator jerked the prisoner to his feet and shoved his face against the burlap bag. In one quick motion the interrogator snatched the burlap cover from the post. The defiant prisoner found himself nose to nose with the mutilated head of a comrade. The prisoner gasped, then began to babble incoherently as he fell to his knees. Their purpose accomplished, the guards grabbed the broken prisoner by his arms and dragged him back into the building.

Dave turned to leave. "I've seen enough. Those sadistic bastards make me want to puke."

"I'll say one thing, they get the job done," said Terry.

The excitement in Terry's voice did not go unnoticed. Dave glanced back and saw that the redhead's face was flushed and he was breathing rapidly. "You seem to be getting a charge out of this," Dave said. "Why don't you stay here with Zung and find out what Charlie was doing out there on the trail?"

Terry smirked. "Roger that. Watching Charlie get his is goddamn near as good as getting laid. What's wrong with you, have you lost your sense of humor?"

Rictor said, "Shut up, Terry!" Stepping close to Dave he said, "Forget it. It's just another happening in a sick fuckin' war. Let's get back to the team house, the chopper should be here anytime."

Dave nodded. "The Vietnamese ain't the only sick ones. Did you see the look in Terry's eyes? He's got the sickness too."

Rictor had noticed Terry's excitement but found further discussion pointless. "If you use the right measuring stick, you can find sickness in all of us."

Dave muttered under his breath but kept moving.

As Rictor walked toward the team house his mind was on Terry. He was aware of Terry's shortcomings, his immaturity. Terry had the build of a muscle beach crowd pleaser and the strength of an ox. His boyish smile was quick and to a stranger completely disarming. But to Rictor the smile was a mask. Behind Terry's green eyes was a mean streak. He was moody, fast with his fists, and prone to turn his animosity on whoever happened to be handy. Recently his outbursts had become more frequent. He was rapidly becoming a team morale problem.

When Rictor and Dave entered the team house, Burt was sitting on the floor next to Terry's rucksack smoking a cigarette. The bottle of bourbon between his feet was half-empty. He glanced up. "You guys weren't gone long."

Most of the strain had disappeared from Burt's face and Rictor attributed it to the bourbon. Dave spotted the bottle and reached for his canteen cup. "Gimme a shot of that. Maybe it will help me forget what a sorry fuckin' war this is."

Burt held out the bottle. "It'll take more booze than this."

Rictor grunted. "Both of you better take it easy on the juice. If you get pushed out of shape, Biggerstaff will blow a fuse."

Dave grinned. "And what would be so unusual about that? If Biggerstaff didn't have something to raise hell about, he'd croak."

The distant sound of a chopper brought Burt to his feet. "I'd better get down to the landing pad and see about the body. You guys coming?"

Rictor picked up a smoke grenade from the table and said,

"Dave, I'll go with Burt. You get the slick pilot on the radio and tell him that we'll mark the landing pad with green smoke."

When the chopper departed with the body, Rictor and Burt headed back to the team house. They found Biggerstaff sitting at the table studying a map. He waved them to wooden crates which served as chairs. "Sit down. I sent Dave to get Terry. When they get back we'll work out the details for the raid."

Burt said, puzzled, "What raid are you talking about, Captain?"

Biggerstaff pushed back his chair. "While we're waiting for Dave and Terry I'll fill you in. The Vietnamese high command has known for some time Charlie was planning a strategy meeting somewhere in this district. A month ago we were sent here to find out when and where the meeting was to be held and conduct a raid.

"We had been here only a few days when we learned the meeting was to take place in a village about fifteen miles north of here. We planned an operation with the district Recon Company but it was compromised and subsequently called off. Since then, based on good intelligence, we have twice cranked up operations but each time came out empty-handed. It's evident that some bastard high up in the district command is warning Charlie. It could be any one, including the district chief himself."

Burt gave Biggerstaff an understanding nod. "Sounds like you've been handed a can of worms. How do my paratroops fit into this thing?"

Biggerstaff grunted. "To make a long story short, our friendly agents report that Charlie's hard-pressed to hold his strategy meeting." Biggerstaff pointed to a red circle on the map. "Our latest intelligence indicates the meeting is to take place tonight or tomorrow at the village of Bien Me. You and the ARVN Paratroop Battalion were brought in to support our raid. A few days ago the VC brought their Binh Dinh Provincial Battalion into the area to secure the meeting place. We've determined the people responsible for this district's entire VC infrastructure, including the VC district leader himself, are supposed to attend."

Burt replied skeptically, "This is the first I've heard about a raid. As far as I know our orders are for a road-clearing operation."

Biggerstaff nodded, saying, "The road-clearing order was a cover. We didn't want to take a chance on a leak this time." Biggerstaff reached into his shirt pocket and produced the envelope Burt had given him earlier. He handed it to Burt and said, "This is a new order for the paratroops. The problem now is to figure out how to get the operation underway without alerting every Charlie in this part of Nam."

Burt shook his head. "That will be a neat trick. When the paratroops entered the camp, they came under the operational control of the district chief. Looks to me like you'll have to show him this new order if you want the battalion. When you do that you're right back where you started."

Biggerstaff exploded. "Goddamnit, Sergeant! You don't need to draw me a fuckin' picture. I know the problem. What I'm looking for is a solution."

Burt's mouth tightened and his voice turned cold. "Captain, I came a long way over a rough road to get here. If you want my help, it's available. But don't try to bully me. I don't work for you." Biggerstaff flushed but before he could respond Dave came in followed by Terry and Zung. Biggerstaff lost interest in Burt.

Terry strolled across the room without speaking and sat down on his rucksack. A long minute went by, and it became obvious that he wasn't going to discuss the interrogation until asked. Biggerstaff zeroed in on him, saying, "Okay, Terry, you've had your little game. You can quit screwing around and tell us what you found out."

Terry grinned but the glint in his eyes was hard. "Charlie was moving to a location near the airstrip where they were supposed to set up an ambush and seal the road before dark."

Rictor nodded, realizing that Burt had guessed correctly about the firefight being a chance meeting. His interest quickened. "Don't fuck around, Terry, what unit are the prisoners from?"

"First company of the Binh Dinh Provincial Battalion."

Rictor knew he was on to something worthwhile. "Where's the rest of the battalion located?"

Terry spread his hands while answering. "The interrogators couldn't find out. The Provincial Battalion supposedly broke camp at daylight this morning and all four companies moved out in separate directions."

Rictor walked over to the table and studied Biggerstaff's map. After a moment he said, "Charlie's apparently trying to seal the entire area around Bien Me. I'd say this, added to what we already know, makes a strong case that the meeting is going to take place tonight."

Biggerstaff grunted. "You're probably right. Now how do we get to Bien Me without giving away the show?"

Rictor said, glancing back to the map, "I've got an idea that might work."

Biggerstaff shrugged, commenting, "It don't cost nothing to listen."

Without taking his eyes off the map Rictor asked, "You think you can talk the district chief into sending the Paratroop Battalion and the Recon Company out to clear the road to the airstrip?"

Biggerstaff was curious. "Maybe, but I don't see how that's going to get us to Bien Me."

"It won't exactly, but I think it'll help. The way I see it, Charlie's sure to have surveillance on the road. When he sees the paratroops and Recon Company moving toward the airstrip and away from Bien Me, he'll probably let them pass." Rictor touched the map with his forefinger and traced the road to a point midway between the camp and the airstrip. "If you can get the paratroops and Recon Company moving right away, I figure we can reach this location by nightfall. Under darkness, it shouldn't be too difficult to break off the Recon Company and head for Bien Me."

Biggerstaff grunted. "What makes you think you can get the recon commander to leave the paratroops?"

Rictor responded, "Just a minute." He got up from the table and crossed the room to his rucksack. Fishing out an envelope he returned to the table. "I admit it's going to take a little doing. In this envelope I've got a copy of the district chief's order for the last raid that was called off. I figure between Zung and me, we can doctor it up so it'll pass for a new order."

Biggerstaff sprang up from the table. "Rictor, you've been spending too much time in the sun! A wild ass scheme like this could get me shit canned out of the army!"

"Maybe, but I figure it's got a pretty good chance of working, and tonight's the last chance we're going to get."

"Anybody got a better plan?" asked Dave. His question was answered by silence. After a moment he said, "It might work. Anyway, it's the only plan we got."

Biggerstaff was far from being convinced. "It's no skin off anybody's ass but mine. In case you have forgotten I'm the one responsible for this operation."

Terry laughed. "I'd say you've got a problem, Captain. If you don't make the raid, it will reflect on your report card. All minuses! If you try Rictor's plan and it's a bust, working relations with the Vietnamese will be shot and when we get back to the 'B' Detachment, Major Strong will have your balls boiled in oil."

Rictor raised his voice. "Shut up, Terry! If this mission is a success we all share in it. If it's a bust everybody gets a share of the crap."

Burt cleared his throat to say, "I know this is a family problem and I probably should stay out of it but you can bet your ass if the raid's a success nobody's going to care about the methods. Besides, if you're leaving right after it, what do you care what the district chief thinks?"

Biggerstaff glanced around the room begging support for his position. The men's faces spoke loud and clear: he was alone. "Okay! We'll try it your way, Rictor, but it had better work. If I get screwed up all of your asses are grass, and I'm the fuckin' lawn mower."

Surprised that Biggerstaff had consented without more of an argument, Rictor said, "It's risky. But even if the Recon Company commander is suspicious of the doctored order, chances are he'll be afraid not to carry it out." He caught Zung's eye and winked. "Besides that Zung's a pretty convincing liar."

Biggerstaff snorted. "If we're lucky enough to get the Recon Company commander to buy the phony order, how do you figure to get past the VC battalion that's securing Bien Me?"

Rictor voiced more confidence than he felt. "Assuming the prisoners are telling the truth about their battalion splitting up and moving out in different directions, Charlie has probably established an outer security ring by setting up ambushes along the roads. If we move cross-country with the Recon Company, we should be able to slip past them and reach Bien Me before daylight. With a little luck we can make a surprise strike at first light."

Biggerstaff interrupted, "What do you expect Charlie to do, sit tight in position while we knock off the village and take his political wheels prisoner? Or do you figure on fighting your way out with eighty half-trained, poorly equipped recon troops?"

Rictor continued, "I hope fighting our way out won't be necessary. But if it is, that's where Burt and the Paratroop Battalion come in."

Burt walked over to the table and stood next to Rictor. "I was beginning to think you had forgotten about my paratroopers."

Rictor indicated the map with a nod. "See the trail that runs through Bien Me?"

Burt leaned forward, squinting. "Yeah, looks like it winds back this way to the river."

Rictor nodded. "If you look closer you'll see that it parallels the river, then crosses over and runs due east until it meets the airstrip road."

Burt took another look at the map and checked the distance. "Could it be that you figure me and the paratroops will reach that trail junction about daylight?" Rictor nodded and Burt continued, "I'll bet that's where you figure on me talking the paratroop commander into turning west toward Bien Me."

Rictor said, grinning, "Now you've got the picture. It's roughly five miles from Bien Me to the river and about the same distance from the river to the airstrip road. The prisoners from Bien Me will slow us down some, but if we hit the village at first light we should be at the river by 0930 hours. When your paratroops meet us at the bridge, we can link up and make it back here before Charlie has time to get organized to stop us."

Biggerstaff was still not convinced. "There's a lot of Ifs in this thing, Rictor. I've seen that river from the air. It's wide and swift, forming a natural barrier east of the village. The bridge you're talking about is the only way out, and Charlie's not stupid. He's probably holding the bridge now. If not, you can bet your ass he will be before we can get there from Bien Me. If he can hold us up at the bridge long enough to consolidate that Provincial Battalion behind us, we'll be outnumbered five to one and trapped against the river."

Rictor said, annoyed, "I said it was risky! That's why it's critical that Burt get the paratroops to the bridge before we arrive."

Burt said, "The paratroop commander's okay. He'll do what I ask him to do. Unless we run into a helluva lot of resistance along the way, we'll be holding the bridge when you get there."

Biggerstaff took a long look at the map. Finally he said, "I still think I'm asking for trouble, but we'll give it a try. I'm going over to see the district chief about the bullshit road-clearing operation. If he gives the okay, Dave, you go with Burt and the paratroops. Rictor and I will take the Recon Company. Terry, you'll stay here, coordinate the artillery support and monitor the radio in case we get into trouble."

Terry smirked, and replied, "That's about what I expected. While you guys go out and make like heroes, I'm supposed to sit here on my ass and play with myself."

"You can take my place as far as I'm concerned. It might even be a good way to get rid of your ass," said Dave.

Terry sprang to his feet and yelled, "You smart bastard! I'll . . ."

"Knock it off!" shouted Biggerstaff. "I'm calling the shots! We'll do it the way I said."

Terry opened his mouth to protest but was stopped by a strangling noise which came through the wall from the rear of the house.

31

There was a mad scramble toward the back door. Burt made it through first. As he stepped outside he yelled, "Hold it, Chinaman!"

Over Burt's shoulder Rictor saw one of the Vietnamese camp laborers lying facedown next to the wall. The squat Chinese who had come to the camp with Burt had his foot resting on the laborer's neck and the muzzle of his shotgun jammed in the man's ear. Biggerstaff bellowed from the door, "What in the hell's going on?"

Burt indicated an overturned wooden box beneath one of the team house glassless windows. "Looks like the Chinaman caught this bastard eavesdropping on us."

Rictor took a quick look around. There were no other Vietnamese in sight. Hopeful the struggle had been unobserved he said, "Quick! Get him inside before anyone sees what's going on."

Once inside, Rictor took a heavy nylon cord and some cloth from his rucksack. Tossing it to Dave, he said, "Tie and gag him."

Biggerstaff motioned Rictor to the radio room. Once they were out of hearing range he said, "Well, that rips it! It's obvious the fuckin' snoop out there speaks English which means he knows our plan. You can bet he isn't going to tell us who he's working for without some coaxing. We can't turn him over to district intelligence without risking compromise."

Rictor nodded and said, "If we lean on him hard enough he'll talk, but I'm not sure that's a good idea. My guess is he works for the district chief."

Biggerstaff exploded. "Goddamnit! I knew this fool scheme wouldn't work. I don't know why I let you talk me into it in the first place!"

Rictor's temper flared. "We're not beat yet! Nobody outside this building knows we caught this fink. We'll just go on as planned."

Biggerstaff said sarcastically, "What do you suggest we do with him—just pretend he don't exist?"

Rictor shrugged. "All this panic might be for nothing. He could be a VC. Let's leave him here with Terry until after the raid. If it turns out he's a VC, we'll turn him over to district

32

intelligence. We'll be pulling out right after the raid. If we find out that he works for the district chief, we'll just toss his ass out of the team house and deny we ever saw him. I don't think the district chief will be anxious to admit that we caught one of his men spying on us."

Biggerstaff lapsed into silence. He had a difficult time making up his mind. Finally he heaved a sigh of resignation. "I'm committed. We'll try it." He took a step toward the door, stopped and looked back. "I'm going to district headquarters and one way or another, I'll get the district chief to send out the paratroops and Recon Company. You get with Terry and work out an artillery fire support plan. If the district artillery is used properly, those 155 howitzers can seal off Bien Me village for us. While you're at it, tell Terry if he lets that agent get away, I'll castrate him."

As he watched the obese captain stalk out of the room, Rictor fought back a grin. He saw no humor in the situation but he felt a certain sense of pleasure watching Biggerstaff squirm.

Chapter III

THE RAID

The district chief listened to Biggerstaff's road-clearing proposal and agreed to dispatch the ARVN Paratroop Battalion without delay but he was opposed to sending out the Recon Company. He took the position that the company's absence would leave the district camp without adequate defense.

Biggerstaff was determined and presented several arguments as to why the company should go, but the district chief was adamant. Finally, Biggerstaff argued that in addition to having been on the move all day the paratroops had just fought a bloody skirmish. To send them out without rest, while fresh local RF (Regional Force) troops remained in the camp, would be an injustice certain not to go unnoticed by the ARVN high command. Fearing reprimand from his superiors, the district chief reluctantly issued the necessary orders.

By 1700 hours the paratroop column was winding its way out of the camp. Biggerstaff, Rictor and Zung waited by the gate for the Recon Company bringing up the rear. Anxious to get moving, Biggerstaff cast a worried glance at the sun and stepped close to Rictor. "If these damn people don't get a move on, it'll be dark before we get clear of camp."

Rictor, checking the time, said, "It's a slow start but we've got almost three hours of daylight left. Unless we run into problems we should make the turn-off point by nightfall."

Biggerstaff grunted, "Maybe," and lapsed into silence.

Rictor scanned the column for Burt and Dave and finally spotted them. Easily identified by the sawed-off shotgun cradled in the bend of his arm and his black pajamas the Chinaman was several steps behind Burt. Rictor saw that Zung was staring at the Chinaman. Curious he asked, "What's bugging you, Zung?"

Zung didn't answer right away. When he spoke his voice was cold and thick with distaste. "He's a Nung, a Chinese mercenary. His gun's for hire and the only allegiance he knows is to the person who pays him."

Rictor scoffed. "So he's a mercenary. I figure there's a little of that in all of us."

Zung busied himself adjusting the straps which held the radio in place on his back. When he was satisfied the radio would ride comfortably, he said, "You're right of course, but some of us do what must be done because we feel it's best for our families and country."

Rictor had never heard Zung speak with such conviction. He was surprised but pleased. Choosing to lighten the mood, he laughed. "I think you've just got a hard-on for the Chinese."

Drawing up to the gate, Dave looked at Burt, then at the paratroops.

Biggerstaff caught the look and turned to Burt. "You people just be where you're supposed to be at 0930 hours in the morning and we'll be okay." Dave gave the thumbs-up signal and moved on through the gate.

Biggerstaff took another look at the sun. "The Recon Company should be coming up any minute now. Are you sure Terry's squared away on the artillery support?"

Rictor nodded. "We worked out the plan together. At 0530 hours in the morning, Terry will go to the district chief and show him the high command's order. He'll tell the district chief that we're in an attack position at the south side of Bien Me and need artillery support to seal off the village. If the district chief's not the one who's been passing the word to Charlie, we'll get an artillery barrage at 0600 hours."

Biggerstaff grunted, "There's that word *if* again. But it's too late to back out now. Here comes the Recon Company."

By sundown the column had wormed its way to within a mile of the Recon Company's turn-off point. As shadows cast by thick jungle vegetation lengthened and gave way to dusk, Rictor breathed easier. He was certain the column's movement along the road was being monitored. The fact that the Viet Cong had done nothing to hinder the column's progress led him to believe that the plan was working. Rictor stretched out his pace to catch Biggerstaff, who was at the front of the company with the recon commander. Coming along beside the large man, Rictor quietly said, "So far, so good. When are you going to spring the bogus raid order on the recon commander?"

Biggerstaff glanced across the trail at the middle-aged Vietnamese lieutenant who commanded the Recon Company. "In about ten minutes. I want to leave enough light for him to be able to read the order but not enough to spot the changes. When I stop the column, you bring Zung up here to do the talking." Rictor slowed his pace until Zung caught up and walked beside him.

When the company came to a halt Rictor said, "Keep going, the captain needs you up front to translate. If you never tell another lie in your life, make this one convincing." Zung's only reply was a brief grin.

Biggerstaff and the recon commander stood in the middle of the road facing each other. As Rictor approached he saw the last of the paratroop column disappear into the fading light. Biggerstaff hesitated for a second, then reached into his shirt pocket and pulled out the bogus raid order. The recon commander was clearly puzzled as he reached for the paper. Biggerstaff said, "Zung, tell the lieutenant that the district chief instructed me to give him the order when we reached this location."

Zung translated Biggerstaff's words but the lieutenant did not appear to be listening. By the time he finished reading the order his expression had changed from one of question to open suspicion. He responded to Zung in Vietnamese but directed his words to Biggerstaff. "Why did the district chief not give me this order before I left the camp?"

Zung made the translation and Biggerstaff answered, "Tell him the district chief thought the plan would be more secure if he received the order out here on the trail."

Even before Zung finished translating, the expression of suspicion on the lieutenant's face had given way to disbelief. He demanded to know if Biggerstaff and the district chief suspected him of being a traitor. Rictor saw that the situation was getting out of hand and interrupted, "Zung, tell the lieutenant that the district chief did this to protect him. There's a security leak back at the camp. By not informing him about the raid until now it keeps him free from suspicion." As Zung spoke, the lieutenant's expression softened and by the time the translation was complete he was nodding in agreement. He immediately summoned his platoon leaders to give them the new route and order of march.

Rictor stepped close to Biggerstaff. "It was touch and go for a minute but it looks like you managed to pull it off."

Biggerstaff grunted. "Don't crow yet. There's still a lot of *if*s in this thing, and I don't think Charlie is going to be so easily fooled." Seeing that the recon commander had finished briefing his platoon leaders, Biggerstaff said, "I'll be back here with the lieutenant. You and Zung stay with the lead platoon and make sure the point squad doesn't swing too far north. If we miss that shallow place southwest of the village we'll never get across the fuckin' river."

The muffled sounds made by troops on the move drifted down the trail as Rictor and Zung hurried to catch up with the lead platoon. Within seconds of doing so, the point squad turned off the trail and was immediately hidden by the dense undergrowth. As he plunged into the undergrowth Rictor felt divorced from the world. The air was hot and humid and long piercing thorns tore at his clothing like a hundred unseen hands. A thick canopy of vegetation completely filtered out the fading light and the pace slowed to a crawl.

With the intrusion of humans, the normal sounds of the night creatures ceased, and a deathly quiet fell over the surrounding jungle. In their struggle to keep moving through the dense undergrowth the recon troops thrashed about like wounded animals and Rictor feared they would alert every VC in the district. He had hoped the march would become less difficult but, if anything, the vegetation grew thicker and the heat intensified. An even bigger concern was that the column had covered less than a mile since leaving the trail, and unless their speed increased there was no chance of reaching Bien Me before daylight.

Zung stopped abruptly and Rictor crashed into the radio. The taste of blood was salty and Rictor's lip began to swell from the impact. The curse which rose in his throat was choked off by the realization that the entire column had come to a halt. A whispered message relayed from the point squad reached Zung and he turned to Rictor to say, "The platoon leader wants us up front."

Rictor spat blood and kept his voice low. "Okay, move out but try not to make any more sudden stops. That goddamn radio nearly knocked my teeth out."

As he clawed his way forward in the dark, Rictor's nostrils picked up the scent of wood smoke. When he reached the front of the column he located the platoon leader kneeling at the edge of a small clearing. Huddled in the center of the clearing were a dozen or more Montagnard grass huts. Aware that the patrol's chances of bypassing the hamlet without being detected were minimal, the platoon leader had sent a reconnaissance team to investigate.

The sound of breaking twigs and whispered hoarse curses announced the arrival of Biggerstaff who flopped down next to Rictor, panting for breath. Rictor was explaining the situation to Biggerstaff when the recon team returned bringing with them two Montagnard women and a newborn baby. After listening to the recon team leader's report, Zung said to Biggerstaff, "These are women from the Rhade Tribe. More than fifty Montagnards used to live in this hamlet, but they have been taken away recently, by the Vietcong. These women are the only remaining inhabitants."

Biggerstaff's whisper was hoarse. "Find out from the women when Charlie was last here."

Zung's ability to speak the tribal language was limited, and the Montagnard women spoke very little Vietnamese. But Zung learned that two weeks previously a squad of Vietcong had come to the hamlet in the middle of the night. They had confiscated all the rice and salt they could find, forced the village inhabitants to become a carrying party and disappeared into the jungle. The two women had been left in the hamlet because the one with the baby had been in labor.

Biggerstaff said, worried, "There's probably a dozen informers hiding in the bush just waiting for us to pull out so they can carry the word to Charlie."

Rictor was concerned, too, but Biggerstaff's pessimism was irritating. He knew that the Montagnards were caught in the middle between the Vietcong and the government and that Biggerstaff might be right. He also knew there wasn't a damn thing they could do about it. He leaned close to Zung to ask, "What do you think? Are the Yards telling the truth?"

Zung responded hesitantly, "Yes, I think they are. The recon team reported that only one hut has been lived in recently. I know for sure that this tribe only helps the VC when there's no other choice."

Biggerstaff grunted. "My map doesn't show a trail. Find out how Charlie got in and out of here."

Zung conversed briefly with the older of the two women then disappeared into the dark. When he came back he was excited. "I've located a footpath, which the old woman says leads to the river where there is a rope bridge for crossing. She also said that on the other side of the river is a trail to Bien Me."

For the first time in days Biggerstaff's voice sounded optimistic. "How about the bridge, is it guarded?"

Zung shrugged. "She doesn't know for sure but she's heard that the VC guard the bridge at night."

The Recon Company commander who had been monitoring the conversation closely through Zung responded, "If this is not a trap, we will be at Bien Me long before daylight."

Biggerstaff had made his decision. "Rictor, you take Zung and the recon team and check the trail all the way to the river. Maintain radio silence unless you make contact. I'll give you a ten-minute head start, then follow with the company." Turning to Zung he said, "Before you leave tell the women they're going with us. If they're telling the truth they'll be rewarded. But if they're sending us into an ambush they're in deep shit. I'm putting them on a leash and they'll be up front with the point squad."

Two hours after leaving the hamlet, Rictor and Zung lay on the riverbank. For more than a half hour Rictor had not moved and every muscle in his body ached. He was watching two VC who sat close to a sheltered cooking fire in a clearing at the end of the bridge. Seemingly unaware of the need for security they talked freely.

Satisfied that there were only two guards, Rictor tapped Zung on the arm and indicated for him to pull back. Once they were a safe distance from the bridge he said, "It's going to be difficult taking out those guards without any shooting. They're sure to spot us if we try crossing the clearing. We've got to figure out a way to make them come to us." Groping for an idea Rictor asked, "Could you hear what they were talking about?"

Zung whispered, "They've been guarding the bridge for weeks and are restless. The older man is anxious for the war to end. He wants to get back to his family. The younger one spoke of rejoining his battalion which he says will attack Qui Nhon soon. He talks of getting a woman and how long it's been since he's had one."

Rictor rapidly formulated a plan. He sent Zung back along the trail to where Biggerstaff was holding the company with instructions to bring the new mother and her baby forward.

Thirty minutes later Zung and the woman stood a short distance from the bridge waiting for the recon team to fan out around the clearing. Zung checked his watch. It was time. He gave the woman an encouraging pat on the back and whispered, "Now!" She walked slowly up the trail to the edge of the clearing, stopped and hesitantly pinched the leg of her sleeping baby.

From a concealed position near the mouth of the trail Rictor heard the baby cry out and saw the guards spring to their feet. The younger one shouted a challenge and the woman stepped forward silhouetting herself against the flickering firelight. Zung crawled close to Rictor. Keeping his voice low he said, "She told the guard that her baby's sick and she must get to Bien Me for medicine. The guard told her to come closer to the fire. I don't think he suspects anything."

Loud voices drew Rictor's attention back to the bridge. The guards were quarreling, and the younger one was shouting angrily. Zung said, "The old man wants to send the woman back to the hamlet, but the younger one is in charge and will make the final decision. He just asked her if she has money."

The young woman had stopped near the fire, and for the first time Rictor could clearly see her. He was spellbound. She wore the traditional wraparound skirt and like most of these women was naked from the waist up. A gentle breeze rippled her waistlength black hair, and the yellow firelight made her skin appear bronzed. She stood with her back straight and her milk-filled breasts were full. The all but forgotten baby on her back let out a squall and the spell was broken.

The younger guard stepped close to the woman and fondled her breast. Zung hissed, "He said that she cannot cross the bridge unless she pays. She told him that she has only her sleeping mat and a small amount of rice which she left at the edge of the clearing."

When the guard laughed and laid his rifle aside, Rictor nodded with satisfaction. The plan was working. After prying the screaming baby from its mother's back, the young VC handed it to the older guard and began pulling the woman back along the trail.

Zung's whisper was filled with disgust. "That son of a whore told the old man to keep the baby while he goes with the woman to place a value on her treasure." Rictor began to inch back from the clearing, but Zung stopped him with a touch. Rictor glanced over his shoulder and caught the glint of unsheathed steel. Then Zung was gone. The woman and guard passed very near Rictor's position. He held his breath. When they had moved a hundred feet father down the trail, Rictor heard the faint rustle of leaves followed by a sickening thud, then silence.

Zung returned as soundlessly as he had departed. Rictor turned his attention to the remaining guard who was sitting by the fire cuddling the sleeping baby. Twenty minutes went by, then thirty and the old man became fidgety. Finally, he stood and began to whistle softly. When there was no response he walked into the clearing and called to the younger guard. The baby stirred in his arms and he soothed it with soft words.

Rictor neither saw nor heard movement, but his instinct told him that the recon team was moving in for the kill. A pair of ghostlike figures detached themselves from the shadows and silently stalked their prey. A minute passed, and it was over, a garrote in the hands of one of the recon people doing its silent, deadly work. The baby, dropped by the dying VC, was caught by the assassin before it hit the ground and was still sleeping.

When the fire was extinguished, Rictor sent the recon team across the river to establish security while Zung was dispatched to bring the company forward. Above the roar of the swirling water, Rictor heard the Montagnard woman humming to her sleeping baby. As he listened he realized that he was standing near the spot where only a few minutes before the Vietcong had stood. He felt no compassion for the young guard but wondered how many children and grandchildren the older guard had at home.

Deep in thought, he failed to hear the Recon Company approaching and was startled by Zung's whistle from the edge of the clearing. He returned the signal and seconds later the point squad was at the bridge. Biggerstaff was with the squad and his whispered directions to Rictor reflected his anxiety. "Zung's already filled me in. You and him stay with the recon team. I'll keep the rest of the company a hundred yards behind. We're well inside Charlie's security screen so once the company is across the river I'm going to cut the rope bridge.

We won't be able to pull back but Charlie won't be able to come in behind us either."

"Where do you want me to hold up with the recon team?" asked Rictor.

"Get as close to Bien Me as you can. We'll use the place you stop as a final coordination point for the attack," Biggerstaff whispered.

Stepping out onto the bridge Rictor turned and asked, "How about putting the women and baby at the end of the column. They've earned their keep." For once Biggerstaff agreed and said, "I'll take care of it. You better get going."

By 0400 hours the recon team had reached a trail junction a hundred yards short of Bien Me. Rictor was surprised to find unmanned Viet Cong foxholes. After positioning the recon team to ambush the junction, he moved back down the trail to meet the company.

Biggerstaff was briefed about the unmanned foxholes and voiced his growing concern. "Why do you think there's no VC security at the trail junction?"

Rictor shrugged. "I don't know. Your guess is as good as mine. They may be overconfident and feeling safe or they may have called off the meeting."

Biggerstaff's curse was barely audible. "Goddamnit, I knew this wasn't going to work."

Rictor was more hopeful. "Maybe Charlie thinks the river is a natural barrier and has deployed his security force between the main bridge and the outlying roads." He whispered, "I think we'll run into some of their close-in security at the very edge of the village."

Biggerstaff said, still unconvinced, "What happens when Charlie discovers the rope bridge is down?"

Rictor could only guess. "First of all, I don't think Charlie is going to be out looking around in the dark. I figure they'll sit in static ambush positions until daylight. By then it will be too late to prevent us from hitting the village. If I'm right, our big problem will come when we get to the main bridge on the way out."

Biggerstaff checked the time. "It's 0450 hours. The villagers are going to start waking up soon. I'm going to send a security squad with a machine gun to the other side of the creek on the edge of the village. When it gets light the gunner should have a clear field of fire and be able to support the attack. Are you sure Terry understood that we need the artillery barrage at exactly 0600 hours?"

Rictor nodded. "He understood . . . but making it happen might be another thing."

Biggerstaff cursed. "You go back and seal the trail junction. I'm going to deploy the company for the attack. Come hell or high water we're going to hit the village at 0600 hours."

Rictor was fifty yards from the trail junction when he heard the muffled sound of an approaching motorbike. He quickened his pace and cautioned the recon team not to fire. Positioning himself by a tree at the very edge of the trail he waited. When the bike rounded the bend and came into view, he could see that its hooded headlight had been adjusted downward causing the reduced beam to strike immediately in front of the wheel. Concealed from the rider's view by the tree, Rictor reversed his rifle, grasped it by the barrel and assumed a baseball batter's crouch. When the rider was within range he swung with all the force he could muster. He missed. The bike sputtered on toward the village without change of speed or other indication that the rider had detected danger.

Rictor's disbelief that he had missed gave way to frustration. He was certain no one had seen him botch the simple task but he was no less embarrassed. As he hurried down the trail to brief Biggerstaff, he silently cursed himself for being incompetent and the M16 rifle for its short length. By the time his anger subsided he had decided that the bike rider must be the luckiest son of a bitch alive.

After briefing Biggerstaff, Rictor stretched out in a prone position to wait for daylight. His mind drifted back to when he was a young farm boy. He could see himself standing in his grandfather's fields watching the first paratroops of World War II making practice jumps. He had been mesmerized, watching them prepare for the war in Europe and the Pacific. By the age of ten he had known that when his time came to go to war he would be a paratrooper. He had listened spellbound to letters from his uncles and cousins in the various services, fantasizing that he was at the front with them.

He had been fourteen when the Korean War started. Big for his age and determined not to miss his chance to fight, he had falsified the necessary papers and enlisted. Eight months later, well-trained and highly motivated, he was anxious to get to the war. Just when he thought he was on his way to Korea, his true age had been discovered and he was discharged.

Two years later, still on the short side of seventeen he could wait no longer. He had signed his own enlistment papers, volunteered for the paratroops and three months later was on his way to Korea.

The rustle of moving men interrupted Rictor's thoughts. Light streaks had begun to appear in the sky, and Biggerstaff was restless. He checked the time. It was 0545 hours. Biggerstaff whispered to Zung, "Tell the company commander to get his men ready."

Rictor heard very little movement but could faintly see silhouettes as the troops moved to form a skirmish line. Biggerstaff estimated it would take five minutes to cover the hundred yards to the village. He wanted to be on the edge of the clearing when the artillery sealed the far side of the village at 0600 hours. He anticipated that the VC would pull back from the artillery barrage and run head-on into the recon troops.

At 0555 hours, the Recon Company began to creep forward. Carefully picking his way along behind the skirmish line, Rictor noted that dawn was rapidly approaching. Early risers in the village had begun stirring, and the smell of smoke from newly lit fires reached his nostrils.

At exactly 0600 hours the recon troops were on the edge of the village clearing, poised for the attack. Biggerstaff gritted his teeth and whispered more to himself than to Rictor, "What's holding up the goddamn artillery!"

Rictor shrugged. "Terry's probably having trouble getting the district chief to fire."

Biggerstaff snorted, "Fuck it! It's daylight. We can't wait any longer." He turned and grabbed Zung by the shoulder. "Tell the company commander to order the attack."

The early morning calm was shattered by bursts of small arms fire, and shrill screams soon filled the air. The company swept forward destroying everything in its path. Straw huts burst into flame as they were put to the torch. Men, women and children were herded toward the center of the village. There was disorganized resistance as the VC Security Force attempted to respond to the surprise attack and a few of the VC formed strong points in an effort to repel the attackers. Others, using terrified villagers as shields, tried to flee across the clearing to reach the jungle. The well-organized attacking troops concentrated their firepower on the VC strong points, and quickly overran them. Deadly fire from the detached machine gun by the footbridge sealed off escape and cut down everything in its path. Not a single VC managed to reach the jungle sanctuary, and the clearing was soon littered with the dead and dying. Ten minutes after the beginning of the attack, resistance had been eliminated. Except for the dead and wounded the entire Bien Me population stood huddled in a frightened mass at the center of the village.

Rictor had stayed near the company commander during the attack. He watched quietly as the troops searched and torched the remaining huts. One of the huts erupted in a fireball and he dove for cover. Stored ammo exploded and secondary explosions came from deep under the ground.

Spotting Biggerstaff and Zung near the village shrine, Rictor moved to join them. As he drew near he saw they were watching an interrogation. He observed that the prisoner, held spread-eagle on the ground by recon troops, wore the orange robe of a Buddhist monk. He also noted that under the robe the monk wore khaki trousers and military boots, instead of the traditional sandals worn by monks. Rictor wondered if the captive was really a monk, and also wondered why a phony monk would make himself so easy to detect.

Biggerstaff snarled, "If these bastards don't let up on the water treatment, they won't get anything out of this guy. They've put him under twice already."

Rictor nodded in agreement. The prisoner had lost consciousness and the interrogators were frantically trying to pound air back into his lungs. Rictor turned to Zung and ordered, "Get the company commander."

The monk gasped for air and went into a coughing spasm as he began to regain consciousness. The overzealous interrogators shotgunned questions at their half-conscious captive but failed to get answers. Once again a wet cloth was plastered over the monk's nose and mouth and held in place. One of the interrogators tilted a canteen over the monk's face and a steady trickle of water soaked the cloth. The resulting suffocation caused the monk to squirm and thrash violently. He gasped, and the wet cloth sank farther into his gaping mouth, but no air came through.

Rictor was disgusted, but he knew it was a touchy situation. The recon troops were not directly under Biggerstaff's command, and to stop the interrogation could cause serious problems with the Vietnamese. He caught Biggerstaff's eye with an unspoken question. Biggerstaff hesitated then threw caution to the wind. Stepping forward he said, "I'm going to put an end to this bullshit!" As Rictor shifted his rifle to cover Biggerstaff, he saw Zung and the company commander approaching.

Suddenly all hell broke loose. The artillery barrage scheduled for 0600 hours had begun. Not only was it late, it was also off target. Screaming 155mm. high-explosive rounds rained down on the village. The monk was forgotten as the interrogators scrambled for cover. Prisoners who had been huddled in the center of the village fled in all directions. Round after round of the heavy artillery ripped the ground and filled the air with white-hot shrapnel and shredded human remains. The recon troops panicked, and it was every man for himself. Rictor, Zung and Biggerstaff took refuge in a gully and hugged the ground. They were out of radio range so there was nothing to do but wait it out. Rictor cursed the gunners and questioned whether the misdirected artillery was an accident.

The barrage stopped as abruptly as it had begun. Amazed that he had escaped injury Rictor scrambled to his feet and surveyed the village. He spotted the still form of the phony monk. Had he been killed by the artillery or died from the water torture? It really didn't matter.

Biggerstaff called out to the stunned and bleeding company commander, who sat leaning against what was left of the Buddhist shrine. Next to the company commander lay the torn and broken body of his radio operator. The radio was in shambles. Realizing that the company commander was out of it, Biggerstaff took command of the situation and began to restore order.

Fifteen minutes after the artillery barrage, Rictor was rounding up civilian stragglers when he heard the sound of a motorbike engine starting. He scanned the trail and saw the bike burst out of a clump of bushes and head for the footbridge that spanned the creek. Rictor snapped off a couple of hasty shots on the run and reached the trail just as the machine gun by the footbridge opened up with a long burst. The motorbike rider crouched low as he approached the bridge. He almost made it, but the machine gunner zeroed in and heavy rounds disintegrated the front wheel of the bike. The rider was thrown clear of the wreckage and headlong into the creek. Masked from the machine gun by the bridge, he struggled out of the water and ran for the jungle. Rictor reached the creek in time to see the rider disappear into the thick foliage. He considered pursuit but decided it was hopeless and instead returned to the village.

By 0720 hours most of the prisoners had been recaptured, and the recon troops were making poncho litters for the seriously wounded. Biggerstaff shouted to Rictor, "Get a body count! We've got to get the hell out of here. I want the column on the trail in zero five minutes!"

Zung was helping a wounded soldier when he heard Biggerstaff's shouted instructions. He called out to Rictor, "There are twenty-six civilians and eleven dead recon troops. Including the children, we still have eighty-one prisoners."

Rictor relayed the count to Biggerstaff who cursed and called to Zung, "I saw a platoon leader over by the footbridge. Tell him the company commander is out of it and that I've taken command. Tell him to leave the dead and get the wounded on the trail. I want what's left of the original recon squad on point with you and Rictor and the rest of the company split to the flanks for security. The machine gun goes on the left flank. We're moving out in five minutes."

From high ground overlooking the peaceful river, the bridge was anything but ominous. It was a primitive structure of planks and wooden pylon spanning the hundred-foot width of the river at a height of forty feet. Swift flowing water lapped at the pylons, but from where Rictor stood the bridge looked safe.

For fifteen minutes Rictor had been studying the riverbanks and surrounding jungle but failed to detect any sign of Viet Cong presence. He shifted his field glasses and scanned the bridge for demolition charges. Detecting none he lowered the glasses.

The sound of gunfire from a mile across the river seemed to be drawing closer. He guessed the fighting involved the ARVN Paratroop Battalion. He saw that it was 1050 hours; the paratroops were almost an hour and a half late and apparently having a helluva time reaching the bridge.

Sniper fire which had plagued the Recon Company and prisoner column during the march from the village had stopped. Rictor was puzzled and disturbed. He had to think. Why had the VC let up? They had attempted to delay the column even though they apparently had a major force on the far side of the river. As the column had drawn near the bridge the harassing fire had abruptly ended. The relief of pressure on the column was intended to cause the column to hold up at the bridge, he suspected, instead of crossing immediately. If he was correct, a major Viet Cong force was moving up behind the column. If so, when the pursuing VC force reached the bridge the column would be trapped.

If Burt and the Paratroop Battalion did not arrive soon, the column had little chance of surviving. Rictor motioned for Zung, who was trying to make radio contact with the paratroops. "Go back to Biggerstaff and tell him to move the column up to this point. I'm going to take a couple of recon

people down to the bridge and attempt to cross. In the meantime, keep trying to contact the paratroops." Zung nodded,
slipped into the bush and disappeared.

Using hand signals Rictor positioned the machine gun
squad to cover the far riverbank, selected two recon people for
the crossing and moved out. As he inched down the slope
toward the bridge he thought he detected movement on the far
bank. He signaled the recon people to hold up and studied the
area intensely, finding nothing. Beneath the bridge abutment
was an opening where he could establish a lookout post. He
signaled the recon people to stay low and follow him as he
crawled the remaining fifty yards to the abutment.

Once in the covered position beneath the bridge he felt less
exposed but trapped. He couldn't understand why the VC
didn't have the bridge ambushed. Using his field glasses he
observed the far bank. Hearing noise to his rear, he turned
abruptly and spotted Biggerstaff and Zung crawling down the
slope. They were within thirty yards of the bridge when a
firefight broke out along the back trail. Rictor guessed that it
was at the tail end of the column. His suspicion about a VC
force closing on the column's rear confirmed, he signaled the
two recon people up and across the bridge. They scrambled
onto the bridge and sprinted for the far side. Halfway across
they disappeared in a cloud of fiery smoke as the center section of the bridge disintegrated.

Rictor was slammed into a pylon by the shock wave, the
impact momentarily taking away his breath. A Viet Cong automatic weapon opened up from the far bank. Splinters filled
the air as angry bullets chipped away at the overhead wooden
structure.

Biggerstaff, Zung and the Vietnamese platoon leader leapt
to their feet and raced for the bridge. Ten yards short of the
abutment the platoon leader's legs were cut out from under
him by machine gun fire. He fell to the ground screaming in
agony. As Biggerstaff and Zung slid under the bridge, Rictor
saw to his dismay that the wounded platoon leader had been
carrying Zung's radio. It lay next to him in the clearing, thirty
feet short of the abutment. Breathing hard Biggerstaff cursed,

"That rips it! If them goddamn paratroops can't pull our asses outta here, we've had the course."

Rictor ignored Biggerstaff. He was studying the radio. Glancing over to Zung he asked, "What's your pay grade?"

Zung eyed the radio with suspicion. "Step eight. Why?"

Rictor held the youthful interpreter's eye while asking, "What's the highest pay level for an interpreter?"

Zung returned Rictor's stare. "Step twelve."

Rictor grinned and motioned Zung to his side. "I think you're going to be a step twelve when you get back with that radio. When I give the signal, you get the radio, I'll get the platoon leader."

Biggerstaff was worried. "Knock off the bullshit and get the radio! If we don't get some help, everybody's pay will be going to their dependents."

Rictor winked at Zung. "Move out!" They broke clear of the bridge on a dead run. Fire from hidden automatic weapons on the far side of the river chewed up foliage and plowed furrows in the ground all around them. Zung scooped up the radio and headed back to the abutment. Rictor grasped the wounded platoon leader by the arms and lifted him in a fireman's carry. The VC gunners had found the range, and as Rictor dashed across the clearing he felt the tug as a bullet clawed at his shirt sleeve. A groan came from the platoon leader—he had been hit again. Rictor dove headlong under the bridge. The platoon leader rolled to a stop at Biggerstaff's feet.

Biggerstaff ignored the platoon leader and reached for the radio mike, saying, "I think I hear a plane!" Rictor was out of breath but, straining his ears, he too heard the distant drone. Biggerstaff switched to the emergency radio frequency and within seconds made contact. The pilot was a FAC who had been called in to support the paratroops, and once briefed as to the column's situation, he quickly agreed to act as a relay between Biggerstaff and the district artillery.

While they waited for the FAC to make contact with district, Rictor studied the twelve-foot breach in the bridge. A loose plank which had been blown free by the explosion teetered precariously at the edge of the breach. The plank appeared long enough to span the gap in the bridge.

Zung nudged Rictor and pointed to the spot where the machine gun had been left behind. Lead elements of the column had reached the machine gun position and were moving toward the bridge. Rictor saw that the recon troops had intermingled with the prisoners for cover during the crossing. Aware that it would be a massacre if the column moved onto the bridge without a way to cross, he motioned to Biggerstaff who was on the radio calling in a fire mission. Biggerstaff failed to respond.

Rictor estimated his chances of successfully spanning the gaping hole in the bridge with the loose plank, then grabbed up the platoon leader in a fireman's carry.

When the first artillery rounds crashed into the far bank, Rictor scrambled up to the trail, stepped onto the bridge and ran for the breach. At the edge of the missing bridge span he dropped to his knees, laid the platoon leader down and wrestled the plank into place. Without looking back he lifted the platoon leader and sprinted for the far side. At the end of the bridge he leaped off and plunged headfirst into the thick underbrush. The platoon leader screamed in agony, and as Rictor crawled toward him, Zung and Biggerstaff came crashing in on top of them.

The artillery had done its work well. The Viet Cong guns along the riverbank were silent so Biggerstaff shifted the artillery across the river, sealing off the column of pursuing VC. Rictor was marveling at the effectiveness of the makeshift fire missions when he heard his name called from fifty yards down the trail. He recognized Burt's voice and responded. Seconds later, Dave, Burt, and the Chinaman appeared on the trail followed by a company of paratroops.

More planks were thrown across the hole in the bridge and the paratroops gave covering fire while the prisoner column crossed to safety. Biggerstaff had the FAC work artillery along the trail to prevent ambush. Within an hour the column closed with the main body of the Paratroop Battalion and headed for Binh Hue District headquarters.

The nearer the column drew to Binh Hue the more concerned Biggerstaff's expression became. Dave stepped close to Rictor. "Biggerstaff's fat ass is dragging," he said. "With this much success you'd think he'd be high stepping."

Rictor grinned and said, "He'd rather be back under the bridge than face the district chief. I don't know that I blame him. The district chief will do his attacking through the chain of command. When Charlie's firing at you at least you get to shoot back."

Dave shook his head. "If it ain't terminal, it ain't serious. With regard to the district chief . . . fuck him if he can't take a joke."

Chapter IV

TIME TO MOVE

When the raid force returned to Bien Hue District headquarters with the prisoners, they found the district chief was livid with rage. He immediately sent a message to the province chief in Qui Nhon, accusing Biggerstaff of questioning his loyalty and undermining his command. The Vietnamese paratroop commander joined in the fray and sent a message to the ARVN high command in Saigon pointing out that the raid's success was more important than the methods used.

Biggerstaff fired off a message to the "B" Detachment advising Major Strong, the "B" Detachment commander, of the situation and requesting new orders. While waiting orders, Biggerstaff interrogated the captive Terry had guarded at the team house. The captive was indeed an agent for the district chief, and Biggerstaff hustled him over to district headquarters to confront the district chief. Unruffled, the district chief released the captive and accused Biggerstaff of trumping up the spy charge. Cursing with every step, Biggerstaff returned to the team house and ordered the team's gear packed. Even Major Strong's message that helicopter transportation had been arranged and that the team would leave Binh Hue District the next day failed to stem Biggerstaff's anger.

Bored with Biggerstaff's ranting and with nothing better to

do, Rictor spent most of the next eighteen hours watching interrogations. From what he heard he was satisfied that the Bien Me raid, even though costly, had been more successful than he had first thought. In the prisoner group were fourteen key Viet Cong infrastructure figures including the wife of the Viet Cong district chief. There were also a number of lesser officials.

When he learned the escaped motorbike rider had been the Viet Cong district chief, Rictor was even more embarrassed than he had been. Yet, he could not help but marvel at the determination of the lucky son of a bitch.

One of the district interrogators satisfied Rictor's curiosity about the phony monk. He explained that the monk was a friendly district agent who was supposed to make himself obvious by his dress so that he would be detected and taken prisoner. Once in the safety of the district camp, he was supposed to identify the Viet Cong among the prisoners. The regional force interrogators had not been informed as to the monk's true identity, thus the water torture. The subsequent death of the phony monk was dismissed by the district chief as unfortunate.

Based on the prisoners' information, the Binh Dinh province chief immediately dispatched two battalions of ARVN Marines to sweep Binh Hue District. The marines arrived on choppers, which then ferried Burt's paratroop battalion to Qui Nhon. One of the slicks was then assigned to shuttle the Americans to the ARVN camp where the truck and other equipment had been left in the care of the MAC-V Detachment. Biggerstaff, Dave and Zung departed on the first lift, leaving Rictor and Terry waiting at the chopper pad for the shuttle to return. Sitting with his back against an equipment locker, Rictor gazed out over the green rice paddies that surrounded the camp. The midafternoon sun was warm and he was relaxed as he watched the trees on the hillside sway gently in the breeze. It was one of those rare moments when he considered just how deceptive Vietnam really was. The sheer beauty of the peaceful Vietnamese countryside was totally disarming. His thoughts drifted back to Korea.

Korea had been a hard country with a well-defined enemy.

The climate and terrain were tough, too. The treacherous mountain ranges were nearly barren of vegetation, with temperatures subzero in the winter and boiling in the summer. By contrast the enemy in Vietnam was ill defined and elusive, the changing of seasons more noticeable only in the volume of rain which fell. The constant tropical climate produced huge rain forests and some of the most beautiful flowers and other vegetation Rictor had ever seen.

Rictor shook his head as he recalled how young and naive he had been in Korea. Life for a combat soldier had been much simpler. All a soldier needed was confidence in his weapons, confidence in his leaders and above all confidence in himself. With those ingredients and a good measure of survival instinct, he could live to savor the exhilaration of one on one combat.

Rictor had been drawn to Vietnam like a moth to a flame. Better trained and more experienced than he had been in Korea, he was ready, even anxious, to try newfound skills. It was the adrenaline high, that feeling of having beaten the odds that comes with winning in combat. The high combined with a good cause gave Rictor a personal sense of fulfillment. The feeling was as addictive as a narcotic.

Terry slapped at a worrisome fly. "I wonder if anybody at home really gives a damn what we're doing over here?"

Rictor studied Terry for a long moment. He suspected the absence of letters was beginning to gnaw at Terry's nerves and his question was a result of building tension. This sign of immaturity annoyed Rictor. Rubbing a three-day beard Rictor said, "I'm sure there're a few people in the world who care what a bright-eyed, bushy-tailed bastard like you is doing no matter where you are."

Rictor's comment lifted Terry's spirits and within seconds he was relating stories about his final fling before leaving the States. Terry rambled on but Rictor only half-listened. He was watching Vietnamese Marines work their way across the floor of the valley as they headed for the high ground.

The sudden crash of mortar rounds and rattle of machine gun fire sent Rictor and Terry diving for cover. The marine column had come under fire less than six hundred yards from the camp. Rice fields and hillsides which had been so peaceful only a few minutes before erupted with the impact of mortar rounds. Within minutes the Vietnamese were heavily engaged in a firefight at the base of the nearest ridge line.

More to himself than Terry, Rictor said, "Huh, looks like Charlie wants to keep the Marines here." Scanning the area around the landing zone the only person he saw was a frail Vietnamese girl walking directly toward him along a paddy dike. She had a large vase balanced on her head and took great care not to get her feet wet. She was within fifty yards of the landing zone when an automatic weapon opened up with a long burst. Hot lead kicked up dirt and made little pockmarks in the LZ (Landing Zone). Using the equipment locker for cover Rictor hugged the ground.

Raising up on his elbows, Terry peered over the locker. The only thing moving was the girl. Cursing he said, "That goddamn slick won't land when it gets back unless we smoke the LZ. What are we gonna do if the area ain't clear?"

Rictor knew their situation and barked at Terry for putting it into words. "Shut up an' look for the damn sniper! We'll worry about the slick when it gets here." He considered withdrawing from the exposed LZ but vowed to himself he would not run while the frail girl continued along the path.

As the last of the Marines disappeared behind the ridge, the girl passed within five yards of the locker. Her face was expressionless. She hesitated then continued toward the camp gate. Terry peered over the locker. "I wonder if I'd like working with ARVN Marines. Considering we're the only Americans left in this district, if that fuckin' sniper opens up again, this might be a good time to find out."

By the time the returning slick arrived over the camp, the Marine firefight had dwindled to an occasional rifle shot and two squads of Regional Force Riflemen moved out of the compound to provide security for the landing. They had barely cleared the gate when the sniper opened up again. Scanning a tree-covered ridge, which protruded into the rice paddies, Terry glimpsed muzzle flashes. Pointing he yelled, "I see the son of a bitch! He's in that tall, lone tree midway up the ridge."

Rictor located the tree but failed to see the sniper. "I don't see anything. Are you sure?"

Terry rested his M16 on the locker and squinted at the tree. "You're damn' right I'm sure. He's hiding in the fork. You wait till those security troops start moving again an' see what happens."

Rictor snapped a glance at the camp gate and saw that the riflemen were already inching forward. Terry opened up with a long burst from his M16. Rictor looked back to the tree in time to see a black pajama clad body topple to the ground. Scrambling to his feet Terry charged toward the ridge. Rictor stood up and shouted, "Where are you going?"

Terry called over his shoulder, "I got the VC bastard good! I'm gonna get his fuckin' ears!"

Rictor shouted, "Get back here, you dumb asshole! He's got friends out there and we've got a chopper to catch." Terry hesitated, defiance plainly written on his young face, then he slowly walked back to the LZ. Dropping down beside the locker he cursed under his breath as he watched the Vietnamese riflemen cross the paddies and work their way up the ridge.

The slick was orbiting at fifteen hundred feet. Rictor tossed a smoke grenade and it began to descend. The slick touched down and was still rocking on its skids when Rictor and Terry shoved the equipment locker aboard and scrambled in behind it. As the slick lifted off, Terry leaned close to Rictor. "How'd you like that shootin'?"

Rictor grunted. "Not bad for a communicator but you wasted a lot of ammo." Terry sneered and made a familiar sign with the middle finger of his right hand.

As they flew south Rictor saw burned villages and blown bridges. The Viet Cong had torn the major coastal route so badly that it was useless. Nudging Terry he pointed to the road. "That's the only major road in South Vietnam. It runs all the way from Saigon to the DMZ. Whoever controls it controls the overland lifeline of the country."

Terry shrugged. "Judging by the damage it's easy enough to see who controls it. Personally, I couldn't care less."

Rictor made a mental note of Terry's indifference and recalled a dozen occasions when his attitude had been less than desirable. He was concerned because communication was essential to the team. He was further concerned because of Terry's open animosity toward Biggerstaff and Dave. Biggerstaff was aware of the problem though, so Rictor put it out of his mind.

The pilot's voice broke through the slick's intercom. "I've picked up a 'MAYDAY' transmission from a Skyraider pilot. He's shot up pretty bad but thinks he can make it to the Qui Nhon Airfield. We're going to follow him south along the coast. If he has to ditch, we'll attempt to pick him up."

Leaning out the door Rictor looked north and immediately spotted the stricken aircraft. Trailing smoke it was closing on the slick fast. The crippled World War II fighter plane passed within a hundred yards and Rictor could see the pilot struggling with the controls. His feeling was one of utter helplessness as he watched the plane become a spot on the horizon and disappear.

The slick was twenty miles north of Qui Nhon when the Skyraider pilot radioed that he was losing altitude fast and would try to belly in on the beach. Seconds later Rictor spotted a bright orange flash several miles up the coast. He pressed the intercom switch but before he could speak the slick pilot said, "I saw it! Looks like he's bought the farm."

A few minutes later the chopper hovered over the charred remains of what had been a mighty war machine. Terry shouted in Rictor's ear, "I wish this damn slick had some guns. I feel like a sittin' duck." Rictor nodded agreement. He too would have felt more secure if a couple of gunships were riding herd. The slick pilot made a low-level search of the area but it was hopeless. The Skyraider had been much too low for the pilot to jump. After regaining altitude, the slick pilot radioed the crash location to Qui Nhon Airfield and made one more run across the crash sight before turning northeast toward the ARVN camp.

Fifteen minutes later, as the chopper orbited the ARVN camp, Rictor saw Biggerstaff standing outside the MAC-V team house.

Dave was waiting at the chopper pad with the three-quarter-ton truck. When the slick touched down, he helped load the team equipment but was uncharacteristically quiet. Rictor saw Dave's sober expression and figured he must have something on his mind. The three-hundred-yard drive to the MAC-V team house was made in silence.

Biggerstaff was waiting impatiently by the door of the team house, and the truck had barely come to a halt when he motioned Rictor to one side. He said that Terry was being replaced by Sergeant Scruggs, who was coming in from the *"B"* Detachment, and Terry would be returning to the Highlands on the next available transportation. Rictor received the news without comment. He was certain that Biggerstaff had decided to have Terry replaced in the best interests of the team.

As Biggerstaff and Rictor entered the team house Dave produced a case of beer he had gotten from the MAC-V people. Setting it on a table in the middle of the room he said, "Help yourself. It took a helluva lot of willpower to wait for you."

Terry fished an opener out of his pocket and uncapped a bottle. Warm beer sprayed his face. "Damn! Where'd you have this stuff, in an oven?"

Dave reached for the opener. "Don't knock it, hotshot, it's free." Handing a beer to Rictor, Dave nodded toward the door, saying, "There's some shade 'round back."

Sure that Dave wanted to talk in private Rictor followed him outside. Leaning against the building Dave asked, "You know about Terry going back to the '*B*' Detachment?"

"Yeah. Biggerstaff told me."

Dave took a sip of beer. "Whatta you think?"

Rictor grunted. "I don't know. It's probably for the best. Terry's got some adjustment problems. Maybe he can work 'em out back there."

Dave snorted. "His only problem's being a punk kid."

Rictor grinned. "I wonder what people thought about you and me before we got old and decrepit?" he asked.

Faking a hurt expression Dave said, "I believe you're trying to tell me something."

"Well, anyway, I'm glad it's Scruggs they're sendin' out as a replacement. I've thought for a long time he ought to be the '*B*' team commo chief," Rictor said.

Dave nodded. "At least we can agree on that. Old Scruggs is hard as a rock and he's got as much combat experience as anybody I know." Pushing away from the building he said, "C'mon, let's get another beer."

Rictor had spotted the MAC-V supply building. He said, "You go ahead. I'll be along in a few minutes. I'm gonna try to scrounge a squad tent from the MAC-V supply sergeant. Biggerstaff's got no idea how long we'll be here. He's going to wait for orders from the 'B' Detachment before moving to Qui Nhon. In the meantime, we'll need some place to call home."

After arranging for the tent, Rictor returned to the MAC-V team house and learned that a slick bringing a passenger was coming in from the Highlands at 1600 hours. Reasonably certain the passenger was Scruggs, Biggerstaff had told Terry to get ready to move.

At 1545 hours Dave and Rictor drove Terry to the chopper pad. When the slick landed Terry picked up his gear and headed toward it without a parting word. Ignoring Scruggs's shouted greeting, Terry climbed aboard. Scruggs strolled over to Dave and Rictor. "What's the matter with our boy Terry? He don't appear to be too happy."

Dave shrugged. "Can't be sure but I think he's suffering from a bad case of lack of nookie."

Scruggs said, "Huh, I think I've got it, too. What's he taking for it?"

Rictor grinned and answered, "We'd planned to get him treated in Qui Nhon but I guess we'll have to treat you instead. What's new in the Highlands?"

"Not much except for a rumor that the whole 'B' team's movin', but you know how rumors are." Looking around he asked, "Where's Biggerstaff? I've got a message for him and the chopper can't leave till he gets it."

Dave grinned. "He's up at the tent suckin' up hot beer. C'mon, let's see if there's any left."

Tossing his rucksack on the truck, Scruggs said, "That's the best suggestion I've heard all day. How're you an' Biggerstaff getting along?"

Dave chuckled. "You know Biggerstaff. He's just as lovable as he ever was."

When they arrived at the tent, Biggerstaff was waiting out front. Scruggs produced a written message from the *"B"* Detachment commander which directed Biggerstaff to proceed to Qui Nhon where he would receive further orders. After instructing Rictor to keep the team ready to move on order Biggerstaff hurried to the chopper pad and departed with Terry.

The following morning Scruggs shook Rictor out of a deep sleep to say, "I just got a radio message from Biggerstaff. We're supposed to make it to Qui Nhon. ASAP."

Rictor rubbed sleep from his eyes and reached for a cigarette. "That suits me just fine. What time is it?"

Scruggs checked his watch. "0600 hours."

Rictor yawned and reached for his boots. "Wake Dave and Zung. We oughta be on the road within an hour."

At 0715 hours Rictor drove the truck through the camp's main gate and turned south on route #1. Within an hour the truck had crawled past a dozen good ambush sites and tension was building. Rictor eased the truck around a hairpin curve and spotted a large group of farmers working in a rice paddy. Many of them were dressed in black rice cloth pajamas, the uniform most commonly worn by the Viet Cong. Aware that a favorite trick of the Viet Cong was to pretend to be farmers and spring ambushes on unsuspecting vehicles, Scruggs swung the machine gun toward the rice paddy. Without taking his eyes off the farmers, Dave reached under the dash and pulled out an M79 grenade launcher. Resting the shotgunlike weapon on the dash he opened his mouth to speak, but his words were choked off as rifle rounds struck the side of the truck.

Rictor shouted, "Hold your fire!" as he jammed the accelerator against the floorboard. He felt certain the shots had been fired from the group of farmers but he would not risk slaughtering so many innocent people to get the sniper. It was possible one or more VC had mingled with the farmers and was holding them at gunpoint. He knew Charlie sometimes used that tactic in an attempt to force a massacre. When he was sure the truck was out of sniper range Rictor reduced speed and looked back. The farmers gave no indication they had heard the shots.

Five miles north of Qui Nhon the road made a sharp turn. Rictor slowed the truck to a crawl and barely missed ramming a bus which blocked the road. Seeing that the passengers were being held at gunpoint by men dressed in black, he stood on the brake pedal and grabbed his M16.

Scruggs yelled, "Duck!" and swung the machine gun around. Leaning out of the line of fire Dave brought up the grenade launcher and flipped the safety switch.

Zung threw himself on Scruggs and screamed, "Don't shoot! They're Regional Force."

One of the men in black dropped his carbine and picked up a long stick. Attached to the end was a small Republic of Vietnam flag. Seeing the flag, Dave lowered the M79. "Goddamnit! I give up. How in the hell are we supposed to fight this stinkin' war when we can't even tell who the good guys are?"

Scruggs leaned on the gun. "Maybe if you ask him the province chief'll give his troops white hats to wear. You figure that would help any?"

Dave's frustration gave way to anger. "You know, Scruggs, you're a real fuckin' comedian. You're wasting your time as a radio operator. What this bullshit war needs is more funny men."

Rictor's frustration was as great as Dave's, but he found his friend's reaction amusing. He tried to suppress a grin, touching a match to a cigarette then shifting the truck into second gear to cover his mirth. The truck coughed a couple of times and rumbled on toward Qui Nhon.

Chapter V

QUI NHON

As the truck nosed its way into Qui Nhon, Rictor noted many changes in the coastal resort town. New gun positions manned by Vietnamese paratroops had been erected and the few civilians he saw appeared to be in a hurry to get off the streets. Waif children that normally crowded the streets begging for handouts were conspicuous in their absence. Tension filled the air, and it was obvious the paratroops were making preparations to defend the city against a major attack.

Instructed to meet Biggerstaff at the MAC-V compound, Rictor drove directly to the beachfront villa. From the gate he saw more signs of beefed-up defenses. Newly installed barbed wire glistened in the sun, and machine guns had been dug in around the troop billets.

The two gate guards gave the truck a casual going-over. They were more interested in the passengers than the truck. Their questions revealed just how little they knew about the Viet Cong and the war in general. Studying their bush hats and low-slung pistols with distaste, Scruggs shook his head. "You reckon these city soldiers are in the same army as the MAC-V people out in the bush?"

Dave grinned. "Yeah, but worse than that, they're in the same army with us."

Scruggs made a face. "I'm gonna cash in my war bonds."

Rictor pulled the truck into a parking area and climbed down. Grinning he said, "Scruggs, you keep Dave and Zung entertained. I'm going to look for Biggerstaff."

Scruggs pointed. "You won't have to look far. Here he comes."

Biggerstaff approached looking more glum than usual. Casting an eye over the truck he asked, "You have any trouble on the way in?"

Rictor shook his head. "None worth mentioning."

"I'm glad you didn't waste any time getting here. We're going to turn the operational gear over to a new detachment that's coming in and fly back to the Highlands, ASAP." Anticipating questions Biggerstaff added, "I don't know why so don't ask."

Dave said, "That's a break. What about the truck? We leave it behind?"

Biggerstaff nodded. "We'll leave it at the airstrip for the new detachment. The only thing we're taking is the voice radio and personal gear." Turning to leave, Biggerstaff said, "After you eat, get the gear squared away. The new team'll be here sometime today and I'm trying to get us on a flight tomorrow morning. I'll know one way or the other this afternoon so meet me in the compound bar at 1700 hours."

Rictor nodded and suggested, "Unless you object I'm going to let Zung go into town to see his wife and baby."

Biggerstaff shrugged. "Suit yourself. I don't care. By the way, Burt Gardner was asking for you earlier. His paratroop battalion is manning the roadblocks. I told him you'd be in later today."

When Biggerstaff had gone, Rictor said as he turned to Dave and Scruggs, "You guys want to spend the night in town?"

Dave grinned and responded, "Well, we promised to get Scruggs laid, didn't we?"

Scruggs said, "Suits hell outta me but I don't think Biggerstaff's gonna go for it."

Dave grunted. "Don't worry about that. If I know Biggerstaff he's already sniffed out a broad for himself. When it comes to pussy he's got a nose like a bird dog."

Rictor turned to Zung. "You can take off but meet us at the Green Beret Hotel around 1730 hours."

Dave said, "If you don't need me, I'm going on downtown with Zung. I'll take a look for Burt Gardner."

Rictor nodded. "Why not. Scruggs and I can handle the equipment transfer."

Scruggs watched Dave and Zung pass through the gate and turn toward town. Reaching for a cigarette he asked, "What do you make of the new order?"

Rictor grunted, "Hell, I don't know. Maybe it's got something to do with the rumor you heard about the detachment moving."

Scruggs said, "What the fuck, I guess we'll find out tomorrow. Let's go to chow. I'm starving."

As they walked toward the mess hall Scruggs mused, "Wonder what Burt Gardner wants."

Rictor shook his head. "Beats me."

Scruggs grunted. "More than likely he's got some of these city soldiers wanting to buy VC souvenirs."

They had reached the entrance to the mess hall and Rictor said, "You're sure down on MAC-V. You'd better be careful what you say, or you won't get fed."

Scruggs opened the door. "I'm not worried about that. These bastards like money too much to turn away any paying customers."

By 1700 hours the detachment equipment had been turned over to the incoming Special Forces people. After learning they would depart for the Highlands on a slick at 1000 hours the next morning, Rictor and Scruggs headed for town. As the truck bounced along the nearly deserted streets, they saw Vietnamese paratroops moving into position for the night. Pointing to one of the sandbagged bunkers Scruggs said, "Looks like these guys are expecting big trouble. What kind of place is this Green Beret Hotel?"

Rictor slowed the truck for an ARVN checkpoint. "It's a rundown hotel owned by an old Vietnamese broad who supplies rice and fish to the Special Forces camps in the area. She keeps rooms and girls for the troops when they're in town. I don't know what the Vietnamese name is for the place, but the troops call it the Green Beret."

When they pulled up in front of the hotel, boisterous cheering and laughter could be heard from the open windows. Spotting Zung near the entrance Scruggs yelled, "What's all the racket?"

Zung shook his head and pointed upstairs. "Many drunk Americans having a party."

Once inside the building Rictor led the way to a stairwell which led to the upstairs bar. As he climbed the steps an unfamiliar voice shouted, "Now, we're gonna have a solo from the best goddamn demolition man in Binh Dinh Province!"

The announcement was greeted by catcalls as a drunken voice, which Rictor recognized at once as Dave's, sang to the tune of "My Bonnie Lies Over the Ocean."

> *My girlfriend's a Montagnard sergeant,*
> *She gets jump pay and per diem to boot,*
> *She works on the corner of Tu Do,*
> *Believe me, she makes lots of loot.*
>
> *Bring back, Oh, bring back,*
> *Oh, bring back my girlfriend to me.*
>
> *My best friend's a part-time gorilla,*
> *He's giving the ARVN a fit,*
> *By selling, for twenty piasters,*
> *A do-it-yourself ambush kit.*
>
> *Bring back, Oh, bring back . . .*

When Rictor entered the bar the first person who caught his eye was a drunk sergeant from one of the outlying "A" camps. The sergeant's pants were down around his knees and he was attempting oral sex on a bar whore who lay spread-eagle on a table while his friends cheered and shouted encouragement. The girl on her knees under the table, giving the sergeant a head job, did not go undetected. A dozen or so bar girls, scattered around the room, squealed and rushed to greet the new arrivals. Rictor pushed his way through the girls and headed for the bar.

Dave stood in the middle of the room clutching a girl under his arm and a bottle of liquor in his free hand.

Scruggs caught Rictor by the arm and pointed. "Ain't that Burt Gardner passed out on the bar?"

Rictor squinted across the smoke-filled room. "Maybe, I can't be sure with him slumped over like that. If it's Burt, he must've been here a pretty good while."

Scruggs laughed. "Let's wake him up. He's missing a good party."

Rictor nodded and started for the bar. He had taken only a couple of steps when he was intercepted by a sergeant who was an old acquaintance. The sergeant caught him in a bear hug and shouted in his ear, "Where'd you drop from, Rictor? I figured some Charlie would be wearing your ears on a necklace by now."

Disengaging himself Rictor shook hands. "I've got a working agreement with Charlie. I let him keep his ears and he lets me keep mine."

The sergeant fingered the nub that had once been his right ear. Laughing, he said, "I'd make a deal with Charlie myself if I knew a way to screw him." Heading toward the bar he said, "Come on, I'm buying—we've got a lot of lies to tell."

Rictor spotted Burt's Chinaman standing in a shadowy corner with the ever-present shotgun cradled in his arm and knew that the sleeping man was Burt. Grinning, Rictor turned to the sergeant. "What happened, partner? Did Dave's singing put Burt to sleep?"

The sergeant shrugged and said, "Nah, he was half-blowed away when he got here. From the way he acted, I figure he's got some kind of problem. He didn't say much, but he was sure trying to drown something."

Rictor was curious. "I've known him a long time but I don't

ever remember seeing him completely wiped out. He's lucky he's among friends."

The sergeant nodded. "He may be MAC-V but as far as I'm concerned he's one of us."

Scruggs had been standing behind the sergeant. "You won't get any argument from me about that. It's too bad I can't say the same for most of the Maggits," he said, using the Special Forces slang for MAC-V.

Dave came over and grabbed a bottle off the bar. "What kept you guys? I'm damn near on my ass," he said. Pointing to one of the bar girls who had her skintight dress hiked up to her thighs, he said, "I know a lot of things more interesting to talk about than MAC-V."

The party picked up momentum, and, as he stood at the bar drinking, Rictor saw Dave and then Scruggs disappear down the stairwell with a girl. The more he drank the better the girls looked. He noticed one girl in particular sitting alone at a table. Her dress was Chinese and her features Eurasian. She appeared to be about twenty years old with shiny black hair which flowed to her waist. Her expression reflected neither happiness nor sadness. If anything she appeared indifferent.

Around midnight Rictor glanced about the room and discovered that the only other American was Burt, still out cold. He looked back to the table and caught the Eurasian girl watching him. Their eyes met. Rictor was not certain whether he saw an open invitation or a challenge but the idea of either was appealing. He took a step toward the table, but the sergeant with the missing ear appeared out of nowhere and intercepted him. Pointing, the sergeant said, "See that lizard crawling on the ceiling?"

Rictor nodded. "What about it?"

The sergeant said, "Well, that particular kind of lizard likes to live around people. When it hollers it makes a noise that sounds just like somebody yelling 'Fuck you.' As a matter of fact most of the guys around here even call it the 'fuck you' lizard. With its long tongue it's able to . . ."

Rictor interrupted. "I'm beat. You'll have to tell me about the lizards tomorrow. Right now I'm going to get some shut-eye." Turning toward the table, he discovered that the Eurasian girl had disappeared. He cursed and headed for the stairwell where Zung sat cross-legged with a folding stock carbine cradled under his arm. Instinctively Rictor glanced to the shadowy corner of the room. Burt's ever-present Chinaman had not moved. When Rictor passed by Zung he scowled and asked, "Where're Dave and Scruggs?"

Zung shrugged. "They went downstairs with two girls over an hour ago."

Rictor glanced over his shoulder. The Eurasian girl was nowhere in sight.

Zung chuckled. "What's the matter, Sergeant, you lose something?"

Rictor grunted and started down the steps. "I guess that depends on how you look at it." At the bottom step he stopped and looked back. "Let's keep the fact that I got hung up without a girl our little secret. I don't feel like listening to Dave's bullshit."

Zung didn't answer but Rictor judged by his amused expression that he could not be counted on to keep the secret very long. Deciding not to press the point he began looking for a place to sleep. He located an unoccupied room at the end of the corridor and considered undressing. The old habit of sleeping in his clothes prevailed. Stretching out on the uncomfortable bed he lit a cigarette and stared into the darkness.

Rictor was startled out of a sound sleep by a gunshot, which sounded like it came from the bar. Cursing under his breath, he rolled out of bed and groped for his automatic. Feeling his way across the dark room he located the door and eased it open. As he stepped cautiously into the hallway, he heard Dave shout, "Don't shoot!"

Dave's protest was drowned out by a rapid series of shots, then shouts of, "You killed him, Burt! You blew his goddamn head off!" Rictor charged down the dark corridor to the stairwell and climbed the steps two at a time. At the entrance to the bar he stopped abruptly. Burt stood on the bar side of the room slowly reloading his 357 magnum. Dave was leaning against the bar with his back to the door. Slowly he pushed himself from the bar, faltered and nearly fell. Regaining his balance he staggered over to Burt. Using the wall for support

Dave pointed to the mangled body of the lizard. "Burt, you shouldn't have done it. He wasn't fuckin' with you."

Burt poked at the lizard with the toe of his boot. Swaying gently he said, "Guess you didn't hear what he said. Lizard or no lizard, nobody talks to me like that."

Rictor glanced to the corner; the Chinaman had not moved. Shaking his head, Rictor jammed the automatic in his shoulder holster and headed for the bar. As others in various states of dress rushed into the room the lizard shooting was told and retold. All thoughts of sleep disappeared, and the party resumed.

At first light Rictor began rounding up the team. Thirty minutes later everyone was on the truck except Dave, who had stopped for a farewell drink. Beeping the horn, Rictor shouted for him. When he finally came out of the hotel, Burt and the Chinaman were with him. Dave said, "Jesus Christ, Rictor! Take it easy on that horn. We got sick people here."

After studying Burt's face, Rictor said, "Get aboard, Dave, and let's get moving."

Dave winked and indicated Burt with his thumb. "You want to give this drunk a lift to his unit?"

Rictor continued to study the thirty-five-year-old, sandy-headed veteran for a long moment. Burt's normally clear piercing eyes were bloodshot, and his tanned face was drawn. He obviously had a dilly of a hangover. Grinning, Rictor pressed the starter. "If we don't, we might have to go through life with him on our conscience. From his looks the walk would kill him."

When the engine caught, it pinged and knocked as though it were coming apart. Scruggs said, "This old truck sounds like it needs a valve job. Maybe giving it away ain't such a bad idea after all."

Rictor shifted into low gear. "Wonder what happened? It didn't sound this way yesterday."

Scruggs said, grinning, "Maybe it knows this is its last trip for us and it's gonna just lay down and quit."

"I hope not before we police up Biggerstaff. I wouldn't like the job of trying to explain why we didn't show," Rictor commented.

A few minutes later Rictor brought the truck to a halt in front of the ARVN paratroop command post. As he climbed down, Burt spoke up soberly. "You guys keep your heads down. Them berets ain't bulletproof."

Rictor shifted to low gear. "We'll do that and maybe you ought to go easy on the booze. They tell me it's bad for the liver. Be seeing you."

As the truck picked up speed Dave leaned over to Rictor. "Did you know Burt extended his tour again?"

"Yeah. This makes three times," Rictor said.

Dave frowned. "Looks like he's pressing his luck."

Thinking Burt had all the symptoms of a man with a big problem, Rictor shrugged and responded, "Maybe so, but he's a pro, and it's the only war we got."

The pinging noise under the hood grew louder. By the time they arrived at the MAC-V compound there was serious doubt in Rictor's mind the truck would make it to the airstrip. He parked next to a troop billet, climbed down and raised the hood. He saw a wire attached to the fan blades and upon closer inspection saw three hand grenade pins dangling from the wire's end. Very gently he lowered the hood and stepped back. It was obvious as to what was causing the pinging noise. Everytime the fan turned, the wire slapped the grenade pins against the engine. Worried it might be a time device, he shouted, "Everybody except Dave get back from the truck!"

Dave scowled. "What's up?"

Rictor lowered his voice. "We've got a problem, and since you're the demolitions expert I'm going to let you solve it." He raised the hood and pointed to the wire. "You'll have to hurry. If it's a time device, it might go any second."

Dave took a quick look, then crawled under the engine. Rictor stepped away from the truck and called to Scruggs, "You and Zung don't let anyone near the truck. Looks like we've picked up a bomb."

Scruggs cursed. "Jesus, all we need is to blow up the fuckin' compound. That'll give the Maggits something to talk about."

Rictor walked back to the truck. All he could see of Dave was his feet. "You find anything?"

72

Dave chuckled, then said, "Yeah. I'll be out in a minute."

"What's so fuckin' funny?" asked Rictor.

Dave slid out from under the truck and lay on the ground grinning. "If I didn't know better, I'd swear the dumb bastard that planted the grenades was MAC-V."

Relieved, Rictor asked, "How about letting me in on the joke."

Still chuckling Dave said, "There are three American-made frag grenades taped to the truck chassis. The Charlie that done the dirty work figured when the truck was cranked, the fan would turn, causing the wire to pull the grenade pins. A few seconds later we were supposed to go up in smoke."

Rictor grunted. "Looks like it worked up to a point. What happened?"

Dave broke out in a wide grin. "When the fuckin' idiot taped the grenades to the chassis he also taped the grenade handles down."

Rictor motioned for Scruggs and explained what had happened. Scruggs said, "If the gate guards had searched the vehicle when we came in like they're supposed to, we wouldn't have brought the damn bomb on the compound."

Remembering that he himself had gotten in the truck and started it without a search, Rictor said, "I fucked up too. Let's just keep it our little secret and don't make the same mistake again."

Dave had replaced the pins and began removing the grenades. Chuckling he said, "I'd give a month's pay to have seen the expression on that Charlie's face when the truck didn't go boom."

Chapter VI

RETURN TO THE HIGHLANDS

Rictor, watching through the open doorway of the descending chopper saw that they were approaching the *"B"* Detachment camp. He spotted Major Strong, the *"B"* Detachment commander, standing near a jeep next to the landing pad. When the chopper touched down, the short, thick-chested major waited patiently for the team to off-load and gather around him. After scrutinizing each man he grunted, "Judging by the red eyes I'd say it was a long night in Qui Nhon. As soon as I've finished with you, they want you over at operations for a debriefing." He got right to the point. "The reason I called you back on short notice is because the '*B*' Detachment will be moving south to assume a new mission. We're replacing a MAC-V team as advisors to Quang Be Province. The move must be completed in five days. An advance liaison team has already departed, and I leave tomorrow with most of the staff. The rest of you will prepare the equipment for air movement, close down the camp, then join us on the fifth day. The executive officer and his strike force of Montagnard paramilitary troops won't be making the move. They're being reassigned to '*A*' camps here in the Highlands." He hesitated, then added, "One more thing. When we get closed in at

Quang Be, there's a MAC-V lieutenant colonel coming in to take command. I'll be staying on as his executive officer."

The major waved off a flurry of questions. "You'll get the details as I get them. It's going to take everybody working together to make this go smoothly. I expect your full coopera-tion." Without further comment he turned and headed for the command post.

Scruggs shook his head. "This whole fuckin' war is turning into a bad joke."

Dave said, "You ain't seen nothin' yet. You got a taste of MAC-V leadership over in the Mang Yang Pass when that Maggit colonel ordered them troops mounted. How do you think you're gonna like serving under some asshole like him?"

"Well, at least we won't have to put up with the dumb bastard who was running the show in the Mang Yang Pass," Scruggs said, still shaking his head. "They've probably re-lieved his ass."

Rictor grunted. "Let's don't paint everybody with the same brush. This new guy could be okay."

Scruggs fumbled for a smoke. "The thing that bugs me most," he said, "is getting saddled with a MAC-V com-mander. They really put a hurting on Major Strong. The way we're shuffled around makes me feel like we're part of a giant chess game."

Rictor's mind flashed back to the ambush, and he said, "If we are, I figure we must be the pawns."

Dave interrupted. "Let's don't stand here shooting the shit all day. My ass is dragging, and I need a bath. Let's get the damn debriefing over with."

As they approached the operations building, Scruggs pointed across the compound. "There's Oink. I'll bet that satchel ass is crying his heart out about having to get the commo gear ready to move." Rictor grinned. The man Scruggs pointed to was Sergeant Hassen, the detachment com-munication chief. He had acquired the nickname "Oink" at one of the local whore houses because of the noises he made while getting laid. When the whores saw him coming they would hold their nose and go "Oink, oink."

"Let's get inside before he sees us," Dave said. "I don't feel like listening to his whining."

After the debriefing, Rictor headed for the team house. At the entrance he nearly collided with Henderson, the detachment's only black. Rictor was genuinely glad to see the tall, lanky radio operator. As they shook hands Henderson said, "Man, I heard you guys really took an ass kicking in that ambush up in the Mang Yang."

Rictor shrugged. "Depends on who's telling the story. How's it with you?"

Henderson smiled, exposing a perfect set of teeth. "Pretty good if I could keep Hassen off my ass."

Rictor shook his head. "If you radio operators were smart, you'd stay out of his way."

"How can you when you work for him?" asked Henderson.

"Don't hand me that crap," Rictor replied. "Not one of you has ever passed up a chance to bump heads with Hassen."

Henderson chuckled. "I don't recall seeing you go out of your way to avoid him."

Rictor shook his head. "That reminds me. I've got to see Hassen about some reports. Let's walk over to the commo shack."

Henderson turned to leave. "Thanks, but no thanks. I'm off shift. If I go over there, you can bet your ass he'll put me to work. I'll see you in a while."

When Rictor entered the commo shack, Hassen didn't hear him. Sprawled in a chair with his feet propped on a field desk, Hassen was munching an apple and reading a paperback novel. He chomped down on the apple and used his free hand to scratch his mammoth stomach. The nickname "Oink" really suited Hassen, and Rictor made no effort to suppress a laugh.

Hearing Rictor's soft laugh Hassen glanced toward the door and gave a half-hearted wave. "When did you get in?"

"A couple of hours ago. I need some information for my after-action report," answered Rictor.

Hassen bit off a chunk of apple. "Sure thing. Come back in about an hour. Terry will fix you right up. I'm just relieving him for chow."

"I don't need to see Terry. I want to go over the message log with you. I'm tryin' to get the report in before Captain Snyder pulls out for his new camp."

Hassen picked up the novel and began searching for his place. "You'll have to come back later. I don't have time to mess with it right now."

Rictor's anger was instant. "Hassen, most of the men in this detachment say you're fat, dumb and lazy. The more I'm around you the more I'm inclined to agree with them."

The door banged open, and Biggerstaff yelled, "Sergeant Rictor! I want to see you out here right away."

"Be with you in a minute, Captain. I need to get something straightened out first," Rictor answered.

Biggerstaff snapped, "Now!"

Rictor hesitated, then headed for the door. Looking over his shoulder he said, "Hassen, when I get back you better damn well have that log ready."

As Rictor stepped outside Biggerstaff said, "Hassen works for me! You stay off his case."

Rictor shook his head with disbelief. "Captain, can't we put this off till another time?"

Biggerstaff shouted, "Goddamnit, Sergeant, I'm giving you an order."

Rictor figured either Biggerstaff was being his normal obnoxious self or maybe the asshole had gone just plain fuckin' crazy. Not really caring which, he said, "Captain, I don't think you heard the entire conversation."

"I heard enough. Hassen's got some management problems, but I won't have you talking down to him like that," Biggerstaff said.

Rictor let out a sigh. "I know that Hassen's a better than average radio operator, but he's a long way from being a commo supervisor."

Biggerstaff snorted. "That's not for you to decide, Sergeant! Like I said he's got some problems."

Rictor knew he was dangerously close to insubordination but threw caution to the wind. "You're right, Captain! He's got three problems. He's fat, dumb and lazy."

Biggerstaff's face turned beet red. "Goddamnit, Sergeant! You stand at attention when you address me."

Rictor put his heels together, but the ass chewing which followed fell on deaf ears. Trying not to hear the ravings of Biggerstaff, he decided that the captain and Hassen had a lot more in common than just being fat.

Nearly winded, Biggerstaff finished by saying, "I'm giving you an order not to make any more derogatory remarks to or about Sergeant Hassen."

Rictor took a deep breath. "Captain, do I have permission to speak?"

Biggerstaff nodded.

"Well, I think you'll agree Hassen is overweight. That makes him fat. You and I both know he's not the smartest man in the world, and you only have to watch him for ten minutes to tell that he's lazy as hell."

Biggerstaff's mouth opened but no words came out. Rictor continued, "And by the way, the moment we arrived at this camp my responsibility to you ended."

Without waiting for a response he stepped back inside the commo shack. Fifteen minutes later, his report finished, Rictor stopped outside the commo shack and lit a cigarette. His mind made up, he headed for the operations building to find Major Strong. He had decided to talk with the major about getting Hassen replaced as commo chief. Entering the building he bumped into Captain Snyder. The young executive officer stuck out his hand. "Hello, Rictor. Good to see you."

Rictor took the extended hand. "It's good to see you, Captain. Sorry to hear that you're gonna be leaving us."

Snyder nodded. "If I had my druthers, I'd be moving with the detachment. Unfortunately what I want doesn't matter."

"When are you leaving?" Rictor asked.

The captain checked his watch. "There's a light aircraft coming for me shortly."

Rictor debated discussing the commo problem with Snyder but decided against it. For all practical purposes the captain was no longer the executive officer. Rictor said, "I just dropped by to say good-bye. I know you've got a lot of things to do so I'll be going."

The captain stuck out his hand again. "I wasn't going to leave without saying so long. You take care of yourself."

Rictor nodded. "Yeah, you too, Captain. We'll probably be going back to the States together. I'll see you then."

Rictor turned to leave but Snyder stopped him, saying, "By the way I've talked to Major Strong. Effective tomorrow Scruggs is the new detachment commo chief."

Hiding his surprise Rictor nodded and stepped through the doorway. He spotted Scruggs and the major standing in front of the team house and waited until the major had gone inside before approaching Scruggs. Pretending not to know about the job change, Rictor said, "I saw the major talking to you. We just got back. Have you screwed up already?"

Scruggs attempted to conceal his satisfaction. "Nope. I've moved up. You're talking to the new commo chief!"

Rictor pretended astonishment. "Well, I guess the major's finally flipped his lid. We'd better get Doc Brown to take a look at him."

"Naw, he's okay. He just knows a good man when he sees one," said Scruggs.

Turning toward the team house door, Rictor said, "I think he'd better get his eyes checked."

Lockwood, the detachment supply sergeant, was in the team house lounge going over a list of shipping weights. As Rictor dropped into a chair, Lockwood glanced up. "You coming to the party this evening?"

"What party?" asked Rictor.

"A going-away party for the Montagnards. Everybody chipped in to buy goodies and the party's laid on for eighteen hundred hours," said Lockwood.

Rictor said, "I didn't know about it but it sounds like a good idea. The Yards have been a good bunch to work with. As a matter of fact, I wish they were going with us."

Lockwood nodded. "Yeah, me too, but there's no chance of that."

Rictor said as he rose to leave, "I've got to get my gear squared away. Figure out what my share of the party cost is and I'll give it to you."

"That can wait. There's something else I wanna talk about," Lockwood said.

Rictor detected uncertainty in Lockwood's voice. "What's on your mind?"

Lockwood hesitated before saying, "It's not my business, but it concerns the team so I'm butting in."

Rictor shrugged. "If something's bothering you, spit it out."

"Well, ever since Terry got back from Binh Dinh Province, he's been bad-mouthing you and Dave. Now that you're back, I figure there might be trouble."

Rictor headed for the door. "Terry's too mouthy for his own good. I'll take care of it." Feeling less confident than he had said, Rictor went in search of Dave. He found him at the camp gate and from the expression on Dave's face knew he had already gotten the word. Fishing out a fresh pack of smokes, Rictor said, "Let's take a walk."

Dave shook his head. "Can't right now. I'm waiting for the truck that went to the village to get supplies for the party."

"Why?" Rictor asked.

"Cause Terry's driving it, and I need to see him."

Rictor said, "Fuck Terry! You and I have been friends for a long time and I've never steered you wrong. C'mon, I want to tell you something."

Dave was determined. "I'll listen to anything you've got to say but I'm not leaving this gate."

Rictor said, "Dave, we've talked about it before. Terry's immature and he's frustrated. Sometimes when a person's frustrated he lashes out at the people he likes most."

"What you say may be true but why us?" asked Dave.

"It's not you and me personally. It's just that we're convenient," Rictor answered.

Dave began to waver. "Well, if he keeps running his mouth, he's going to wish I wasn't so damn convenient."

Rictor saw that he was gaining ground. "There's something else. If we have a big flap with Terry, the rest of the team is going to take sides. It could get out of hand and bust the detachment wide open. Give Terry a little time. He'll come around."

Dave relaxed. "Okay! I'll let it go for now, but Terry had better watch his mouth. I'm not taking any more of his crap."

Satisfied, Rictor headed back to the team house wondering if he could practice what he had preached.

Shortly after 1800 hours everyone in the camp except the security guards and the Vietnamese Special Forces (VNSF) assembled for the party. The VNSF had been invited but declined the invitation. They seldom, if ever, associated with the Montagnards. Like most Vietnamese, they thought themselves far superior to the tribesmen. The feeling was mutual, and the Montagnards were not overly concerned when the Vietnamese failed to appear.

Major Strong and his staff sat in a circle around one of the clay urns which had been set around the building and drank with the Montagnard leader. The remainder of the detachment mingled with the tribesmen. The group Rictor sat with consisted of Dave, Scruggs, Hassen and five Montagnards. The eldest tribesman placed a long reed in the urn and began sucking on it. When he had his fill he passed the reed to Rictor. After a long drink Rictor passed the reed to Dave and it continued to move in a clockwise circle. Every so often one of the Yards would pour more booze into the five-gallon urn. Scruggs grunted. "This damn thing's like a perpetual fountain. It'll never run dry."

Rictor learned from Scruggs that Major Strong had given Hassen a chance to transfer to another unit but Hassen had decided to stay with the detachment. Rictor's opinion of the ex-commo chief improved. After the food was served, the Montagnards sang and performed tribal dances. In return the SF (Special Forces) men sang a few verses of the only song they all knew: "I've Been Working on the Railroad." The singing, dancing, and serious drinking showed no signs of slowing down by 2300 hours when Rictor decided he had had his fill. He had just asked Dave and Scruggs if they were ready to leave when Hassen made a strangling noise. Rictor glanced around in time to see Hassen pull the reed from his mouth and puke. When Hassen was finished being sick, he looked drunkenly around the room and made a loud *ouu-uuuuuuu* noise.

Rictor rose to leave and was joined by Dave and Scruggs. At the door they all stopped and looked back. Hassen was sucking on the reed again, and the midget-like tribesmen were breaking up with laughter as they patted Hassen on the back.

As they walked toward the team house Scruggs asked, "You guys know what Hassen's new job is? He's leaving with the major for the new camp tomorrow. He's going to be the detachment mess sergeant."

Dave made a strangling noise. "I don't believe it."

Rictor grinned. "There's one advantage—as well as he likes to eat we should always have plenty of chow."

The lyrics of "North to Hanoi" blared from the team house. Dave said, "Sounds like somebody's started their own party. Let's go take a look. Maybe they've got some decent whiskey."

In the team house lounge, Terry and four other men were sitting at a table drinking. Spotting Dave and Rictor, Terry slurred, "Everybody bow down! The two 'Big Men' from Binh Dinh Province have arrived."

The room grew quiet and all eyes were on Dave and Rictor. Dave flushed with anger. "Terry, you're a punk. You wouldn't know a big man if he stepped on you."

"Why don't you try stepping on me, lightweight," Terry sneered.

Dave took a step toward the table, but Rictor stopped him. "Take it easy, Dave. He's drunk."

Doc Brown, the detachment medic, rested a hand on Terry's shoulder. "You guys knock it off and let's all have a drink."

Terry snarled, "Get your hands off me, Doc. This crap's been building for a long time."

"I don't know what your problem is, Terry," Rictor said quietly. "But let's talk about it tomorrow when our heads are clear."

"I'll tell you what the problem is. I'm tired of every son of a bitch that ranks me telling me what to do. My ass is hanging out just as far as yours."

Seeing there was no way out, Rictor walked over to the table and stood facing Terry. "You including me in that 'son of a bitch' category?"

Terry started to rise, saying, "You rank me, don't you?" Shifting his weight to his right foot Rictor threw a left hook to

Terry's mouth followed by a straight right to the jaw. Terry dropped to the floor like a wet sack of flour but he was tough and came up swinging.

Everyone in the small room was moving at once. Some were trying to separate Rictor and Terry. Others were just trying to get out of the way. Rictor ducked under a wild right hand and landed a solid left hook to the kidney. Terry sucked air through clenched teeth and flurried with both hands. Rictor took a chop high on the head and threw a right cross which caught Terry flush on the nose. Blood flowed freely from Terry's nose but he only shook his head and lunged forward. He was hurt but a long way from being whipped. Backpedaling, Rictor tripped on the overturned table and fell on a broken whiskey bottle which cut a deep gash in his right hand.

Scruggs grabbed Terry and shoved him into the hallway where half the detachment had crowded to watch. Doc Brown had not been quick enough to avoid the falling table, but it took a lot to shake the thin blond medic. After picking himself up from the littered floor and removing a sliver of broken glass from his arm he said, "You guys sure make it hard on the family doc. C'mere, Rictor, an' let me take a look at your hand."

Scruggs offered Terry a drink. Terry snatched the bottle from his hand and sucked out the remaining two inches of bourbon. Lowering the bottle he shouted, "I'm going to kill that fuckin' Rictor!"

Scruggs grunted. "Terry, you're not only drunk you're a fool! I've had just about all I can take of you myself."

Doc heard the shouted threat and caught Rictor's eye. "Let's go to the Aid Station. Your hand needs treating."

As Rictor stepped into the hallway, Terry swung at him with the empty whiskey bottle. Scruggs was standing too close. The bottle struck him high on the shoulder and shattered. He pivoted to his left and threw a looping right hand. Terry took the punch square on the jaw and staggered. Scruggs grabbed him by the collar and measured him for another punch. Terry was tough but the second punch nearly tore his head off. He fell to the floor and lay still. The fight was over. Scruggs and Dave picked Terry up and carried him to his room.

At the Aid Station, Doc Brown examined Rictor's hand more closely. He decided the cut needed stitching and went to work. When the repair job was completed, he cautioned, "Take it easy for a while. That cut is awful close to a tendon."

On his way back to the team house Rictor heard boisterous arguing. Near a partially completed well on the far side of the camp, he thought the voices belonged to Dave and Terry but he wasn't sure. At the team house entrance he sensed rather than saw someone in the shadows. Squinting, he saw Henderson standing motionless with his head cocked toward the well. "What's up?" Rictor asked.

Henderson chuckled softly. "Right after you left for the dispensary Terry woke up. Still drunk and roaring mad, he threatened to shoot you. Dave policed up all Terry's weapons and tossed them in that thirty-foot dry well. When Terry found out about it he went ape shit. He wants to go down in the well and get them. If Terry's dumb enough to go in the well, Dave's going to cut the rope. The flap you hear is Dave taunting Terry to go down. It sounds to me like Terry's just about to chicken out."

Shaking his head Rictor said, "It's been a hard day. I'm going to sack out."

Rictor awoke with a pounding headache, a cut lip and a sore hand. Long after he had gone to bed he could still hear Dave's and Terry's raised voices. He wondered if Terry had spent the night in the well. Before he could decide whether to get up or go back to sleep the door burst open and Dave came in. "How's the hand?" he asked.

Rictor grimaced. "It don't hurt any worse than my head."

Dave laughed. "Hope you feel up to a trip."

"Why?" Rictor grunted.

"Cause you're making one whether you feel like it or not. The Old Man (Major Strong) found out about the fight and he thinks some fresh air will be good for all of us. He's ordered that everybody involved in the fight is to escort the Montagnards to their new 'A' camp," Dave finished, smiling.

Rictor groaned and climbed out of bed. "Did Terry spend the night in the well?"

84

Dave's grin broadened. "Naw. While we were arguing he sobered up and chickened out."

"Would you really have cut the rope?" Rictor asked.

Laughing, Dave asked, "Is the Pope a Catholic?" Heading for the door he said, "By the way, if I were you I'd stay clear of Biggerstaff for a while. I overheard him crying to the Old Man that you were insubordinate yesterday. The Old Man told him to stay the hell out of the enlisted men's disagreements. He said we had a way of working out our own problems. From what I gathered the major figured your description of Hassen was pretty accurate."

"How did Biggerstaff take it?" Rictor asked.

Dave shrugged. "He puffed up like a toad but didn't have much to say. Looks like you won this round, but, like I said, if I were you I'd stay out of Biggerstaff's way until he's cooled off."

Rictor nodded. "Sounds like good advice. I was half-expecting an ass-chewing from the major."

By 1000 hours, six trucks loaded with Montagnards were ready to roll. Climbing up into the passenger seat of the lead truck, Rictor was surprised to find Terry sitting behind the wheel. Frowning, Terry started the engine and eased the truck through the gate. Without waiting for the other vehicles he picked up speed and headed for the Montagnard's new camp. The route was relatively secure but for the next two hours Rictor kept a close watch for any sign of ambush. Neither he nor Terry spoke during the entire trip.

When they arrived at the "A" camp, the Montagnards off-loaded quickly and fifteen minutes later the convoy pulled out for the return trip. "How's the hand?" Terry asked, breaking the silence.

Rictor thought he detected a note of concern. "Sore. How's the jaw?"

Terry rubbed his chin. "Scruggs has one helluva right hand." Rictor relaxed. There was no trace of animosity in Terry's voice.

When the convoy returned to the "B" team camp, Hassen was waiting at the gate. Telltale marks from the party the night before were evident on his fat face. When Dave's truck stopped to be searched, Hassen climbed aboard and rode to the parking area. Heading for the team house, Dave said to Rictor, "I just found out from Hassen that I'm leaving for Quang Be Province this afternoon with the major."

Rictor grimaced. "I knew all along that you'd figure out a way to beat helping with the packing."

Hassen grinned. "Do you know who the major is leaving in command here?"

Before Rictor could answer, Dave said, "Hassen's buddy, Biggerstaff."

"That little piece of news is all I needed to make my day." Rictor said drily.

Shortly after 1600 hours Rictor and Scruggs drove the advance party to the airstrip. They returned to the camp in time to attend a briefing by Biggerstaff, who issued timetable instructions for packing the remaining equipment and supplies. He planned to release the camp to MAC-V control on the fourth day and depart by air with the equipment on the fifth.

The following three days were hectic for Rictor. He divided his time between helping Lockwood with the equipment and keeping an eye on the Vietnamese Special Forces. With both the American and the Vietnamese detachments preparing to move, supplies were being shuttled in all directions. Rictor knew that regardless of the VNSF's other qualifications, they were experts when it came to pilfering. In an effort to prevent the supplies from disappearing, he spent most of his time at the camp gate inspecting loaded trucks as they departed. Being at the gate served an additional purpose; it kept personal contact with Biggerstaff to a minimum.

By noon of the fourth day the heavy packing was finished. The detachment trucks had been loaded with tons of mortar and machine gun ammo which was to be shipped on the first aircraft. Most of the detachment members were either loafing around the camp or packing their personal gear. Rictor was almost finished packing when Scruggs came to his room waving a slip of paper. "Take a look at this message to Biggerstaff from Major Strong."

Rictor read it aloud. "New commander feels due to good

security and limited space this location, no need for mortars, machine guns and ammo for same. Take appropriate action for disposal."

Scruggs scratched his ear. "What do you make of it?"

Rictor reread the message before answering, "If security's as good as this message says, I wonder why we're being sent down there?"

Scruggs reached for the message. "Beats me, but there's one thing for sure. Biggerstaff's got a problem with those loaded trucks, but I think he's going to move the ammo like he planned. With the planes arriving tomorrow, he don't know what else to do except blow it up."

"There's enough waste around here without that," Rictor said.

Heading for the door Scruggs said, "By the way, scuttlebutt has it that I was right about them relieving that dipshit colonel who was in charge at the Mang Yang ambush. His name is West, and he'd only been at II Corps ten days. Apparently the senior corps advisor has sent his ass packing."

"It would be better if they sent him back to civilian life. Thanks for the info. I'm going over to check with Lockwood."

On the way to the supply building, Rictor spotted Zung walking across the compound. He wondered if Zung planned to move his family to the new camp. "Hey, Zung! C'mere a minute," he called out.

Zung walked over and Rictor asked, "You going to leave your family in Qui Nhon?"

Zung nodded. "I was hoping maybe I could move them from Qui Nhon to the new camp, but it's too far and there's no time."

Rictor was concerned. "You'd have to go to Qui Nhon to get them and then make the trip south by bus and on foot. With the roads out and Charlie all over the place I doubt if you'd make it."

Zung nodded again. "That's why I decided not to ask for permission."

After a moment Rictor said, "Let me see what I can do. I'll talk to you later."

As Rictor entered the supply building he heard Lockwood say, "I think you're right, Captain, but I'll bet there's a flap when we get there."

Biggerstaff finished signing some papers and threw down the pen. "I don't give a good fuck how much they flap. The ammo and weapons are already loaded and I refuse to take the responsibility for destroying them. They go!"

Seeing that Biggerstaff was in a worse mood than usual Rictor hesitated, then asked, "Captain, what's the chances of letting Zung go to Qui Nhon to pick up his family? He can meet us at the new camp in a few days."

Biggerstaff was concerned with his own problems. Without looking up he said, "I don't give a damn what Zung does!"

Lockwood caught Rictor's eye and indicated the door with a nod. Rictor made a hasty retreat from the building. It had been too easy and he was not going to give Biggerstaff time to change his mind. Thirty minutes later, he had finished writing two letters. One was to the team sergeant of the Qui Nhon Special Forces detachments. He had requested the sergeant to arrange air transportation for Zung and his family from Qui Nhon to Saigon. The other letter was to the air liaison sergeant at Tan Son Nhut Air Base in Saigon. He had asked the liaison sergeant to arrange transportation for them to Quang Be Province.

With the letters out of the way, he left for the airstrip to see the MAC-V air movement sergeant. An hour later Zung was booked on a supply plane which would depart for Qui Nhon the following afternoon. Finding Zung in the operations building, Rictor gave him the letters and instructions. Zung was stunned. Before he could recover, Rictor walked away, inwardly smiling with the feeling he had made a friend for life.

Late in the afternoon, Dave returned from Quang Be Province. He had been sent by Major Strong to brief the remainder of the detachment. Rictor listened as Dave described the new camp as being small but plush and part of a large complex which surrounded the provincial capital. Not a camp in the true sense of the word but rather a fenced area between the province chief's home and a regional force compound.

Dave said, "According to the briefings the advance party

had received from MAC-V on arrival at the new camp, there's very little need for security."

Rictor interrupted. "What makes you think security is not important?"

Dave responded, "I didn't say that's what I thought, but it's the impression you get down there. The province chief's favorite joke is that there are only two VC in Quang Be Province and both of them are friendly to the government. I guess it's been quiet down there for a long time. The MAC-V colonel—I mean the new detachment commander—says there hasn't been any overt VC activity around the capital in over a year."

Scruggs asked, "What kind of officer is the new colonel?"

Dave shook his head. "No comment. You can decide for yourself when you get there."

Henderson asked, "And what do you mean *plush?*"

"That'll be a surprise, but I'll tell you this much. MAC-V troops go there from all over the country for rest and recreation." Holding up his hand to ward off more questions, Dave said, "Before you pick me to pieces, I've got some more info. Some of the MAC-V people assigned there now ain't leaving. They'll be integrated into the 'B' Detachment."

There was a moment of silence followed by a barrage of grumbling and questions. Scruggs summed it up when he said, "It ain't bad enough we're being saddled with a Maggit commander. Looks to me like we're being deactivated as a Special Forces unit."

Rictor felt like something was wrong, but he decided to hold his questions until he could talk to Dave alone. He couldn't help but think the new camp sounded too good to be true. He didn't believe there was any place in Vietnam as secure as the one Dave had described.

Later, as he and Dave walked toward the MAC-V compound, he asked, "What's the new colonel's name?"

Dave cursed. "I've been hoping you and Scruggs wouldn't ask me that. The new commander has been down there for the last couple of years. About two weeks ago he was sent up here as deputy corps advisor. His name is West. After that stupid ambush fuckup in the Mang Yang Pass, the corps senior advisor very quietly sent him back to Quang Be Province and diverted his replacement up here."

Rictor grunted. "Amazing! Utterly fuckin' amazing!"

Dave said, "Think of God. That'll give you a pretty good idea as to how he pictures himself. In the short time I was there, I got the idea he'd do just about anything the province chief asked. He's a real ass kisser." Dave hesitated. "I figure we oughta keep the Colonel West story quiet for a while. Biggerstaff won't say anything. He's too worried about his goddamn report card."

Rictor and Dave stopped at the entrance to the MAC-V club. "How many troops are we getting?"

Dave shook his head. "None. There's an understrength Ranger Battalion and some RF troops down there but they've got MAC-V advisors. There won't be anybody on our compound but MAC-V and us."

Rictor was apprehensive but he decided not to ask any more questions for the time being. He said, "I'll brief Scruggs. If you don't want to answer a barrel of questions, make yourself scarce for a while."

Inside the club Rictor spotted Scruggs sitting alone at the bar. He took the seat beside him and asked, "Where is everybody?"

Scruggs motioned toward the game room. "They're in there watching Henderson get fleeced."

Rictor shook his head. "Is that American Montagnard shooting dice again? I thought he learned his lesson the last time he went up against those people." Then he said, "I want to talk to you alone for a minute. I've something to tell you that you're not going to like."

Scruggs frowned. "Sounds serious." He listened quietly, but by the time Rictor had finished, his face was red with anger and his lips were trembling. "That fuckin' colonel got Shay killed. If he fucks up anybody in this detachment, I'll waste him myself."

Rictor knew that Scruggs didn't make idle threats. He said, "Well, just keep this quiet for the time being and let's see what happens."

Scruggs nodded agreement.

Rictor said, "Good. Come on, let's see what the Maggits are doing to Henderson."

The next morning C123 providers began landing at 0700 hours. When the last aircraft was loaded, Rictor climbed aboard and watched through the window as the plane taxied into takeoff position. Catching a glimpse of Zung standing by the flight shack, Rictor wondered if he would ever see the young interpreter again.

Chapter VII

THE RESORT

The heavily laden transport made a slow descent and broke out of the clouds over a jagged, jungle-covered mountain which looked out of place in the midst of so much flat terrain. Rictor studied it through the window, assuming it was the Binh Tien Mountain that Dave had spoken of at the briefing. Near its base lay a sprawling village, and to the north, the provincial capital and military complex. He spotted the American compound, which lay on the west side of the complex bordering the river valley. As the plane banked to the south the crew chief signaled that they would land in four minutes. Rictor snapped his safety belt into place and tried to relax, but something tugged at his subconscious.

Once on the ground the pilot taxied alongside a mountainous pile of supplies which had been deposited by other aircraft and brought the plane to a halt. Rictor walked down the ramp to where Doc Brown was loading ammo on a three-quarter-ton truck. "Where's the brass band and dancing girls?" he asked.

Doc spread his hands. "Beats me. I'm just low man on the totem pole and got stuck with shuttling this stuff to the compound. Where's Lockwood?"

Rictor glanced back inside the aircraft before saying, "He'll be along in a minute. He's talking with the crew chief."

A MAC-V sergeant came around the truck carrying a case of ammo. Acknowledging the sergeant with a nod, Doc said, "Meet Sergeant Campbell. He's coming into the detachment as a medic." As they shook hands Rictor wondered what qualifications the MAC-V medic had for assignment to a Special Forces Detachment.

Olga, the detachment demolition sergeant, yelled from the front of the truck, "You guys can quit fuckin' off now. The truck's loaded! Get aboard and let's head for the compound. I'm starved!"

Lockwood came off the plane with a satisfied expression on his face. "The Air Force is going to unload the plane," he said. "Who's staying back as security?"

Campbell pointed to a Vietnamese civilian standing near the plane. "That national policeman over there has been detailed as a guard."

Lockwood said, "No chance! Vietnamese cops are so slick they can steal your radio and leave the music. I'll stay till the truck gets back."

Rictor was as surprised as Lockwood that anyone would consider leaving critical supplies to be guarded by a Vietnamese civilian even if the civilian was a cop. Olga said, "I'll stay too. The major would flip if he found out that one of us was out here alone."

As soon as Rictor and Doc were on the truck, Campbell cranked up and headed for the compound. Just north of the airstrip he pointed out Binh Tien District headquarters. Rictor made a mental note of the large number of regional force troops lounging around the compound. With so many troops available for maintenance he wondered why the defensive gun positions were in such poor condition. Two miles north of the district headquarters they passed a Steing tribal village. Rictor was aware that the Lowland tribesmen lived separate from the Vietnamese and held the same social status as Montagnards. He was curious about the village dwellings. Pointing to one of the larger rundown buildings he said, "Those block houses look like they might have been built by the French."

Campbell nodded, replying, "The French once had a prison camp here. When they left the Steing moved in and set up housekeeping."

Doc grunted. "Judging from the condition of the village, the health conditions must be awful. Has MAC-V ever had a medical patrol out here?"

Campbell snorted. "Are you kidding? With the amount of medical supplies we get, I've been lucky to keep a first aid kit together."

"Well, at least that problem is solved," Doc said. "The 'B' Detachment has plenty of supplies and we can damn sure get more."

"In that case, I'm ready to come out here anytime you say," Campbell said.

A few minutes later, they came to a village that had many new huts. Campbell slowed the truck. "That's the refugee village. It's jammed with people from all over the province. They're fed and otherwise supported by the Overseas Mission." Rictor thought it was odd to have a large refugee village in an area described as pacified. Something was nagging strongly at his subconscious.

The narrow dirt road wound around the base of the mountain and entered Quang Be Village. The inhabitants Rictor saw on the streets were moving about freely, and the tension and fear that had been so evident in Qui Nhon were conspicuous in their absence.

They drove north of the village, past a chopper pad, and turned onto a street which ran due north through the military complex. Rictor tried to recall the American compound as he had seen it from the air. As the truck moved slowly along the street, he saw the ARVN ranger and regional force compounds, noting that their meager defenses were in need of repair. He was still looking at the rundown RF fighting positions when Campbell announced, "Welcome to the resort."

Scanning the compound, Rictor saw that it was roughly the size of a football field and enclosed by an eight-foot wire fence. The fence was lined with neat beds of flowers, and he wondered who had time for such trivialities. The four buildings were well constructed and painted. Except for a huge pile

94

of recently arrived supplies just inside the gate, the grounds were as neat as a pin.

Campbell drove through the unattended gate and parked close to one of the buildings. Climbing down from the truck he said, "Now that the whole team is here, we'll have to double up in rooms. Rictor, you can bunk with me if you want to."

Rictor nodded. "Suits me. Let me get my gear, and you can show me where."

Campbell said, "Let's eat first. After chow, I'll show you to the room."

Following Campbell into the largest building on the compound, Rictor saw that most of the detachment was already eating. Hassen stood in the middle of the large room shouting instructions to the waitresses, who scurried back and forth between the kitchen and dining area.

The ex-commo chief saw Rictor and called out, "What do you think of this joint?"

Rictor answered, "Looks great. How's the chow?"

Hassen motioned for a waitress. "Find yourself a seat and give it a try."

Scruggs sat at a table which had a couple of empty chairs. With his mouth full of food he waved Rictor over. Rictor pulled out a chair and said, "If you'll stop eating long enough, I'll introduce you to Sergeant Campbell here."

Scruggs swallowed hard. "Already met him and I ain't got time to talk about anything but commo. I've got a blue million problems to take care of."

Rictor sat down. "Don't tell me about them. They might spoil my appetite."

Scruggs pouted. "Okay, but seeing as how we don't have a chaplain, I thought maybe you'd listen."

"Nope. Not interested."

One of the waitresses approached the table with a tray of grilled sandwiches and salads. Finding the food delicious, Rictor decided he was going to like the mess whether he liked anything else about the new compound or not.

"Who are those guys?" Scruggs asked Campbell as two Americans in civilian clothes entered the room.

"Watts and Mendoza. They're the USOM representatives assigned to Quang Be Province. They come here once in a while for chow or a drink but most of the time they stay clear of the compound."

Rictor asked curiously, "Why?"

"Well, being with the civilian aid program, they think it hampers their progress to be closely tied to the military effort. They say they're trying to win the hearts and minds of the local civilians."

"What they're trying to do with a handful of rice is being done all over the country a lot more effectively by Charlie," Scruggs scoffed.

"Yeah," Rictor agreed, "but Charlie's not using rice. He's using the business end of a Russian or Chicom rifle."

"Which method is getting the best results?" Scruggs asked. The answer was obvious, and Rictor didn't bother to respond.

When he was finished eating, Campbell said, "I hate to rush you, but let's take your gear to the room. I've got to get back to the airstrip."

Rictor took one final bite and pushed his chair back from the table. "No problem. I'm finished."

Scruggs said, "I might as well help too. I've got so much to do that a few more minutes lost won't hurt anything." At the mess hall door they met Callahan, the detachment operations sergeant, who informed Rictor that he was to be at the operations building at 1400 hours for an operations and intelligence briefing.

When they reached the truck, a large black monkey was plundering through the supplies. Campbell shouted, "Git down from there, your hairy bastard!" The monkey casually climbed down and headed for the mess hall. Campbell laughed. "That was Deuces, the compound mascot. He's friendly enough most of the time but a thief all the time."

Scruggs grinned. "You sure he's a monkey? Sounds like he might be a Vietnamese in disguise."

Rictor said, "Be nice, Scruggs. Maybe he's a VC. I'll check him out when I get time."

Carrying Rictor's duffel bag Campbell led the way toward the rear of the mess building. At the alley entrance formed by two rows of troop billets, Rictor saw a large sign which read Keep Off The Grass. Scruggs nodded toward the sign. "Man, seeing that makes me homesick. It's the first one I've seen since we left Fort Bragg."

Rictor grunted. "There are a lot of things around here that seem more like stateside garrison than a combat outpost."

Campbell stopped at the door to one of the rooms. "This is it. C'mon in." The room was more than adequate, with two beds and a large wardrobe with a mirror. Dropping the duffel bag on one of the beds Campbell said, "Watch this." He stepped over close to the doorway and pulled down on a rope. Canvas, which draped the front wall, rolled up like a shade exposing the alley through large screened windows.

Scruggs said, "I'll be damned. I've stayed in stateside hotels that weren't this nice."

Campbell moved toward the door. "I've gotta get back to the airstrip. Make yourself at home. I'll see you later."

Rictor sat down on the nearest bed and felt for his cigarettes. "Okay, Scruggs, I can see that something is bothering you. What's up?"

Scruggs heaved a deep sigh. "These Maggits have been operating on a shoestring. They don't even have a commo bunker and the major has given me a week to rig an operational system to the 'A' teams. It'll take a miracle. I'm going to use the commo van we brought in until we can dig a bunker but I've got to have some antenna poles right away. Rictor, we could have big problems."

Checking his watch Rictor saw it was almost time for the briefing. He hurriedly unpacked and headed for the operations building. As he approached the building, he stopped abruptly and made a 360-degree visual search. He had finally realized what had been nagging at his subconscious. There was not one defensive gun position on the entire compound.

Chapter VIII

FRUSTRATION

The small operations room was crowded, but Rictor managed to work his way to a seat next to Dave. The briefing was conducted by a MAC-V captain who explained the working relationship between the Americans and their Vietnamese counterparts. Each morning Colonel Nam, the Quang Be Province chief, held a briefing at the capitol building and both the military and civilian staff attended. The new *"B"* Detachment commander, Colonel West, was Colonel Nam's personal advisor and at these briefings the previous day's military activities were discussed and future operations planned. Colonel West offered advice and assistance on both civil and military matters. After a plan of action was decided on, Colonel Nam issued orders to the agencies concerned.

The captain described Colonel Nam as a cooperative officer unafraid to make a decision. He further explained that all of the MAC-V advisors enjoyed good working relations with their Vietnamese counterparts. To insure a smooth transition, Colonel West had decided that the outgoing MAC-V personnel would continue to run the show for a week, while the *"B"* Detachment monitored and got settled from the move.

At the conclusion of the operations briefing, Rictor stayed behind for an intelligence briefing. When the room was clear the briefing captain picked up a pointer and walked over to a wall map. He pointed out the provincial boundaries and explained to Rictor that Quang Be Province was subdivided into four districts of which Binh Tien was the largest. He said that the most recent overt VC activity in Binh Tien District had been more than a year ago. It had been a long-range mortar attack on the capital and caused only minor damage. Almost as an afterthought he added, "From time to time the Viet Cong distribute propaganda leaflets but even that activity is limited."

Curious as to how much the MAC-V people actually knew about what went on in the province, Rictor asked, "The area sounds quiet enough. How close do you work with the local intelligence agencies?"

The captain appeared embarrassed. After a pause he answered, "The Vietnamese handle all the intelligence collection but they keep us informed as to what's going on."

Rictor knew that the Vietnamese gave just enough information to the Americans to keep them satisfied. Remembering the lack of compound defenses, Rictor said, "If you don't mind, I'd like to take a look at the compound defense plan."

The captain shook his head. "You don't need to bother with that. The Vietnamese Regional Force troops on the adjacent compound are responsible for our defense."

Rictor persisted. "I'm talking about the American defense plan. What action do we take if the compound comes under attack?"

"We don't have a separate plan. We're a part of the overall defense plan. But don't worry, we're prepared. Have you seen the large hole at the end of the alley formed by the billets?" asked the captain.

Rictor shook his head. "No, I haven't had much time to look around yet."

"If the compound is ever attacked by high-angle fire, everyone is to take cover there until it lifts," continued the captain.

Rictor had a difficult time hiding his concern. "What happens if there's a ground attack?"

The captain grinned. "That's not very likely. The Viet Cong

would have to come through a lot of Vietnamese troops to get at us."

Rictor got up to leave. He couldn't believe that anyone with the rank of captain could be so gullible. "Maybe you're right, but you put more confidence and trust in the Vietnamese than I do."

He was almost to the door when the captain stopped him. "I received some information today that might interest you."

"What's that?" asked Rictor.

"An ARVN Ranger Patrol returned from a three-day search operation today at 1200 hours. Yesterday the patrol uncovered a VC cache about ten miles south of here. The cache contained propaganda handbills and detailed drawings of the capital complex," said the captain.

Rictor was interested. "I'd like to take a look at the drawings."

The captain spread his hands. "Sorry, they've already been turned over to the province intelligence section. I didn't get to see them myself."

Rictor frowned. "Do you know if this compound was included in the drawings?"

"I'm not sure, but I think it was. Lieutenant Maxwell, one of the ranger advisors, was with the patrol, and he's here on the compound if you want to talk with him," added the captain.

Rictor nodded and said, "Thanks for the information."

He left the building thinking about the drawings. They were not significant by themselves but were worth studying. He would like to have seen them. At the rear of the mess he decided to look in the alley for the position the captain had said would be used for shelter in the event of an artillery attack. Locating the hole near a brick wall at the west end of the alley he estimated the eight-foot rectangle to be four feet deep. Seeing it had no field of fire Rictor muttered to himself, "They'll never get me in that fuckin' death trap."

Terry squeezed through a small opening between the brick wall and a corner of the troop billets. "You talking to me?" he asked.

"No, I was just mumbling," Rictor said.

Terry pointed to the hole. "What's it for?"

"It might be a grave under the right circumstances," Rictor said laconically.

"What'cha mean by that?"

"Nothing. I was thinking out loud."

"Rictor, sometimes I think you're loony as a fuckin' bed-bug."

Rictor glanced at his watch and saw that it was almost 1700 hours. "C'mon, Terry. I think the bar's open. I'll buy you a drink."

"Okay, you've talked me into it, but I still think you're crazy."

Entering the mess hall by the rear door they found the bar crowded. Spotting Dave and Lockwood, the supply sergeant, on the far side of the room, Rictor worked his way toward them. As he approached, he heard Dave say, "Sorry, Lockwood, but you know I can't do a damn thing until I get the materials and the labor!"

Lockwood raised his voice. "Well, something's got to be done and fast. Just to find room for it, I had to put most of the mortar and machine gun ammo over on the RF (Regional Force) compound."

Resting a hand on Lockwood's shoulder, Rictor said, "What's the matter, Supply Sergeant, you got problems?"

Lockwood spun around, saying, "You'd better believe it! I've got supplies piled all over the fuckin' compound. With the goddamned rainy season starting any minute they're gonna get wet. When they do, we can kiss 'em good-bye."

"How about a little help, Rictor?" Dave pleaded. "This guy is about to eat me alive. He thinks all I hafta do is twitch my ass and a quartermaster depot will materialize."

Before Rictor could respond, Lockwood snapped, "Quit being a smartass! I know it's gonna take some time. All I'm asking is how long?"

Dave said, "Like I already told you, I can't do anything until Colonel West gives his okay. Olga and I have drawn up some building plans, and Major Strong is gonna talk to the colonel about them this evening. Maybe we can get started tomorrow."

"Well, I don't know of anything that can be done today so let's have a drink," Rictor said, changing the subject.

Terry said, "Give me your order, guys, Rictor's buying."

Scruggs came up behind Lockwood. "Did I hear somebody say Maverick was buying?"

Rictor smiled. "Looks like Terry's got me committed. Whatcha drinking?"

Scruggs said, "Bourbon and water." Shifting his eyes from Lockwood to Dave, he said, "Ain't this a happy little group? Who died?"

"Go away, Scruggs, nobody needs you," Dave said.

"You remember that the next time you want to send a radio message," Scruggs responded.

Hassen passed by on his way to the bar. Dave called to him, "Hey, Hassen, you getting enough to eat?"

Hassen patted his massive stomach. "Just between you and me, I never had it so good."

Rictor had been concerned that there would be trouble between Hassen and Scruggs over the commo chief position, but Hassen seemed to be satisfied with his new job. Terry returned with the drinks, scowling. "Who's the Vietnamese sergeant at the bar?"

Hassen said, "That's Sergeant Lee, Colonel West's interpreter."

Terry snorted. "To hear him talking to that Maggit lieutenant, you'd think he was a fuckin' colonel."

Dave reached for his drink. "I think you've got a hard-on for all zipperheads."

Terry shrugged. "Maybe, but you don't have to listen to this guy very long to tell that he's no fuckin' good."

Facing the bar Rictor studied the slight Vietnamese sergeant for a moment. Shifting his gaze to the man with whom Lee was talking Rictor asked, "Who's the lieutenant?"

"He's a ranger advisor named Maxwell," Hassen said. "He just came in from a three-day operation."

Rictor started for the bar to talk to the lieutenant about the captured Viet Cong documents but stopped when a waitress announced it was time to eat. Hassen glanced at his watch and hustled off toward the kitchen. Terry called after him, "Watch

102

out, Hassen, or she'll be the mess sergeant and you'll be a waitress!" For a reply Hassen patted himself on the rump, farted and kept moving. The message was clear, and Terry laughed. "Look at the hams on that joker."

At 1900 hours the barmaid came to work and Campbell introduced her as Coa Kim. Rictor noted that she was beautiful and from the glances she and Campbell exchanged, he suspected they had more than a casual interest in each other.

As Colonel West and Major Strong approached the bar Rictor observed them. The colonel was of medium build and had dark, well-groomed hair, and the way he carried himself left no question in anyone's mind that he felt superior to everyone in the room. It was clear from his manner that the colonel thought himself a hardened field grade officer and expected subordinates to act accordingly. Rictor joined Campbell and Doc at a table and learned that they planned to take a medical patrol to some of the nearby villages the next day. Rictor volunteered to accompany them to become familiar with the area around the capitol. Campbell said, "The USOM folks, Watts and Mendoza, are coming too."

Rictor said, "Then it's settled. I think I'll turn in. Tomorrow looks like a busy day."

Campbell gulped down his drink. "Just a second and I'll go with you. I'm ready for some sack time myself."

At 0745 hours the following morning Rictor stood in front of the operations building watching Deuces. The monkey was amusing himself by running up and down the tennis court. When the command group came out of the building Rictor fell in behind them for the two-hundred-yard walk to the capitol. The capitol building was a three-story concrete structure which looked out of place when compared to the shacks in the nearby village. The command group climbed a winding stairway to a large conference room on the second floor that was crowded with both military and Vietnamese civilians. Colonel West and Major Strong took their reserved seats in the front row while Rictor moved to the rear of the room.

Promptly at 0800 hours Colonel Nam, the province chief, entered, accompanied by Sergeant Lee who called the assembly to attention. The colonel walked to the front of the room and shook hands with Colonel West and the major. Lee mounted a low platform at the front of the room so he could be seen by the Americans for whom he was to translate.

One after the other, the different civilian and military agency heads mounted the platform and briefed those present. As each speaker finished, Lee summarized in English what had been said. Rictor found the briefing boring, and it struck him as odd that not one of the agencies appeared to have any problems.

The province intelligence officer's presentation was short and made no mention of the drawings and propaganda documents brought in by the ranger patrol. Rictor began to suspect that the common method of operation at the capital was for the various agencies not to share information with each other.

When the last agency head finished, Colonel Nam mounted the platform. Indicating a large wall map with his pointer he spoke in Vietnamese. Turning to Colonel West, he spoke in English. Pointing to the map he indicated two areas he had selected for air strikes. After a brief discussion about the number of aircraft to be used, Colonel West agreed to request the strikes.

Bothered by the fact that nothing had been said during the intelligence briefing which justified air strikes, Rictor understood why the Americans and Vietnamese had a good working relationship. The province chief made a decision and the Americans agreed.

After the briefing Rictor returned to the American compound. Work details had been organized and most of the detachment personnel were busy erecting temporary storage tents.

The medical patrol which Rictor was to accompany was nearly ready to depart. Lee was to be the patrol's interpreter. Campbell and Doc had just finished loading the medical supplies on a four-wheel drive carryall when Watts and Mendoza, the USOM people, arrived. After Campbell made the introductions, Mendoza said, "You won't need your weapons. The only shots we're going to pass out are hypos."

Mendoza, Watts and Lee were unarmed. Rictor caught Doc

Brown's eye as he responded to Mendoza, "I'll take it along anyway. We might run across a snake."

Doc rested his carbine on the fender of the carryall. "I've brought a snakebite antidote, too."

Biggerstaff came out of the operations building and called to Rictor, "Check on the possibility of recruiting some laborers from the villages."

Before Rictor could answer, Lee said, "Any civilian labor you need will be obtained through the provincial labor minister."

Rictor noticed the authoritative tone Lee used. After waving acknowledgment to Biggerstaff, he turned to face Lee. Looking the interpreter directly in the eye he said, "It won't hurt to take a look." Without further delay Campbell cranked the truck and headed for the gate.

As they bumped along the winding rocky road, Rictor had second thoughts about having left Zung in the Highlands. He instinctively disliked Lee and knew there would be trouble between the two of them.

They arrived at the refugee village, but it appeared to be deserted. Campbell directed Lee to move about the village, repeatedly calling out in Vietnamese that the American doctor had come to treat the sick. Lee had repeated the call several times when an old man carrying a small baby hobbled from one of the huts. They both had festered jungle ulcers on their feet and legs. The old man's sores were so badly infected he had a difficult time walking. He was obviously frightened but concern for the child's welfare had brought him out of the hut. Campbell and Doc began to work on the sores immediately. Their gentle manner encouraged other villagers to come out of hiding. Within fifteen minutes, there were nearly a hundred people, all in need of treatment, crowded around the carryall. Their medical problems ranged from malaria to tuberculosis.

Reaching for a roll of gauze, Watts said, "The most important civic action done over here is providing medical treatment."

Rictor nodded. "There's no question about it. If the Saigon government wants to make friends with the people, this is the way to do it."

Doc and Campbell did all they could with their limited supplies, and after promising to return, the patrol departed for the Steing tribal village. During the drive, Rictor asked Watts where he and Mendoza lived.

Watts said, "We've got a house in the main village just south of the compound."

Rictor was skeptical. "Is security so good around here that you don't sweat the VC?"

Mendoza answered, "It's not a matter of physical security. The VC are hesitant to harm us because to do so would cost them civilian support."

Rictor shook his head. "I admire your courage but I question your wisdom. Don't you realize that an effective aid program can hurt the VC more than an infantry division? How long do you figure they'll let you move around free as a bird?"

Unimpressed, Mendoza said, "Well, we haven't had any trouble so far."

Rictor nodded. "Charlie's got the patience of Job. Maybe you oughta consider moving to the compound."

Campbell turned off the main road and headed toward the Steing village. Lee sat up straight in his seat. "Where are we going?"

Campbell grinned. "We're gonna treat the people in this village."

Lee was shocked that the Americans would waste their time and medicine on the tribesmen. Rictor was familiar with that attitude. It was typical of most Vietnamese, especially the ones from Saigon. On impulse he turned to Lee and asked, "Where's your home?"

Lee sneered, his face filled with open animosity. "Saigon."

Rictor laughed and shook his head.

Campbell stopped the carryall near the village and Rictor saw that living conditions were worse than he had suspected. He had visited many Rhade and Jarai villages in the Highlands but the living and health conditions of the Steing were by far the worst he had ever seen. A few of the villagers spoke Vietnamese, but for the most part, they spoke only the Steing tribal language. Luckily, the village chief and some of the

106

elders spoke French. Between Lee's Vietnamese and Mendoza's limited French, the patrol managed to communicate.

The patrol was the first medical assistance the villagers had received from the American or Vietnamese governments. While questioning the chief about the villagers' skin diseases (obviously caused by filth), Doc learned that the village did not have a fresh water supply. When the French departed, they had left a water pump but it hadn't worked in years. After inspecting the pump, Watts and Mendoza agreed to replace it. They also promised to send rice to the village as soon as possible.

Rictor noted he had not seen male inhabitants in either village between the ages of fifteen and forty-five. He knew that the absence of young men normally indicated the government or the VC were placing troop levies against a village, and he decided to check it out with province intelligence. With Mendoza's assistance, Rictor questioned the village chief about laborers and found him eager to help. The village obviously needed the money.

Late in the afternoon when the patrol returned to the compound, Rictor saw two nearly erected squad tents. Assuming that they were for supplies, he hoped the added storage space would keep Lockwood pacified for a while. On his way to the operations building he saw the detachment weapons sergeant erecting an 81mm. mortar. He wondered if the major had convinced Colonel West to build defensive positions.

Locating Biggerstaff in the operations building, Rictor informed him that laborers could be obtained from the Steing village. Biggerstaff looked up from the map he was studying. "You're not going to check with the provincial labor minister?"

Rictor shrugged. "I plan to see him in the morning right after the briefing. If he can come up with some laborers I won't bother with the tribesmen."

Biggerstaff nodded. "Find out from Dave and Lockwood how many people they need."

After briefing Biggerstaff on the patrol, Rictor left the building to look for Dave and located him near the gate. "How many laborers do you need?"

Dave scratched his head. "It's hard to say. I could use a dozen right now." Pointing to the compound water tower he said, "That damn thing has got to have a storage tank. It's not big enough to handle the load."

Rictor grinned. "Sounds to me like an engineering problem. Spare me the sad details and just tell me how many people you need."

"I've already checked with Lockwood and the weapons sergeant," Dave said. "With the help we're gettin' from the detachment, we still need about fifteen laborers."

"I didn't know that the weapons sergeant needed any help?"

Dave replied, "You don't expect him to dig in the mortars by himself, do you?"

Rictor didn't mention that he had seen a mortar being erected. "Diggin' crew serve weapons positions is news to me. Last I heard, Colonel West wanted them left in the Highlands."

Dave shrugged. "All I know is that Major Strong and the colonel had a long meeting this afternoon and when it was over the major came back here mad as a Russian jumpmaster with a planeload of quitters. He told us to dig in the mortars."

Rictor nodded. "It might cost us a major but it looks like we won the first round."

Dave started for the mess hall. "C'mon, it's chow time. We can talk about mortars later. I hear we're having roast beef."

Following Dave into the mess hall Rictor noted that the dining room was almost segregated. With the exception of a couple of ranger advisors and Campbell who shared a table with Doc, the MAC-V people ate on one side of the room and Special Forces on the other.

Rictor finished eating and lit a cigarette. He looked to the next table where Terry and Scruggs were wolfing down their food. "How's commo shaping up?" he asked.

Scruggs swallowed and answered, "I think we'll make the one-week deadline. It's difficult because I'm supposed to support everybody on the damn compound with detail men."

Terry stopped chewing long enough to say, "If some of the Maggits would get off their ass and help, things would move a lot faster."

Dave leaned back in his chair. "You're right, Terry, but seeing as how we don't have any control over them, you might as well forget it."

Terry snorted. "Maybe so but they live here and it gripes my ass to see them loafing around the compound or sitting in here drinking coffee while every man in the 'B' Detachment is busting his ass."

Rictor said, "Most of them will be leaving in a few days. In the meantime, it won't help matters any to have a feud. Have you forgotten that our commander is MAC-V?" Not feeling up to a long Special Forces versus MAC-V debate, he stood up and headed for the bar.

Terry washed down a mouthful of food with tea. "No, I ain't forgot, but I still don't understand it! Do you?"

Ignoring the question Rictor continued toward the bar. He settled into a seat next to Henderson. "How's my favorite Montagnard?"

The black radio operator smiled. "Hello, Maverick. What's new on the riverboat?"

Rictor laughed. "Not much. You want a drink?"

"No, I just came over to get a closer look at Coa Kim."

Pretending secrecy, Rictor looked both right and left. Lowering his voice he said, "Don't let the word get around but that's why I'm here." He ordered bourbon and when Kim brought it he asked, "Did you know you've got a couple of secret admirers?" Kim smiled and held out her hand for payment. She hadn't understood what Rictor said but her smile was warm and friendly.

Rictor finished his drink and decided to take a look around the compound before going to bed. At the rear door he stopped and looked back to the bar. Henderson was trying to explain to Kim the meaning of secret admirer. Prepared to give odds that she would never understand, Rictor smiled and stepped outside.

At 0745 hours the next morning, Rictor was standing in front of the operations building waiting for the command group. He looked around for Deuces but the monkey was no-where in sight. When the command group came out of the building and headed for the capital, he followed along, wondering if today the VC drawings and documents would be mentioned.

The briefings went as usual—there was no mention of the documents. When Rictor returned to the compound, Dave was perched on top of the water tower taking measurements. He motioned Rictor to the base of the tower and yelled, "Zung and his family got here while you were gone!"

Rictor was surprised that Zung had been able to make the long trip so quickly. "Where's he now?"

"He's down in the village looking for a place for his wife and baby to stay."

"Did he say when he'd be back?"

"No, he's been gone a good while. He oughta be back soon."

Rictor nodded. "I'm glad he's here. I'd just as soon not use that bastard Lee any more than I have to. When Zung comes back tell him to wait here for me. I'm going to find out where the labor minister's office is located."

A few minutes later, Rictor came out of the operations building. When he saw Zung standing at the base of the tower he realized how much he had missed the young Vietnamese. He had not given it much thought before, but the interpreter had become more a friend than a soldier. He approached Zung from the blind side and growled loudly. "Where in the hell have you been? You should've gotten here yesterday."

The twinkle in Zung's eyes showed that he was not fooled by Rictor's pretended irritation. "I came as fast as I could, Sergeant Rictor. Your letters prevented it from taking a lot longer."

Rictor snorted. "Well, you're here now and that's the important thing. Did you get your family squared away?"

"Yes. I found a house in the village. They'll be okay."

Rictor stepped through the gate. "Well, let's not stand around here talking all day. C'mon, we're gonna see about hiring some laborers."

When they were out of Dave's hearing, Rictor said, "If you need more time to get your family settled, let me know. You can have as much time as you need."

At the labor building, Rictor and Zung were ushered into the minister's office by a male secretary. Zung made the introductions and Rictor got right to the point. The discussion moved slowly because Zung had to translate every question and response. It took fifteen minutes to find out that it would take three days for the minister to supply fifteen men. Unhappy with the three-day delay Rictor inquired about wages. The minister said that each laborer would receive 110 piasters ($1.25) per day.

Rictor had been authorized by Biggerstaff to pay up to fifty-five piasters per day. Aware that the national wage scale for common labor was forty-six piasters, he asked why the pay rate was excessively high. The minister said there was a severe labor shortage in Quang Be Province. From his conversation with the Steing village chief, Rictor knew the minister was lying. He told Zung to find out how the money was to be paid. After a brief exchange with the minister, Zung looked at Rictor and shook his head. "All wages will be paid to this labor office once a week. I am sure that more than half of the piasters will be kept by the minister."

As Rictor started to leave he said, "Tell him to get fucked! We don't need labor bad enough to stand for his petty graft."

When Zung translated the minister's mouth dropped open but no words came out.

Rictor stomped out of the office and headed for the provincial intelligence building to check the security risk in hiring Steing tribesmen. When he was introduced to the intelligence officer, Rictor was surprised to learn that the gaunt Vietnamese captain spoke perfect English. Ten minutes later, he knew that the provincial officials had conspired to force the Americans into hiring laborers at twice the normal wage scale. The intelligence officer had said, "It will take from three weeks to six months to conduct a security check on the tribesmen. Without the investigation, my agency cannot accept the responsibility for their loyalty."

Rictor said, "I need laborers and I need them now. What do you suggest?"

The Vietnamese captain hesitated a moment. "There is a way to solve the problem. I can provide all the men you need from the Regional Force Unit at Binh Tien District, if you are willing to pay one hundred and ten piasters a day for each man. But there are conditions."

"What are they?"

The captain's voice was steady. "The wages will be paid to me, and our agreement will be, shall we say, confidential."

Thoroughly disgusted, Rictor's first impulse was to drag the intelligence officer from behind the desk and kick his ass. Realizing the consequences of such an act he stood up to leave. "Forget it, I don't need your fuckin' help. As far as I'm concerned you can take your RF labor and cram it!"

Back at the compound Rictor explained the situation to Biggerstaff, who became enraged. After getting the okay to hire labor from the Steing village, Rictor left operations looking for Dave. Halfway to the gate he could still hear Biggerstaff cursing.

Dave and Olga were in a waist-deep hole they were digging at the base of the water tower. Rictor called to Dave, "You got time to go with me and Zung to hire some laborers?"

Dave said as he climbed out of the hole, "I'll make time. Where are they?" After Rictor's brief explanation, he said, "If that's the way the Vietnamese wanna play the game, it suits the hell out of me. I'd rather work with the tribesmen, anyway."

Olga stopped digging and leaned on the shovel. "If I had my druthers, I'd druther be back in the Highlands."

Dave pointed to mud-splattered Olga. "I've already got one Montagnard on the payroll."

Olga gave him the finger and resumed digging. Dave chuckled. "Did you see that? You'd think they would have at least taught this boy some respect for his elders before they booted his ass out of that big-time college."

Olga tossed a shovel of mud out of the hole and splattered Dave. "Sorry about that, boss. I must've lost my head."

When he was well out of Olga's hearing range Dave said, "Olga's learned almost as much about demolitions in a year an' a half as I have in fifteen but he shouldn't be here. He oughta be back in school."

For the first time in all the years Rictor had known Dave,

the tough engineer had come very near showing real affection for someone. Rictor said, "Don't expect me to pin a rose on you but I guess you've done a pretty good job of teaching him. As far as school's concerned he's got plenty of time for that when he gets back to the States."

Dave frowned. "You mean *if* he gets back!"

Catching Dave's meaning Rictor said, "Well, let's just say it's up to people like you an' me to make sure."

At the village it didn't take long for Rictor to learn that the village chief was a good horse trader but with Zung's help he finally reached an agreement. Each laborer was to receive fifty piasters per day and the village chief was to get pants and shoes for services rendered.

When Rictor stopped the truck jammed with tribesmen at the compound gate Olga had a reception committee waiting. Doc was there with soap and buckets of water. Lockwood had old fatigues and boots he had scrounged from team members. After the tribesmen had scrubbed themselves and discarded their loinclothes for fatigue trousers, Rictor photographed and fingerprinted them for identification. By midafternoon the weapons sergeant had some of them digging a mortar pit and Lockwood had the remainder shuttling supplies around the compound.

Late in the evening as Doc and Rictor were searching the tribesmen as they left the compound, one old fellow complained of a stomachache. Doc directed him to remove his shirt to be examined. When he unbuttoned his shirt a dead rat, weighing about a pound, fell out. The old man retrieved the rat and Zung told Doc he was taking it home for food. Doc spread his hands and grinned at Rictor. "Can't say for sure but just offhand I'd say this old fellow's diet is causing his stomach trouble." Glancing up at the sky he said, "Looks like we're in for some rain."

Rictor had already noticed the clouds moving in. "Yeah, I think Lockwood was right about the rainy season. We're lucky the tents are up."

Doc indicated the partially dug 81mm. mortar pit with a nod. "The tents won't keep water out of that hole. If it rains tonight that damn thing'll be a swimming hole tomorrow."

The words were barely out of Doc's mouth when a light rain began to sprinkle the compound.

By 1900 hours rain was coming down in sheets. Rictor had remained in the mess hall after chow. He spotted Lieutenant Maxwell, the ranger advisor, sitting alone at the bar. After introducing himself, he inquired about the documents and drawings that had been discovered by the ranger patrol. The lieutenant said, "I can't tell you much about them except that the second day the patrol was out one of the ranger squads uncovered a Viet Cong cache which contained two Chicom carbines and the documents."

Rictor nodded. "You figure the cache was part of a recon patrol base?"

"Maybe, I can't say for sure. We searched the area but didn't make any contact."

"How detailed were the drawings?"

"I only got a quick look but the whole capital complex was drawn in detail."

"Were the ARVN gun positions plotted?"

"Yeah. From what I saw it looked like all the ARVN and RF positions were plotted. By the way, I noticed that you people started digging a mortar pit today."

Rictor nodded. "I don't understand why it wasn't done a long time ago."

The lieutenant glanced around the bar and lowered his voice. "There are a lot of reasons. The main one is Colonel West. He feels that heavily fortified American compounds give the Vietnamese the impression that the American effort is defensive in nature. The impression he wants to give is one of mobile offense. That's the reason we've got flower beds where gun positions should be."

Rictor studied the young blond lieutenant and decided he was going to like him. He was lean and sharp, and Rictor suspected he was eager to fight. Rictor replied, "That's a positive point of view, but a positive point of view gives very little protection if you come under attack." The young ranger nodded in agreement. Rictor excused himself, picked up his drink and joined Dave and Scruggs at a table in the corner.

As Rictor pulled out a chair Dave asked, "Did you guys

know that Lockwood's teaching them mangy tribesmen to speak English?"

Scruggs was dubious. "I think it'd be easier for him to learn to speak Steing."

Dave shrugged and said, "I don't know. Every time I looked at one of those long-haired jaspers this afternoon, he would say 'Okay!' or 'Airborne!'"

The lyrics of a popular country-western song blared from the bar's tape player. Scruggs grinned. "Maybe he can teach them to sing. We might even end up with the only Steing hillbilly band in the world."

Dave pointed to the bar. "If we do, I don't think they'll be practicing here." Rictor glanced toward the bar. He saw Colonel West pointing to the tape player while speaking to Biggerstaff, who turned and spoke to Kim. She hurriedly turned off the tape player. Apparently the colonel thought the tape belonged to Biggerstaff. He raised his voice. "Captain, country music is generally identified with ignorance and a definite lack of dignity! It will not be played in this mess as long as I'm in command! Is that understood?" Without waiting for an answer, he whirled on his heel and left the building. The door had barely closed behind him when a roar of protest arose. The colonel had made a serious mistake.

When Rictor left the mess hall, he found that the driving rain had slackened to a drizzle. He decided to check the security. The RF guard posted by the gate was bundled up in a poncho: the guard would have a difficult time hearing or seeing a herd of elephants approaching. Entering the alley formed by the billets, he tripped and sprawled headlong on the wet ground. He groped to find what had tripped him and let out a few choice four-letter words when he discovered a Keep Off The Grass sign under his foot.

Near the brick wall he took care not to fall into the water-filled mortar shelter. He squeezed between the wall and the billet corner and finally reached the west fence. The guard who was supposed to be there was nowhere in sight. After a five-minute search Rictor saw the RF soldier coming out of a tin building where he had taken shelter from the rain. Thoroughly disgusted with the guard and Vietnam in general, Rictor retraced his steps. Reaching his room, he removed his wet clothes and went directly to bed.

Rictor awoke early, and, on his way to breakfast, discovered that Doc's prediction had been accurate. The mortar pit was overflowing with water from the previous night's rain. As he walked out of the alley, Rictor saw Deuces streak by clutching a huge ham bone. A four-month-old shepherd pup, which had been brought from the Highlands by the weapons sergeant, was hot on his heels. After scrambling to the mess hall roof, Deuces turned and taunted the pup with the bone.

Rictor ate alone and was having a second cup of coffee when Hassen approached his table. Lowering his enormous hulk into a chair Hassen said, "The major wants to see you at eight hundred hours."

Rictor sipped his coffee. "Did he say why?"

"Nope. He just told me to pass the word."

"Thanks," Rictor said. "At least I won't have to make the province chief's briefing, if you can call that abortion a briefing."

Hassen's expression tightened as he said, "I heard a rumor that Colonel Nam owns a rubber plantation just north of here."

Rictor nodded. "I've heard the rumor. What's your point?"

Hassen leaned across the table and lowered his voice, "I also heard he's made a deal with the VC. He won't bother them if they won't mess up his rubber operation."

Rictor said, "That might be true but I wouldn't go around repeating it unless I had proof."

Hassen faked a hurt expression. "I'm not saying it's true. I'm just telling you what I heard. You're the one that's supposed to figure out if it's true or not."

Rictor shoved back his chair. "The only thing I know for sure about this goddamn place is that the living is plush, security is bad, the provincial officials are opportunists, and Deuces is a thief!" At the door he stopped and looked back. "And the damn mess sergeant talks too much."

Long after Rictor had gone, Hassen sat at the table sipping coffee and chuckling to himself.

At 0800 hours, Rictor entered the major's office and found the ex-commander going over backlogged correspondence.

The major looked up and motioned to a chair. "Be with you in a minute." He laid a letter aside, and said, "We need a better intelligence picture of this area. I'm sending you to Saigon for a 'C' Detachment briefing."

Mother's Day was only a few days away and Rictor had hoped to get to Saigon to buy a gift. He also wanted to call home. It was difficult to hide his enthusiasm. "When do I leave?" he asked evenly.

The major toyed with a letter opener. "A slick will come for you tomorrow afternoon. You can spend the weekend in Saigon and report to the 'C' Detachment intelligence officer Monday morning. But I want you back here Monday afternoon." Without waiting for a reply, the major turned his attention back to the correspondence.

Rictor waited to be dismissed. "Is there anything else?"

Looking up the major said, "Not unless you object to spending the weekend in Saigon."

Rictor left the office looking forward to the trip. He had not met the "C" Detachment intelligence people, and he was anxious to get their provincial area assessment.

By early afternoon Rictor had compiled a lengthy shopping list. Almost everyone in the detachment needed something from the Saigon PX. He was crossing to the mess hall from the operations building and watching Colonel West, who had come through the gate and stopped at the tower. The colonel said something to Olga but Rictor could not hear. When the colonel moved on, Olga climbed out of the hole and slammed down his shovel. He was flushed with anger and muttering to himself. Rictor walked over and asked, "What's up?"

Olga pointed to the departing colonel. "I've had it with that bastard! He's more concerned with what some damn VIP who might come by the camp would think of the compound's appearance than he is with having drinkable water. He must've forgot that the big boys down in Saigon don't let the visitors come in unannounced. If they did, they might really see something they ain't supposed to."

Rictor said, "Cool down and tell me what happened."

"The asshole said that we'd just arrived," Olga continued, "and already had the compound looking like a pigsty. He said he would be ashamed for any visitors to see it. He gave me twenty-four hours to get this crap cleaned up. It ain't possible."

Rictor shook his head. "It's a little early but I need a drink. C'mon, we'll open the bar."

Except for one waitress the mess hall was deserted. After pouring the drinks, Rictor lifted his half-filled glass and studied the contents. "Olga, they say that it takes all kinds to make a world. I guess it takes all kinds to make an army too." After pausing to take a sip he said, "I'll talk to the major about the water tower. In the meantime don't worry about it."

Olga sipped at his drink. "I guess you're right, but I figure we could get along without the colonel's kind. He'd better wake up to the fact that the detachment can lose him and still get the job done. But if he loses the detachment, he's screwed." He reached for the bottle and continued. "It looks to me like he's doing everything he can to lose us."

Rictor dug out his cigarettes. "It appears that way but I don't think that's the colonel's intent. He's got tunnel vision. He's from the dress right dress army with very little combat experience. He just don't understand the way Special Forces operates."

The side door opened and the USOM people came in. Mendoza pointed to Olga's drink. "You got two more of those?"

Rictor nodded and reached for glasses. "I think we can fix you up. How's the 'Heart and Mind' business?"

Watts scowled. "It'd be a lot better if the crooked politicians would keep their hands off the supplies!"

Mendoza nodded to Olga. "Our boy here looks like he's been in a mud-ball fight."

Olga stood up to leave. "That reminds me, I've got a lot more mud that needs moving." As he walked toward the door he said, "If you guys get bored, c'mon out. There's a couple of extra shovels."

Watts grinned. "No, thanks. We just stopped by to drop off our PX shopping list. We heard someone was going to Saigon."

Rictor snorted. "It's no wonder the damn VC are winning the war. How'd you find out I was going to Saigon?"

Mendoza reached in his shirt pocket and produced a shopping list, saying, "We've got spies everywhere."

Rictor reached for the paper. "It wouldn't surprise me if Ho Chi Minh himself showed up with a list."

In a more serious mood Watts said, "We sent a truckload of rice out to the Steing village. The water pump has been ordered and should be here any day."

Rictor nodded approval. "That's good. The laborers we hired from out there are doing a good job."

"The tribesmen working for you people are probably the first ones ever to work for wages," Watts said. "The Vietnamese don't pay them. Sometimes the Vietnamese dole out a little of the rice they're supposed to provide free under the aid program, but that's about it."

Rictor came from behind the bar. "I'll see you later. I'm going to give Olga a hand."

At the door he nearly collided with Hassen who was carrying a film can. Hassen tapped the can with his forefinger. "We're having a movie tonight."

"What time?" Rictor asked.

"As soon as chow's over. It's a western." Anxious to avoid another discussion with Hassen about the province chief, Rictor nodded and kept moving.

By 1920 hours that night, chow was finished. The mess hall chairs had been rearranged and almost everyone in the detachment except the radio operator on duty had gathered to watch the movie. Campbell made final adjustments on the projector and announced that the movie would begin in ten minutes.

Rictor sat at the back of the room discussing his Saigon trip with Dave and Scruggs. Dave said, "Maybe you oughta bring some life preservers for those laborers to use. Looks to me like some of them are gonna drown in that mortar pit."

Scruggs grinned. "I got a better idea. You bring a dozen or so of those big-titty Saigon whores to dig the mortar pits. Me and my radio operators will make like lifeguards."

Henderson came through the back door and stopped to remove his wet poncho. Spotting an empty couch near the movie screen, he strolled over and sat down. Campbell said,

"You can't sit there, Henderson. The couch is reserved for Colonel West."

Henderson got up slowly. "Does your Maggit colonel need the whole damn couch to watch a movie or are you afraid he'll get sick if he sits next to a nigger?"

Campbell flushed. "Knock off the crap! I don't give a rat's ass who he sits next to but he's invited Colonel Nam and I was told to keep the couch empty."

Scruggs called to Henderson. "C'mon back to the rear of the bus with the rest of us peons! You might catch something yourself sitting up there with the brass!"

Drinking bourbon straight from the bottle, Hassen shouted to Campbell in a half-drunk slur. "I'm the goddamn mess sergeant and I say screw anybody that's not here! Let's get this fuckin' show on the road!"

Scruggs leaned close to Rictor. "Looks like Hassen's getting ready to tie one on," he whispered.

Rictor nodded. "I've been wondering when he'd get around to it."

Henderson took a seat between Scruggs and Dave. "I didn't like the front of the lousy bus anyway but it gripes my ass to hafta move for one of them zipperheads."

Staggering slightly, Terry came over and wrapped his arm around Henderson's shoulders. "Don't worry about it, Buddy. Just between you and me this whole goddamned place sucks with a capital *S*."

Lockwood came from the bar carrying his beer. He dropped into a chair next to Rictor. "Anyone got an extra size-seven beret?"

Noting that Lockwood's beret was almost new Rictor asked, "What's wrong with the one you're wearing?"

Lockwood took a slug of beer, then said, "Nothing, I don't need one. The major told me to get one for Colonel West."

Rictor had an extra beret but he was not going to give it to the colonel. When no one volunteered, Lockwood said, "I know that most of you guys have more than one. C'mon, cough up."

Dave snorted. "You're damn right but nobody's going to give that bastard one! If he wants a beret let him earn it! Or better yet, maybe he would like to go up to the Mang Yang Pass and find Shay's."

Rictor caught Dave's eye. "You know what they say about loose lips and sunk ships?"

Lockwood was puzzled. "What the fuck does that mean?"

Scruggs said, "Nothing, let's drop it."

Lockwood cursed. "I don't give a shit about your little secrets but I'm the goddamn supply sergeant, and the major told me to get a beret!"

Terry laughed. "Give him yours."

Lockwood pulled off his beret. "This is the only one I got and colonel or no colonel there's no way I'm going to give it away."

Dave grinned. "Looks like you've got a problem. You oughta be able to get one through normal supply channels—in about six months." Lockwood gave up and turned his back.

A couple of minutes later Colonel West arrived with Colonel Nam and about half the provincial staff. Many of the Vietnamese officials had brought their wives or girlfriends, and it was necessary for some of the Americans to give up choice seats to make room for the colonel's guests. Scruggs said, "I don't mind watching a movie with a bunch of slopeheads but this is too much." Seeing Sergeant Lee, the interpreter, sit down on the couch next to the colonel, Scruggs said, "It'll be a cold day in hell when I give up my seat for that sorry bastard!"

Dave grunted. "Then you'd better get yourself a coat. I've gotta feeling these guys are going to get anything they want."

Scruggs stared at Colonel Nam. "Speaking of getting anything they want, word's around that there's a kickback on labor and USOM supplies all the way from district to the corps commander. I hear it's real big, in the millions maybe."

Rictor said, irritated, "You must've been talking to Hassen. Sometimes I think he's got diarrhea of the mouth."

"Well, from what I understand, everybody between here and Saigon knows about it already but nobody wants to rock the boat. It's easier just to close your eyes. That way there're no waves," said Scruggs.

Rictor grunted. "Hell, that's true all over the country."

The lights snapped off, and the movie began. Halfway through the first reel a plane roared over the complex at such a low altitude the sound track was drowned out. Dave nudged Scruggs. "Man, I'd sure hate to be up there tonight. The ceiling is less than five hundred feet not to mention the rain."

A couple minutes later the plane returned. The side door of the mess banged open and the duty radio operator shouted, "There's a plane circling the complex dropping flares!" The movie watchers broke for the door.

Rictor had just stepped outside when the plane came directly over the compound. It was an AIE Skyraider and obviously in trouble. The engine coughed and sputtered as the pilot attempted to gain altitude. At five hundred feet he leaned out of the open cockpit and dropped two small hand flares. He made a sharp bank to the right and brought the plane around.

It was obvious to everyone watching the pilot was searching for a place to land. Scruggs yelled to the radio operator who had sounded the alarm, "Have you made contact with him?"

The operator shook his head. "We've been trying ever since the first time he came over. Either his radio's out or he's a slopehead. I think it's his commo because ARVN can't raise him either."

Dave and several others ran by headed for the trucks. Scruggs yelled, "What's up?"

Without breaking his stride Dave called over his shoulder. "We're gonna try lighting the street that leads to the capital. Maybe the poor bastard can belly in."

As Scruggs and Rictor scrambled aboard a truck driven by Terry, the Skyraider blasted over the compound at seventy-five feet narrowly missing Scruggs's antenna poles. The plane began to climb and the screech made by its straining engine sounded almost human. At four hundred feet the engine gave a gasping cough and died. The plane slipped into a glide and came back across the complex. In the orange flare light the silent ship looked like a giant bird of prey soaring to its death. Terry braked hard and brought the truck to a sliding halt. He leapt to the ground and when the plane was directly overhead he screamed at the top of his voice, "Jump, you bastard! Jump!"

Terry's yelling got to Scruggs. He shouted, "Shut up, you fool! Can't you see that he's too low to jump? He's had the meat!" The words were barely out of Scruggs's mouth when the plane plowed into a tree at the end of the street then burst into flames. Even as he ran toward the crash site Rictor knew it was too late to help the luckless pilot.

Doc Brown was the first to reach the crash site. He shielded his face with his arm but thirty feet from the plane he was driven back by the intense heat. Several others tried to reach the plane but retreated with singed hair and eyebrows. Stopping long enough to pick up an object the size of a basketball, Olga was the last to pull back.

Scruggs nudged Dave. "What did Olga find?"

Dave shrugged. "Beats me but we'll know in a minute. He's coming this way."

Olga came up carrying a flight helmet. "Looks like the pilot was Vietnamese. I found his headgear and judging by the blood in it he was lucky. I doubt if he even knew what he hit." Hearing that the pilot was Vietnamese, Dave and Scruggs lost interest and headed for the compound.

Rictor returned to the mess hall. He was listening to a noisy debate about what had caused the crash when Henderson noted that the colonel and his guests had not returned. Still smarting from having to give his seat to a Vietnamese, Henderson raised his voice to make himself heard. "I don't know what caused the crash but it sure got rid of the colonel's friends."

Hassen yelled from the bar, "Well, at least he's got some friends. That's more than I can say." He hoisted a bourbon bottle and took a long pull. "But I don't give a damn if anybody likes me or not. I don't need anybody."

Terry winked at Dave. "Looks like Hassen is up to his ears in that jug."

Dave grinned. "Sounds more like his old self, doesn't he?"

Swaying unsteadily, Hassen looked around the room. When it was obvious he was not going to get a rise out of anyone, he grasped the bottle by the neck and shouted, "Who wants a drink? I'm buying." The invitation was greeted with silence. Hassen's massive face twisted out of shape and tears appeared on his cheeks. He screamed at the top of his voice, "I hate every goddamn one of you! Do you hear me? I hate every fuckin' last one of you!" He turned to the bar and yelled at Kim. "I hate you, too, you slopehead bitch!" He raised the bottle and smashed it against the bar. Kim ducked to avoid flying glass and cringed against the wall. Hassen rested his head on the bar and hideous racking sobs came from deep within his body.

Campbell leapt to his feet and headed for the bar. His expression made his intention clear. Dave stood and blocked his path. "I figure I know how you feel about that chick but it's all over. Look at him. He's had it." Campbell tried to push by but Dave grabbed him. "I said let it go, Campbell." Their eyes locked and except for Hassen's sobbing the room was silent.

After a long tense moment Campbell relaxed. "Okay, Dave, but I'm gonna get Kim and leave. It's time for her to go anyway."

Terry opened his mouth to speak. Scruggs said, "Shut up! Don't even think it. If you want to do something, give me a hand getting Hassen to his room." Terry quietly got up from the table and followed Scruggs toward the bar.

Disgusted, Rictor headed for the side door. As he stepped outside, he caught a glimpse of Campbell and Kim passing through the compound gate. Campbell had his arm wrapped around her waist. There was no question in Rictor's mind about their relationship. Walking toward the gate he mumbled, "Why not!" and began looking for the RF guard who was missing as usual.

Rictor overslept and barely had time to catch a cup of coffee before going to the morning briefing. While walking toward the capital he reflected on the events of the previous night. Apparently the whiskey had brought out Hassen's true feelings. The way Rictor saw it, Hassen's situation in the detachment was one of his own making.

When Rictor arrived at the capital, the briefing was already in progress. He located an empty chair at the rear of the conference room and half-listened as the briefing ran its normal boring course. But when the provincial police chief took the speaker's platform Rictor's interest quickened. He had not met the police chief but, according to the MAC-V operations officer, he was the most powerful member of the provincial staff. The chief's report was brief and his words sent a ripple of laughter through the assembled Vietnamese officials. Standing on the edge of the speaker's platform, Sergeant Lee translated to Colonel West, "The police chief has challenged you to a return volleyball match. He said he would like to give the Americans another chance."

Colonel West grinned. "I accept. Tell him that we've been practicing while he was away, and he doesn't have a chance. We'll play on the tennis court at the American compound. He can choose the time."

The police chief made a comment about the Americans' chances of winning which brought another wave of laughter. When the laughter died down, the provincial intelligence officer moved to the front of the room. He mounted the platform and looked Rictor straight in the eye but gave no sign of recognition. His briefing was short. Lee translated that there was no change in the intelligence situation. Rictor decided it was time someone asked about the captured VC documents. He stood and called to Lee, "Ask the intelligence officer what he's learned from the documents found by the ranger patrol and find out why they haven't been mentioned." Lee glanced to Colonel Nam and hesitated. During the brief silence Rictor felt the scrutiny of every eye in the room. He knew the intelligence officer had understood the question and judged from his startled expression that he was caught off guard. By the time Lee repeated the question, the intelligence officer had regained his composure. He gave a curt nod and answered in Vietnamese.

Lee translated, "The documents are being studied. When the evaluation is completed, the Americans will be informed." Rictor nodded and sat down. He made a mental note that the intelligence officer was a corrupt bastard, but a smart corrupt bastard.

Colonel Nam mounted the speaker's platform and disclosed plans for a three-day Heliborne Operation by the rangers. After a brief discussion of the operation, Colonel West agreed to coordinate through American channels for helicopter transportation.

When the briefing terminated, Major Strong motioned Rictor to one side. "Colonel West wants to see you right away. When you talk to him be cool. He's got his ass on his shoulders about your document inquiry." The major hesitated, then said, "If you get in a jam, I can't help much. I'm on shaky ground myself because of the mortar pit and that goddamn water tower."

Rictor nodded and headed back to the American compound, where he went directly to the operations building. Through the open doorway he saw Colonel West sitting behind his desk studying a manual. Rictor knocked and stepped inside. "You sent for me, Colonel?"

The colonel looked up from his reading. "I don't know why I expect the junior members of this detachment to act regulation, when a senior sergeant apparently doesn't know how to report to his commanding officer properly."

Rictor's face flushed. He stepped in front of the desk and rendered the hand salute. "Sergeant Rictor reporting as directed, sir."

The colonel ignored the salute. "I'll get right to the point, Sergeant. I'm not accustomed to having enlisted men acting in an officer's capacity, and that's a situation I intend to remedy as soon as possible."

Rictor dropped the unanswered salute. "I'm not sure I follow you, Colonel."

The colonel raised his voice. "In your capacity as detachment intelligence officer, you embarrassed me in front of the province chief and his staff."

"How did I embarrass you?" Rictor asked.

The colonel responded, "By inquiring about matters which are clearly in the Vietnamese area of responsibility. Just as soon as I can find a suitable replacement I'm going to relieve you."

Rictor shook his head in disbelief. "Colonel, if you're not going to let me do my job you might as well relieve me now."

The colonel stood up, shouting, "Goddamnit, Sergeant, I'll

decide when the change is to be made. In the meantime you will . . ."

Rictor's frustration had turned to cold anger. "Colonel," he interrupted, "may I speak off the record?"

The colonel's face was still livid but he had regained his composure. "It's the only opportunity you'll have, so speak freely."

Rictor didn't hesitate. "In the best interest of the detachment, there are a number of people who have tried to cover the fact that you fucked up and were responsible for the massacre at the ambush in the Mang Yang Pass. Your arrogance and obvious distaste for Special Forces are killing morale and tearing this detachment apart. It's clear I'm finished here, but in the best interest of the mission I suggest that you make some attitude adjustments that will put an end to the petty bickering."

The colonel pointed to the door. "You're dismissed, Sergeant. I'll deal with you when you get back from Saigon."

Rictor left the office without bothering to salute. He was certain that he would be relieved upon return from Saigon and had mixed feelings. The prospect of leaving the detachment left him cold, but at the same time he was relieved. He could no longer work under Colonel West's command, and that was that.

Deciding to keep the encounter with Colonel West quiet, Rictor busied himself preparing for the trip to Saigon. He finished compiling the PX shopping list, packed a small overnight bag and went to chow. While he was eating Scruggs came to the table. "We just got a call from an inbound chopper. The pilot estimates his arrival time as thirteen hundred hours."

Rictor glanced at his watch. It was 1245 hours. "How much ground time does he figure?"

"It's touch and go. He'll be on the ground just long enough to drop off a couple of Air Force people and a ranger advisor. He'll be heading straight back to Saigon. If you wanna go with him, you'll hafta be at the chopper pad when he lands."

Rictor pushed his plate aside. "Who are the Air Force people?"

"Some captain and his radio operator. I understand the captain's the forward air controller assigned to this province. I guess that's his spotter plane parked down at the airstrip."

Rictor said as he got up and headed for the door, "Thanks for the info. I'll grab my bag and make it to the chopper pad."

Scruggs said, "If you hurry, you can get a lift with Olga. He's taking a jeep to pick up the Air Force people."

When Rictor reached the gate, Olga and Zung were waiting for him. He tossed his bag to Zung and climbed in the jeep next to Olga. As they pulled through the gate he heard the chopper approaching from the south. He sensed something was bothering Olga. "What's the matter with you, Slick?"

Olga shrugged. "I'm okay, but I've got a funny feeling about this place and I can't seem to shake it. Don't stay in Saigon too . . ." The noise made by the landing helicopter drowned out his voice. Rictor grabbed his overnight bag and hopped out of the jeep. Holding onto his beret to keep it from being blown away, he ran to the chopper and scrambled aboard. As the chopper lifted off Zung yelled something which Rictor could not understand.

Chapter IX

SACRIFICE

During the hour-long flight to Saigon, Rictor studied the green jungle canopy and peaceful rice paddies below. From the chopper it was hard to believe that a vicious war was being waged all over the country. When Tan Son Nhut Air Base came into view, it was easier to believe. As the chopper circled the sprawling air base, everywhere Rictor looked he saw evidence of war. Camouflage-striped Skyraiders and sleek B57 Canberras were lined up in takeoff positions. Bombs were being loaded on planes that had just returned from missions, and new planes were being made ready for combat. He had never seen so many supplies in one area.

When the chopper landed, Rictor went directly to air operations to make arrangements for his return trip. He was assigned space on a supply plane scheduled to depart on Monday at 1300 hours. Satisfied with the booking he left the building wondering where he was going to stay while in Saigon. He had stopped to light a cigarette when the sound of a racing engine caught his attention. Turning, he saw a jeep bearing down on him fast. He dropped the overnight bag and made a diving roll to avoid being hit. The jeep came to a sliding halt less than three feet from where he was lying. He scrambled to his feet and reached for the black pajama clad

Chinese driver. Just as his hand closed on the driver's arm, a low, familiar voice said, "Turn him loose or you don't get a ride."

Rictor relaxed his grip and looked past the driver. Burt Gardner was sitting in the passenger's seat grinning. Rictor leaned across the Chinaman and pumped Burt's outstretched hand. "You're the kind of guy that could kill a man with kindness but I'm glad to see you. I'm walking and don't have a clue as to where I'm going to stay," he said.

"Climb in, your problems are solved. I'll fix you up with a pad at my hotel and the jeep is yours for the taking. I'll even furnish the driver."

Rictor recovered his overnight bag and climbed into the back seat. "Sounds like a good deal to me." He was barely seated when Burt nodded to the Chinaman and the jeep lurched forward. Burt turned in the seat. "What brings you to Saigon?"

"I'm supposed to get a briefing at the 'C' Detachment headquarters Monday. You don't happen to know where it's located, do you?"

"Sure! It's a couple of blocks down the ramp from where you were standing. You couldn't miss it if you tried."

Rictor grinned. "You look a helluva lot better than you did when we left you up in Qui Nhon. How long did it take to get rid of the hangover?"

Burt winced. "Don't mention it. My paratroop battalion moved out on an operation the same day you left. I saw lizards and threw up for two days."

Rictor laughed. "That should teach you not to try drinking the country dry in one night. What are you doing in Saigon?"

"This is home base for my unit," Burt said. "We closed in here a couple of days ago, and it looks like we're going to stay a while. I almost didn't see you back there. If you hadn't been wearing a beret, I wouldn't have noticed you at all."

"I'm sure glad you came along. I don't know a damn thing about Saigon," Rictor responded.

"I'm almost a native. I'll take care of you."

More than satisfied to let Burt take charge, Rictor leaned back and relaxed.

At Tan Son Nhut's main gate, a Vietnamese policeman stepped from the guard shack and held up his hand. When he saw that Burt was an American, he waved the jeep on and went back inside. The Chinaman eased through the gate and turned onto a busy four-lane street. As the jeep picked up speed Rictor expected a collision at any moment. The thousands of bicycles and cars which jammed the street seemed to move independently without regard to right of way.

During the forty-five-minute drive across the city Burt pointed out several places of interest, including the palace. Rictor was impressed by the French colonial style government buildings and their beautiful gardens. The wealthy Vietnamese appeared to live in the same manner the French colonial aristocracy had, while the masses existed on a day-to-day basis with little hope for the future. The contrast was startling.

Engrossed in his thoughts, Rictor failed to realize that Burt was speaking to him. He was jolted when Burt said, "And I want you to meet my wife."

Not sure that he had heard correctly Rictor said, "Sorry, Burt, I was thinking about something. Did you say you wanted me to meet your wife?"

Burt nodded. "She's waiting for me at the hotel."

Rictor grinned. "You're putting me on. All the American dependents were ordered home a long time ago."

Burt's face became strained. "This is home for her—she's Vietnamese." Rictor knew that Burt had a wife in the States and was momentarily at a loss for words. The silence was embarrassing.

The jeep swerved to avoid a bicycle, and Rictor grabbed the back of Burt's seat. Leaning forward, he said, "If the Chinaman can get us to the hotel in one piece, I'd like very much to meet her."

Burt flashed an appreciative smile. "You're the only person I've told about Dinh. I don't think most of my friends would understand."

Rictor nodded to give assurance but he didn't understand either. Making an effort at conversation he said, "You're pretty good at keeping a secret. How long you been married?"

"A couple of months," Burt responded.

Rictor said, "You must've still been celebrating when we were at the Green Beret Hotel in Qui Nhon. You were drunk enough for two people."

Burt shook his head. "I haven't had any reason to celebrate for a long time." Rictor was still puzzled but Burt was so obviously troubled he decided to drop the subject.

The Chinaman turned off the main street into a narrow alley. Five minutes later they arrived at the Tan Loch Hotel. Climbing out of the jeep Burt said, "This is it. My home away from home."

Rictor grunted. "I've got so many homes away from home, sometimes I wonder if I've got a real one." He took in the hotel with a glance. It was an eight-story building sandwiched between two clothing shops. It might have once been one of Saigon's better hotels, but time had taken its toll.

Inside the hotel Burt went directly to the manager's office and quickly made arrangements for Rictor to have a room next to his own. As he followed Burt toward the stairwell Rictor said, "You must really be tight with the Vietnamese for them to give you a jeep for your own personal use."

Burt grinned. "I get a few fringe benefits."

"Is the Chinaman one of them?" Rictor asked.

Burt shook his head. "No. I hired him. He works for me."

Rictor nodded. "I figured as much. He looked like he knew his business on the Binh Dinh raid. He also gave you good cover while you were passed out at the Green Beret Hotel."

Burt grinned. "He's the best I've seen. His only problem is having too much guts for his own good."

When they reached Rictor's room, Burt said, "After you get settled, c'mon over to my place for a drink. It's the next room down."

Rictor stepped inside. "I'll be over just as soon as I get cleaned up. I haven't had a decent bath in weeks." He found the room less than what he had hoped for. The bed was lumpy and the water cold. Deciding against a shower, he shaved and peeled off his camouflage fatigues. He removed the shoulder holster which cradled a compact 7.65 automatic and started to put it in the overnight bag but changed his mind and strapped it on again. A few minutes later, feeling a little awkward in civies, he headed for Burt's room, deciding not to ask any questions about Burt's marriage.

When the door opened, any question he might have had was answered. Standing in the doorway was the most beautiful Vietnamese woman he had ever seen. She appeared to be in her late teens. He nodded politely and stepped inside. He gave no indication that he had noticed she was in the late months of pregnancy.

Burt was leaning over a washbasin brushing his teeth. He waved to a chair and mumbled, "Be with you in a minute."

Rictor took a seat at a small table and fished out a cigarette. The girl had not moved after closing the door. Rictor smiled at her, and she returned his smile but made no attempt to speak. He wished he was someplace else. "Burt! You didn't tell me she was so pretty."

Burt used a towel to wipe toothpaste from the corner of his mouth. "I decided to let you see for yourself. Dinh's kinda shy around Americans. She don't understand much English." He turned and spoke to Dinh in Vietnamese, and she came over to be introduced. Rictor took her outstretched hand and used his limited Vietnamese vocabulary to express his pleasure. Dinh nodded and smiled but did not speak. Burt strolled over to the bed, picked up a leather overnight bag and took out a bottle of sour mash bourbon. "How about a drink?"

Rictor nodded. "You must have been reading my mind." Dinh quickly brought ice and glasses from the sink. After placing them on the table next to the bourbon she retreated to a chair by the door.

Burt and Rictor had been drinking and reminiscing for several hours when Burt suggested they go upstairs to the hotel bar. Rictor realized that Burt was drunk and looked across the room to get Dinh's reaction. He studied her face and realized that she had not spoken. "Look, Burt, I don't want to interfere with your plans. I'll find my way to the bar and see you tomorrow."

Burt held up his hand for silence. "I don't want to hear it! I don't have any plans, and I feel like getting drunk." Without waiting for a reply he gulped down his drink and stood up.

Rictor set his half-finished drink on the table and got up.

"In that case, lead the way." Burt was already moving toward the door. He passed Dinh without a glance.

As Rictor followed Burt down the corridor, he thought of Dinh. He had stopped at the door for a moment to say good-bye and made a curious observation. Her brown eyes were filled with naked fear and terror. It was kind of terror he had seen in the eyes of trapped animals waiting for the deathblow. He considered asking Burt about it but decided it wasn't his business.

The hotel bar was crowded with American soldiers, typical of a thousand other such bars Rictor had patronized. A record player in the corner blared out the latest stateside tunes. Twenty-five or thirty busty *"B"* girls moved among the GIs, hustling drinks. The girls wore thin, skintight dresses and heavy makeup. Most of them were young in years but old in experience. The fact that they were prostitutes made no difference to the sex-starved men from the bush. In the dim light the women looked like exotic queens and the soldiers were more than willing to shell out a couple of bucks for an imitation drink called Saigon Tea. For the price of a drink they were allowed to dance with and fondle the girls' bodies.

Standing at the bar, Rictor was sipping on his second bourbon, when Burt spotted an empty table in the corner. They worked their way across the crowded dance floor and were barely seated when one of the waitresses came over. Resting a hand on the table she leaned forward. Her low-cut blouse drooped at the neck, and even in the dim light her firm white breasts were visible. When she was sure that Burt had an eyeful, she asked what he wanted to drink. Burt held up two fingers. "Double bourbon and water. Go easy on the water."

Without taking her hand from the table, she pivoted the upper portion of her body toward Rictor and he received the full benefit of the drooping blouse. In broken English she asked, "What you drink, honey?"

Rictor shifted his eyes to meet hers. "Bourbon and water. A single."

She smiled and there was confidence in her voice when she said, "Baby, you buy me whicky coke and I luv you too much!"

Rictor suppressed a laugh. He hesitated just long enough to let doubt creep into her eyes. "Sweetheart, you get anything you want." He had been exposed to this act a hundred times in other bars. His answer was usually no, but he liked the way she smiled. On the way to the bar she passed a candle-lit table. He found her even more interesting from the rear than she had been from the front.

Burt called after her, "Hurry up! We don't have all night." He turned to Rictor. "I hope you ain't still getting sucked in by the blouse trick."

Rictor grinned. "It hasn't been too long since I saw you chomping at the bit over a loose blouse. You haven't forgotten Pleiku, have you?"

Burt shook his head. "I ain't forgot, but I've got more than enough female problems to last me a lifetime."

Rictor assumed he meant Dinh. "You want to talk about it?"

Burt hesitated. "No, but I figure I owe you some kind of explanation."

Rictor shook his head. "What you do is your business. You don't need to explain anything to me but if you want to talk, I'm a good listener." Burt started to reply but the girl came back with the drinks. Taking a fistful of piasters from his pocket, Rictor shoved them across the table. "My friend and I want to talk so you run along and play but keep an eye on the table and when our glasses get empty bring more drinks." She was puzzled but nodded her understanding and headed for the bar.

Burt took a slug of bourbon and mechanically lit a cigarette. Toying with his glass he let out a deep sigh and looked up. "I'm going to tell you a story. It's not very pretty, but the truth usually ain't." He took another slug of bourbon before continuing.

"Eight months ago, me and the Chinaman were out on a platoon-size patrol with one of the Vietnamese airborne units. We were operating in an area about eighty miles northwest of here and on the third day out I started feeling bad. By the fourth day I was really sick and had a pretty good idea it was malaria. I should have radioed for a Medevac ship and got out, but we only had two more days to go. I figured if I took them damn little pills, I could tough it till we got to the chopper pickup point. Late in the evening of the fourth day we came across one of those little villages you find in the jungle and made contact with a VC squad. We drove them out in a hurry but during the firefight a couple of the paratroopers got scratched. The platoon leader decided to occupy the village for the night and rest his troops. We put out security and sacked out. I knew better than to stay in the village with the VC knowing we were there but by then I was too sick to give a damn."

Burt paused for a moment to light a cigarette and take a drink. Appearing anxious to get something off his chest, he said, "I guess it was close to midnight when the Chinaman woke me up. I remember him saying, 'Viet Cong,' then all hell broke loose. Everything that happened after that is foggy.

"It was several days later when I came to my senses. I awoke and saw Dinh for the first time. She was leaning against a dirt wall. We stared at one another for a minute before she realized I was conscious. She let out a yell and took off through an opening in the wall. It was then I realized that I was in a cave. I figured I must be a prisoner and tried to get up. I was too weak and my right leg was stiff as a board. I leaned back to rest and felt something hard under my shoulder. It turned out to be my carbine. It was in working condition and loaded. I covered the cave entrance and waited. A few minutes later, the Chinaman came in grinning from ear to ear."

The big-chested waitress came to the table with fresh drinks, and Burt stopped talking just long enough to gulp one down. Rictor remained silent and waited. He had never seen Burt so keyed up.

Burt cleared his throat. "The Chinaman filled in the blank space. Just after midnight on the fourth day of the patrol he had heard movement in the jungle and discovered that a large VC attack force was surrounding the village. Knowing that I was in no shape to fight, he dragged me to one of the huts. It turned out to be the home of Dinh and her mother. I was barely inside before the VC counterattacked. Lying unconscious on the dirt floor I took a stray bullet in the right leg.

The Chinaman told me the fight was fierce but short. The badly outnumbered paratroops had put up a helluva fight, but it had been hopeless from the start. Satisfied that the paratroops had withdrawn, the VC made only a token search of the village. During the confusion, the Chinaman and Dinh managed to move me to the cave. I had been there three days when I woke up and saw Dinh."

Rictor said, "I think I pretty well know what happened after that. Why don't you let it go for now?"

Burt shook his head. "There's a lot more to it than you think. I was lucky the Chinaman had dragged me into Dinh's hut rather than someone else's. As it turned out, Dinh's father, who had been chief of the village and loyal to the government, was murdered by the VC several months before we arrived. Nearly everyone in the village was loyal to the VC, some by choice and others out of fear.

"During the days after I woke up, the Chinaman pulled guard while I rested. I recovered from the malaria attack pretty fast, but the wound in my leg got infected. The village was less than a mile from the cave so we never built a fire. For almost a month I stayed in that damn cave. I had a fever from the infection and lying there alone almost drove me nuts. If it hadn't been for Dinh, I would have climbed the walls. She came to the cave almost every evening to bring food and care for me. At first she was very shy but after a few days we began to talk in Vietnamese. She stayed longer with each visit and I taught her to speak a little English. In the daytime I'd lie in that goddamn cave wishing for night because I knew when it got dark she would come.

"Toward the end of the second week she failed to show up two days in a row. Knowing what the VC would do if they caught her helping us, I imagined a million things that could have happened. Finally on the third night she came. When she entered the cave she was scared to death and I held her close for a long time. She told me that two nights before when she started for the cave she discovered that she was being followed. She doubled back toward the village and saw a man who was known as a VC informer following her. She quickly hid the food she carried, returned to her hut and waited two days before trying again.

"That night we became more than patient and nurse. We slept together. From that night on, sometimes she came late but she never failed to show.

"Toward the end of the fourth week I was well enough to travel and the Chinaman was anxious to be moving. I promised Dinh that I'd come back for her and we pulled out. Moving only at night, it took nine days for the Chinaman and me to get back to friendly territory. By the time I reached Saigon I knew that I wasn't in love with Dinh but I intended to keep my promise to go back."

Rictor caught the waitress's attention and held up two fingers. Burt gulped down the bourbon and lit a cigarette before continuing. "You know how ARVN operates. It took four damn months to convince them to run another operation into that area. The paratroops I work with wanted to avenge the loss of the platoon but the high command was afraid of losing more troops."

Rictor frowned and said, "I'm familiar with that problem."

"Well, we finally got a battalion-size operation cranked up and moved out by chopper. Landing a day's march from Dinh's village we ran into heavy resistance but the paratroops were looking for vengeance. They left dead VC all over that part of the jungle. The Chinaman and I were with the first platoon to reach Dinh's village and there was no resistance from the villagers. The Chinaman guided me to Dinh's hut, but it had long since been burned to the ground. We moved through the village asking about Dinh and her mother, but the villagers were scared and wouldn't talk.

"When the Airborne Battalion commander arrived, he decided to evacuate the village and burn it. I gave up hope of finding Dinh and began to look for the Chinaman—he'd disappeared. The last time I had seen him he was at the edge of the jungle talking with some farmers. I was looking for him when he and two paratroopers came out of the jungle carrying a stretcher. Even as I walked toward them I knew it was Dinh on the stretcher. The paratroopers put the stretcher down and stood to one side. When I saw her, I wished to hell that I'd never come back to the village. She was filthy and almost naked. Her pregnancy was even more pronounced than now because she was so thin. She was conscious and horrible strangling noises came from her mouth.

"The Chinaman came out of the jungle and walked over to one of the farmers that I'd seen him with earlier. I called to him but he ignored me. The farmer pointed to a villager who broke for the jungle on a dead run. The Chinaman brought up his shotgun, took deliberate aim and shot the running man in both legs. The man tried to crawl into the jungle but the Chinaman caught up with him. While the wounded man lay there pleading for his life, the Chinaman unsheathed his machete. With one swift blow, the Chinaman hacked off the wounded man's head. When a few of the more curious paratroopers came over to take a closer look, the Chinaman wiped his machete on the dead man's shirt and said, 'Viet Cong.'

"When the troopers walked away, the Chinaman told me the dead VC was the informer who had followed Dinh the night she turned back from the cave. He had been watching the last night she came to the cave and stopped Dinh on her way back to the village. He had tried to force her to have sex by threatening to report her to the VC. She refused, and he ratted on her. It was too late for the VC to do anything about me but they forced Dinh to watch while they disemboweled her mother and burned the hut.

"As a reward for his treachery the VC made that fuckin' informer chief of the village and gave him Dinh. Time after time the bastard beat her into submission and raped her. After a week he turned her over to the VC squad that guarded the village. They took her to their jungle camp where she was raped again. When she went into deep shock, some of the VC wanted to let her go. But the VC leader knew if she told what they had done, it would hurt their status with the villagers. The VC leader developed a hideous plan. They'd cut out her tongue and turn her loose in the jungle. He figured she'd die but if she survived she wouldn't be able to talk. The bastards were drunk when they tried to operate. They hacked her up pretty bad but failed to cut out all of her tongue. Days later a farmer found her wandering in the jungle. He'd been a friend of her father's and knew about the cave. He took her there and cared for her as best he could. She was still in the cave when the paratroopers and the Chinaman found her."

Unable to hear, Rictor leaned across the table. Burt's voice was barely a whisper. The forgotten cigarette Rictor was holding burned his fingers and brought him back to the present. Snuffing out the butt he motioned for the waitress.

Burt seemed almost asleep, then roused himself and said, "She stayed in the hospital here in Saigon for two months. The doctors said that she would probably be able to talk a little, but it would take a long time. They decided to send her to a refugee camp. My tour of duty was up about the time she got released from the hospital. I couldn't go back to the States knowing the baby she carried might be mine. I extended my tour again and pulled a few strings to get her released in my custody. We went through the formality of a Buddhist wedding. It has little if any weight with the Army, but I guess I'm a bigamist. She's been living here at the hotel ever since."

Burt continued. "I wrote my wife back in the States and told her that I was thinkin' of adopting a child. I didn't tell her why, but since she can't have any children I thought she might go for the idea. She wrote back that under no circumstances would she consider it. The baby is going to be born in about a month. If it turns out to be mine I don't know what in the hell I'm going to do."

Burt stopped talking and fumbled for a cigarette. Rictor kept quiet. He held a light for Burt's cigarette and suggested another drink. Burt gave no indication that he had heard.

The record player was blaring, and Rictor looked to see what idiot had turned it up. When he turned back to Burt to suggest they call it a night, Burt was facedown on the table and out cold. He took his friend back to the room he shared with Dinh and crawled into bed.

A steady pounding on the door snapped Rictor out of a restless sleep the next morning. He barked, "Who is it?"

Burt's voice came through the door. "It's Ho Chi Minh! Who in the hell did you think it was?"

Rictor was amazed that anyone who had been as drunk as

Burt could be so cheerful the following morning. He threw back the covers and went to the door without bothering to put on his trousers. Burt came in grinning. "For a guy that's got a lot to do today you sure are slow in getting started. The Chinaman's downstairs with the jeep waiting for you."

Rictor slipped into his trousers. "You coming with me?"

"No. I'll be busy most of the day but you won't have any problems. The Chinaman knows Saigon like the back of his hand. He'll take you anywhere you want to go."

Rictor said, "If he can understand me. My Vietnamese leaves a lot to be desired."

Burt laughed. "Don't worry. When the Chinaman wants to communicate his English is better than yours and mine."

Fifteen minutes later, Rictor and Burt stood in front of the hotel discussing where they would meet later in the day. Burt said, "There's a floating restaurant on the river called the Mekong. It's got the best seafood in Saigon. Why don't we meet there around 2000 hours?"

Rictor nodded. "Sounds good to me. I should be through running around long before that."

Burt hesitated. "I'm going to bring Dinh. She spends too much time in that damn hotel room."

"Good idea," Rictor agreed. "If the Chinaman can find the place, I'll see you there about eight."

Burt turned to the Chinaman who was sitting in the jeep with the engine idling. "You know where the Mekong Restaurant is?" The Chinaman nodded and raced the engine. Without further delay Rictor climbed in, and they headed for the PX.

The Chinaman enjoyed offensive driving. Using the horn as a substitute for brakes he charged at every small opening in the traffic. Narrowly missing a bicycle he grinned and shifted to second gear. Glancing at Rictor, he said, "I drive pretty good, huh?"

Rictor grunted, "Yeah. You got the makings of a real race car driver if you live."

At the PX compound the Chinaman parked near the gate and waited in the jeep. The PX was so crowded that Rictor could barely move. He spent three hours pushing and shoving until he finally filled the team's shopping list.

After dropping the packages at the hotel, he ate lunch and went shopping for a Mother's Day present. The Chinaman suggested he try the jewelry stores on Tudo Street. Tudo, with a heavy French influence, was wall-to-wall people. It reminded Rictor of the Pigalle in Paris. There was a carnival atmosphere, the entire area catering to American servicemen and wealthy Vietnamese. Even in the early afternoon the street girls were out in force. They openly advertised their wares on street corners and from shaded doorways.

Rictor browsed through several jewelry shops and finally selected a gold cross and chain for his wife and an ID bracelet for his son. Selecting the gifts was the easy part: it took fifteen minutes, with the Chinaman's help, to establish a purchase price.

Rictor wanted to telephone home, and the Chinaman informed him the Saigon radio station had an overseas radio telephone system. When they arrived at the radio station it was jammed with people trying to make telephone calls. Rictor filled out a call slip and located a seat. While waiting for his call he drifted off to sleep.

The telephone operator's touch startled Rictor, and he jerked violently. Embarrassed, he glanced at the wall clock. He had been sleeping for almost three hours.

The radio phone patch was poor, and he was forced to yell in order to make himself understood. The brief conversation with his wife and son was well worth the wait but he was left feeling lonely. For a fleeting moment he thought maybe he should not have reenlisted, but the thought was gone as quickly as it had come. As much as he missed his wife and son, he knew he could never find fulfillment and satisfaction in marriage and homelife as long as he'd left his friends behind, here, where he couldn't help them. He was where he belonged.

He hurried to the jeep and instructed the Chinaman to take him to the restaurant. When they reached the Saigon River, Rictor checked his watch. It was 2030 hours. He turned to the Chinaman and said, "We're thirty minutes late. How much farther is it?"

The Chinaman blew the horn and swerved to avoid a taxi.

"Not far now. Maybe two more min—" His words were lost in an earsplitting explosion from the next street. The Chinaman yelled, "Viet Cong!" and floorboarded the accelerator. At the first intersection he barely made the turn and almost flipped the jeep. The street was jammed with curious pedestrians making their way toward a short pier which led to a houseboat. Orange flame licked at the boat's roof and smoke billowed from the windows. The flickering fire made it difficult to see but the name written on the boat's marquee was unmistakably MEKONG.

Unable to keep the jeep moving in the sea of people, the Chinaman killed the engine. He reached under the dash and grabbed his sawed-off shotgun as he leapt from the jeep.

Rictor stood in the passenger's seat attempting to see over the crowd. He caught a fleeting glimpse of Burt and Dinh struggling to get off the boat. A second blast knocked Rictor to the pavement. Scrambling to his feet he heard the familiar whine of bullets followed closely by the rattle of an AK47. Using the jeep for cover he reached for his automatic and peered over the hood. The street was covered with dead and wounded civilians.

Firing as he ran, the Chinaman zigzagged his way across the street. A shadowy figure clutching an AK bolted from a dark doorway and ran down the sidewalk. The Chinaman knelt and cut down the fleeting figure with a series of blasts from the shotgun. A second VC rushed from the doorway and dove for the AK dropped by his dead comrade. The Chinaman sprang to his feet and attempted to fire but the shotgun was empty. He charged and reached the VC just as his hand closed on the AK. Without breaking his stride the Chinaman raised the shotgun and there was a squashing sound as the barrel crushed the VC's skull.

Carefully picking his way through the dead and dying, Rictor walked toward the pier. He felt numb as he stood looking at the torn and twisted bodies of Burt and Dinh on the edge of the dock where the blast had flung them. He was used to seeing violent death, but he grew cold with rage at the senselessness of mass murder in the streets.

Light from the burning restaurant reflected Burt's defiance, even in death, in the pistol clutched in his right hand and the fierce expression on his face. Stooping to remove Burt's dog tags, Rictor saw Dinh's eyes and nodded unconsciously. The terror he had seen at the hotel was gone. When Rictor straightened up, the Chinaman stood a couple of yards away staring at the still figures. Tears on his cheeks reflected in the flickering light, and Rictor wondered if the tears were for Burt or Dinh. He suspected it was Dinh.

When the police arrived, Rictor was tying an improvised tourniquet on the mangled leg of a civilian. He heard an American MP call out, "Hey, Fred! C'mere, this guy's an American."

Having done all he could for the wounded man, Rictor walked over to the MP and held out Burt's dog tags. The MP flashed a light on Burt. "Did you know this guy?"

Rictor lit a cigarette and took a deep drag. "He was Sergeant First Class Burt Gardner, Regular United States Army. In answer to your question, I don't think anybody really knew him. I'm not even sure he knew himself."

Chapter X

VIET CONG DEFECTORS

The girl snuggled closer as Rictor slowly awoke. Her breath was warm on his neck and her soft yielding flesh pressed close against his bare back. He lay with his eyes closed for a moment, trying to recall the events of the previous evening. He could remember leaving the waterfront and vaguely recalled being on Tudo Street. Everything else was a blank. Disengaging himself from the girl's arms he sat up. When his feet touched the floor, he let out a groan. His head felt like someone was pounding on it with a sledgehammer.

After a cold shower he felt somewhat better but could not remember how he had got back to the hotel or where the girl came from. He checked the time and found that it was almost noon. Feeling the need for a cold beer he removed two thousand piasters from his wallet and walked over to the bed. As he stood looking down at the sleeping girl, he recognized her as the waitress who had performed the blouse trick at the hotel bar. He started to wake her but changed his mind. Dropping the money on the bedside table, he quietly left the room.

There were only six people in the bar. Thankful that the record player was mute he took a chair at a corner table. He had been nursing a beer for about thirty minutes when the Chinaman came in. Rictor learned that the Chinaman had taken him back to Tudo where he had drunk his way through almost every bar on the street. Just prior to curfew, the Chinaman had guided him back to the hotel. He could only guess what had happened after that.

After a few drinks Rictor's hangover gave way to a mild buzz. He made arrangements with the Chinaman for a ride to the airport the following morning and returned to his room. As he had hoped, the girl was gone.

Rictor tossed and turned most of the night. Waking early, he had breakfast at the hotel bar and went for a long walk through the open air market. Burt and Dinh dominated his thoughts. He had never been one to waste time mourning the dead, but the irony of Burt getting killed in a restaurant after the many close calls in combat left a bitter taste in Rictor's mouth.

By 1100 hours Rictor was impatiently pacing back and forth in front of the hotel. In less than two hours his plane would depart for Quang Be, and he still had to attend the intelligence briefing. He had just made up his mind to catch a taxi when the Chinaman came roaring down the street and brought the jeep to a sliding halt.

As they drove through the heavy midmorning traffic, Rictor considered his own uncertain future at Quang Be. He finally decided to offer the Chinaman a job with the *"B"* Detachment. The Chinaman had spent the morning making arrangements for Dinh's funeral. With Burt gone there was no reason for him to stay in Saigon. He accepted the job.

When they arrived at the *"C"* Detachment, Rictor went directly to the intelligence office. He was guided to a room that had two walls covered with maps. The briefing was basically the same as the one he had received from MAC-V. The intelligence officer concluded by saying, "To be perfectly frank, we have very little hard intelligence to offer you. Your detachment is the first we've had in that area and our information is based on secondhand MAC-V and ARVN reports. We can't give you a detailed assessment of the enemy situation. We had hoped to get one from you."

Rictor shrugged. "Have you recently received a report on captured drawings of the capital?" he asked.

"No. What kind of drawings?"

"I'm not sure," Rictor replied. "I didn't get to see them myself, but from what I can find out Charlie's been reconning and drawing sketches of the defensive positions."

The intelligence officer picked up a pencil. "When, where and how were they captured?" After relating all he knew about the documents Rictor got up to leave. The officer said, "Wait a minute," and turned to the wall map. Rictor saw that he was studying two red lines which paralleled each other as they ran northeast toward Quang Be. The lines stopped about forty miles short of the province boundary. Without taking his eyes off the map the officer asked, "When did you leave the 'B' Detachment?"

"Three days ago. Friday afternoon to be exact. Why?" Rictor asked.

"I've got some info you probably don't have. We received a message from your detachment last night saying that province intelligence has a Viet Cong defector. The preliminary report said that he had deserted from a VC recon patrol but the interrogation report hasn't come in yet." He tapped the map with his forefinger. "These red lines represent the movement pattern of two large unidentified VC units. We tracked them through agent reports for several days, but Friday we lost them. They could be almost anywhere by now."

Rictor moved to get a better look. After calculating the distance between the end of the red lines and the Quang Be Province capital he turned away from the map. "What do you think?"

The briefing officer appeared concerned. "I think I'm gonna get busy and try to locate those documents," he said.

Rictor checked the time. "My plane leaves in fifteen minutes. How about letting me know what you find out?"

The officer nodded. "I'll keep you posted and when you get back to Quang Be try to speed up my copy of the interrogation report on that defector."

Rictor hurried out of the office. He double-timed the fifty yards to the jeep where the Chinaman was sitting behind the wheel with the motor running. When they arrived at air operations, a Caribou was taxiing into takeoff position. The Chinaman wheeled past operations and followed the plane. Near the end of the runway the plane stopped just long enough for Rictor and the Chinaman to abandon the jeep, throw the PX purchases onto the open ramp and scramble aboard. After locating a seat Rictor waited impatiently for the takeoff. He felt a great urgency to get back to the detachment and interrogate the VC deserter.

When the Caribou came to a grinding stop on the Quang Be airstrip, Rictor and the Chinaman hurriedly collected the PX purchases. Doc Brown backed a truck up to the Caribou's loading ramp, and Henderson climbed over the tailgate. From the rear of the aircraft he called, "Hey, Rictor! Did you get my goodies?"

"I got the stuff, but if you want it you'd better get your ass over here and help. There's no way I'm going to carry this crap any farther," Rictor said.

Doc shouted from the driver's seat, "Give him a hand, Henderson, so we can get back to the compound and find out what all the excitement's about."

Rictor tossed Henderson a package. "What's going on at the compound?"

Henderson shrugged. "Beats the shit out of me. A VC deserter turned himself in to province this morning, and the whole damn place is in an uproar."

Climbing aboard the truck Rictor said, "I believe you're a little mixed up. I heard about the deserter in Saigon. He came in yesterday."

Henderson shook his head. "There are two of them. The one they're making all the fuss about came in two or three hours ago."

Henderson saw the Chinaman climbing over the tailgate. "Who's the Chinese dude with the shotgun?"

Rictor said, "He works for us. It's a long story. I'll tell you about it later. What do you know about the deserters?" he asked Doc.

Doc eased the truck into gear. "The only thing I can add to what Henderson said is that Colonel Nam's called an emergency staff meeting at fifteen hundred hours."

Rictor glanced at his watch. It was 1430 hours. "Who's going to the meeting from the detachment?"

"Colonel West and the major as far as I know," Doc said.

The report of a second defector made Rictor even more anxious to get to the compound. When they arrived, Major Strong was waiting at the gate. Motioning for Doc to stop the truck he called to Rictor, "Climb down. I want you to go with me to the capital."

Rictor grinned. "Last I heard I was persona non grata at the capital."

The major snorted. "Forget about that crap, the colonel and I have an understanding. You work for me."

Rictor read concern in the major's eyes. "What's the big meeting all about?"

"C'mon, I'll fill you in on the way," the major responded.

As they walked toward the capital the major said, "Yesterday a VC armed with a Russian SKS rifle gave himself up to the national police. He said that he was a member of a ten-man patrol which was reconning the airstrip and the area around Binh Tien District headquarters. Just before noon today another deserter came in. I don't know what he told province intelligence, but ever since he got here the capital's been buzzing like a beehive. This meeting should bring us up-to-date."

At the capital excitement filled the air like an electrical charge. Junior Vietnamese officials scurried in and out of the second-floor briefing room, and staff officers clustered in small groups. Colonel Nam was pacing up and down in front of the speaker's platform questioning one of the deserters. Colonel West and Lee stood nearby listening. Colonel Nam fired questions so rapidly that Lee had difficulty translating.

As Rictor walked toward the speaker's platform he observed that the outward appearance of self-confidence and superiority Colonel Nam normally displayed had disappeared. He was extremely nervous and from all indications frightened.

The colonel continued the questioning but little was learned. Rictor wanted to question the prisoner and asked Major Strong to get permission. Colonel Nam overheard the request and immediately opposed an American interrogation.

The major insisted, and after a lengthy argument the colonel agreed.

Rictor didn't want to give the province chief time to change his mind so he told Lee to bring the prisoner and headed for the door. As they walked toward the American compound Rictor scrutinized the deserter. He appeared to be about twenty-five years old, a little over five feet tall and weighed around 135 pounds. His outward appearance was as calm as a Sunday school teacher, unlike most deserters and captives who were either sullen, defiant or frightened. He was also much cleaner and healthier looking than any Viet Cong defector Rictor had ever seen.

At the American compound, Rictor chose a small room at the end of the operations building to insure privacy. He told Lee that he wanted the prisoner to tell his life story beginning with where he was born and ending with his desertion. Lee shook his head. "We're not interested in his life story. We want to find out the mission of the patrol that he was on."

Rictor cursed. "I'll decide what's to be asked. You just ask the fuckin' questions!"

Lee smirked. "I don't take orders from you or any other American," he said.

Taking care not to expose his anger to the prisoner, Rictor strolled over and opened the door. He spotted Henderson coming from the mess hall and yelled, "Find Zung and the Chinaman. Tell them to get over here on the double!" He turned to Lee, smiled and spoke softly. "Beat it, you smart bastard, and don't come back."

Lee was shocked and then fearful. "I'm sorry for the way I spoke. I will translate any questions you have."

Rictor was momentarily puzzled by Lee's quick change of attitude. But he laughed when he realized that Lee had probably been instructed by Colonel Nam to ask certain questions and to report the responses as soon as the interrogation was over. Lee was frightened because he was going to have a difficult time making a report on an interrogation in which he had no part.

Zung ran into the building and stopped at the door. Lee gave no indication of leaving. Rictor barked, "Maybe you didn't understand me, asshole! I said get the fuck out!" Zung stepped to one side to let Lee pass but Lee remained in place. The Chinaman had been watching from outside. He stepped through the open doorway, leveled his shotgun at Lee's stomach and flipped the safety. Lee left the room without comment. Rictor caught the Chinaman's eye and nodded. "Close the door. We've got a lot to do and I don't think there's much time."

A rap on the door broke Rictor's concentration. He was not finished with the interrogation but had the information he needed for the moment. He opened the door and found the provincial intelligence officer and two RF soldiers.

Having expected someone immediately after he threw Lee out, Rictor was not surprised. The Vietnamese captain spoke in English. "I have orders to take the prisoner."

Rictor motioned him inside. "Okay, take him but it's time to quit playing games. As soon as I've made my report to the major, you and me better get together and compare information."

The intelligence officer nodded. "I'll wait for you at the capital."

Rictor dismissed the Chinaman and directed Zung to get the major. He had been evaluating his notes for ten minutes when the door banged open. His expression one of concern the major said, "Jesus Christ, Rictor! With all the turmoil at the capital I had to stand still for an ass chewing from Colonel West. You didn't really threaten to shoot that fuckin' useless interpreter, Lee, did you?"

Rictor shook his head. "No. The Chinaman did."

The major cursed. "Shit, that's the same as you doing it." He dropped into a chair and lit a cigarette. Taking a long drag he exhaled and blew smoke toward the ceiling. "Colonel West was hot enough to fuck. Having momentarily forgotten that Lee is a goddamn interpreter I told the colonel there must be some misunderstanding because of the language barrier. He nearly had a stroke and ordered me to investigate. I guess we'll both get our asses relieved over this." He snuffed out the cigarette and was silent for a long moment. Finally he said,

"Fuck it! I didn't care much for being his executive officer anyway." A slow grin spread across the major's face, then he chuckled. "You should have seen that silly bastard. He came totally unglued. He was screaming with every breath."

Rictor said, "It looks like the good news is that Colonel West is going to kick us out of here. The bad news is that it's not going to be today."

The major's grin disappeared. "What's up?"

Rictor pushed his notes across the desk and waited.

After he finished reading, the major leaned back and lit a cigarette. His eyes had turned hard and his voice was all business. "What's your estimate?"

Rictor said, "I'll walk through it with you." Picking up the notes, he continued, "The defector said he was kidnapped and forced into service by the VC about six months ago. That may be true but I don't think so. He was too informed to be a conscript private as he professed to be. According to him, he's a member of the Q762 Viet Cong Regiment, which after a seven-day forced march arrived in the vicinity of Binh Tien District headquarters yesterday. He said that along the march route, the Q762 had been joined by the Q761 and Q763 regiments plus an artillery battalion. All of those units supported by several hundred civilian food and ammunition bearers are supposedly deployed in jungle assembly areas around the capital."

Using a yardstick for a pointer Rictor walked over to the wall map and indicated several red dots near Binh Tien District headquarters and the airfield. "The deserter drew in these assembly areas." Moving the point of the stick to the base of Bien Tien Mountain he pointed to several more red dots. "This is supposedly the current location of the Q762 and Q763 regiments." He picked up a red grease pencil and drew two parallel lines south from the capital toward the Mekong Delta. Returning to the desk he said, "When I was briefed in Saigon, the briefing officer said he had been tracking two large unidentified units moving along that axis for several days, but had lost them. I think we may have found them."

The major got up and walked over to the map for a closer look. Nodding, he said, "If the defector's telling the truth, it looks like the Q761 Regiment is targeted for the district head-quarters and airfield."

"Take a look at the dot on the high ground overlooking the airfield," Rictor said. "That's supposed to be the VC artillery battalion. If so, from that position, the artillery could very easily support all three infantry regiments."

Moving back to the wall map, Rictor pointed to the dots at the base of Bien Tien Mountain. "If that really is the Q762 and Q763 regiments, they could move to an attack position south of the village in a couple of hours. If they attacked the capital through the village and caught us unprepared our position would be untenable."

The major returned to the chair. Worry lines had appeared on his forehead and his jaw muscles tightened. He checked the time. "Anything else?"

Rictor nodded. "The defector said the Q762 commander has stated that the regiment is going to seize Quang Be Capital and ordered all units to recon and make preparations for the attack. The defector said he was with one of those recon patrols and slipped away while crossing the Plei Be River."

The major moved back to the map. Studying the lines and dots, he asked, "How much of the defector's story do you believe?"

Rictor shook his head. "Unfortunately most of it. The problem is, I know that conscript privates don't read maps and certainly can't plot divisional-size deployments. And to think that some Charlie regimental commander would make his attack plans known to his rear ranked privates is ludicrous. By the way, the bastard says he has no idea when the attack is to start, but he has additional important information he's prepared to give as soon as he's safely in Saigon and rewarded."

The major cursed. "I've got a reward for that fuckin' ass-hole. What's your estimate?"

Rictor said, "I didn't get to see the documents captured by the ranger patrol, but I understand the capital defense positions were plotted. The route of advance plotted by the defector is almost identical to the one I saw on the 'C' Detachment map in Saigon. If Charlie hopes to overrun the capital he will need the darkness and some element of surprise. Assuming that he knows that two of his soldiers have defected, the attack must occur soon or be called off because his chances of success are extremely poor if we have time to prepare. I want to take a look at the interrogation report from the first defector, but I'm already convinced that Charlie has consolidated too many troops and too much equipment to abort. After dark as soon as he can move into position he'll attack."

Chapter XI

HOLD AT ALL COST

After presenting his interrogation report to the major, Rictor hurriedly prepared a message for the "C" Detachment and headed for the commo van. He found Scruggs struggling with the rear door of the van. Scruggs snorted. "Gimme a hand with this damn thing. It's stuck."

Rictor grinned. "You make a helluva commo chief. You can't even get in the van."

Scruggs threw the full force of his 190 pounds against the door and it burst open. "You really know how to hurt a guy. What did you find out from that Charlie?"

Fishing the message out of his pocket Rictor said, "Send this to the 'C' Detachment."

As he read the message Scruggs let out a low whistle. "You really figure they're coming, huh?"

Rictor nodded. "Looks that way, but keep it under your hat for a while. The major is going to get the detachment together for a briefing."

"I'll keep it quiet but everybody knows something's up. They figure it must be big, because when the major came back from the meeting he put out the word to drop everything and get busy on the defenses. How much time you figure we got?"

"No way of telling for sure. My guess is at least until midnight. I hope the rain holds off."

Scruggs glanced at the sky. "I doubt it. It ain't missed a night in the last seven."

Rictor turned to leave. "How about getting that message out as soon as you can. I've got to go to the capital."

At the gate he met Terry and Dave who were shuttling ammo from the adjacent RF compound. Lowering the box of mortar ammo he was carrying, Dave snapped, "What in the hell's going on, Rictor? The major's got us digging and stock-piling ammo like he was getting ready for a siege."

"That might be a pretty good guess, but I haven't got time to talk about it right now. I've got to get over to the capital. There'll be a briefing for everybody before dark."

Dave cursed him. "Thanks for nothing."

Terry shifted the box he was holding. "C'mon, Dave, can't you see he's stalling? Whatever it is ain't too important or half the Maggits wouldn't be sitting on their asses in the mess hall."

Dave shouldered the box of ammo and said, "If you use the fact that the Maggits are sitting on their asses to say that nothing's up, I can see why you're not in the intelligence business."

Inside the capitol building he found Callahan, the detachment operations sergeant, pacing up and down the corridor. Rictor indicated the closed doors of the conference room with a nod. "What's going on now?"

Callahan shrugged. "Search me! I've been trying to get in there for an hour. I want to take a look at their defense plan."

"I'd like to see it myself," Rictor said. "Wonder if they plan to put early warning outposts on the roads and trails leading in here?"

Callahan shook his head. "Beats me. I'm trying to find out how much fire support we can count on from the RF company that flanks the compound."

"If they don't bug out, we oughta get plenty. They've got at least three light machine guns and an armored car. The car's got a fifty-caliber on it."

Callahan nodded in agreement. "Even under heavy attack,

they oughta be able to hold for a long time. I just want to make sure they're going to be there. With them on our left flank and the security company holding the province chief's house on our right, we can deploy most of our people to the east and west ends of the compound."

Rictor nodded. "How many people we got?"

"Thirty-one, but if the ranger advisors decide to stay with their battalion, there'll be four less."

"How about Watts and Mendoza?" asked Rictor.

Callahan shook his head. "I don't know what they're gonna do. Colonel West doesn't have any control over USOM."

"Is that forward air controller that came in when I was leaving for Saigon still here?"

"Yeah, him and his radio operator are included in the count," said Callahan.

"Well, I hope . . ."

The doors banged open and Vietnamese officials spilled out of the conference room. Rictor moved close against the wall to let them pass. Most of the officials had worried expressions, and all of them were in a hurry. When Colonel West came out he appeared to be in deep thought. He caught Rictor's eye but did not speak and kept moving.

As the crowd thinned Rictor stepped inside the conference room. He spotted the Vietnamese intelligence officer studying a wall map at the far end of the room and walked over to take a look. The captain turned to face Rictor. "I'm glad you've come. The situation is very bad."

Rictor nodded. "If the information I have is correct, we're in for big trouble." He scanned the map and noted that battalion-size VC units had been plotted in several places. Two were several miles east of Binh Tien District headquarters. One was near the bridge three miles south of the capital where the road from the airstrip crossed the Plei Be River. Two units just south of Binh Tien Mountain were shown as moving north toward the capital. Two more battalions were on the high ground across the river due west of the American compound.

Upon closer inspection, Rictor saw that one of the units located south of the mountain bore the artillery symbol. None of the other units had identification markers. He picked up a red grease pencil and drew the lines which he had seen on the "*C*" Detachment's intelligence map. He marked the unit designation Q762 between the route of march lines and added it to the units just south of the mountain. Seeing the captain's puzzled expression he explained he had gotten the information from the "*C*" Detachment and the defector.

After a detailed exchange of information, Rictor concluded that if the VC attacked they would have a minimum force of five infantry and one artillery battalion. From the disposition of the VC units, it appeared they would simultaneously attack Binh Tien District headquarters and the province capital. The units attacking the district would have an additional mission of seizing the airstrip. If they were successful there would be no chance of reinforcement by air. The VC units along the road would establish ambushes and the isolation of the capital would be complete.

Mulling the new information over, Rictor walked to the window. From the second-floor conference room he had a good view of the American compound. He looked farther west across the jungle-covered river valley and studied the high ground. There was no question in his mind that Charlie could hide a division out there. He studied the steadily darkening sky and shook his head. If Charlie was able to isolate the capital and the weather knocked out friendly air support, things were going to get awful tough.

Callahan came up scowling. "I didn't get to see the capital defense plan. I'm not even sure these lazy bastards have got one, but the operations officer says the RF and security companies will stay on our flanks."

"I hope to hell they're working on their defense positions."

"The operations officer showed me on his map where they've got security patrols," Callahan said. "According to him they'll have squad-size early warning units on all avenues of approach. There's one thing I don't understand. I noticed that most of the national police are working on their compound defenses. It looks to me like they oughta be trying to find out what Charlie's doing."

Rictor lit a cigarette and blew the smoke out the window. "I understand from the intelligence officer that Colonel Nam is bringing just about everybody in to protect the Capitol building."

"Well, I hope to hell he's smart enough to put good people on the patrols south of Quang Be Village. If Charlie gets in the village without us knowing it, there'll be hell to pay. There are over a thousand civilians down there. I'd hate to be the one to have to give the order to fire on them," Callahan remarked.

Rictor nodded. "Surely he's not dumb enough to leave that road poorly protected."

Callahan pointed. "Speak of the devil, here he comes."

Rictor started to turn from the window but movement across the river caught his attention as several figures came into view. As they drew near the center of a clearing he identified them as Montagnards—one man, two women and four children. He nudged Callahan and pointed to the tribesmen. "I'd sure like to talk to them Yards. They just came out of an area where province has two VC battalions plotted. I'm gonna see if the intelligence officer will send out a patrol to pick them up."

Shouts rang out from the other side of the room as Colonel Nam dressed down two members of his staff. Callahan said, "It's a little late, but it looks like the province chief is getting worried about what's happening around here. I guess he knows what'll happen if Charlie gets hold of him."

Studying the province chief, Rictor saw signs of worry and panic. The colonel looked frightened. Rictor motioned for the intelligence officer and pointed to the Montagnards. "What's the chances of getting a patrol out there to pick them up for questioning?"

Before the officer could answer, Colonel Nam approached the window. When he saw the Montagnards, he began shouting orders to the operations officer in Vietnamese.

The intelligence officer tried to interrupt and was told to be quiet. Rictor was not sure what was being said but he knew that it had something to do with the Yards.

The operations officer hurriedly checked the wall map and picked up the field phone. A few minutes later, two 105mm. howitzers located at the rear of the capitol building boomed out a twenty-round fire for effect. Rictor realized what was happening and watched with disgust as the hill across the river was blanketed by artillery fire. When the smoke cleared he saw the remains of the Montagnards strewn all over the clearing. Satisfied that he had killed seven Viet Cong, Colonel Nam wheeled and left the room.

Callahan, who was small in stature and usually mild in manner, let fly a barrage of four-letter words. Consumed by anger he turned from the window. "During my twenty-five years in the army, I've fought in three wars and seen all kinds of idiots, but this son of a bitch takes the cake! Panicky bastards like him worry me more than Charlie!"

Rictor made no effort to control his own anger. He faced the intelligence officer. "You going to get a patrol out there to see if any of the Yards are still alive?"

The officer spread his hands. "Colonel Nam said to leave them there as a warning to the Viet Cong."

Rictor snorted. "C'mon, Callahan, let's get the hell outta here before I puke."

When they arrived at the American compound, they found most of the detachment clustered at the west fence discussing the massacre. Major Strong lowered his field glasses and turned to Biggerstaff. "Get somebody over to province. I want to know what in the hell's going on."

From behind the major, Rictor said, "I can tell you. Colonel Nam just murdered seven Montagnards! For one reason and one reason only, he's scared to death."

The major nodded. "All we need on top of everything else is for the Vietnamese to panic. Get a message off to the 'C' Detachment and find out what they know about the 'Q' regiments."

Rictor turned to leave. "I've already requested a report. Maybe Scruggs has it. I'll check. What time is the detachment briefing?"

"Soon as we're finished with the defense plan," the major responded. "Probably around nineteen hundred hours."

Rictor nodded. "After I check on the message, I'm going to give Dave a hand with his mortar pit. That's where I'll be if you need me."

At the commo van Rictor learned that the *"C"* Detachment had sent a negative reply to his request for information on the *"Q"* regiments. He accepted the lack of enemy information as one more shortcoming in a screwed-up war and went to his room for cigarettes. As he was leaving the room, he collided with Lockwood who was struggling with two boxes of hand grenades. Lockwood stumbled and dropped one of the boxes. Regaining his balance he said, "When I signed on as supply sergeant for this outfit, I didn't know they planned to make a damn mule outta me."

Rictor picked up the dropped grenade box. "Where you headed? I'll give you a hand."

"I'm trying to get these damn grenades to Dave's mortar pit and it's the last trip I'm making. He's got enough crap back there to fight a one-man war."

Rictor laughed. "How much of the ammo is still on the RF compound?"

"At least half. It would all have been moved over here by now if the damn laborers had showed up."

It dawned on Rictor that he had not seen a laborer all afternoon. "Where are they?"

"Search me. Dave and Scruggs went to the village this morning to pick them up, but they wouldn't come."

Rictor cursed. "Charlie's probably got them hauling ammo for him by now." As they approached the end of the alley he noted that the hole by the wall was empty. "How come you're not storing ammo in there?"

Lockwood shrugged. "Colonel West said no. He wants it left empty."

Dave called out from the other side of the wall, "Is that you, Lockwood?"

"It's me," Lockwood yelled. "What'cha want?"

"How about giving me a hand setting up this mortar?" Dave said.

Lockwood shoved the grenade box up on the wall. "Not a chance. I've got to get back to the RF compound."

Rictor squeezed through the narrow opening between the wall and troop billet. "Lockwood's busy moving ammo. I'll help you. Where do you want these grenades?"

Dave surveyed the cluttered hole. "Just put them there on the edge. Soon as we get the mortar set up, I'll figure out where to store them. There ain't room enough in here now to cuss a cat without getting pussy in your mouth."

Rictor grinned. "Then you had better keep your mouth shut."

Dave picked up the mortar tube and locked it to the base plate. Without looking up he said, "Scruggs showed me your message to the 'C' Detachment."

"You believe everything you read?"

Dave looked up. "Depends on who wrote it. Hold the bipods still."

Rictor frowned. "Who else saw it?"

"Far as I know I'm the only one, but the whole detachment has a pretty good idea as to what's going on. Why all the secrecy? We need to know what to expect," Dave said.

Rictor snapped the mortar sight in place. "Nobody's denying that and everybody'll get the word in about an hour. The major doesn't want rumors to get started before he's ready to pass out the straight poop."

Dave squinted through the mortar sight. "That should do it. Let's get the ammo squared away."

When the ammo boxes were in the pit, there was barely space to stand, and no room to work the mortar. Ready for a break, Rictor lit a cigarette and took a long drag. He let the smoke out slowly. "Burt Gardner got killed while I was in Saigon."

Dave cursed and fitted the last ammo box into place. "How'd he get it?"

"Charlie blew up a restaurant he was in."

Dave climbed out of the hole. "It's a cruddy war. Burt was a good trooper." He reached for a cigarette. "Olga's putting in an automatic rifle position over by the tennis court. C'mon, let's give him a hand."

As they rounded the corner Rictor noted that a lot of work had been done. Ammunition brought from the RF compound was stacked high around the nearly completed 81mm. mortar pit. A two man rifle position had been dug to provide security and a 60mm. mortar had been erected between the billets and the commo van.

On the far side of the tennis court Olga, Zung and the Chinaman were fitting sandbags around a hastily dug automatic rifle position. Dave indicated the Chinaman with a nod, "I see you brought Burt's chink back with you."

Rictor said, "He was out of a job."

"He'll do. What do you think of Olga's position?"

Rictor glanced along the vulnerable west fence. "Not much cover. It needs a lot of fortification, but the location's good. He should be able to cover the entire west end of the compound except for the corner where your mortar's located."

Dave nodded. "Maybe this damn tennis court will be good for something after all. It's the only clear field of fire on the compound."

Rictor made a visual search. "Where are the machine guns?"

"Terry and Scruggs are cleaning one of them. It will go in the trench just in front of my mortar. The Maggits will put the other one in by the mess hall porch. They'll cover the gate."

"That trench is too close to the fence. One well-thrown grenade, and it'll all be over for whoever's manning the machine gun."

Dave shrugged. "It's either move up close to the fence and run the risk of grenades or move back and not have a field of fire."

"I guess you're right but it could get tough in that corner. By the way is Lockwood going to move the truck parked between your mortar and the RF fence?"

Dave shook his head. "No place to put it. Most of the trucks are loaded with supplies and he can't leave them bunched up."

"You guys figuring on playing tennis?" Olga called from his rifle position.

"It beats hell outta filling sandbags!" Dave yelled.

Olga grinned. "Lockwood's got a truckload of thirty caliber ammo up by the mess hall. I need some for this AR."

Dave took a step toward the mess hall. "C'mon, let's get it for him. He's almost as good with that AR as he is with explosives."

Rictor nodded. "Did he ever get the water system fixed?"

Dave laughed. "We've got plenty of water. As a matter of fact we've got too much. Everytime I look around the fuckin' water tower is overflowing, but Olga's still working on it."

At the corner of the operations building, they met Campbell. He was pulling Deuces along on a chain. The monkey grabbed Dave's leg and refused to budge. Dave tried unsuccessfully to pry him loose. "Get this hairy bastard off me, Campbell! I've got work to do."

Campbell shook his head. "I can't do anything with him. That's the reason he's on the chain. Doc and me are trying to inventory the medical chest. Everytime he catches us not looking he runs off with something."

Dave snorted. "I never have liked the thieving bastard! If he doesn't let go of my leg he's going to need some of that medicine."

Hassen came out of the mess hall munching a sandwich. Dave said, "Give this damn monkey some of whatever it is you're eating so he'll let go."

Hassen shook his head and let out a nauseating belch. "Not a chance. Besides, this sandwich is my supper; I doubt he likes tuna fish."

Irritated as much with Hassen as Deuces, Dave snapped, "Knock off the crap, you fat bastard, and see if you can attract his attention!"

"Okay! Okay! Don't get excited," said Hassen, as he crammed half the sandwich into his mouth. He tossed the remainder of the sandwich on the ground. Deuces cocked his head to one side but held fast. Finally his curiosity got the best of him. He let go of Dave's leg and cautiously inched his way toward the sandwich. One sniff told him that he was not interested. He whirled and lunged for Dave's leg but Dave had already gotten clear.

At 1920 hours every American on the compound was milling around the dining room waiting for the briefing. When Colonel West and the major arrived, the colonel made a brief statement of the situation and took a seat. Major Strong stood and began issuing the defense order.

As the major spoke, Rictor studied the colonel's face. The air of aloofness was gone. It had been replaced by nervousness and concern.

"As all of you know, there's no possibility of night time reinforcement," the major was saying. "We'll have to make do with what we have. There are thirty-one of us, and our flanks are protected by Vietnamese. With our backs to the capital, we can make it hard on any would-be attackers. One of the MAC-V officers will be staying over at province. He'll maintain radio contact and keep us informed as to what's happening over there. Everyone else will be assigned a specific position. A fifty percent alert goes in effect at twenty-one hundred hours and will remain until further notice. Doc and Campbell will establish an Aid Station here in the mess hall. Colonel West and I will be located at the sixty mortar position between the billets and the commo van. It will serve as the CP."

After a short pause he continued. "The Viet Cong have never captured a provincial capital, and I don't intend for this to be the first. If we come under attack, there will be no withdrawal. *We will hold at all cost!*"

Rictor had taken it for granted that there would not be a withdrawal, but when it came as an order he felt a tingle of excitement run through his body.

When the briefing was finished the group quickly broke up. Rictor had been assigned to the 60 mortar position with Dave. He hurried outside to take advantage of the remaining daylight. He was busy unpacking ammo when Terry and Scruggs arrived with a 30-caliber machine gun. The gun was positioned in the recently dug trench located twenty feet in front of the mortar. Terry called over to Rictor, "Who was the major trying to kid with that 'No withdrawal—hold at all cost' shit? If there's as many VC out there as he says, where in the hell would we go?"

Scruggs traversed the gun and checked the field of fire. "Everybody knows we ain't going no place. The major just said that for the record. Quit dickin' around and start fixing a place for the ammo. The Maggits will be here any minute."

Surprised that Scruggs had been assigned to the trench,

Rictor asked, "What are you doing back here? I figured you'd be at the commo van."

"I left Henderson at the van. He's got that Air Force kid that works for the FAC helping him. They're young but they can handle it. Besides I figured you and Dave might get lonesome." Rictor saw through Scruggs's smoke screen. Henderson and the FAC's radio operator were young and inexperienced. Scruggs had put them in what he figured was the safest place on the compound.

Dave finished making a mortar adjustment and stood up. "Speaking of the FAC, where's he going to be? He just might get to be an important man around here before the night's over."

Terry sat on the lip of the trench cleaning his M-16. "I saw him working on the machine gun position up by the mess hall porch. He'll probably be up there."

The sound of footsteps announced the arrival of two MAC-V men who were assigned to the trench with Scruggs and Terry. They came up laden with machine gun ammo. Henderson poked his head around the wall and shouted, "Hey, you guys! Biggerstaff wants some help at the other 60 mortar position. It's supposed to be the CP but there's no time to dig in. We're gonna lay sandbags."

Dave climbed out of the hole. "We might as well get over there. I knew that fat ass Biggerstaff would be hollering for help sooner or later." He motioned for Scruggs. "Leave Terry to sort out the ammo, and let's get to it. It's getting late."

By dark, a two-foot-high sandbag wall shielded the mortar from the west fence, but the makeshift command post was unprotected from the rear and they were out of sandbags. Rictor recalled seeing bags near the water tower and went to look for them. In the fading light he failed to see the hole Olga had dug at the base of the tower and fell headfirst into a foot of mud. He climbed out of the hole, cursing and spitting slime.

A voice he recognized as one of the MAC-V officers called to him from the gun position by the mess hall porch. "Watch your step around the tower. There's an open hole!"

"Thanks a lot! I already found it. What happened to the sandbags that were over here?"

The officer suppressed a laugh. "We used them on this position, and I think they were the last ones on the compound."

"That figures," Rictor said as he headed back to the CP. Stopping to light a cigarette, the murmur of voices by the gate attracted his attention. He couldn't distinguish what was being said but it sounded as though some kind of disagreement were taking place. The gate opened and closed and a few seconds later Lockwood came by muttering to himself. Rictor stepped out of the shadows and asked, "What was all the ruckus about?"

"I was trying to talk the USOM people into staying here on the compound tonight. In so many words they told me to get fucked. Both of them, especially Mendoza, are convinced that Charlie wouldn't dare lay a hand on them. How stupid can they get?"

Rictor shook his head. "Forget it. You did your best. Just between you and me I'm about to get a bellyful of simple people, Vietnamese and Americans."

"I'll buy that, but it looks to me like Colonel West could have ordered Watts and Mendoza to stay here tonight," said Lockwood.

"He can't. He doesn't have the authority," Rictor replied.

Lockwood shrugged. "If I was him, I'd make the authority. What's he doing anyway? The only time I've seen him today was at the briefing."

"He's in his room, and my guess is he's got a lot of things on his mind," Rictor said.

"I'll bet he has, but it's too late now to start worrying about something that he should have done months ago."

It seemed pointless to continue the discussion. Rictor said. "I'm going to get a cup of coffee. The lights are going out pretty soon."

Rictor entered the mess hall by the side entrance and saw Doc and Campbell sorting medical supplies. They had rearranged the bar's couches to serve as beds in the event they were needed for casualties. Doc stood up and surveyed the hastily arranged Aid Station. "Well, it ain't exactly Walter Reed, but it's better than nothing."

Campbell nodded. "If we had a small light, we'd be in a lot better shape."

Rictor poured a cup of coffee and walked over to Doc. "Try Lockwood. He might have a lantern."

"Already did, but he doesn't have one in working condition. We could rig a battery, but there's no way to keep the light from bleeding through the windows. I don't think it would help matters to advertise that we're in here. I guess flashlights are the best we can do. How's it going outside?" asked Doc.

"I guess it's as good as can be expected," Rictor said. "It looks like it's going to start raining any minute."

"That will make everything just dandy," Doc replied. "If Charlie does attack, how much warning do you think we'll have?"

Rictor was noncommittal. "That's the sixty-four-dollar question. If I was Charlie, I'd launch my main attack through the village and use the civilians as a shield. Province says they've got security out, but I'd bet a fat man that every cop in the area is buttoned up in the national police compound."

Doc nodded in agreement. "I guess the RF troops and rangers will be slow to fire on the village, considering that most of them have families who live down there. Why don't you send Zung home? If anything is going on, he can get his tail back here and let us know."

Rictor shook his head. "I'd like to, if for no other reason than so he could be with his family. The problem is, we might need him here."

Lieutenant Maxwell, the ranger advisor, had entered the bar unnoticed. After listening for a moment he said, "Lee should be able to handle anything that comes up. If you think Zung can be of more use in the village, you ought to let him go."

Rictor grunted. "After the run-in I had with Lee this afternoon, I didn't expect to see his sorry ass around here anymore."

"He's not too happy about it but he's here now. Colonel Nam sent him over to spend the night," said the lieutenant.

Rictor drained his coffee and headed for the door. "In that case, I don't see any reason why Zung shouldn't go."

By 2100 hours, when the 50 percent alert went into effect, the sky was overcast and the ceiling was less than a thousand feet. The lights were turned off, and, like a blanket, darkness shrouded the compound. At the 60 mortar pit Dave and Rictor were unpacking grenades. Dave tossed an empty canister out of the pit and snapped off his flashlight. "What did Zung say when you told him he could go home?" he asked Rictor.

"Not much. He'd rather have stayed here, but with his family down there he felt he had to go," said Rictor.

"You reckon he'll get the word to us if Charlie shows up in the village?" Dave asked.

Rictor shook his head. "I don't know but I'd rather count on him than any other Vietnamese I know."

"You're right about that but . . ." A heavy thud followed by soft cursing came from the alley side of the brick wall. Dave laughed. "Sounds like somebody found the colonel's mortar shelter."

"Is Sergeant Hollister over there?" a voice called from behind the wall.

Under his breath Dave said, "Here comes bad news. That's Lieutenant Maxwell, and he's calling me sergeant." Dave climbed out of the pit and said, "I'm here. What's up?"

The lieutenant said, "The Ranger Battalion commander sent a man up here to see if we'd put some claymore mines around the chopper pad. I've talked to the major, and he said to check with you and Olga."

"That figures." He snapped the flashlight on and squeezed past the wall. "Soon as I can locate Olga and get some mines together, I'll meet you at the gate."

At 2205 hours on a trail half a mile south of the capital, a squad of RF troops detected a large force of VC moving single file toward the village. The RF squad leader decided to stay quiet until they passed. Five minutes later he realized his mistake. His squad was cut off and surrounded. Out of fear of discovery, he decided not to use the radio and thus failed his mission of early warning.

As the VC closed in on the village, the only sound in the dark USOM house was Mendoza's ragged snoring. Watts was in bed but wide-awake. He lay rigidly listening for familiar night sounds, but they were not there. Even the irritating bark of mongrel dogs was absent. As the minutes dragged by he wished he had not decided to spend the night in the village but rather had stayed in the American compound.

The feeling of impending disaster continued to grow. Startled by a light tap at the front door he eased out of bed. The glowing face on his watch indicated it was 2240 hours. He fumbled for a bedside candle and considered waking Mendoza but the flare of candlelight brought a surge of confidence. He went to the door and his challenge was answered by a familiar voice. He quickly opened the door and admitted a middle-aged prostitute with whom he had spent many a lonely night. She handed him a bundle of black clothing similar to that worn by peasant farmers and the Viet Cong. The prostitute cautioned Watts to silence and whispered that VC were moving into the village in force. Fearing for Watts's life she had come to take him to a safe hiding place. She motioned for him to get dressed.

Awakened by the sound of voices Mendoza walked into the room rubbing sleep from his eyes. When he saw the prostitute he said, laughing, "It's a little late for a social call, isn't it?"

Watts tossed Mendoza a shirt and pants. "Put these on. The VC are moving in, and she says they've got us marked for assassination. She's going to hide us but we don't have much time."

Mendoza ignored the clothes. "I think she's wrong, but if she's right we'll have a better chance of escape if we split up. You go with her. I'm gonna stay here."

Watts's lips formed a protest, but he saw that Mendoza's mind was made up. He blew out the candle, clutched the prostitute's hand and followed her into the night.

The door had barely closed before Mendoza was feeling his way toward his bedroom. He dropped to his knees beside the bed and groped until his hand made contact with a 45-caliber submachine gun which he kept for just such an emergency. He stood and waved his arm above his head until he located a rope ladder suspended from an opening in the ceiling.

On the far side of the village, Zung sat in the dark beside the bed he shared with his wife and baby. His concern for their safety was mounting. A sharp metallic sound in the yard brought him to his feet. Barefoot he made his way across the room and cautiously opened the door. He eased himself outside and had taken less than a dozen steps when the muzzle of an AK47 was jammed in his side. A guttural Vietnamese voice rasped, "Back inside, come out again and everybody in the house dies."

He knew better than to resist and made a hasty retreat. Unmistakable sounds at the corner of the house told him that the VC were erecting a mortar. Once inside he tried to decide what to do. He knew it was unlikely that he could get to the capital or the American compound without being detected. If he was discovered, the shots would surely give an alert. He was not afraid for himself, but he knew if he was captured his family would be killed.

While he pondered the dilemma, two battalions of VC moved into the village, thus eliminating any chance he might have had of reaching the capital.

After Dave and Olga left for the ranger compound, Rictor drifted over to the 81 mortar pit. He found Lockwood and the weapons sergeant using a penlight to set mortar time fuses. Lockwood recognized Rictor's footsteps. "Who was that I heard going out the gate?" When told it had been Dave and Olga and where they were going, Lockwood snorted. "Bullshit! Why didn't some of them candy ass Maggits go. Better than that, why weren't the claymores put in before dark? Anybody between the ranger compound and the village is a sitting duck."

The weapons sergeant lay the fuse wrench aside and patted his shepherd pup, which was curled up next to the mortar.

"Most of the MAC-V people don't know anything about clay-mores. As a matter of fact they don't know much about weapons at all."

Rictor nodded agreement. "What are you going to do with the pup? If you have to fire the mortar, the concussion will ruin his ears."

"Haven't decided yet. I can't keep him here, but I don't want to shut him up in a room either."

"If he was mine," Lockwood said, "I'd turn him loose. Dogs have a way of looking out for themselves."

Rictor turned to go. "See you later. I'm going over to check with Doc about some pills. If the going gets tough it won't hurt to have some eye-openers. We may be awake for a long time."

Lockwood patted his pocket. "You're way behind time. I'm already squared away."

On the way to the mess hall Rictor felt a light sprinkle of rain. He glanced up at the low cloud cover and cursed. After getting the stay-awake pills from Doc, he poured himself a cup of coffee and spent the next few minutes discussing the situation with Doc and Campbell. As he left the mess hall by the side door, he heard a steady splash of water as it spilled from the overflowing tower.

The shuffle of approaching footsteps and murmur of voices told him that Dave and Olga were returning. Olga came through the gate cursing. Dave said, "Look at it this way, Olga, working on the tower is better than being out there in that field laying mines."

"That's not the point," Olga grumbled. "With a little coop-eration, I could've had the damn tower fixed days ago." Olga turned on his flashlight. "Be back in a minute. I've got to get some tools."

Rictor walked over to Dave. "I don't blame him for being pissed off about the tower. Did you get the mines in?"

"We got them in, but I wouldn't swear they'll work. It's so dark out there we couldn't see a damn thing. Every Charlie in the country could've had us surrounded and we wouldn't have known it. Olga and I were less than a hundred yards from the village, and you'd think it was deserted. We didn't see a light or hear a sound."

Olga returned with his tools. "He ain't kidding about it being dark. It's black as a witch's belly button. I had a spooky feeling the whole time I was out there."

Dave grunted. "If you want me to help, quit jacking your jaws, and let's get started."

"I wondered why you were still hanging around. I don't need any help. Besides that there's only room up there for one person."

Dave turned to leave. "In that case I'm gonna get some sack time." Turning to Rictor he said, "Wake me up when you get tired. I'll relieve you on the mortar."

Rictor remained at the base of the tower until he was certain that he could not be of any assistance to Olga. He spotted the orange glow of a cigarette in front of the operations building and walked toward it. He found Lockwood sitting behind the wheel of a jeep. Rictor climbed in the passenger's seat and lit a cigarette. "You fixing to take a trip?"

Lockwood chuckled. "If there's anything to this VC scare you've come up with, it looks like a good time to go some place."

"Sounds like you don't believe Charlie's out there."

"It's not that. If you say he is, I believe it. But if there are as many of them as you say and you gotta pretty good idea where they are, why no air strikes?"

Rictor shook his head. "One look at the situation map and you can see that Charlie's not stupid. He picked his assembly areas either in or near rubber plantations."

Lockwood was puzzled. "Charlie might not be stupid, but I must be. What have rubber plantations got to do with it?"

"You know that most of the rubber is owned by the sorry ass French. Our chances of getting an air strike on a plantation is less than a snowball in hell. One good strike would rattle cages in Saigon, Washington and Paris."

"Them fuckin' Frogs already got their asses whipped down here," Lockwood cursed. "Are they gonna help us get ours kicked too?"

Rictor shook his head. "I haven't seen any indication otherwise and don't expect to. Best I can figure is they want us out of Vietnam as much as Charlie does."

A sprinkle of rain pelted the compound, bringing a murmur of protest from unseen men manning the dark alert positions. Lockwood turned up his shirt collar. "If Charlie is coming he couldn't have picked a better night. Rain just about stacks the deck in his favor."

Rictor checked the time. "It's 0145 hours. If they're gonna attack, it'll be soon. They can't wait much longer because daylight will catch them in the open."

Chapter XII

THE ATTACK

The rain stopped as suddenly as it had begun. Sure that the letup was only temporary, Lockwood climbed out of the jeep. "I'm gonna mosey over to the eighty-one pit." Studying the soft glow made by Olga's flashlight, he said, "I'd sure hate to be caught on that tower, if Charlie . . ." His words were lost in the ear-shattering explosion of an artillery shell slamming into the roof of the operations building.

Hot shrapnel and debris filled the night air as incoming artillery ripped at the compound. Rictor grabbed his M16 and leapt from the jeep. As his feet touched the ground, mortar fire erupted near the gate, showering him with dirt and gravel. In the brief flash of light he caught a glimpse of Olga jumping from the tower.

The rattle of small arms fire along the west fence told Rictor that a VC assault force had managed to reach the compound undetected. Realizing that flare light was needed to prevent penetration, he crouched and sprinted the forty yards to the CP. He leapt over the two-foot sandbag wall and crashed into Biggerstaff.

Cursing, Biggerstaff groped for an illumination round. Grabbing one, he clawed out the safety pin and fitted the round to the mouth of the mortar. The sucking sound made by the round sliding down the tube was followed by a thunderous boom. Rictor's ears rang as he watched the comet-tailed round streak skyward and disappear into the overcast. Seconds later, the dark cloud cover turned bright orange and gradually changed to yellow as the parachute flare drifted earthward, bathing the compound in soft light.

Small arms fire from the west fence grew more intense. Resting his M16 on a sandbag, Rictor leaned forward and waited. When his eyes adjusted to the light, he saw shadowy figures in black trying to hack their way through the fence. He fired a burst and saw several of the figures collapse. While he was reloading, the major and the Chinaman charged into the CP and took up firing positions.

Satisfied with the range of the first flare, Biggerstaff dropped two rounds down the tube and yelled for the Chinaman to break out the high explosives. While the firefight raged at a distance of forty yards, Lockwood and the weapons sergeant got the 81 mortar cranked up and began lacing the river valley west of the fence.

Bending close to the ground and favoring his right leg Olga hobbled by the CP. Ten yards short of the tennis court, he took a bullet in the side, and his body spun like a top. Dropping to his hands and knees, he crawled forward and lunged into the automatic rifle position. When the flare burned out, the compound was plunged into darkness. The VC mortar and artillery gunners had found their range, and the indirect fire was murderous. As he waited for the next flare to fire, Rictor hoped that by some miracle the men who had been sleeping in the billets had managed to get out.

Scruggs and Hassen had been in the trench in front of Dave's mortar before the first round went off. Discovering that he was out of cigarettes, Scruggs had headed for the billet he shared with Dave to get a pack. Squeezing past the brick wall he was careful to avoid Colonel West's mortar shelter. He worked his way through the pitch-dark alley to the door of the room, where ragged snoring told him Dave was asleep. As he stepped inside, the incoming artillery shell crashed into the operations building, and all hell broke loose.

Awakened by the explosion Dave's still-groggy mind refused to accept Scruggs's yell that the compound was under attack. When the words finally broke through, he rolled out of bed, grabbed his rifle and followed Scruggs out of the room. Turning toward the brick wall he had barely cleared the door when the room took a direct hit and exploded into a shower of broken timber and smashed furniture. The blast knocked Dave off his feet and sent him tumbling down the alley. Stunned but conscious, he landed in the open mortar shelter. When his mind cleared, he realized the hole was jammed with people.

A flare burst overhead, lighting the alley and exposing Colonel West who stood frozen on the elevated walk in front of his room. Dave yelled for him to get down, but the warning was too late. The area around the colonel erupted with fire, leaving him broken, crumpled facedown in the alley.

"You people in that hole get the hell outta there," Callahan called from the fence side of the wall. "It's a death trap! Try to make it over to this side. Hassen and I will cover you."

Dave made a quick head count. There were five other people in the hole: Scruggs, Terry, Lieutenant Maxwell and two enlisted ranger advisors. Dave grabbed Scruggs by the shoulder and said, "As soon as that flare burns out, work your way around the far end of the wall to the trench. Take Terry and the ranger sergeant with you. I'll take the lieutenant and the corporal. We'll try for the mortar pit."

Just before the flare burned out the ranger sergeant caught sight of Colonel West's body and screamed for a medic. "Shut the fuck up and get ready to move!" Scruggs barked. "There ain't nothing you or anybody else can do for him."

As Lieutenant Maxwell crawled out of the hole, machine gun fire chipped away at the wall, ricocheting in all directions. He took up a firing position at the end of the wall and opened up with his carbine.

When the flare burned out, Dave and the ranger corporal scrambled out of the hole. Squeezing past the lieutenant they crawled around the wall and dropped into the mortar pit.

Sliding on their bellies, Scruggs and Terry made it past Callahan and Hassen into a two-man foxhole between Dave's mortar and the trench. Bringing up the rear, the ranger sergeant made the mistake of standing up. The blast from a mortar explosion slammed him against the wall, but he managed to stagger to the trench.

Scruggs grabbed the machine gun and raked the fence line with 30-caliber rounds. Spotting the muzzle flash of a large weapon on the high ground across the river, he yelled for Dave to concentrate his mortar fire on the hill. Two flares popped overhead exposing VC infantry bunched up at the corner of the compound fence. Scruggs shifted the machine gun and raked them with a long burst. The combined firepower of six M16s and the machine guns cut down a dozen VC, leaving their shattered bodies dangling in the wire.

When the artillery round crashed into the operations building, Lee had panicked and run out the mess hall side door. He had taken only a few steps when a jagged piece of shrapnel slashed a gash across his left ear. Clutching his head with both hands, he ran back inside.

With the aid of a flashlight, Doc bandaged Lee's head. Flare light poured through the open back door, and seconds later yells for a medic came from the alley. Doc grabbed a stretcher and hurried out the door. Before his feet touched the ground a burst of rifle fire caught him in the right shoulder and arm. Campbell reached the doorway in time to see Doc topple from the stoop. He leapt to the ground and dragged Doc back inside.

Crouched close to the billet wall at the mouth of the alley, Henderson waited for the VC artillery barrage to lift. When the incoming rounds stopped, he made a mad dash for the commo van. Finding that the Air Force radio man was already in contact with the *"C"* Detachment, Henderson figured he could be of more use in one of the fighting positions and headed for Dave's mortar pit. Halfway down the alley he was buried by a collapsing billet. Flare light lit the alley, and he could see several people in the hole by the wall. He screamed for help, but his voice was drowned out by incoming mortar and artillery fire. Struggling frantically, he used his one free hand to throw off rubble and broke free just as the flare burned out. Unable to locate his M16, he crawled down the alley. At the hole he rolled over the lip and found it deserted. Unarmed and uncertain of his next move, he waited.

The rattle of carbine fire at the end of the wall told him that he was not alone. He scrambled out of the hole just as flares popped overhead. A burst of machine gun fire forced him to hug the ground. When he looked up, he saw Lieutenant Maxwell leaning against the billet clutching his stomach with both hands. Henderson crawled forward and pulled the lieutenant behind the wall. Seeing that he was gut shot and pouring blood, Henderson lifted him in a fireman's carry and stumbled up the alley toward the mess hall.

From his automatic rifle position, Olga poured deadly fire across the tennis court to the west fence. He was determined to make Charlie pay for the wound in his side. Every few seconds he changed the point of aim, making certain not to establish a pattern that would give the VC a chance to advance.

From the command post, Rictor watched the arc of tracers from Olga's rifle and nodded with approval. There was a break in the mortar and artillery barrage, but rifle and machine gun fire were increasing. Beyond the west fence Charlie was massing his fire for an assault. Bullets whined and buzzed in all directions, filling the air with a sound like angry hornets. The sandbagged front of his position was taking a hell of a beating.

Alternating high explosive and illumination rounds, Biggerstaff and the Chinaman fired the mortar at maximum rate. Lockwood and the weapons sergeant elevated their mortar and pumped round after round into suspected assembly areas.

When the anticipated assault came, the VC made easy targets in the flickering flare light. Three times they regrouped and charged the fence only to be cut down or driven back by automatic weapons fire.

When it became apparent the VC were not going to try again, at least for the moment, the major leaned over to Rictor to say, "See if you can get a casualty report." Rictor eased out through the open side of the command post and zigzagged his way toward the mess hall.

Entering through the back door he saw Campbell bent over Lieutenant Maxwell, who was lying on the bar. Doc, in pain from his own wounds, leaned against the bar holding burning scraps of paper which provided light for Campbell to work by.

Rictor peered over Campbell's shoulder. "How bad's he hit?"

Campbell shook his head and said, "If we don't get a Medevac pretty quick, he's had it."

Indicating the burning paper, Rictor asked, "Is that all you've got for light?"

Doc nodded. "I lost my flashlight when I got hit, and Campbell lost his when he came to get me."

Rictor fished a flashlight out of his pocket. "Take mine. You need it more than me. How many wounded you got, and what can I do to help?"

Campbell finished applying a pressure bandage to the lieutenant's wound and said, "There are only three wounded in here, but I know there'll be more coming. We might run short on bandages. If you can get some bed sheets, it'll help."

Rictor ducked out through the back door. He stopped momentarily and listened to the roaring firefight taking place around Dave's mortar position. Something new had been added, the muffled sound of exploding hand grenades.

He stepped into the alley and entered the first room on the left. Finding it in shambles, he climbed over broken furniture to the bed. Quickly gathering up the blankets and sheets, he worked his way back to the door. As he stepped outside he heard movement farther down the alley. Before he could call out a challenge, he was engulfed by the multicolored flashes of light and the hot blast of a mortar round. He pitched forward, ricocheted off the billet wall, and landed on a pile of rubble. Dazed and numb, he discovered that shrapnel had slashed through the palm of his left hand between the middle and ring finger. As he pushed up to his knees, a sharp pain in his side made him clench his teeth. Running his good hand over his rib cage, he found no open wound. Tender lumps told him that he had fractured ribs.

He located his M16 and was feeling around for the blankets and sheets when his hand brushed against a body. It was warm but had the clammy feeling of the dead. A flare burst out of the overcast west of the compound. In the shadowy half light he identified the still form of Colonel West. The arrogant colonel was dead. He had taken a hunk of shrapnel through the chest, and his lungs had spilled out through the hole.

A scraping noise at the end of the forty-yard alley caused Rictor to look up. He saw Henderson attempting to free a case of machine gun ammo which was trapped in a pile of rubble. Assuming it was Henderson he had heard just before the mortar round came in, he located the sheets and carried them to the mess hall.

There was nothing more he could do to help Campbell, so he left by way of the side door and sprinted for his position. As he scrambled through the open side of the mortar position, Biggerstaff was screaming at the major, "You've got to get out of here and do something! You can't just sit here while the compound comes down around us!"

Rictor saw that Biggerstaff was in a panic and shouted him down. "We've already lost one commander!" Turning to the major he said, "You're in command. Colonel West is dead!"

Rictor gave the casualty report, crawled out of the CP, worked his way past a supply tent and banged on the door of the commo van. The door opened slowly, and the Air Force radio operator appeared. Rictor leaned close to make himself heard over the rattle of small arms fire. "Have you got contact with the 'C' Detachment?" Getting a nod he said, "Find out how long till we get a flare ship."

The airman said, "There's one on the way. It would've been here already but the pilot's having trouble finding us in this overcast."

"When you make contact, try and guide him in. We're running low on illumination rounds," Rictor said.

As he worked his way back to the command post, Rictor was concerned about the lack of communications. There was no field phone connecting the fighting positions, and the van was their only contact with the outside world. Fortunately, the van was situated close to the operations building, which gave it some protection from mortar and artillery, but it was vulnerable to small arms fire and had already been punctured in several places.

At the command post Rictor noted that small arms fire from the west fence had dwindled to an occasional burst. He took advantage of the lull to bandage his hand. He listened to fire-fights raging in other sections of the complex and figured the Viet Cong had attacked simultaneously on three separate sides. A force supported by mortar and artillery from Binh Tien Mountain had come out of the village and attacked the ranger compound from the south. A second force moving in from the east had engaged the ARVN Artillery Unit and the national police compound. And a third force had attacked the RF and American compound from the west.

Rictor felt some admiration for the simplicity and effectiveness of Charlie's strategy. If the units attacking from the east and west could penetrate, thus forcing the defenders to withdraw toward the center of the complex, the larger force moving north from the village could easily drive the disorganized defenders toward the capitol building. If the three numerically superior VC forces linked together, they would overwhelm the capital with firepower and drive the defenders into the river valley. If the plan was successful, it would be a simple maneuver for the VC to mass artillery and mortar fire on the valley and eliminate any chance of counterattack.

Meanwhile, the small arms fire was increasing in volume. Rictor fitted a full magazine to his M16 and scanned the west fence. Biggerstaff shortened the 60mm. mortar range until the rounds barely cleared the compound. The Chinaman laid his shotgun aside, grabbed a 40mm. grenade launcher, and waited.

When the VC charged, Rictor singled out sappers carrying explosives. He took well-aimed shots and saw a few go down before the flares burned out, once again pitching the camp into darkness.

Biggerstaff cursed as he searched through empty ammo boxes for more illumination rounds. Olga locked his automatic rifle on the fence and continued to pour a murderous stream of fire into the area. The sound of Olga's heavier rifle was comforting, and Rictor held his fire and waited. From the second mortar pit, Lockwood fired two hand-held flares exposing VC along the fence. The concentrated fire of Olga's AR, several M16s and the grenade launcher was devastating for the VC. Badly mauled, they pulled back, leaving their dead and wounded behind.

Rictor reloaded and focused his attention on the firefight taking place in the vicinity of Dave's mortar. Fifty-caliber tracers from the RF compound screamed and whined as they ricocheted over the billets. The dreaded rushing of rockets indicated that VC gunners had found the range, and the number of explosions increased.

At the trench in front of Dave's mortar, the blast from an incoming mortar round ripped the machine gun out of Terry's hands. Concussion caused the ranger sergeant to drop his carbine and claw at his ears with both hands. He lurched out of the shallow trench, staggered blindly past Dave's mortar position, and headed toward the mess hall.

Bleeding from a deep gash in the head, Scruggs righted the machine gun and fired a long burst at the corner where the two compounds linked together. Dazed and in agony from shrapnel wounds, Terry struggled out of the trench and crawled toward the alley. Seconds later, a grenade landed in the trench. The blast lifted Scruggs like a rag doll and slammed him against the ground. Blood poured from a jagged wound in his upper left arm. Standing up he slowly stumbled toward Dave's mortar. A machine gun burst caught him in both legs. He pitched forward and landed on the edge of the hole.

Dave grabbed him by the shoulders and hauled him in. Aware that Scruggs was badly hit, Dave shouted in his ear. "If the corporal and I cover for you, do you think you can make it to the mess hall on your own?"

Scruggs shook his head. "Gimme a rifle," he said. "I can still shoot."

Ignoring Scruggs's plea, Dave picked up his rifle and nudged the ranger corporal. "When I signal, you start lobbing grenades along the fence line." Resting a hand on Scruggs's shoulder, he said, "There's no way we can patch you up, and you're going to be in the way. When I start firing, you crawl around the wall and try for the mess hall. Doc will take care of you." Scruggs started to argue, but Dave looked him long in the eye. "Beat it, I'll see you later."

Scruggs nodded and pulled himself up to the edge of the hole. Dave snapped his M16 on full automatic and tapped the corporal. When the grenades began exploding, he shouted, "Get moving!" Scruggs climbed out of the hole and dragged himself around the wall.

From a shallow hole twenty feet to the right of Dave's mortar, Callahan, Hassen, an MAC-V private and a radio operator named Bryant poured rifle fire into the corner. A near miss VC rocket sprayed the hole with shrapnel, and a jagged piece slashed through Bryant's right arm, severing the bone and leaving his arm dangling from the shoulder by the large muscle.

Cut and bleeding from less serious wounds, Callahan used his own first aid packet to make a tourniquet for Bryant's arm. Unable to stop the bleeding, he shouted to Hassen, "Cover for me! I'm gonna try to get Bryant to the mess hall."

He pulled Bryant out of the hole and pushed him toward the alley. As they squeezed past the wall, a flare popped overhead. Callahan spotted Terry lying in Colonel West's mortar shelter. He knew at a glance what had happened. Terry had come around the wall just as an artillery round had ripped through the billets. The blast had torn out part of the wall and blown Terry into the hole.

Callahan pushed Bryant toward the mess hall. "Keep moving! You can make it. I'll be right behind you!" He jumped into the hole and began pulling rubble off Terry's nearly naked body.

When the flare went off, Hassen glanced around to see if Callahan and Bryant had made it past the wall. He caught sight of two VC on the RF fence and screamed, "Watch out, Dave! They've got us flanked. They're on the RF compound!" Standing, he brought his M16 to the shoulder and fired several short bursts. Impact from the small high-velocity rounds almost tore one of the VC in half. The second VC was gut shot and dangled screaming in the wire. Hassen took careful aim and with a single shot blew off the top of his head.

Dave realized then that the RF troops had retreated from the west fence, giving the VC free access to his unprotected flank. He cursed ARVN for a bunch of cowards and shouted for the ranger corporal to break out more hand grenades. Attempting to cover the RF fence, he found his field of fire blocked by the supply truck. The VC on the RF side of the fence took advantage of the blind spot, using the truck for cover to shower Dave's mortar position with grenades.

Crouched low in the hole, Dave fired, but most of his rounds either plowed into the ground or ricocheted harmlessly off the truck. Laying the rifle aside he grabbed two grenades and arched one over the fence. His first throw was long, but the second found its mark and brought screams from the far side of the truck. With both Dave and the corporal throwing, the supply of unboxed grenades was quickly used up. Struggling frantically to open a new box, the ranger corporal didn't see an incoming grenade. It lodged in the soft dirt directly beneath him and exploded. His body absorbed the shrapnel, smothering the blast. Disemboweled, he died instantly.

Spattered with blood and the corporal's flesh, Dave bled from the ears and mouth. He leaned against the mortar and vomited. When the world stopped spinning and his eyes focused, he saw that his M16 was twisted and useless. Shoving the corporal's mangled body aside, he broke open the grenade box.

At the front of the compound, the position next to the mess hall porch was overcrowded. Three MAC-V officers and the forward air controller were jammed against each other. Using his air to ground radio continuously, the FAC was unsuccessful in contacting the missing flare ship. The VC had not pressured the east fence, but the sight of ARVN rangers withdrawing toward the capital and the sound of advancing fire from the village meant the situation was deteriorating fast. Lieutenant Savage, one of the MAC-V officers, detected movement behind the flowers which lined the fence. Resting his grenade launcher on the sandbagged front of the position, he leaned forward and waited. A moment later, a shadowy figure inched out from behind the shrubbery and crawled toward the gate. "Get ready," Savage whispered. "Here they come!" Taking careful aim, he squeezed the trigger. The impact of the 40mm. grenade tore the VC in half.

At the command post there was growing concern over the dwindling supply of illumination rounds. Biggerstaff took a count and shouted to the major, "There's only nine flares left and I think the other position is already out of 'em. If that flare ship don't get here pretty fuckin' quick, it's gonna be too late. When we run out of flares, Charlie'll pour through the fence and be all over our ass."

The major heard the panic in Biggerstaff's voice and attempted to hide his own concern. "Shut up and take advantage of the lull. When Charlie tries again, you're going to need all your energy. We'll worry about flares when we have to." He turned to Rictor. "Sounds like things are getting nasty around Dave's mortar, and I haven't heard Scruggs's machine gun lately. See if you can get a casualty report."

Rictor nudged the Chinaman. "Cover the major. When I come back, if he's dead I expect to find your body too." Without waiting for a response he crouched and ran as fast as his injured ribs would allow to the back door of the mess hall. He stepped inside and was met by a whispered challenge, "Who's there?"

He recognized Scruggs's voice and identified himself. When his eyes adjusted to the dim light he saw that Scruggs, unable to stand, had propped himself against a table and was sitting with his M16 covering the door. Rictor knelt and rested a hand on Scruggs's shoulder. "How bad you hit?" he asked.

"I guess it could be worse. How does it look outside?"

"Not too good. I've gotta talk to Doc and Campbell for a minute. Is there anything I can do for you?"

"Yeah! You can help me down the alley to Dave's mortar."

Rictor listened to the close-quarter battle at the far end of the alley. He knew that Scruggs couldn't walk but suspected that he was a long way from being out of the fight. Leaning close Rictor said, "Charlie's putting a lot of pressure on the fence. If he gets on the compound, somebody's got to cover this door."

Sudden pain made Scruggs clench his teeth. When it

passed, he said, "I get the message. You got yourself a door-man."

Rictor stood. "I'll see you on the way out." He made his way over to where Campbell and Doc were working on Terry. The number of wounded in the room had increased to eight, and Campbell reported that several of them were dying.

Struggling to get up Terry screamed, "Get your goddamn cold hands off me! I gotta find some clothes before I freeze."

Certain that Terry was in shock, Rictor asked, "How about our boy here, is he gonna make it?"

Doc grunted. "If it was anybody else, I'd say he didn't have a chance, but he's one tough son of a bitch."

Rictor nodded. "Yeah, I know. What about the lieutenant?"

Doc shook his head. "Just a matter of time."

Turning to leave, Rictor said, "I've got to get going. The major's waiting for a casualty report." A burst of 50-caliber machine gun fire from the RF compound ripped through the mess hall and plowed into the ceiling. Rictor cursed. "Either the fuckin' RF people are firing wild, or Charlie's captured one of the armored cars. Keep everybody down."

"We've been taking a lotta fire from over there," Campbell said. "I figure Charlie's on the RF compound."

Hoping that Campbell was wrong, Rictor said, "Put the wounded where they can get the most protection, and don't use the light any more than you have to." Remembering Scruggs's pain he turned to Doc. "You got something you can give Scruggs? He's hurting pretty bad."

"He can't take any more morphine," Doc said. "It might kill him."

Rictor nodded and walked over to Scruggs. Reasonably certain that Charlie was on the RF compound, he placed half his ammo where Scruggs could reach it. His voice barely above a whisper, Rictor said, "Keep your eye on the back door, and don't let any uninvited guest in. There may be some any time now."

Scruggs spat blood and patted his M16. "You got it."

Rictor eased outside and waited for his eyes to adjust. Suspecting the letup in mortar and artillery fire meant the VC were regrouping, he studied the pitch-black RF compound for a long moment. He couldn't see any movement so he headed for the CP.

After making his report to the major, Rictor took up a prone position at the open side of the command post. A light rain was falling, and smoke from burned gunpowder hung in the air like fog. His eyes ran, and the acid smoke made his mouth so dry he couldn't even spit. Dry as his mouth was he had never wanted a cigarette more. He fished out his lighter. Hugging the sandbags to shield the light, he reached for a cigarette. His hand closed over the forgotten package containing the cross bought in Saigon. Fingering the package he thought of home, his wife and son, then counted his grenades and tightened his grip on the M16.

Chapter XIII

THE PENETRATION

Minutes after the attack began, the Regional Force troops adjacent to the American compound began retreating from their west fence positions. Poorly trained and even more poorly led, they had no stomach for close combat. As the assault intensified and the VC attackers broke through the fence, even token resistance by the RF troops ceased. Terrified, they abandoned an armored car without firing a shot. Using the captured vehicle's guns, the VC drove the remaining defenders from the compound.

The main VC attack force pursued the retreating RF troops toward the capital while a smaller group of VC, using the RF barracks for cover, attacked Dave's mortar position with hand grenades and small arms.

A sapper squad carrying lengths of iron pipe filled with explosives worked their way along the unprotected fence of the American compound setting breaching charges. A perfectly timed barrage of VC mortar fire pounded the American compound just as the pipe charges blew large holes in the fence. The breaching explosions were masked by the barrage and went undetected by the Americans. Racing through the openings, some of the VC turned toward Dave's mortar position while others headed for the mess hall.

189

The only defenders to observe the penetration were two RF soldiers hiding in a shallow culvert near the fence. Armed with carbines but paralyzed with fear, they did not fire.

Splinters of wood and bits of concrete sliced through the air as artillery rounds ripped at the billets. Crouched low in the mortar pit, Dave yelled over to Hassen, "I just saw people running along the inside of the RF fence. If it's Charlie, we'll be in deep shit when the artillery lifts."

Hassen knew that if the VC came down the alley using the wall for cover, he and Dave and the others would be sitting ducks. He turned to the MAC-V private who had come sliding into the hole a few minutes earlier and said, "Go up the alley and cover our rear. Looks like Charlie's on the compound. If he gets in the alley, we're dead meat." Certain that he could not get through the alley alive, the private shook his head. Hassen grabbed him by the shirt collar. "Get your ass up the alley, or I'll blow your fuckin' guts out. Now get moving!"

The private crawled slowly out of the hole and inched his way around the wall, then dropped into the mortar shelter. While he waited for his eyes to adjust to the darkness, the artillery barrage shifted from the American compound to the capitol building. During the brief silence which followed he strained his eyes and ears for sound or movement. Failing to see or hear anything, he took a deep breath, climbed out of the hole and crawled forward. As he felt his way along the alley, fear gnawed at his nerves and tightened his throat until he could barely breathe. Midway up the alley he brushed against a dead body. He stifled a scream and scrambled to his feet. Regaining control, he inched forward.

Near the mouth of the alley he detected movement and ran head-on into three Viet Cong. Instinctively, he fired. The nearest VC took the heavy 7.62 slug in the belly and let out a shrill scream. The private shifted his M14 and squeezed the trigger, but the gun was jammed. He saw muzzle flashes and felt the rounds slam into his chest, but the sound of the AK47 seemed far away and unimportant. All at once he was very tired. As the cool darkness of death settled over his dulled mind, he pitched forward and let out a deep sigh.

Dave heard the burst of AK fire in the alley. Aware that the private was armed with an M14, he shouted to Hassen, "Sounds like the Maggit ran into trouble. Cover the wall!" His words were lost in the explosion of a grenade thrown from the corner of the billet. Bleeding from dozens of needlelike shrapnel punctures in his arms and shoulders, Dave grabbed a grenade and hurled it at the corner. The grenade ricocheted off the billet and exploded harmlessly. A VC sapper cradling a homemade bomb in his arms leaped around the corner and charged.

The VC's intent was clear. Scrambling out of the pit Dave dove in the hole with Hassen, who was already taking aim. "Cut the bastard down, Hassen! Shoot or we'll go up with him!" Hassen froze. Pounding the giant mess sergeant in the kidney, Dave screamed, "Shoot! Shoot, you fat son of a bitch!" At the very last second, Hassen squeezed off a long burst. The high-velocity rounds took the VC in the stomach. His guts spilled out on the bomb, and he stopped in his tracks. Hugging the wall Dave covered his ears with both hands. When the ten-pound charge exploded, it gouged a deep crater and the VC disintegrated.

Before the dirt and debris stopped falling, Dave was out of the hole. Halfway to the mortar pit he stopped and went back. Crouching on the lip of the hole he said, "Hassen, you motherfucker, if you quit me, I'll kill you myself." Without waiting for a reaction he whirled and headed for the mortar pit.

At the mess hall Campbell was working on Terry's wounds when he heard Vietnamese voices along the RF fence. Not knowing if they were friendly troops or VC, he began moving the wounded into the kitchen, where thicker walls gave more protection. Lieutenant Maxwell lay unconscious on the bar. Terry was conscious but in shock. He lay on a couch between the bar and the door. Scruggs, having refused to be moved, covered the rear door.

A flare popped over the compound. From a window at the end of the bar, Campbell saw a small group of VC moving along the RF fence. He unholstered his 9mm. pistol and yelled to Scruggs, "Charlie's on the compound!" Taking careful aim, he fired. The nearest VC took the round in the throat and dropped. Before Campbell could fire again, the rear door of the mess burst open and two VC were silhouetted against the orange flare light. Scruggs braced himself and fired from the hip. Both VC went down. Hoping to get the door closed before the flare burned out, Scruggs rolled over on his side and pulled himself along the floor toward the door.

"Pull back, Scruggs!" Campbell yelled from the window. "Charlie's pouring through the fence like water. They'll be coming through the door any second! Try and make it to the kitchen. I'll cover for you!"

Scruggs glanced to the couch at the end of the bar. Terry should have been dead but his heaving chest said he was still alive. Scruggs continued moving toward the door and shoved it closed. Jamming a fresh magazine in the M16, he crawled over to the couch. Bracing himself in a sitting position, he said, "Hang on, Terry. We're gonna see this through together." The door squeaked, and Scruggs fired a long burst. He heard the answering scream but in the darkness failed to see the heavy satchel charge that arched over his head and landed behind the bar. It slid up against Campbell's feet and exploded.

The blast tore at the floor and ripped apart the wooden bar. The flying splinters gouged deep cuts in Terry's already battered naked body. Scruggs rolled headlong across the floor and crashed against the wall. When his head cleared, he cursed under his breath. He had lost his rifle.

Two grenades exploded just inside the door, and AK fire sliced through the darkness. A movement by the door alerted Scruggs that Charlie was inside. Unsheathing his commo knife, he flattened out on his stomach and waited. It was a short wait until a pair of strong hands, searching for weapons, worked their way along his body. Pretending to be dead, Scruggs nearly gagged from the VC's body stench. When the hands reached his shoulder, Scruggs flipped over on his back, locked his left arm around the VC's legs and pulled downward while thrusting the knife upward. The sharp blade penetrated the VC's groin slashing open his stomach. Screaming with agony, the VC collapsed on top of Scruggs, he drove the knife deep into the VC's neck and the scream became a gurgle.

Intestine and blood covered Scruggs's face. He shoved the dying VC to one side, rolled over on his stomach and pulled himself along the floor toward the side door.

The satchel charge explosion had left Terry lying on his back, unable to move. Grenade explosions had blown out his eardrums, and showered him with hot shrapnel. He only wanted to sleep but his eyes wouldn't close. He was confused. In his silent, painless world he could tell that people were around him but couldn't make out what they were doing. A flashing light just above his face caught his attention. The light came closer and made his eyes water. He wished somebody would turn it off. The VC gunner, manning the light machine gun resting on Terry's chest, fired through the doorway and down the alley. As the gunner depressed the barrel, muzzle flashes seared Terry's face, and concussion ripped his already punctured eardrums.

At the other end of the dining room, most of the wounded who could move on their own had crawled through the kitchen onto the screened porch. Doc had located an M16 but was having trouble operating it with one hand. He lay just inside the kitchen entrance listening for movement. It had grown deathly quiet at the far end of the dark mess hall.

Certain he had heard someone brush against a table, Doc strained to hear. Detecting the faint sound of movement near the side door, Doc touched the wounded ranger sergeant lying at his side and offered him the rifle. The sergeant declined and crawled out onto the porch. Doc lay very still. The only sound in the building was his own ragged breathing. After what seemed like an eternity, there was an unmistakable bump near the side door. He was uncertain as to what action to take. If he called out and it was Charlie, he would give away his position. Yet he knew he was in no condition to fight. He was aware, too, that if he remained silent and any of the wounded in the bar area were still alive, they might die needlessly.

A sliding sound moving in his direction made up his mind. He hugged the floor and called toward the dining room, "Campbell, if you or any of the wounded can crawl, try to work up this way!" He got a quick response. A burst of AK fire splintered the wall above his head. Reluctant to fire, Doc crawled toward the porch.

At the corner of the mess hall porch, Lieutenant Savage peered out of the sandbagged position. A flare popped west of the compound and he saw the side door of the mess hall slowly opening. He raised his carbine and fired through the door. Hearing movement in the kitchen, Savage shifted the carbine and fired through the screen wire. From inside the kitchen Doc yelled, "Hold your fire, you shaky bastard! I'm coming out!" His shout was masked by another long burst and carbine rounds ricocheted off the walls. The sound of running feet in the dining room told Doc that Charlie was closing in fast. He yelled at the top of his voice, "Hold your fire!" and crawled for the door.

Callahan, with shrapnel wounds in the arms and chest, lay in a dark corner on the porch. He heard Doc's yell and called to Savage, "Hold your fire! It's Doc. He's coming out!"

Rolling onto the porch, Doc spun to cover the kitchen doorway. He shouted to the wounded men huddled together, "Get the hell off the porch! Charlie's right on my ass!" His warning was too late. Three VC loomed in the kitchen doorway. Doc cut down the closest one, but the remaining two pulled back into the dark kitchen. Before any of the wounded could crawl off the porch an unseen grenade rolled from the kitchen and exploded.

Doc was blown across the porch. His arm came off at the shoulder, and he was dead before he stopped rolling.

Shrapnel ripped at Callahan's face, and the blast tore out his right eye. Blinded, he struggled to get through the screen, finally lowering his head and using it as a battering ram. Once through the wire, he dragged himself along the foundation to the sandbagged position at the corner of the porch and called out for help. Savage yelled, "There's no room for you in here! Find yourself some cover!"

"Give me a hand! I can't see!" Callahan hissed.

The Air Force FAC stood up. Savage grabbed him by the arm and said, "Where are you going?"

"To get Callahan. He needs help!"

"There's no room," Savage screamed in the FAC's ear.

"Stay on the radio. We need that goddamned flare ship." The FAC hesitated, then sat down and picked up the radio. Savage called to Callahan, "Crawl straight ahead! You'll find a hole on the other side of the water tower with all kinds of room."

A burst of machine gun fire ripped through the mess hall roof. A slightly wounded ranger sergeant panicked and ran screaming from the porch. "They're on the roof! Do something, Charlie's on the goddamned roof!" Ten feet from the porch he took a round in the side and fell. He struggled to his feet and staggered to Savage's position, collapsing against the sandbags. When the ranger sergeant went down, the interpreter, Lee, realized he was the last living person on the porch. He broke through the screen, leapt over the sandbags and landed on the FAC. His wounds were minimal, but he was frightened out of his wits and babbled a steady stream of Buddhist prayers.

Early on in the battle Henderson had realized the fighting positions would need ammo resupply. He had appointed himself to the job. After taking a box of ammo to Olga's AR position, he zigzagged his way to the 81 mortar pit. A couple of minutes later he slid into the command post. Dropping down on his hands and knees next to Rictor he said, "Man, that flare ship better get here in a hurry, or we won't need it." Beads of sweat covered his shiny black face and formed rivulets as they rolled down his neck and bare back.

Seeing Henderson was unarmed, Rictor said, "Find yourself a weapon and stay put. I think Charlie's on the compound."

The major called to Henderson, "What's the flare situation with Lockwood's mortar?"

Henderson shook his head. "Bad. He said they've only got six left."

The Chinaman, who was helping Biggerstaff man the mortar, crawled over to the major. "I remembered seeing some hand-held flares in the supply tent behind operations," he said. Without waiting for a reply, he bolted out of the CP and ran for the tent. A few minutes later he returned with a dozen flares. The weapons sergeant's pup was tagging along behind him.

Henderson called to the dog but an incoming mortar round sent it scurrying back to the tent. Henderson started after the dog but Rictor stopped him. "Stay here. The dog can take care of himself."

A series of explosions in the mess hall ended Henderson's attempt at arguing. Leaping to his feet he screamed, "The goddamn VC are in the mess hall! They're throwing grenades on the wounded."

Before Rictor could stop him, Henderson charged for the rear door of the mess hall. Rictor started to go after him. "Come back, you fool, you haven't got a chance!"

"Stay put, Rictor! That's an order!" yelled the major.

As Henderson's foot touched the bottom step at the rear door of the mess hall, the VC manning the machine gun elevated by Terry's chest pulled the trigger. Henderson never knew what hit him. His lifeless body fell facedown blocking the doorway.

When the machine gun stopped firing, Biggerstaff turned to the Chinaman. "Find out what happened to Henderson."

"Disregard that!" the major said, whirling to face Biggerstaff. "An Oriental in black pajamas won't stand a fuckin' chance. If you want somebody to commit suicide, you go!"

"What about the mortar?" Biggerstaff hedged.

"We can handle it," the major grunted.

Seeing no way out, Biggerstaff inserted a fresh magazine in his M16 and moved to the open side of the command post. The Chinaman picked up his shotgun and joined him. "I'll go with you, captain."

"No, you won't!" the major barked. "Biggerstaff, you don't hafta go either."

Biggerstaff shrugged. "That's what you think, Major."

Rictor considered trying to stop Biggerstaff but decided against it. He watched in silence as Biggerstaff eased out of the CP and disappeared into the darkness. A few seconds later, he heard the machine gun at the rear end of the mess hall firing again. There was no answering rifle fire. Cursing softly, Rictor shifted his M16 to cover the open side of the CP.

The rattle of carbine fire from the position by the screened porch was followed by grenade explosions and screams. The Chinaman eased over to Rictor. "Sounds like the VC are in the mess hall."

"There ain't nothing we can do!" Rictor snapped. "Be quiet and keep your eyes open."

A flare from the 81 pit burst several hundred yards to the west, and light flooded the compound. The Chinaman whispered, "Viet Cong!" Rising to one knee he fired the M79 grenade launcher too quickly and missed. The grenade exploded harmlessly against the mess hall. Rictor and the major fired simultaneously. The VC sapper was caught in a withering crossfire. Faltering, he took several steps before wilting to the ground.

As Rictor watched the mess hall for signs of movement, the drone of a lone aircraft announced the impending arrival of the flare ship. It was still a long distance away, but the feeling of being completely isolated vanished and Rictor's spirits rose. A string of flares broke through the cloud cover two miles northwest of the compound. Realizing the pilot was still having difficulty finding them, the major crawled over to Rictor. "Go to the commo van, and tell the Air Force kid to talk that ship in."

Crouching low, Rictor zigzagged the thirty yards to the van. When he grabbed hold of the door handle, an electrical shock ran through his body. The van was short-circuited. He tried again, and the shock was even worse. He was reaching for the handle a third time when it occurred to him that if he was inside the van and knew Charlie was on the compound, he would shoot anyone who tried to open the door. Standing well clear of the door, Rictor jerked down on the handle. As the door swung open a hail of bullets brushed past his arm.

Shouting his name, Rictor leaned around the door and found himself looking into the muzzle of a carbine. Even in the dim glow of the van's red night-light, he could see that the Air Force radio operator's face was slashed and torn. The kid said, "Sorry, man, but I wasn't taking any chances. The last time I opened this door somebody tried to change my looks."

Rictor said, "Forget it. The flare ship is a couple miles

northwest of here. Bring it in." Turning to leave he said, "Charlie's all over the place. Keep the door covered. If anybody tries to come in unannounced, kill him." On the way back to the command post, Rictor wondered if he would have the guts to sit bottled up in the vulnerable van.

When Dave saw the distant flares from the flare ship, he had been exchanging grenade throws with VC at the corner of the billet for what seemed like an eternity. Painful shrapnel wounds made his entire body ache. Cursing under his breath, he wished for a rifle. A low whistle from the alley attracted his attention. He strained to hear and caught the sound of whispering Vietnamese voices. They appeared to be coming from the colonel's mortar shelter. He carefully judged the distance, lobbed a grenade over the wall and waited. Screams and groans from the alley told him the grenade had found its mark.

He kept his voice low and called over to Hassen, "Cover your end of the wall! The bastards are in the alley!"

Hassen yelled back, "Let's get the hell outta here! I'm just about out of ammo."

"Don't be a fool, *Hassen!* There's no place to go. If we lose this corner it's all over. Ration your ammo. Don't shoot unless you've got a target."

"You can stay if you want to, but as far as I'm concerned it's all over now. If things don't get better pretty quick, I'm going up the alley."

Dave snorted. "Suit yourself, but be quiet. All we need is to attract more VC."

The flare ship was still off target. As a faint glow from its flares reached the compound, a creaking noise caught Hassen's attention. Glancing to the billets, he saw a window shutter directly behind Dave's position slowly open. Taking careful aim he fired. The shutter opened wide exposing a VC dangling from the window. He switched the M16 fire selector to semi-automatic and fired a couple of insurance rounds. The lifeless body toppled from the window and a grenade came sailing over the wall. Hassen dropped his M16, caught the grenade and threw it back. With no chance of shooting through the wall, he grabbed an empty ammo box. A second grenade arched over the wall, he swung and made contact. The grenade sailed like a baseball toward the fence and exploded harmlessly. When the next grenade came he lashed out with the box but his timing was bad, he missed. The grenade dropped in the hole and lodged between his feet. Before he could move, it exploded.

Dave called out to Hassen, but there was no answer. A grenade rolled to the edge of Dave's mortar pit and dropped in. Unable to reach it, Dave dove headlong out of the pit. He hugged the ground and waited for the explosion. An automatic weapon opened fire, and a bullet burned a shallow furrow along the inside of his right thigh. The seconds dragged by, but the grenade failed to go off. Hoping it was a dud, he crawled back into the pit.

The VC with whom Dave had been exchanging grenade throws stepped around the corner of the billet with one in his hand. Standing in the open he calmly pulled the pin and threw at Dave's mortar pit. He missed. Dave was sure then that the VC, who had ducked back around the corner, knew he did not have a rifle. Immediately following the explosion, Dave grabbed his last six grenades, sprang out of the pit and scrambled over to Hassen's position. He dove headfirst into the hole and landed on what was left of Hassen's mangled body. One touch told him the huge mess sergeant was dead. Groping in the dark, he located Hassen's M16 and peered over the lip of the hole.

The grenade-throwing VC had not seen Dave move and eased into the open to study the mortar pit. Mistaking the dead ranger corporal for Dave he inched forward. Standing, Dave fired from the hip. The VC's belly opened up and vomited intestines. The VC was dead in his tracks, but Dave kept firing until his rifle was empty. Kneeling to reload, he hurriedly ran his hands over Hassen's body. The search produced a loaded 45-caliber pistol but no M16 ammo. Cursing himself for wasting precious ammunition, Dave tossed the useless rifle aside.

Small arms fire from the west fence was increasing. Dave had no way of knowing for sure if any of the other positions were holding but the steady *chug chug* of an automatic rifle led him to believe Olga was still alive. Sure that Charlie was preparing to assault the fence again, Dave laid his six grenades side by side on the lip of the hole, shoved the 45 pistol into his belt and leaned back to wait. Resting a hand on Hassen's body, he said, "Oink, when Charlie comes through the fence, we're gonna take the price of admission out of his ass."

At the command post, Major Strong checked his watch as he listened to the growing sound of assault fires. He cast a worried glance at the sky. The flare ship was beginning to pay off. Ammunition was running low, and he felt sure Charlie was preparing for another assault. Crawling over to Rictor he said, "Looks like we're caught in a crossfire. I figure when the main force hits the fence, the VC in the mess hall and billets will pour it on from the rear."

Rictor nodded. "You're right about the crossfire, but I don't think the VC outside the fence know about the position by the mess hall porch. If Savage and the rest of the Maggits are awake, they should make it awful hard on anybody coming from the billets or mess hall. If we can hold on until daylight and the clouds break, we might make it."

The major glanced at his watch. "How long you figure until first light?"

"Maybe an hour, but Charlie knows that too. You can bet he's going to use that hour to kick ass," Rictor said.

The major turned to the Chinaman, who was removing sandbags from the front of the command post and placing them at the exposed rear. "Help me adjust the mortar. I want the rounds to come in on the fence in front of Dave's position. I don't think Dave or anybody else is alive down there. If Charlie comes through that corner and up the alley, he'll be all over us before we know it." Shouting to be heard over the steadily increasing small arms fire, he called to Lockwood's pit, "Don't fire until Charlie reaches the fence. When you open up, pour it on. We've gotta buy some time."

The almost constant *chug* of Olga's big automatic rifle told Rictor that Olga still had plenty of ammo. He checked his own supply and found less than fifty rounds. He was feeling around the base of the mortar to see if he had overlooked any ammo when an artillery round crashed into the operations building. He opened his mouth to reduce concussion and hugged the ground.

For fifteen minutes VC gunners poured a deadly barrage of mortar and artillery on the compound. Lockwood peered out of his 81mm. pit and was slashed across the ear and forehead by shrapnel. He cursed, wiped blood from his eyes and called to the weapons sergeant, "When the bastards hit the fence, you handle the mortar. I've got a personal score to settle."

The barrage lifted as suddenly as it had begun, but the small arms fire intensified. When the support fire reached saturation, the first wave of assaulting VC hit the fence and ran head-on into a hail of fire from Olga's AR. He fired methodically from left to right killing VC with every burst.

The Chinaman dropped round after round into the 60 mortar and the heavier 81mm. boomed out a fire for effect. Everyone able to fire a weapon was firing as fast as they could. The main VC force hit the fence and the VC in the mess hall and billets opened up on the command post, creating the crossfire Strong had feared. Every time the VC in the mess hall and billets attempted a charge, they were driven back by fire from the position near the mess hall porch. The determined VC continued to hit the fence in waves, but the defenders held their positions. As daylight began to break, light from the flare ship flooded the compound. After eight costly charges, the VC along the fence gave up and began withdrawing into the jungle.

Rictor could hear the whir of helicopter gunships and the roar of fighter bombers as they circled above the cloud cover waiting for enough visibility to join the fight. Viet Cong small arms fire dwindled and became sporadic. Rictor shoved the last twenty-round magazine into his M16 and waited. Time dragged and he felt an overpowering weariness. Fishing in his pocket, he dug out the bottle of speed Doc had given him and took a couple of the bitter tablets. The minutes that followed seemed an eternity, as if the dawn would never come. Although the battle raged in other parts of the complex as ARVN and Viet Cong units battled for the advantage, the American compound was silent.

Bathed in the eerie orange glow cast by dying flares, the compound seemed to belong to a different world.

Chapter XIV

DAYLIGHT—
COUNT YOUR LOSSES

Crouched in the dark musky attic of the USOM house in the village, Mendoza had spent a sleepless night. The smell of mildew was strong in his nostrils, and his cramped body ached all over. Red-eyed from straining to see through a small crack in the wall, he continuously cursed himself for not having gone with Watts.

As the initial artillery rounds landed on the military complex, Viet Cong soldiers were hammering at the front door of the house, demanding that he and Watts come out at once. Finally, they broke down the door and searched the house. They fired into any place large enough to conceal a person, but in the darkness failed to find the small opening in the ceiling.

Lying motionless in the attic, Mendoza understood enough of their shouted conversation to know that their orders were to assassinate Watts and himself. He also knew that with the coming of daylight he would be discovered. Sure that the Viet Cong were in complete control of the capital, he decided to surrender.

When the first streaks of dawn appeared in the sky, Mendoza reluctantly discarded his unused submachine gun. He dropped the rope ladder through the hole and slowly climbed down from the attic. Hearing harsh VC voices in front of the house, he decided to take a look out back and make certain there was no chance of escape before surrendering. He eased through the back door and climbed the eight-foot wooden fence which surrounded the house. In the gray light he saw dozens of Viet Cong. Knowing there was no escape, he pulled himself to the top of the fence and called to the nearest soldier, "Don't shoot. I'm the USOM man!" The VC raised his carbine and took careful aim. Mendoza threw up his hands and screamed, "Don't shoot! Don't shoot! I'm the USOM man!" He saw the muzzle flash and felt a searing pain in the gut as he pitched forward off the fence. Landing on his back, he watched horrified as the VC unsheathed a small razor-sharp shovel. Spitting blood, Mendoza let out a strangled scream. "I'm the USOM man, you fool. Goddamnit, can't you see I'm a USOM ma—" Mendoza's jaw continued to move, but the only sound was the sucking noise made by his severed windpipe.

Rictor crouched at the open side of the CP and weighed the chances of reaching the mess hall without being seen by the Viet Cong. Almost as if he were reading Rictor's mind the major said, "The mess hall's got to be cleared before the light gets any better. In ten minutes, we'll be sitting ducks."

Rictor nodded to the Chinaman. "Cover me. I'm gonna work my way around the operations building and try to cross by the water tower. I oughta be able to get some help from the MAC-V people up at the porch."

"Don't take any unnecessary chances," the major said. "If Charlie's still in there, you'll hafta kill him to get him out."

Rictor eased out of the CP and slowly made his way past the commo van. At the corner of the operations building, he heard movement in the shadows. He hugged the wall and froze. It was growing lighter by the second, and afraid of being caught out in the open, he took a deep breath and stepped around the corner. There was no one in sight, but something told him that he was not alone. He stayed near the wall and inched forward. He was almost past the building when a loose board squeaked directly over his head. He dropped to the ground, rolled away from the building and fired.

Screeching at the top of his lungs, Deuces leapt from the roof and locked his long hairy arms around Rictor's legs. Cursing under his breath, Rictor broke free and scrambled to his feet. The fear-crazed monkey was chained. Rictor fingered the trigger of his M16 and mumbled under his breath, "You poor bastard. If I had more ammo, I'd put you out of your misery."

"Who's there?" an unfamiliar voice called out from the hole at the base of the water tower. Rictor identified himself and kept moving. The voice asked, "You got any water?"

Annoyed, Rictor snapped, "If you want water, there's a tower full right over your head! All you gotta do is get your ass out of that hole, climb up there and get it." Without waiting for an answer, he dashed toward the mess hall and flattened himself against the wall. In the growing light, he made out the twisted form of the VC that he and the major had killed at the corner of the building. He glanced toward the porch and saw the back of a bandaged head protruding out of the sandbagged position. Even in the hazy light he knew it was a Vietnamese. Easing away from the wall he brought up his M16. As his finger tightened on the trigger the head turned to face him. He exhaled and lowered the rifle. It was Lee. Motioning for Lee to join him he moved along the wall to the rear of the building.

At the corner he stopped short. The lower portion of a body clad in camouflage fatigues protruded from the back door. The head was not visible, but the bare, black feet left no doubt in his mind that it was Henderson. He saw no way to reach the body without exposing himself to fire from the half-open door. He was pondering his next move when Lee and Lieutenant Savage came up behind him. Savage said, "I told the people up front to cover the porch. We can go in from this end and flush Charlie toward the kitchen. If he goes out the kitchen door, he's wasted."

Rictor nodded. "Let's try something else first." He turned to Lee and said, "Step around the corner and yell to the VC that they've got ten seconds to come out unarmed. Tell them if we have to come in after them, we'll take no prisoners."

Lee shook his head. "If I go around the corner, they'll kill me."

"Stay close to the wall," Savage said. "You'll be all right."

Lee leaned against the building and refused to budge. Stepping up close, Rictor jammed the muzzle of his M16 in Lee's stomach. "You've got less than ten seconds. Do what you're told or you're dead."

Slobbering with fear Lee slowly crawled forward. At the corner, he whirled and brought up his carbine. Rictor side-stepped and Savage took the point-blank burst in the chest. Before Rictor could fire, a shotgun blast tore off Lee's face. The Chinaman darted across from the operations building and flattened himself against the wall. Rictor knelt to help Savage but the lieutenant was beyond help. Cursing, he stood up and turned to the Chinaman, who held his shotgun at the ready. Their eyes locked and held for a brief moment. Rictor nodded. "You take the left side. I'll take the right." The Chinaman grinned and eased around the corner. One quick look was all that Rictor needed to tell him that Henderson was dead. Crawling over the mutilated body he made his way on his stomach into the building. In the half-light, he bumped into a couch and found himself face-to-face with Terry, whose lifeless eyes stared at the ceiling. Hurrying to get clear of the lighted doorway, he rolled to the left and kept moving. He worked his way around a pile of rubble which had been the bar and reached the side door without drawing fire. He had just about decided there were no VC in the building when he heard movement near the kitchen. Aiming at the ceiling to prevent hitting any surviving wounded, he fired a long burst and rolled to get clear of his exposed position. An answering burst from an AK slammed into the wall over his head and running footsteps told him that the unseen VC were trying to get outside. Seconds later, heavy automatic fire from the porch told him the VC had run head-on into the waiting MAC-V men.

Rictor sprang to his feet and charged for the kitchen. He had taken only a few steps when he tripped over the body of a

VC. Reaching the kitchen he saw three dead VC and counted six more bodies on the porch. Rictor called the all clear to the Chinaman. But he couldn't help but wonder why Charlie had quit the building without a fight. On his way out he stopped at the back door. On impulse he bent close and looked into Terry's staring eyes. Gurgling noises came from Terry's throat, and bubbles of blood built on his lips. Rictor shouted for the Chinaman. "Give me a hand. Terry's still alive!" With the Chinaman's help, he put Terry on a couch and dragged it out into the light. Not only was Terry alive, he was conscious. But after one quick look, Rictor wished they had left him inside. There wasn't a place on his entire naked body large enough to lay a hand without touching a wound.

Terry strained to speak, but only animallike noises came out. The effort caused a deep wound in the neck to spurt blood. Realizing there was nothing he could do, Rictor turned to the Chinaman. "Watch him. I'm gonna see if I can find Doc."

The Chinaman shook his head. "He's up by the porch but he can't help. He's dead."

"Maybe I can find some morphine," said Rictor, heading for the porch. Rounding the corner, he saw the weapons sergeant's shepherd pup licking at a VC's body. The top of the VC's head was missing, and the pup was lapping at his spilled brains. Noting the blood-matted 4 × 4 gauze bandages stuck to the bottom of the VC's sandals, he knew they could only have come from the mess hall. Recalling how Terry and Henderson had looked, he kicked the dead VC and kept moving.

He was almost to the front of the building when the voice he'd heard earlier, asking for water, called out again. This time he recognized it. Crossing over to the tower he peered down in the hole. Lying half-submerged in the slimy muck was Callahan. Remembering his brusque reply to the request for water, Rictor cursed and stepped down in the hole. Seeing that Callahan was blind and had taken several hits, including a bad chest wound, he was hesitant to move him. He rested a hand on Callahan's shoulder. "You just lie here and take it easy for a little while. Soon as we can get a Medevac ship, we'll get you out."

Callahan strained to sit up. "That you, Rictor?"

"Yeah, it's me. Lie back, and take it easy."

Callahan was weak but his spirit wasn't gone. "You think you're dealing with a punk recruit or something? We both know I've had it. Now get me outta this goddamn pigpen before I hurry the end by drowning."

Rictor knew it was useless to argue. Reasonably certain the billets were clear of VC, he lifted Callahan in a fireman's carry and headed back to where he had left Terry. He had just placed Callahan in a protected area when the familiar whirring noise made by helicopters grew loud in his ears. Glancing up he saw two gunships drop through a hole in the overcast and run head-on into a hail of automatic fire from the ranger compound. Banking off to the south they gained altitude, made a wide circle and came in for a strafing run.

Major Strong came to the mouth of the alley and motioned for Rictor. "The compound is clear of VC, at least for the moment, but we're almost out of ammo. If Charlie counterattacks, we've had it. I want you to get all the wounded collected here in the alley. Anyone who can walk and carry a rifle is to report to me. I'll be up by the gate with the air controller. As soon as you've got a complete casualty report get the most critically wounded ready to move and let me know how we stand."

Rictor said, "If it hasn't been destroyed there's plenty of ammo in the storage building on the RF compound."

The major nodded. "The FAC's got the gunships on the radio. He's trying to guide them in along the fence. If they can suppress Charlie's fire long enough, Lockwood and the weapons sergeant will make a try for the storage building."

Thinking about Terry and Callahan, Rictor asked, "How long you figure it will be till we get Medevac ships?"

The major spread his hands. "No way of telling. Except for the capitol building and the national police station, it looks like Charlie is in control of the entire area."

"When Charlie overran the mess hall," Rictor said, "a grenade landed in the medical chest and destroyed the supplies. If we don't get plasma and other medicine right away, some of these people are gonna die."

"Do what you can for them," the major called over his shoulder as he moved toward the gate. "Soon as the overcast clears maybe we can get some supplies parachuted in."

Dave came limping up the alley and stopped to take a look at Callahan. He saw the open chest wound and spat. Then he called to Rictor, "Give me a smoke. I'm about to have a nicotine fit."

"You're outta luck. I've been wanting one for hours. Let me look at that cut on your neck."

Indicating Callahan with a nod Dave said, "Forget it. There's a lotta people here that need help more than me. Where's Scruggs?"

Rictor shook his head. "Don't know. I'm trying to get a head count now. You leave anybody at the mortar pit?"

"Yeah, Hassen and that ranger corporal. But they won't be coming up. They're dead."

Rictor nodded. "The major's at the gate. He wants you up there."

Indicating his empty 45-caliber pistol Dave asked, "You know where I can get some ammo for this goddamn thing?"

"No, but Lockwood and the weapons sergeant are going to try the RF compound as soon as Charlie pulls back."

"Where's Lockwood now?"

"On the other side of the billets, waiting."

Moving off to the billets Dave said, "I'm gonna give them a hand. When you find Scruggs, tell him I'm okay."

Within a few minutes Rictor had accounted for everyone except Biggerstaff, Lieutenant Maxwell, Campbell, and Scruggs. Reluctantly, he returned to the mess hall. From the rear door he spotted a barely visible hand protruding from the shrubbery. He parted the thick foliage and found Biggerstaff lying facedown in a pool of blood. After pulling Biggerstaff's body from the shrubbery, Rictor stepped over Henderson and entered the building. Light filtering through shattered blackout windows formed eerie little patterns but made it possible to see. He climbed over broken furniture and made it to the far end of the bar. Lying in a small opening he found the upper portion of Campbell's body. The satchel charge had completely torn away the medic's legs. Fighting back nausea he noted that part of the bar rack was still on the wall and a bottle of scotch teetered on one of the shelves. In bad need of a drink he crawled over the rubble to get it. He was almost to the rack when his hand brushed against cold clammy flesh. Straining to see in the dim light he found a leg protruding from rubble. Unsure if it belonged to a VC or an American, he took hold and pulled. It wouldn't budge. Finally the body broke free: there was no head. A silver bar pinned to what was left of a blood-soaked shirt left no doubt in his mind that it was Lieutenant Maxwell.

He snatched the bottle off the rack, climbed out from behind the bar and took a drink. The whiskey burned all the way down, and he immediately felt better. After taking another belt he continued the search. Ten minutes later, he had found several dead VC but no Scruggs. Hoping that somehow Scruggs had managed to get out of the mess hall, he headed for the alley.

As he stepped out of the building a pair of gunships belching machine gun fire and rockets made a run on the RF compound. A flight of sleek B57 Canberras followed them in but rolled off to the south without firing. Spotting a wounded ranger sergeant kneeling next to Terry, he walked over to inquire about Scruggs. The sergeant said, "The last time I saw him was just before Charlie came in the mess hall. As far as I know, I was the last one out. Unless he managed to make it through the side door, he's still in there."

Lockwood came charging up the alley with Dave and the weapons sergeant hot on his heels. Seeing Rictor he yelled. "Where's the major? Charlie's massing on the RF compound for a counterattack!"

The major and the FAC came around the corner of the mess hall. Having heard the shouted warning, the major turned to the Air Force FAC. "Bring the B57s in," he ordered. "I want that goddamn Regional Force compound leveled."

The FAC shook his head. "The pilots have orders not to strike any built-up areas."

"I don't give a goddamn what their orders are. I want that strike, and I want it now!"

"Okay, Major, it's your show." Shouting to the wounded in

the alley he said, "Everybody take cover. The Canberras will be dropping five-hundred-pounders!"

After dragging Callahan up close to the billet wall, Rictor knelt next to him. From the rasping noises Callahan made as he labored to breathe, Rictor knew the old soldier was very near death. Callahan attempted to speak but blood gushed from his mouth and ran down his chin. Wiping away the blood with his hand, Rictor said, "Don't talk. Save your energy."

Callahan groped until his hand made contact with Rictor's leg. His voice was barely a whisper. "Rictor, if you manage to get out of here, don't ever let a bunch of ass-kissing incompetents and thieves get you fucked up again. This whole stinking country ain't worth the life of one rout stepping rear rank private."

Before Rictor could reply, a five-hundred-pound bomb exploded on the RF compound, sending a shock wave sweeping through the alley. He ducked and waited for debris to stop falling. When he straightened up, Callahan was dead. Reaching down to close the old soldier's one staring eye, Rictor's voice was barely a whisper. "Callahan, I make you this promise. If I survive this fiasco, I'll never subordinate myself to bungling, incompetent leadership again."

For the next ten minutes the ground trembled from the impact of bomb strikes, and a roaring secondary explosion on the RF compound spelled the end of the ammunition storage building there. When the Canberras broke off, three gunships, which had been circling well clear of the strike area, came in at two hundred feet on a strafing run. As they crossed over the compound, the armored car which Charlie had captured earlier from the RF troops pulled out of its camouflaged position at the edge of the village and opened fire. The trail chopper was hit in the fuel tank and burst into a ball of fire as it spiraled earthward.

When the two remaining choppers broke off and gained altitude, Dave entered the alley yelling for Lockwood and the weapons sergeant. Spotting them he hollered, "Let's go see if there's any ammo left on the RF compound. It doesn't look to me like Charlie is ready to quit, and we don't have enough ammo to fight off a WAC platoon!"

When the trio disappeared around the billets, Rictor returned to the mess hall to look for Scruggs. Midway through the dining room he discovered a trail of blood. Near the side door the trail widened, and bullet holes in the door showed that someone had tried to get out but had been turned back by fire from the MAC-V position near the porch. Picking up the trail again, he followed it until he came to the VC body that he had tripped over the first time he entered the building. Satisfied that the trail was made by the dead Charlie, he all but lost interest. But when he turned the body over for a search, he discovered that the VC had been stabbed to death. His curiosity was aroused. He was looking around for a knife when he spotted another blood trail. It led him into the poorly lighted windowless kitchen. The trail ran under two large sinks then turned back sharply toward a small food storage room. Remembering that he had not searched the tiny pantry earlier, Rictor pulled the door open, expecting the worst. He was totally unprepared for what he found. Staring wide-eyed, Scruggs was sitting under a shelf directly in front of the door. Stepping inside, Rictor reached for the commo knife Scruggs held as if to ward off an attacker. Unable to pull the knife from Scruggs's clenched fist, Rictor cursed silently. Scruggs was dead and had been for several hours.

Rictor left the building by way of the porch, located Major Strong and gave him the casualty report. "With any luck," the major said, "we'll be able to get some of them out before long. The chopper pilots say the force that hit us is pulling back to the west. I figure the VC are either withdrawing to the jungle to mass for another try, or they're quitting altogether. We ought to know one way or the other pretty soon."

Rictor nodded. "I don't think the bastards are fool enough to try again long as those Canberras and gunships are up there."

The major shrugged. "I don't know. The units attacking the capital and police station don't show any signs of letting up. If anything, they're increasing the pressure."

Casting an eye at two Canberras circling out of small arms

range, Rictor asked, "Why doesn't the Air Force blast them out?"

Looking up the major said, "The pilots have orders not to bomb the village or any of the constructed area. I'm probably going to catch hell for bringing them in on the RF compound."

Rictor grunted. "You don't look too worried. Maybe that's because you know that anybody who wants to raise hell has gotta come out here to do it."

"I'll cross that bridge when I have to. In the meantime, we've got to clear an area to bring the Medevac ships in."

Olga came up and asked about ammunition for his AR. "There's a detail over at the RF compound trying to get some now," Rictor said. "C'mon, we'll give them a hand."

"If you're talking about Lockwood and Dave," Olga said, "forget it. They're back. All they found were two cases of M16 ammo and a few loose grenades."

The FAC called out from the position by the porch, "Major, I've got the pilot of a cargo ship on the radio! He's on the way in with medical supplies and ammo. Where do you want the drop?"

"How much time we got?" the major asked.

"The pilot estimates ten minutes."

Studying the open area between the compound and the capitol building, the major said, "Tell him to orbit. We have to clear a place to receive the drop. When we're ready, we'll mark the DZ with red smoke." Turning to Rictor he said, "Get that M16 ammo distributed and position the walking wounded where they can cover the west fence. Soon as that's accomplished, bring me everybody who can collapse a parachute and carry ammo. We'll clear the street between here and the capital and use it for a drop zone."

Ten minutes later, Rictor returned to the gate with several men, including Lockwood and the weapons sergeant.

Approaching the major he said, "I left Dave in charge back there. He knows about Scruggs, and I figure he'll make it awful hard on any VC that show up while we're gone."

The major nodded. "Everybody gather around and listen close. Here's the plan. The FAC will bring gunships in to suppress fire while we cross the clearing. Rictor, you take Olga, Lockwood and the Chinaman and link up with the rangers at the capital. Get them to shift their fire so Charlie can't cross the street. The rest of you go with me. We'll move up to the corner opposite the capital and put fire on the VC dug in around the police station. Soon as everybody's in position, the FAC will throw red smoke in the street to guide the plane in. Questions?"

The FAC pointed to a lone high-flying plane approaching from the south. It was a long way off but was identifiable by its twin engines as a Caribou. He said, "Here comes the supply plane, Major. The gunships are ready when you are." Stepping over to the gate, the major lifted the latch and shoved it open.

The distance to the capital was less than two hundred yards, but to Rictor it seemed more like a mile. When he finally reached the protected side of the capitol building, he was gasping for breath. His injured ribs were giving him a fit. He sent Olga and Lockwood to coordinate with the ranger commander and dropped down on one knee to catch his breath. A few seconds later, the province intelligence officer came around the corner and stopped. The rattle of gun fire made it impossible for Rictor to hear what he was saying, but the Vietnamese captain was obviously enraged. Rictor leaned close. Shaking his head with disgust the captain said, "The situation is very bad. Many of our soldiers have been killed and even more have deserted." Lowering his voice he said, "Colonel Nam is considering surrender."

Rictor leapt to his feet. "Has he lost his goddamn mind? With the Air Force we can hold our own until a relief force gets here. He must have forgotten what the VC will do if they get their hands on him."

Olga came sliding around the corner of the building and dropped next to Rictor. "The rangers will cover us and the major is almost in position. There's gonna be hell to pay when the Caribou comes in to drop. Charlie's got a fifty-caliber machine gun hidden in the tower of the church."

Looking down the street toward the village Rictor could see

the church, but there was no sign of the gun. "Where's Lock-wood?" he asked.

"He went to warn the major. You figure the Old Man can get the church bombed?"

Rictor shook his head. "I doubt it. The pilots have orders not to strike the village unless they're fired on. Charlie knows it, and he'd be pretty damn foolish to start anything with the bombers."

Pointing to a growing cloud of red smoke billowing up from the street Olga said. "It's too late anyway. The FAC's already thrown the signal smoke."

The Caribou made a final orbit and lined up with the street. As it nosed down and came roaring in, the captured armored car in the village and the machine gun in the church put up a barrage of 50-caliber tracers. The heavy rounds tore at the Caribou's fuselage and ripped a gaping hole in the right wing, but the pilot held it on course.

Olga shouted, "He's too low! The chutes won't have time to open!" Rictor nodded and watched the plane roar over at a hundred feet. When it was directly over the smoked area, two bundles of supplies rolled off the tailgate. As Olga had pre-dicted the chutes only partially deployed. The bundles crashed in, scattering desperately needed ammunition and medical supplies in all directions.

The major and Lockwood charged into the street to see what could be salvaged but were driven back by a hail of fire from the machine gun in the church. The major's covering force opened up, but their M16s were too light to penetrate the stone church wall. "That rips it," Olga snapped. "Unless the Canberras come in we're screwed."

The MAC-V liaison officer, who had spent the night in the capitol building, came running up. Dropping down between Rictor and Olga he said, "The ranger commander is getting some people together on the other side of the building. He's gonna try to knock out that gun in the church."

Recognizing the MAC-V officer as the captain who had briefed him the day he arrived from the Highlands, Rictor was disgusted. "How does the ranger commander figure on getting by the VC dug in around the police station?"

The captain shrugged. "I don't know. He's wounded and about half out of his mind. He lost three-fourths of his troops when the ranger compound was overrun."

Olga stood up and headed for the corner of the building. Rictor stopped him. "Where're you going?"

"I'm tired of lying here on my ass doing nothing. I'm going with the rangers."

"Like hell you are. If the ranger commander's fool enough to lead his people down the street, it's okay by me. But the way I see it, fools and incompetents have gotten too many people killed already."

"What are we gonna do," Olga yelled. "Just lie here waiting for Charlie to come and get us?"

Rictor said, frustrated, "No, and I don't want to be a hero either! We're not through yet. Sooner or later Charlie will make the mistake of firing on the bombers. When he does, he's hurting."

Unconvinced but knowing further argument was pointless, Olga dropped down next to the MAC-V captain and watched in silence as a dozen rangers came around the building and headed down the street. Rictor turned to the captain. "You've been here all night, what's ARVN's situation?"

The captain shook his head. "Hopeless. The VC have overrun Bien Tien District headquarters and are in complete control of the airstrip. They've occupied the village and are using the villagers as a shield to ward off the aircraft. The police station is still holding, but a VC unit is dug in less than a hundred yards from its wall. The only ARVN troops left are the Regional Force and ranger survivors who are defending this building. I think the VC will try to hold their position. If they can continue to hold the airstrip and ambush the roads, when night comes and it starts to rain, we've had it. No airstrip, no planes. No service roads, no resupply trucks."

Rictor grunted. "What's this I hear about Nam being ready to surrender?"

The captain was surprised. "I wasn't going to mention it. The situation is bad enough without a break with ARVN. But since you've heard something already, I may as well tell you. Colonel Nam has lost his mind. He's up there babbling like an idiot. The intelligence officer told me Nam plans to surrender the capital and use us to bargain for his own safety."

Olga interrupted, "By us, you mean the Americans?"

The captain nodded. "I was on my way to tell Colonel West when I stopped here."

Olga cursed. "Forget it. Colonel West has been dead for hours."

Without taking his eyes off the rangers who were halfway to the church Rictor asked, "What's Nam waiting on?"

"He received a message that an ARVN relief force is on the way. He doesn't think the relief force can get through, but he's going to wait and see before trying to deal with the VC."

Rictor pointed down the street. "Look!"

Olga could hardly believe his eyes. A hundred yards short of the church, the rangers had formed a skirmish line which extended the entire width of the street. He said, "Jesus, look at those crazy bastards! They're really asking for it!" The words were barely out of his mouth when the VC on the far side of the police station opened fire with everything they had. Three of the rangers were cut down immediately. The remaining nine broke into a run and charged. The VC in the church waited until the rangers were within fifty yards before firing. The rangers continued to advance. Caught in the withering crossfire, they went down one after the other and ten seconds after the first shot they all lay dead or dying in the street.

Cursing with every breath Olga fired at the church windows. Knowing that Olga was wasting precious ammunition, Rictor shouted for him to knock it off. But if Olga heard, he gave no indication. Attracted by the screech of jets, Rictor glanced up in time to see a flight of three B57s peel off and dive toward the church. He grabbed Olga by the shoulder. "Watch this!" The lead Canberra flashed over the church at three hundred feet but failed to drop bombs. Rolling off to the south it gained altitude and came around for another run.

Puzzled, Olga asked, "What do you figure they're up to?"

"A dry run. They're trying to draw fire," Rictor said. The second bomber zoomed in even lower than the first, and the VC in the church fired on it. Taking several hits, the Canberra faltered and made a slow turn to the south trailing black smoke. The third bomber came in at a higher altitude. Diving through a wall of machine gun and small arms fire, the pilot planted a five-hundred-pound bomb dead center on the church. Masonry and debris sailed hundreds of feet in the air and, when the smoke cleared, the church was a pile of scorched rubble. The lead Canberra came back around for a strafing run on the VC dug in around the police station. A rope of 50-caliber tracers arched up from the armored car in the village and many of them found their mark. Shuddering under the impact of the heavy rounds, the Canberra belched rockets and cannon fire on the exposed positions.

Taking their directions from the FAC, a flight of three Sky-raiders peeled off and came in strafing. One of the pilots spotted the armored car and veered off in a shallow dive. Gunning the engine he cut loose his napalm tanks and began to climb.

Rictor's view of the armored car was obstructed by buildings, but after the napalm drop, the car's machine gun was silent. Glancing across the street, he saw the carrying detail coming out for the scattered supplies. He nudged Olga and leapt to his feet. "C'mon! While the fly-boys have got Charlie's head down, let's see if any of that stuff is worth saving."

The canvas containers were in shreds but Rictor salvaged some pressure bandages and a few morphine syringes. Lockwood and four other men came by laden with ammunition. Lockwood yelled, "The major wants the critically wounded and dead brought to the compound gate! Soon as the Air Force knocks out the VC dug in around the police station, the FAC is gonna try to bring in the Medevac ships." Satisfied that he had located all the supplies worth salvaging, Rictor motioned for Olga and headed for the compound.

While Lockwood distributed ammunition to the walking wounded, Rictor and Olga located a stretcher and helped move the critically wounded. As they neared the gate with Terry, he struggled and tried to speak. Placing his end of the stretcher on the ground, Olga studied Terry's mutilated body with awe. Shaking his head he said, "Terry must be the toughest son of a bitch in the world!"

"Stay here and do what you can for him," Rictor replied. "I'm gonna look for more stretchers." He shouted to three

MAC-V men who were milling around the gate. "Start collecting the dead. When the choppers come in, we won't have much time to get them loaded!" Spotting a stretcher near the entrance to the mess hall porch he picked it up and headed for the alley.

As he approached Colonel West's body, he saw that the colonel was sprawled on a fallen Keep Off The Grass sign. Studying the tortured expression on the dead commander's face, Rictor felt neither remorse nor hatred. But he couldn't help but wonder if the high-handed colonel had realized before he died what a damn fool he had been.

Rictor turned and found Dave staring at the sign. Shaking his head with disgust, Dave said, "The poor bastard is probably better off dead. If he had survived, his life would have been a living hell!"

Rictor nodded and reached for the colonel's shoulders. "Give me a hand getting him on the stretcher. We'll try to get him out."

Dave reached for the colonel's feet. "I guess there's somebody that wants what's left of him," he said.

Laboring under the weight of the stretcher, Rictor and Dave were almost to the mouth of the alley when Olga came sliding around the corner of the mess hall. Clutching his injured side, he said, "The major sent me to tell you we've got about five minutes till the Medevac choppers land. The people up at the gate have got most of the wounded and dead loaded on jeeps. If you hurry, we'll be ready to move when the choppers touch down."

"Has Scruggs been loaded yet?" Dave asked.

Olga shook his head. "When I came by he was still lying on the porch."

Dave indicated his end of the stretcher. "Here, take this. I'm going to see about Scruggs."

Olga grasped the wooden handles and watched in silence as Dave disappeared around the corner of the mess hall. Rictor said, "Let's get moving. Don't worry about Dave, he'll be all right." Without taking his eyes off the corner where Dave had disappeared, Olga nodded and began walking. Rictor asked, "What's the situation over at the police station?"

"Man, you should've seen it. I had a ringside seat. First the Skyraiders came in low over the exposed foxholes and opened up with rockets and cannons. They were barely out of the way when the Canberras made their bomb run. A lot of VC stood up in the knee-deep holes and fired, but it was like pissing in the wind. The bombs must have killed half of them. The gunships followed the bombers and hosed the area with machine gun fire to make sure none of the VC got away, but it wasn't even necessary because they refused to give an inch. A lot of them even climbed out of the holes to get better shots at the planes.

"When the Skyraiders were back in position, the FAC called off the choppers and brought the fighters in for a napalm run. I've never seen anything like it. The whole area around the police station was on fire, and the heat was so bad that some of the national police were forced out of their defensive positions." After a short pause Olga said, "They were VC, but I'll tell you one thing—they had guts. Not one of them tried to run. They stayed and died to the last man."

"Other than the rangers," Rictor said acidly, "it's too bad we can't get some of these so-called friendly Vietnamese to show some guts." After loading the colonel's body on a jeep, Rictor headed for the porch to help Dave with Scruggs's body. Through the screen wire he saw Dave straining to pull the knife from Scruggs's death grip. Stepping onto the porch Rictor said, "Forget it, Dave. The Graves Registration people will take care of it."

Dave continued trying to pry Scruggs's clenched fist from around the knife. "I think the detachment oughta keep the knife to make damn sure we don't forget."

Olga stood next to Rictor, watching the struggle for a long moment. Finally he said, "Nobody's gonna forget. Let him keep the knife. It might even wake up some of the Maggits back in Saigon that think we're playing a game out here."

Dave released his grip on the knife. "Maybe you're right. Give me a hand with him."

When the jeeps were loaded and ready to go, Rictor took a head count to make sure that no one had been overlooked. He couldn't find one of the wounded radio operators and asked, "Has anyone seen Bryant?"

Lockwood responded, "When we were bringing Hassen's body up, I saw him down at the far end of the alley. He was trying to treat one of the wounded Maggits, but it looked like he needed help worse than the other guy. His arm is all but off."

Rictor was almost to the mouth of the alley when he heard Olga yell, "Get the jeeps moving! Here come the Medevac ships!" Glancing over the roof of the mess hall, Rictor saw three choppers dropping toward the capital street; the medical cross painted on their sides was unmistakable. Breaking into a run he raced into the alley, but Bryant was nowhere in sight. Continuing down the alley, he squeezed past the concrete wall and saw Bryant standing in the open staring out over the west fence. Coming up behind him Rictor said, "C'mon! You're going for a chopper ride." When Bryant gave no indication that he had heard, Rictor realized that he was in shock. Grabbing him by the belt, Rictor half-dragged, half-carried him up the alley.

At the gate Rictor stopped to catch his breath. Glancing across the clearing, he saw the last of the wounded being transferred from the jeeps to the choppers. When two of the ships lifted off, he shoved Bryant out the gate and yelled, "Get moving! If you don't help me, we'll never make it!" Getting no response, he dropped his M16 and lifted the radio operator in a fireman's carry. Though moving as fast as he could, he was still fifty yards short of the landing zone when the remaining chopper revved its engine for takeoff.

Waving and yelling at the top of his voice, Rictor finally attracted some attention. Dave and Lockwood ran to meet him. Between the three of them they managed to get Bryant to the landing zone. As they lifted him aboard Rictor caught a glimpse of Colonel Nam huddled among the wounded. Cursing at the sight, he pushed Bryant aboard and stepped back to get clear of the rotary blades.

At the same moment the chopper lifted off, the resupply plane came roaring in at five hundred feet. The Caribou pilot spotted the Medevac ship directly in the path of his parachutes, but it was too late to abort the drop. Grabbing the stick, he gunned the engines and banked over the capitol building, trailing a string of heavy-laden parachutes which drifted toward the VC-infested river valley.

The first chute to touch the ground landed in a small clearing. A dozen VC swarmed out of the thick underbrush to claim the precious ammunition and medical supplies. The rangers defending the rear of the capitol building had a clear field of fire and opened up with everything they had. Within seconds the clearing was littered with VC bodies.

The Americans at the landing zone could see the slaughter through the fence that surrounded Colonel Nam's house. As more VC charged into the clearing Dave said, "If I had that Caribou pilot by the balls, he'd wish to hell he had never heard of a parachute. He couldn't have made a worse drop if he had planned it."

Pointing to the Caribou, which had gained altitude and headed south, Olga said, "If you were close enough to the pilot to get hold of his family jewels, you'd have it made. He's probably on his way to Saigon to get knee-walking drunk and laid."

A pair of Skyraiders roared over the clearing at treetop level strafing the area around the supplies. Gaining altitude, they made a victory roll and came around for another run.

Dave snorted. "The fly-boys had better destroy them damn supplies, or Charlie's gonna get them sure as hell."

Rictor shook his head. "I don't think so." Pointing to a small single-engine plane which was circling over the valley, he said, "I figure there's a forward air controller in that bird dog, and he's using the bundles for bait. If I'm right, when Charlie presents a good enough target he'll bring in the bombers."

Major Strong stepped away from the fence. "There is nothing we can do here, and we're still a long ways from being out of the woods. Let's get back to the compound."

As Rictor turned to follow the major, three Canberras roared over the capital. Glancing back to the valley, he saw white marker smoke boiling up from the jungle. Under the impact of the Canberra's heavy bombs the area around the smoke erupted like a volcano, sending splintered trees and broken limbs sailing high into the air. Olga shouted, "Holy shit!"

Dave had already seen dozens of VC pouring out of the jungle, trying desperately to get out of the strike area. Leaning against the fence he raised his M16 and snapped off ten shots before realizing the VC were out of range. Lowering the rifle he glanced to the rear of the capitol building. "What in the hell are the rangers waiting on? They'll never get a better target. There must be two hundred Charlies out there," he said in frustration.

The words were barely out of his mouth when the rangers opened up with machine guns and rifles. Their fire was deadly accurate, and more than twenty VC were cut down. Knowing it was suicide to remain on their feet in the withering fire, the surviving VC hit the ground and attempted to crawl across the clearing. As if by magic a flight of Skyraiders appeared out of nowhere. Peeling off they picked up a trail formation and came in strafing. Panic-stricken, the VC scrambled to get out of the beating zone. They were doomed.

The lead ship dropped napalm, and half of the clearing was turned into a fiery inferno. The trail ships made overlapping drops, and the VC who had been lucky enough to survive the initial blast were turned into human torches by the jelly gasoline. The distance from the fence to the jungle clearing was several hundred yards, but inhuman screams of agony could be heard by the men along the fence. As they watched in silence, intense heat set fire to the supply bundles, and the ammunition began to explode. When the napalm burned out, the clearing was scorched black and littered with smoldering bodies.

As the bird dog spotter plane waggled its wings overhead, Dave said, "I'm glad that son of a bitch is on our side. Looks like he's headed for the village."

Feeling a sudden wave of nausea Rictor snapped, "C'mon, we're wasting time." Walking toward the compound he wondered if his queasy feeling was caused by lack of food and loss of sleep, or if he was just sick of the killing.

By 1000 hours, the battle had shifted from the capital complex to the village. The leaderless ARVN forces deployed around the capitol building were satisfied to let the Air Force do the work and held their defensive posture. Ground action came to a virtual standstill, and air attacks increased as more planes arrived.

Needing cloud cover and darkness to continue the assault, the VC in the village were using the villagers as shields in an attempt to buy time. As the air strikes increased, they realized the village was no longer tenable. But to attempt a mass withdrawal would be disastrous. Breaking into small groups, they herded the civilian hostages like cattle in front of them, trying to reach the sanctuary of the jungle. Some of them made it, but the price was high. The sky was crowded with aircraft of all types. Unable to distinquish the villagers from the VC, the pilots slashed and ripped at everything that moved. They bombed the fringes of the village and struck at gun positions in the surrounding jungle. Several planes went down, disabled by heavy ground fire.

By midafternoon, the village was an abandoned heap of rubble. The VC had managed to break contact and take cover in the jungle. Certain that they were regrouping to renew the attack, the Air Force continued to blast suspected assembly areas. Just prior to 1500 hours, a Caribou loaded with medical supplies and ammunition made a perfect resupply drop. Nearly all the American survivors were suffering from some type of wound, and, after recovering the supplies, their first order of business was to patch each other up.

Leaning against the sandbagged position at the corner of the mess hall porch, Lockwood waited impatiently for Rictor to finish bandaging his injured eye. Placing a final piece of tape on the bandage Rictor stepped back to take a look. Nodding approval he said, "That oughta hold you for a while. Let's get the rest of the ammo distributed."

Heading for a stack of ammunition boxes near the gate, Lockwood said, "If I were you, I'd be careful what I lifted. If you jam one of those busted ribs into your lungs, you're going to be in a world of hurt."

Rictor was more concerned about the gash in his hand than

he was about his ribs. "The tape job you did on me should hold till the relief force gets here."

Lockwood's expression was doubtful. "You really figure that ARVN can get through?"

Rictor shrugged. "Depends on what Charlie has in mind. The major said that province has got radio contact with an ARVN regiment that's moving in on foot. Their last reported position was five miles south of Bien Tien District."

Sounding even more skeptical, Lockwood said, "If Charlie's still holding the district headquarters and airfield, you can bet your ass he's not going to give them up without a fight."

Rictor agreed. "That's the way I see it, too, but we've got no way of telling for sure. And province flat refuses to send out any patrols. The acting province chief is as screwed up as Nam was, if that's possible. He's got all his troops pulled in tight around the capitol building and won't budge an inch."

Lockwood scoffed. "Capitol building! Capital of what? Except for the couple of stinking acres we're occupying, Charlie is in complete control of the entire province. Don't the dumb bastards realize that the village is deserted? Can't they see that the little bit of influence the government had over these people went up in smoke with the village?"

Rictor said, "I agree. The whole system is fucked up. We both know that there is no way the Saigon government can send a bunch of puppet opportunists out here and expect to gain the support of the people. As a matter of fact, right this minute we've got something in common with the people. It's called survival. The way I see it, the acting province chief's plan is to button up and bury his head like an ostrich. It couldn't be a worse defense plan if Charlie had drawn it up for him." Stooping to pick up a box of machine gun ammunition he continued, "In the meantime, we'd better get busy beefing up defense. I, for one, intend to survive!"

Lockwood flipped the safety on his M16 and pointed down the street toward the village. "Look what's coming!" Rictor dropped the ammunition box and walked over to the gate to get a better look. He saw a black pajama clad figure struggling under the weight of what appeared to be a body.

With his rifle held ready Lockwood eased up behind Rictor. "What do you think?"

Rictor shrugged. "He looks too big for a Vietnamese, but if he keeps coming this way we ought to know pretty quick."

Lockwood exclaimed, "Well, I'll be damned. It's Watts! I never expected to see his USOM ass again. Wonder if that's Mendoza he's carrying?"

"Too far away to tell. C'mon, let's give him a hand." When Watts drew near Rictor reached out to take the body. Like a man in a trance Watts ignored the offer of help and continued toward the compound gate. As he stumbled past them Rictor and Lockwood got a look at the body. The head was missing.

Lockwood spat. "Jesus Christ! I tried to warn that poor simple bastard last night, but he wouldn't listen. You reckon he changed his mind before he died?"

"Knock it off!" Rictor snapped. "Let's find out if Watts knows anything about Zung and his family."

Just inside the compound gate, Watts collapsed. As he lay on the ground gasping for breath, tears ran down his cheeks and a whimpering sound came from his mouth.

Producing a canteen Rictor knelt to give him water. Indicating Mendoza's body with a nod, Rictor told Lockwood to move it to the generator shed. As an afterthought he added, "And cover him with something. There's no telling when we'll get him out, and the flies are going to get bad."

Ten minutes dragged by before Watts was able to talk. When he spoke his voice was barely above a whisper. He related how he had been hidden by the prostitute, and how he had found Mendoza's body. By the time he finished telling his story, it was obvious that he blamed himself for Mendoza's death.

Rictor asked, "What about Zung? Have you seen anything of him or his family?"

Watts nodded. "You know how thick the jungle is on the south side of the village. Well, I couldn't see a damn thing from the hole I was hiding in, and the planes were striking all around. About ten o'clock this morning my curiosity got the best of me, and I crawled out of the hole to see what was going on. I inched my way forward to the edge of the jungle and was almost caught by some VC who were using villagers as a shield against the aircraft. Before I could get back to the hole, another group of VC came out of the village. When they were halfway to the jungle, a woman clutching a baby in her arms broke and ran. One of the VC cut her down with a burst of submachine gun fire. The baby was screaming its head off.

"A man broke away from the group and raced toward the woman. It was Zung. The same VC that had killed the woman raised his AK, but before he could shoot, a Skyraider opened up with machine gun fire, then dropped napalm. I tried to get the baby, but it was impossible. The entire area was on fire. There were no survivors!"

Olga stepped over to Rictor and held out a pack of cigarettes. "When we finally win this cruddy war do you reckon there will be any people left? Between the VC and us it might just be one big graveyard that nobody wants."

Reaching for the offered cigarette Rictor said, "Your guess is as good as mine, but sometimes I catch myself wondering if the victory is worth the price."

Dave came from behind the operations building and motioned Rictor to one side. In a low voice he said, "Commo's got contact with the Maggit advisors with the relief force. They've run into heavy resistance south of Binh Tien District, and there is no way they'll get here today."

Rictor took a long drag of the cigarette. Inhaling he let the smoke out slowly and glanced at his watch. It was 1630 hours. Looking up, he searched the sky. There was no sign of clouds, but he knew they would come. He nodded to Dave and left the gate in search of the major.

Chapter XV

THE AWAKENING

Sitting on the edge of Dave's mortar pit, Rictor gazed out over the shattered west fence and the valley beyond. The jungle appeared peaceful, but he knew that beneath the green canopy there were a lot more Viet Cong. Surveying the fence, he thought about how few Americans had survived the attack and how small the detachment had appeared when the major had called them together for the defense orders. The combined force of MAC-V and Special Forces was only fourteen men. The major had told them, too, that the province chief refused to send out security patrols. Rictor reached for a cigarette.

The sound of trucks moving out from the capital attracted his attention. He had started to the gate to see what was going on when he heard footsteps in the alley. A few seconds later, Dave squeezed past the wall. Seeing Rictor he said, "A bunch of empty trucks just left the capital and headed south. Wonder what ARVN's up to?"

Shaking his head Rictor said, "There's no telling, but one thing is for sure, the trucks can't go any farther than the village and even that's risky. Charlie's still got his artillery, and I'm surprised we haven't heard from it already. I'd say the trucks make a pretty fat target."

Dave stepped into the pit and leaned over to check the mortar. "If I hadn't seen for myself that the trucks were empty, I'd say the bastards were trying to cut out on us."

Rictor grunted. "If they're stupid enough to try and ride out, we're probably better off without them."

Dave sat down on the lip of the hole and lit a cigarette. He said, "Well, you can count on one thing, if ARVN's not already trying to pull out, he will be if the going gets any tougher." Taking a long draw from the cigarette he continued, "I don't mind telling you that just before daylight this morning I thought long and hard about running myself. I saw them sorry-ass RF troops cut and figured the rest of you guys were dead. Sitting over there in that hole with Oink's body, I had a helluva time convincing myself to stay and fight for something the Vietnamese wouldn't fight for."

Rictor said, "You should have gone out with the Medevacs. I heard the major tell you to."

Dave snuffed out the cigarette and glanced at the sky. Studying the growing cloud formations he said, "I don't give a damn what happens to this capital, and I'm not interested in being a hero. But after seeing what Charlie did to Scruggs and Terry, I've got a personal debt to settle with him. I figure right here is a good place to do it."

As Dave talked, Rictor studied a wilted flower bed near the fence. Rousing, he said, "I'm just as ready as you are to make Charlie pay the price, but I don't give him all the credit for what's happened. It was made easy for him here just like it is everywhere else in this phony ass war."

Dave indicated the flower bed. "Is that what you're talking about?"

"That's a big part of it." Stepping out of the mortar pit he said, "I'm going to take a look around the compound. I'll be back before dark."

Rictor found Lockwood busily sorting ammunition at the rear of the mess hall. "How's the eye?" he asked.

Lockwood fingered the bandage. "This damn thing is more trouble than the wound."

Lockwood was tall and blond. Rictor supposed he would have been described as handsome before the shrapnel tore away part of his left ear and ripped his face above the eye.

"Are you going to be able to handle the machine gun?" Rictor asked. Lockwood glanced along the RF fence. "You let Charlie try to come in this way tonight, and you'll find out."

Satisfied that Lockwood would be okay, Rictor walked on. As he approached the commo van, he heard the bird dog pilot's voice coming over the radio loud and clear. "The soup's getting so thick up here I can't see. I'm heading for home, but there'll be a flare ship here before dark. Good luck!"

Poking his head inside the van, Rictor nearly collided with the FAC's radio operator. He noticed the gashes in the youth's face and had second thoughts about not having sent him out with the Medevacs. Concerned, he asked, "Do you need any help with the radio?"

Gently touching his face with his forefinger the operator answered, "No, I've got everything under control, but I can tell you one thing, I'm through fuckin' around with broads that scratch."

Rictor saw that the radio operator, for all his wounds, seemed to have been strengthened in spirit, if not in body, by the hellish night. He said, "I'll make you a deal. You keep the radio working, and I give you my word that your mother won't find out from me about the girls. If you lose radio contact, I won't promise you anything."

The high-pitched chattering of Deuces made Rictor turn. Glancing toward the operations building, he spotted the monkey perched on the rooftop. He mumbled, "You hairy bastard, this morning you almost gave me a heart attack."

Walking back to the mortar pit, Rictor passed near Olga's automatic rifle position. Olga and the Chinaman sat on the lip loading magazines, and Olga called out, "I don't know what you're selling, but we don't want any."

Rictor shrugged. "That's too bad because I'm giving away expense-paid trips to Frisco."

"In that case, I can spare you a couple of minutes."

Rictor grinned. "There is one catch. You hafta complete a year over here before you can go."

Olga said, "Forget it. I really don't have the time for a long trip. I'm busy planning a surprise party for a large number of guests, and I don't know exactly what time they'll be arriving."

Rictor nodded. "I'll be with Dave. If you and the Chinaman get more guests than you can handle, we'll try to give you a hand."

Rictor had taken only a few steps when Olga asked, "Do you think that bastard Nam would have turned us over to Charlie?"

Rictor knew the answer was yes. Over his shoulder he said, "I'm glad we didn't hafta find out."

When he returned to the mortar position, Rictor found Dave sitting on the edge of the hole blowing cigarette smoke at a swarm of flies. Studying the overcast sky Dave said, "You'd think sooner or later we'd get a break. Sure as hell it's going to rain."

"Maybe rain will get rid of the flies. Which reminds me, tomorrow we've got to do something about the VC bodies. One more day in the sun, and they will really be ripe."

Dave took a final drag on his cigarette and flipped it toward the fence. "You seem pretty sure there's going to be a tomorrow."

Ignoring Dave, Rictor let his thoughts drift to Olga and the radio operator. He knew their bantering was camouflage. As for his own feelings, he knew that in a very short time he might be dead, but the desire to live swelled up inside him.

Dave's shout of "Look over there!" interrupted Rictor's thoughts. Tracing a line from Dave's extended finger to the high ground west of the river, he saw two ropes of orange machine gun tracers arching toward the clouds. The object of their fury was nowhere in sight.

He scanned the clouds and asked, "Where's the aircraft?"

"Three Skyraiders just disappeared in the clouds," Dave said. "Unless I miss my guess they'll be back. If so, some fuckin' VC gunners are going to be awful sorry they opened fire."

Seconds later the Skyraiders broke through the overcast. The pilots had pinpointed the machine gun positions by the tracer fire. One of the planes peeled off and barreled in low over the jungle. Rictor lost sight of the aircraft, but a rising fireball meant the plane had dropped its napalm. The two remaining planes nosed down and hurled earthward. Three hundred feet from the ground, they leveled off, also releasing their napalm tanks. The jungle around the VC guns turned into a sea of fire. Dave nodded his approval. "Ho Chi Minh can scratch them guns. Another bunch of dumb shits that won't live to regret their mistake."

Holding up his hand for silence Rictor cocked his head and looked south of Binh Tien Mountain. Dave asked, "What's up?"

"Be quiet and listen," Rictor snapped.

Rifle and machine gun fire was barely audible, but without question there was a firefight occurring on the road between the mountain and Binh Tien District headquarters. Rictor knew the relief force could not have advanced to that location in such a short period of time. He wondered who was involved in the fighting.

Dave stood and cupped his hand to his ear. "What do you make of it?"

"I don't know unless Charlie's mopping up Regional Force survivors from Binh Tien District." As he spoke another thought occurred to him. Climbing out of the pit he said, "Jesus Christ! You don't suppose those dumb-ass ARVN drivers took the empty trucks that far south, do you?"

Dave shrugged. "I wouldn't put anything past ARVN, but if they did, it's the last trip they'll ever make."

Rictor turned. "I'm going to find the major. Maybe he knows what's going on."

"Unless he's got a direct line to God or a Ouija board, I wouldn't give any odds on that. I'd bet a fat man the Vietnamese haven't told him anything."

There was little doubt that Dave was right, but Rictor wanted to make sure. Approaching the CP, he spotted the major sitting on the sandbag wall with his head cocked toward the south. In the fading light, his haggard face made him look as though he had aged ten years. Hearing footsteps the major glanced around. At Rictor's question he said, "Your guess is as good as mine!"

Before Rictor could comment, the Air Force radio operator

came running toward the command post. Coming to a sliding halt, he yelled, "I just had one of the MAC-V people with the relief force on the radio. His battalion is caught in an ambush just south of the mountain, and I've lost radio contact with them."

The major was skeptical. "Are you sure they're just south of the mountain?"

The operator nodded. "That's what he said!"

The major was puzzled. "How in the hell could they have gotten that close? The last contact we had with them they were a good ten miles farther south and planned to hole up for the night."

The operator shook his head. "I don't know, sir. After giving his location all the guy on the radio said was that half the trucks had been knocked out, and they were catching hell."

Rictor knew that the relief force had been on foot. His suspicions about the empty trucks was confirmed, and he was filled with rage. Stepping close to the major he said, "The son of a bitch standing in for Nam sent out trucks with orders to bring in part of the relief force!" After a short pause he continued, "I can almost see Charlie's mouth watering as he watched the trucks go south knowing they'd be back loaded with troops. There's only one road leading in here and it was a pretty simple process for them to set up an ambush. You can bet it was effective."

The major snapped at the operator. "Get back on the radio and keep trying to make contact." Turning to Rictor he said, "I'm going to the capital," and stomped off toward the gate.

When Rictor returned to the mortar position, the sound of firing had stopped, and the last rays of light were fading. Dave called out, "What did you find out?"

"Looks like at least part of the relief force got ambushed over on the south side of the mountain," Rictor answered.

Dave cursed. "How in the hell did that happen?"

"It was them fuckin' trucks," Rictor said. "There's no way of telling how bad they got hit unless the major can find out from the Vietnamese. He's over at province now."

Half an hour later a disgusted and mad major came to Dave's mortar pit. Dropping down on one knee next to Rictor he said, "Your guess about the trucks was right. The fool that's acting province chief was afraid we wouldn't be able to hold tonight and sent out trucks with orders to bring back a relief force battalion. Charlie let the empty trucks go through, but when they came back with the troops on board, he was waiting. The poor devils on the trucks didn't have a chance. When I left the capital, the Vietnamese had radio contact with the survivors. They're on the way in now, but only one truck got through."

Dave cursed. "What about the Maggits that were with them?"

The major shook his head. "I couldn't find out, but ARVN's bringing in a truckload of dead and wounded."

Disgusted with the sheer stupidity of the Vietnamese commander, Rictor asked, "How many Americans were involved?"

"I've got the radio operator trying to contact the main body of the relief force," the major said. "In the meantime, I want you to go to the gate and wait for the survivors. When they get here, see what you can find out. I'll be at the CP."

As the major walked away, Rictor picked up his M16 and climbed out of the mortar pit. Dave snorted. "I guess you know you're wasting your time!"

"Maybe. But I just felt a sprinkle of rain, and I'd rather be moving around than sitting here in this damn mud hole soaking up water like a sponge."

"You've got a point, but don't be gone too long. It gets awful lonesome down here."

An hour later rain was coming down in sheets. Soaked to the bone Rictor was trying to light a cigarette when a Vietnamese runner came to the gate and said that there were some Americans at the chopper pad. Unable to get any further information from the runner, Rictor went to the rear of the mess hall and got Lockwood. When they arrived at the chopper pad, Rictor spotted a parked truck and called out identifying himself. There was no response. Cautiously approaching the truck he climbed up on the side and snapped on his flashlight. As the yellow beam swept the cargo compartment, he discovered more than thirty mangled bodies. He would have to pull them apart in order to locate the Americans. He cursed and called to Lockwood for help. Climbing up next to Rictor, Lockwood took one look and vomited. Wiping his mouth he took a deep breath. "You figure the Maggits are under the pile?"

Rictor didn't answer, he was watching fresh blood mix with the rain. Lockwood swore. "What do you want to do?"

Rictor let out a sigh. "Here, hold the light. I'll take a look."

Five minutes later he located the body of a young MAC-V captain. As he and Lockwood lowered the body to the ground, Rictor saw that the captain had died from a head wound and judged from the powder burns that it had been inflicted at close range. Continuing the search he located the body of a MAC-V sergeant he knew named Turk. Satisfied that there were no more Americans on the truck, Rictor pulled the sergeant's body to the tailgate and motioned to Lockwood. "Gimme a hand."

The body was laid on the ground next to the captain's and Rictor saw that he had been mistaken about how the captain had died. Both he and the sergeant had obviously died of multiple body wounds. Anger burned in Rictor like a hot flame. It was just as obvious that they had been given the coup de grace. Lockwood swore. "Ain't that Bill Turk?"

Rictor nodded and stripped off his poncho. "Let's cover them up. There's nothing we can do tonight." As he stooped to get the dog tags, he saw that the captain was not more than twenty-four years old. To keep out the driving rain, Rictor reached down and closed the young officer's eyes.

Lockwood pointed to Turk. "Why do you suppose Charlie took time to mutilate them?"

"For the psychological effect. It's Charlie's way of telling us what to expect. C'mon, let's get back to the compound."

Lockwood snorted. "Well, I got a message for Charlie, and I plan to deliver it to just as many of the bastards as possible."

Walking along the muddy road leading to the compound gate, Rictor's thoughts were of Turk. The huge sergeant had too much battle savvy to have gotten on a truck without putting up a flap. He guessed that Turk had agreed to ride to keep from being embarrassed in front of the Vietnamese or because he had been ordered to do so.

A challenge from the sandbagged position at the corner of the mess hall startled Rictor. He identified himself and kept moving. At the gate Lockwood said, "If you don't need me anymore, I'm going back to my gun position."

Rictor secured the gate. "After I report to the major, I'll be with Dave. See you in the morning." Lockwood didn't respond, and Rictor persisted. "Yeah, I said in the morning!"

Moving toward the gun position Lockwood called out, "Damn, Rictor! Just because one of my eyes is fucked up don't mean I can't hear. I heard you the first time."

Rictor grinned and headed for the CP. He found the poncho-clad major huddled in the sandbag enclosure fighting a losing battle with the rain. The major asked, "What did you find out?" When Rictor had finished his report, the major said, "That means one American is still out there."

Rictor frowned. "How do you know?"

The major stood and threw off the rain-soaked poncho. "While you were gone I had radio contact with the main body of the relief force. There were three MAC-V people on the trucks."

Rictor cursed. "There's not a fuckin' chance in a thousand that the missing Maggit is still alive. Even if he is there's nothing we can do to help him. I'll be with Dave if you need me."

As Rictor picked his way across the dark compound, he cursed the war, the rain, the acting province chief, the VC and the world in general. Drawing near the mortar pit, he could hear Dave grumbling as he restacked ammo to keep it out of the mud. Rictor said, "There's one thing for sure, we don't have to worry about Charlie finding us. He can hear you a mile away!"

"Fat chance they don't know where we are," Dave snapped. "What did you find out about the ambushed Maggits?"

"There was three of them. Two are dead and one's missing."

Dave blurted out a few choice four-letter words and then lapsed into silence.

For the next half hour Rictor stood with his back to the driving rain. When the rain let up, he took out his pill bottle, let a couple of the tiny pills dissolve in his mouth and took a seat on an ammo case. As his mind rambled, he thought about Terry and wondered if he would live. Rictor's thoughts turned to Scruggs. He remembered Scruggs's saying at the Highlands airstrip that the way they were shuffled around was like a giant chess game. Like waking up from a deep sleep. Rictor realized at that moment his true value in the war. Like Scruggs, Henderson and the rest, he was a pawn, trapped in a war without victory or end and likely to be sacrificed by bungling incompetents. The realization was chilling.

Shortly after 2200 hours incoming mortar rounds exploded along the fence, and small arms fire raked the west end of the compound. Rictor dropped to the muddy floor of Dave's mortar pit and grabbed an illumination round. He was too slow. Dave was already dropping one down the tube. On the other side of the compound, the 81mm. mortar boomed out a ten-round fire for effect, but when Dave's flare popped there were no VC at the fence and no answering fire. "Looks like Charlie wants to play games," observed Dave.

"Maybe, but we'd better keep this end of the compound lit," Rictor suggested.

"Okay, but we're not fat with flares. Wonder where that damn flare ship is?"

Rictor scanned the overcast. "It's around some place. I imagine the pilot is staying clear unless he's called."

"Well, as far as I'm concerned, somebody can call him now. I feel better when I hear him up there." Five minutes later the drone of a lone aircraft announced the arrival of the flare ship. It was hidden from view by the cloud cover but a string of perfectly timed flares broke through the soupy overcast and bathed the entire compound in soft light.

For nearly four hours the night remained quiet. Just before 0200 hours a machine gun on the high ground west of the river fired a long burst at the compound. As Dave adjusted the mortar to return fire, three incoming mortar rounds exploded near the pit, and shrapnel ignited a hand-held flare which lay on the lip of the hole.

The burning flare dropped at Rictor's feet and set fire to the contents of an ammunition box. Silhouetted by the firelight, Dave and Rictor leapt out of the hole and sprinted for the corner of the billets. At the edge of the tennis court, Olga mistook them for VC and fired. Rictor scrambled behind a mound of freshly dug dirt. Lying on his belly Dave yelled, "Knock it off, you dip shit. It's Dave and Rictor!"

Olga stopped firing, but when Rictor attempted to get up, he found he had taken shrapnel in the lower left leg. Cursing, he glanced back to the mortar. The fire had burned out, and he said, "Let's get back to the pit and see what we can salvage."

"Okay, but if Olga starts shooting again, I'm going up there and strangle his ass with my bare hands."

From somewhere in the ruins of the billets a lizard, disturbed by the incoming rounds, hissed, "Fuck you! Fuck you!"

Dave swore. "Even the goddamn lizards are against me. If I'm still alive tomorrow, I'm gonna find that bastard and show him what the word means!"

"Shut up and give me a hand," Rictor snapped. "I'm hit."

By the time they crawled back to the mortar position, the compound was quiet again. As Rictor bandaged the shallow but painful wound in his leg, he noticed a break in the overcast. Fifteen minutes later, barely visible behind the thinning cloud cover, he was able to make out the flare ship. Aware that they were finally getting a much needed break, he relaxed.

The night passed slowly. Occasionally, the VC fired harassing mortar rounds, but the flare ship provided almost continuous light. The expected attack failed to materialize. By daylight the sky over the capital was once again filled with planes and gunships which ripped and slashed at the surrounding jungle. Under their cover, a lone chopper touched down and dropped off a doctor. He brought a message from the *"C"* Detachment that the camp would be reinforced by an American paratroop unit.

At 0800 hours, Rictor and Lockwood stood in front of the

operations building trying to decide what to do with the deteriorating VC bodies scattered around the compound. Rictor said, "While the doctor was bandaging my leg, he told me that the bodies had to be moved. I told him there was no way we could bury them but that we might be able to burn them. He said he didn't give a damn what we did, but that we have to do it today."

"He won't get any arguments from me," Lockwood grunted. "One more day, and the flies will have all of us sick. The smell is awful. Let's pile them outside the gate and burn them."

Rictor shrugged. "Suits me."

With a nod, Lockwood indicated the generator shed. "What about Mendoza's body?"

Rictor hesitated. "No. Leave him where he is. Maybe we can get him out on a chopper. C'mon, let's find a place to build a fire."

Rictor was surprised to find Kim, the bartender, waiting at the gate. He figured that she was either dead or had fled south with the rest of the villagers. Kim's English was poor, but Rictor knew she was looking for Campbell. Shaking his head, he made the palms-together sleep sign and said, "Saigon." Not sure that she understood, he yelled for the Chinaman.

While the Chinaman explained what had happened to Campbell, Rictor studied Kim's face. Like most Orientals, her expression did not reveal any emotion as she listened to what was surely bad news. She was haggard and dirty and her clothes were in shreds, but her poise and beauty were still evident.

Rictor said, "Ask her what she plans to do."

The Chinaman translated the question. After listening to Kim's answer, the Chinaman said, "Her home was destroyed, and she has no place to go. She wants to know if she can stay here and help us?"

Rictor hesitated. After considering her relationship with Campbell and the fact that they had no cook, he said, "Tell her she can stay till we can get her on a chopper to Saigon."

The Chinaman conveyed the message. Kim smiled and

headed for the mess hall. The Chinaman said, "She's going to try and find some food for us."

Rictor had not eaten in two days but did not feel hungry. He said, "As long as I keep taking these damn pills, I won't have much need for food."

Lockwood agreed. "Me either. But if I quit taking them, it's all over. You wouldn't be able to wake me with a hand grenade."

"Did Kim say where she was during the attack on the village?" Rictor asked.

The Chinaman nodded. "She was one of the lucky ones that managed to make it to the jungle. She's been hiding there since night before last."

"How come she didn't move south with the rest of the villagers?" Rictor asked.

The Chinaman grinned. "You know the answer to that—Campbell. She said the villagers pulled out because the VC are telling them they will continue attacking until they win. The VC say they don't care what the cost is or how long it takes. The villagers know they were caught in the middle and would be killed."

Rictor was aware that the villagers usually had accurate information about what the VC were doing. He turned to Lockwood. "Get some people to start moving the bodies. I'll be along later. I've got to talk to the major."

He located Major Strong at the CP and passed on the information which Kim had given. He and the major agreed that the main VC force was probably west and southwest of the capital. However, they had no way to confirm it. The major said, "I've been trying all morning to prod the acting province chief into sending out recon patrols, but I could have saved my breath. He's scared he'll make another mistake so he won't issue the order. His only concern is to hold the capital."

"Don't the dumb son of a bitch realize that if he knows Charlie's location and strength, he'll be in better shape to defend the capital?"

"I think he knows it, but he's afraid."

"Has he sent anybody to the ambush site to look for survivors?"

The major shook his head. "He's not sending anybody any place for any reason."

"He was fast enough to send out the fuckin' trucks yesterday!" Rictor swore. "What are we going to do about the missing Maggit?"

"Rictor, I told you already I've done all I can. He's not sending anyone out. If the paratroops come in, I'll send a patrol. Nobody here is in any shape to go out, and you know it."

Aware the major was frustrated and very close to losing his temper, Rictor said, "You don't sound too sure the paratroops are coming."

The major was uncertain. "There's no suitable place for a parachute drop within a day's march of here, and Charlie's holding the airstrip. Besides that, from what the 'C' Detachment says, there's a flap going on in Saigon as to whether or not to use American troops. This would be their first offensive ground action."

"What about the main body of the ARVN relief force?"

The major shook his head. "After losing a battalion in the ambush, the relief force commander doesn't figure he's got the strength to fight his way here. He's dug in five miles south of the airstrip waiting to be reinforced himself."

Rictor opened his mouth to protest, but a tug on his sleeve cut him off. Turning, he saw Kim. She motioned for him to follow her to the mess hall. Once inside, he saw that Kim had cleaned up some of the rubble but the stench of death and smell of blood was almost overpowering.

On a table near the center of the dining room, Rictor found the object of Kim's concern. Charlie had left behind a banana leaf–wrapped bomb large enough to bring the building down. Remembering that the VC had abandoned the building with only token resistance, he surmised that when he and the Chinaman entered the building Charlie had set the charge and attempted to escape by the porch. Aware of what would happen if the charge exploded Rictor motioned Kim out of the building and went looking for Olga.

When Olga entered the mess hall, he took one look and let

out a whistle. "Jesus Christ, Rictor! That damn thing must weigh fifty pounds!"

Rictor nodded. "Can you handle it?"

Olga walked around the table to get a better look. Lightly touching the charge he said, "There's only one way to find out for sure." Twenty minutes later he had the bomb disarmed, and they were on the way to the gate with it.

"I would have gotten Dave to handle this," Rictor said, "but he's pretty well banged up. Anyway, I wanted to find out if he'd taught you anything."

Olga grinned. "Just because I'm a college dropout don't mean I'm stup—"

A piercing female scream from the rear of the mess hall cut off Olga's words. Whirling, Rictor said, "Get rid of the bomb!" Snatching out his automatic, he ran back to the mess hall as fast as his fractured ribs and wounded leg would allow. A second shrill scream cut through the air, and when he rounded the corner of the mess hall he saw Kim standing in the doorway. Her eyes were clenched shut, and she was sobbing hysterically. Rictor was puzzled. Her hands were bloody, and she was obviously in shock but there was no one else in sight. Then he saw it. Lying at her feet was a severed human leg. He saw the ripped boot top which bore the name Campbell in bold letters. Taking hold of Kim's arm, he attempted to lead her away from the door, but she refused to budge and only continued to scream. Not knowing what else to do, Rictor holstered his automatic and slapped her. She began to cry.

Lockwood came charging up the alley. "What the hell's going on?"

Rictor pointed to the leg. "Get it out of here! Burn it, bury it, or put it with Mendoza. I don't care, but get it out of here!"

Lockwood cursed, picked up the leg and headed for the generator shed.

Chapter XVI

TIME FOR A WALK

By 1500 hours, Rictor felt sure there would not be a relief force. He had been sitting on the edge of Dave's mortar pit mulling over the situation. He felt certain he knew the VC strategy, but it was all guesswork. Turning to Dave, he said, "Charlie's not stupid. And he knows that as long as province thinks he's in the area, there'll be no patrolling. I think he's withdrawing southwest, leaving just enough people behind to create the illusion that he's still here in strength. That leaves him free to move without pursuit. If he can make it to the Phu Ring Rubber Plantation sanctuary, he's home free."

Dave was interested. "What makes you think that?"

Rictor lit a cigarette. "Well, Charlie knows the longer he waits to continue the attack the stronger we'll be. If he was waiting for cloud cover, he had a beautiful opportunity last night. All he did was toss us a few mortar rounds and a little automatic weapons fire. I think that was to convince us that he's still out there in force."

Dave was skeptical. "How do you explain the ambush?"

"I figure a chance sighting of the trucks presented a target that Charlie couldn't pass up. The ambush also helped strengthen the illusion that he was still here in force and trying to seal the area."

243

"If you're right," Dave said, "by sitting here bottled up we're playing right into Charlie's hands. Once he breaks contact, we've lost him."

Rictor nodded. "Except for the bodies he left behind, we've got no idea how badly he's hurt."

Dave climbed out of the mortar pit. "Are you going to be here for a while? I need to talk to Olga."

Rictor flipped the half-burned cigarette toward the fence and stood up. "I'll be at the operations building. I want to check the ambush location on the big map. We've still got a Maggit out there somewhere." Dave nodded and headed toward Olga's AR position.

Twenty minutes later, Rictor was studying a badly damaged wall map in the operations building. He heard footsteps to his rear and turned to find Dave, Lockwood, Olga and the Chinaman. All four carried rucksacks and extra ammo. Guessing their intent, he pretended ignorance and asked, "What's up?"

Dave stepped over to the map, "We're gonna take a walk down to the river. Do you want to come along?"

Rictor scoffed. "Get serious. You guys look more like two weeks in the hospital than a patrol."

"We're going. Aré you coming?" Dave said shortly.

Rictor glanced from Lockwood to Olga. Their grim faces told him the decision was final. He turned to Dave. "If you ask the major for permission, he'll say no. If you don't ask him, when you get back your ass is grass."

Dave pointed to the map. "Is that red circle south of the mountain the ambush site?"

Rictor nodded and stepped toward the door. "Wait here. I'll be back."

Minutes later he returned with his rifle and a radio tuned to the air ground frequency. Sticking his head inside the room he said, "Let's get moving. I instructed the radio operator to give us thirty minutes before telling the major that we're gone."

With Dave leading the way, they worked their way across the deserted RF compound, eased out through a hole in the west fence and entered the jungle. Reaching the area the VC had used for an assault position to attack the west fence, Dave discovered a well-used trail which led toward the river.

As they worked their way along the trail, the stench from the decaying bodies was stifling. Just short of the river they discovered several shallow mass graves. Adding the number of bodies they found along the trail with the ones found on the compound, Rictor figured the VC had been badly mauled. It was easy to see that they had moved in from the west. Indications were that they had also withdrawn to the west.

The discovery of a cache containing tons of rice and equipment strengthened Rictor's belief that the VC had been hurt badly. They had departed the area in great haste, otherwise they would never have left so much food and equipment behind. On the bank of the river near a shallow fording site, he found an American pistol belt and load-bearing harness with Callahan's mark on it. The equipment could only have been dropped or discarded by someone who had been on the compound. The VC route of withdrawal was fixed.

Rictor motioned for Dave. Holding out the belt he said, "Take a look."

Spotting Callahan's mark, Dave cursed. "The bastard that dropped it had to have gotten it from the mess hall. Wonder if he was the son of a bitch who killed Scruggs?"

Olga came over to see what the discussion was about. Rictor said, "Get Lockwood and take a break. It's decision time."

"You saying it's time to decide whether to keep going or turn back?"

Rictor nodded. "I figure everybody should decide for himself. If Charlie left a covering force, chances are we'll make contact just across the river. Besides that, those planes and gunships up there don't know we're down here. That makes us as likely to be attacked as Charlie."

Dave shrugged. "We came out here looking for Charlie. If we run into a covering force, that means we've found him. I don't intend to pussyfoot around the compound while the bastards do a disappearing act. As far as the planes are concerned, you've got a radio and I'm willing to take my chances."

Lockwood added, "I'm with Dave. Let's find them."

Rictor turned to Olga who was examining his M16 and trying hard to look disinterested. Realizing that they were waiting for him to decide, Olga looked up. "I've been putting you guys on long enough. They didn't boot me out of college, I dropped out and enlisted because I wanted to find out about the war firsthand. Now that I know, I'm ready to hurt some people."

Rictor caught the Chinaman's eye and held it. The Chinaman's nod was barely visible. Shifting his eyes to the far bank of the river, Rictor adjusted the radio carrying straps. "I've had enough of the resort myself. If this trail swings south on the far side of the river, it should run close to the ambush site. We'll take a look for the missing Maggit."

Dave stepped into the small clearing adjacent to the ford. "I'll take the point. When I spot Charlie, do you want to engage him or try to avoid contact till we've checked on the Maggit?"

Rictor glanced from Lockwood to Olga and said, "I figure the Maggit's dead. Like the rest of you, I've got my own score to settle. If we find Charlie between here and the ambush site, let's kick ass." Daved nodded and waded out into the river.

At the provincial capitol building, the acting province chief stood at a conference room window scanning the jungle-covered river valley. Catching a glimpse of movement in a small clearing near the river, he grabbed his binoculars. When five figures, four camouflage clad and one wearing black, came into focus he nodded with satisfaction. Without taking his eyes off the clearing he yelled to the operations officer, "Get the artillery on the radio! I've got a target!"

Chapter XVII

RETRIBUTION

Major Strong listened impatiently. The Air Force radio operator was nervous but obviously pleased with himself. He took a deep breath. "I know I should have told you about the patrol sooner, but Rictor said if I didn't give him a thirty-minute head start he'd kick my ass all the way to Saigon."

The major cursed and checked his watch. Figuring the patrol was still short of the river, he instructed the operator to establish radio contact and order Rictor to abort and return to the compound immediately. Concerned the Vietnamese would spot the patrol and mistake it for Viet Cong, he ran the two hundred yards to the capitol building and took the steps to the second floor two at a time. Pausing at the operations center doorway he took the large room in at a glance. The provincial intelligence officer and national police chief were in a corner at the far end of the room talking in hushed tones. The operations officer was shouting into the field phone. He spoke rapidly and was obviously excited. The acting province chief stood at an open window observing the river valley through his field glasses.

The major headed across the room to see what was happening. He was halfway to the window when one of the artillery pieces at the rear of the capitol building fired a spotter round.

He stepped up to the window and scanned the valley. Detecting movement, he fixed his binoculars on a small clearing at the edge of the river and spotted four men in waist-deep water working their way toward the west bank. Shifting his glasses to the far bank he saw a fifth man disappear into the jungle. He was certain it was the patrol.

The spotter round exploded in the clearing, and the acting province chief called out a fire adjustment for relay to the artillery.

To the major it was déjà vu. His mind flashed back to the time when the province chief had indiscriminately used the artillery to massacre the helpless Montagnards on the hillside west of the river. He grabbed the Vietnamese colonel and yanked him around. "Cease fire, you son of a bitch! Those are my people you're shooting at."

The colonel slowly lowered his glasses and stared straight into the major's eyes but gave no indication he had heard. The guns at the rear of the capitol building fired ten rounds for effect.

The major cursed and reached for his holstered pistol. "I know you understand English, you no-good son of a bitch! Give the cease fire order, or I'll blow your fuckin' head off!" The colonel continued to stare. Realizing the colonel's mind had snapped, Major Strong raised his pistol and pulled the hammer back.

The Vietnamese intelligence officer raced across the room. "Don't shoot, Major! The artillery has been canceled."

The national police chief approached cautiously. Placing himself between the major and the colonel he said, "You won't need the pistol, Major. The intelligence officer has taken command." Grasping the colonel by the arm, he led the unresisting officer out of the room.

Major Strong turned to the window and saw the artillery rounds exploding along the riverbank. They appeared to be short of the water, but smoke and debris obstructed his line of sight. When the smoke cleared, the patrol had vanished. Cursing with every step, he hurried back to the American compound.

* * *

The spotter artillery round landed fifty yards short of the river sending a shock wave across the muddy surface.

Rictor stumbled in the waist-deep water, regained his balance and glanced back to see if Olga and the Chinaman were okay. Satisfied they were not hit he struggled toward the west bank. Aware that a fire for effect would follow the spotter round, he yelled to Lockwood, "We've got about a minute to clear this goddamn river! Tell Dave to move three hundred yards due west and set up security." Before Lockwood could respond, Dave signaled he understood and disappeared into the thick undergrowth.

Olga called out to Rictor, "Don't sweat it. Them sorry-ass ARVN gunners never got on target with one spotter round in their lives."

Rictor shouted over his shoulder, "Shut up and keep moving. This whole damn valley is preregistered." As he spoke he heard the capital guns boom out ten rounds. He struggled forward and was within twenty feet of the bank when the first high-explosive round landed. The sound was deafening. Shrapnel sprayed the river and centrifugal force from the blast threw him facedown in the murky water. He held his breath and stayed submerged until his lungs felt as though they would burst. Surfacing, he took a deep breath. Smoke lay on the water surface like thick fog, and the taste of burned powder nearly gagged him.

Lockwood crawled up the slippery west bank and stopped to catch his breath. Seeing Rictor surface, he called out, "You okay?"

"Yeah," Rictor shouted. "Catch up with Dave. I'll look for Olga and the Chinaman."

The smoke was thinning, but Rictor's vision was limited to ten feet. He called out to Olga and the Chinaman. There was no response. Olga had been twenty feet behind him when the artillery came in. He waited ten seconds and called out again. There was no answer but a splash to his left told him someone was moving.

Rictor called out, "Is that you, Olga?"

The Chinaman gasped for air. "No, it's me."

Rictor said, "Olga should be somewhere between us. Work your way toward me and search for him."

When the smoke lifted Rictor had a clear view of the river from bank to bank. Olga was nowhere in sight.

Cursing softly he signaled to the Chinaman. "Let's get the hell out of here before we attract every Charlie in a hundred miles!"

When they reached the bank, Rictor scrambled out of the murky water and turned to the Chinaman. "Stay about ten yards behind me. I don't want Dave and Lockwood mistaking your black pajamas for Charlie."

He made a final visual search for Olga, shook his head and turned west.

As he laboriously worked his way through the thick undergrowth, Rictor's mind was on Olga. He felt responsible. Olga was a good man, and he was dead because of Rictor's decision to cross the river.

A hundred yards west of the river the undergrowth began to thin. The trees were still double canopy, but visibility improved. Rictor was glad to be clear of the clinging vines and thorns. He had a better chance of finding Dave and Lockwood, but conversely, any VC waiting in ambush had a better field of fire.

Rictor signaled for the Chinaman to hold up and give cover while he scouted forward. Movement forty yards to his front, followed by a low whistle, caused Rictor to freeze in his tracks. Rifle at the ready he searched the area with his eyes. A camouflage-clad figure stepped from behind a tree and motioned him forward. Rictor let out a sigh of relief as he signaled the Chinaman to advance. He couldn't decide whether to reprimand Olga or give him a bear hug. Putting on his best poker face he whispered, "How in the hell did you get this far out front!"

Olga grinned. "I'm not prepared to swear I walked on water, but there's precedence for it and I came pretty damn close. What kept you guys?"

The Chinaman said, "I lost my shotgun in the river and we had trouble finding it." Rictor gave the Chinaman an appreciative look and said, "Let's get moving. We've still got to locate Dave and Lockwood."

Olga grinned again. "Hell, that's no problem. I've already found them. They're about a hundred yards straight ahead. I came back to find you guys."

Aware that Olga had totally disregarded security to have covered that much distance in such a short time, Rictor grumbled, "You're lucky some Charlie don't have your ears in his pocket. Take the point and hold down the speed." Turning to the Chinaman he said, "I'll follow Olga, you bring up the rear."

Olga had advanced only a few yards when he heard movement on his left flank. Dropping to the ground he flattened out on his belly behind a tree and waited.

The sounds of breaking vegetation and metallic clanks were faint but growing louder. Rictor could hear people struggling with the thick undergrowth as they moved in his direction. Unable to determine the number of approaching VC, Rictor crawled over to Olga and whispered, "Those metallic noises sound like they're carrying a crew serve weapon. If they keep coming in this direction, they're going to pass between Dave and us. Make your way over to Dave, and tell him if there are ten or less of them, he's to open fire. If any of them come in this direction, the Chinaman and I will be waiting." Olga nodded and crept forward.

Motioning the Chinaman to his side, Rictor said, "Unless we're detected, don't fire until Dave does. If possible I want a prisoner, but no one gets away." The Chinaman nodded and positioned himself five yards to Rictor's left.

The noises made by the approaching Viet Cong grew louder. Rictor tightened his grip on the M16, squared his shoulders and relaxed his breathing. The VC point man came into view. He was closer to Dave's position than Rictor's. His AK at the sling position, the VC stopped, took off his helmet and called out to someone behind him. A second VC carrying a mortar tube joined the point man. They appeared to be waiting for the remainder of the squad. Rictor figured the VC with the mortar tube was the gunner and probably the squad leader.

A third and fourth VC carrying bipod and base plate joined the first two. Rictor took aim and waited.

Seconds later the remainder of the squad broke out of the undergrowth and closed on the squad leader. The point man moved forward and the nine-member squad formed a single file. Signaling the Chinaman to take the last man in file, Rictor zeroed in on the point man. When the VC came within twenty yards, Dave, Olga and Lockwood opened fire. Four VC including the point man were killed instantly. Rictor fired at the squad leader's legs. The high-velocity rounds exploded the luckless VC's left knee. He dropped the mortar tube and pitched forward. Screaming in agony, he grabbed his mangled leg and flopped around like a fish out of water.

Rictor scanned the killing zone looking for a new target. Eight VC were down but the ninth was nowhere in sight. Detecting movement to his front left, he fired too quickly and missed. Springing to his feet for a second shot, he tripped over a loose vine and sprawled backward. As he rolled to his right he felt AK rounds tearing at the radio strapped to his back. He was halfway to his feet when the VC crashed into him headfirst. The impact sent Rictor sprawling again. He dropped his M16, grabbed the VC by the throat and reached for his boot knife. Even as he plunged the knife deep into the VC's kidney he realized the man had quit struggling. Shoving the VC to one side he grabbed the dropped M16 and scrambled to his feet. The dying VC lay facedown with a machete lodged between his shoulder blades. He glanced to his rear and saw the Chinaman standing ten feet away with the shotgun at the ready.

The firing had stopped. Rictor looked to the killing zone and saw the rest of the patrol searching bodies. He bent down and pulled the machete from the VC's back. Handing it to the Chinaman he said, "I thought I told you to try and take a prisoner." The Chinaman grinned and headed for the killing zone.

Olga called out, "Hey, you guys, this dude with the mortar tube is still alive, and he's got a map."

Lockwood pushed Olga aside and placed the muzzle of his M16 against the VC's head.

"No, Lockwood! We need him," shouted Rictor. A long burst from Lockwood's M16 disintegrated the VC's head, spewing blood, bone fragments and brains in all directions. "Jesus Christ, Lockwood! Give me a fuckin' break," moaned Olga as he wiped blood and brains from his face.

"Knock off the shit, and let's get moving!" shouted Dave. "We need to put some distance between us and this fuckin' place."

Rictor called to Olga to bring the map. Turning to Dave he said, "We'll move south paralleling the river. If there're any more VC in the area, they're going to be dead on our ass! We'll hold up at the road leading to the convoy ambush site." Seeing the Chinaman pick up a VC helmet, Rictor said, "Get an AK and take the point. If we run into Charlie, your black pajamas just might give us an edge."

The Chinaman located an AK and checked its action. After stripping a body of ammo, he headed south.

It was relatively easy walking along the open jungle floor and visibility was good, but Rictor was concerned about the radio. Its batteries had been destroyed by the AK rounds.

The attack on the VC squad had been a morale builder. They had bloodied Charlie without losses, and spirits were high. Rictor looked at Dave who was cut and punctured in half a dozen places. He turned his attention to Olga and Lockwood. The bandages covering the deep flesh wound in Olga's side showed signs of fresh blood. Part of Lockwood's left ear had been shot away, and his eye was badly swollen.

Marveling at the fact that the Chinaman was unscratched, Rictor turned his thoughts to his own wounds. The exposed tendons in his hand throbbed continuously, but the pain from his bruised ribs was thankfully reduced by the tight tape. His main concern was the shrapnel gash in his leg. It was infected and badly swollen.

The rush of adrenaline caused by close combat had begun to subside, and Rictor was weary. He dug in his pocket for the bottle of pills and took two speed tablets.

As they drew near the site of the ARVN relief force ambush, Rictor was deep in thought and had come to a decision. When the search for the missing American was accomplished, it would be time to return to the compound. He instinctively knew that terminating the patrol was not going to be simple. The encounter with the Viet Cong mortar squad had whetted an appetite for revenge that wasn't going to be easily controlled.

The Chinaman signaled that he had reached the road. Rictor halted the patrol and took out his map. Dave eased up next to Rictor. "How far do you figure to the ambush site?"

Rictor fingered the map. "We're at the base of the mountain where the road turns south. My guess is the site is four or five hundred yards from here." Using his index finger as a pointer, he said, "I guess about here."

Dave studied the map. "Since the terrain drops east of the road I'd guess the ambush was initiated from the high ground to the west."

Rictor nodded agreement. "If Charlie left a covering force, they're somewhere up there on the high ground." He paused before saying, "The killing zone is probably covered by artillery."

Dave continued to study the map. "You got a plan?"

Rictor shook his head. "I know the problem, but there's no easy solution." He turned, exposing the damaged radio. "If we had a battery we could bring in air cover while we search."

Dave cursed. "Fuck the radio, we're committed. I'm for checking out the ambush site. Let's just make sure we stay on this side of the road. If we cross over and get caught between the road and the river, we've had it."

Rictor nodded and took a final look at the map. "You and Lockwood figure eight our back trail and see if we're being followed. I'm going to pull the Chinaman a hundred yards west of the road and parallel south to the ambush site. When we spot the trucks, we'll hold up and wait for you."

Dave turned to leave. "We should catch up in an hour. If you make contact, fall back along the road. Me and Lockwood will try to cover for you."

Rictor signaled Olga and the Chinaman back from the road and briefed them. Without being told, the Chinaman took the point and headed south. The jungle floor was open, but the steep terrain made progress slow.

Forty-five minutes later at the crest of a jagged finger the Chinaman stopped and motioned Rictor and Olga forward. From the top of the ridge Rictor had a clear view of the road. A hundred yards farther south he counted nineteen burned-out trucks. Decaying bodies in grotesque positions were strewed along both sides of the road. Gagging from the stench, Rictor scanned the carnage. He silently cursed the acting province chief for having sent the relief force into the ambush but marveled at the efficiency of the Viet Cong. Not one body was more than twenty feet from the trucks.

Dave worked his way up the ridge and stopped just short of the crest. Breathing hard he said, "Our back trail is clear. Did you find the ambush site?" Rictor nodded and motioned him forward. Dave studied the wreckage and bodies for a long moment. "We can forget about locating the missing Maggit. Even if he's down there he's so fucked up we couldn't identify him."

The wind shifted and the odor was overpowering. Dave spat. "Jesus Christ! Let's get the fuck outta here. I don't see any reason to go down there and expose ourselves to any Charlie that might be watching."

Rictor nodded. "You're probably right, but we might find a usable radio battery. Without one we might as well abort and head back to the capital."

Dave was anxious to get moving, but his appetite for vengeance had not been satisfied. He scanned the high ground west of the road. "Let's figure out how to take a look without getting creamed."

Rictor had already formulated a plan. "Get Lockwood up here. I've got an idea." Motioning the Chinaman closer, Rictor said, "I'm going to ask you to hang your ass way out."

The Chinaman grinned. "You mean it's not hanging out now?"

Rictor suppressed a laugh. "You haven't heard yet what I want you to do."

When Lockwood arrived, Rictor explained, "If we're going to pursue Charlie, we need a battery. There may be one around the trucks. If Charlie is running true to form, he's got an artillery observer up there on the high ground waiting for

ARVN to check out the ambush site. The guns could be any-where, but if I'm right you can bet your ass they're zeroed in on the trucks."

Dave was impatient. "So what's the plan?"

Ignoring the interruption, Rictor continued. "If there's an artillery observer, there's no way he's closer than five hundred yards from the trucks. Nearer than that and he'd run the risk of being hit by his own guns." Rictor pointed to the ridge west of the road. "I see a lot of places up there where an observer could see the road and still be clear of the beating zone." Turning to Dave he said, "You take Lockwood and check out the high ground. If you find an observer, try to take him out without firing. But under no circumstances are you to let him get off a transmission. If you make contact between here and the high ground, fall back to the road a hundred yards north of here. We'll meet you there."

"We'll work our way along the backside of the ridge and come down hill," Dave said. "We'll need an hour."

Rictor checked his watch. "We've got plenty of daylight left." Turning to the Chinaman, he said, "Leave that shotgun with me, put on the VC helmet and make your way down to the road. When you come into the killing zone, walk in like you owned the fuckin' place. Keep the trucks between you and the high ground. If Charlie is up there, he'll probably think you're a VC straggler. In any event he won't fire the artillery at one man, but he may come down to take a look. Olga and I will cover you from here."

Dave motioned for Lockwood to follow and started up the ridge. "Give us half an hour before you put the Chinaman on the road."

Rictor fixed his field glasses on the high ground and searched for signs of VC. He had been observing twenty min-utes when he remembered the map Olga had taken from the wounded VC squad leader. Hoping it might hold some spe-cific clue as to the VC route of withdrawal, he unbuttoned his shirt pocket. As his fingers touched the map he changed his mind and checked the time. Turning his attention back to the high ground he scanned the ridge line. There was no sign of movement. Lowering the glasses he signaled the Chinaman to move out. Rictor saw the Chinaman had the captured AK slung on his right shoulder and the ever present shotgun in the crook of his arm. Concerned the shotgun might compromise the Chinaman, Rictor's impulse was to stop him. Still, the Chinaman was the one taking the risk, so Rictor just watched silently as the man in black worked his way down the road and disappeared.

Fifteen minutes later Rictor was again scanning the high ground when Olga tapped him on the shoulder and pointed to the road. The Chinaman strolled up to the lead truck and peered into the burned-out cab. His curiosity satisfied he moved on. He stopped briefly to investigate an object lying in the road before disappearing behind the second truck. Rictor checked the time. Satisfied that Dave was in position, he told Olga to cover the Chinaman and turned his attention to the high ground.

The Chinaman had worked his way past five trucks when Rictor detected movement on the hillside. He focused the binoculars and spotted two VC slowly working their way toward the killing zone. He alerted Olga and glanced toward the road. The Chinaman stood in front of a truck urinating on the bumper. Certain the Chinaman had not spotted the VC, Rictor considered the options. If he opened fire, he was probably inviting an artillery barrage. If he didn't, he might be sacrificing the Chinaman. While he pondered the dilemma, the advancing VC reached a covered spot sixty yards short of the trucks and well within his rifle range. Hoping Dave could prevent an artillery strike Rictor took careful aim at the nearest VC.

From behind a truck the Chinaman called out in Vietnamese and the VC froze. Rictor held his fire but maintained his aim. The Chinaman's weapons were at the sling position, and he was holding a burned radio in his hands. Stepping into the open the Chinaman called out again. After a brief dialogue with his companion, one of the VC shouted a response. Rictor didn't know what was said, but the exchange was lengthy. Apparently satisfied, one of the VC began working his way down the hill. Certain that the Chinaman could not pass muster face-to-face, Rictor nudged Olga and whispered, "When

257

that Charlie moving toward the trucks spots the Chinaman as a phony, waste him. I'll take the other one."

The advancing VC stopped at the edge of the road. His AK was leveled at the Chinaman's midsection. The Chinaman shook the burned radio and laughed as loose parts fell away from the casing. Speaking in a casual tone he tossed the useless radio aside, motioned the VC to follow and stepped behind the truck. The VC relaxed and followed.

Olga cursed softly. "What now?"

Rictor shook his head. "I don't know, but keep your eye on the Chinaman. It's his show."

The VC on the hillside was getting fidgety. Rictor kept him in his sights and waited.

Five minutes dragged by with no sign of the Chinaman or the VC. Rictor whispered to Olga, "We'll give it five more minutes before taking out the guy on the hillside. If the Charlie behind the truck reappears, kill him."

Olga said, "Fuck it! Hit him now. I'll go down and look for the Chinaman and take car—" The sound of exploding grenades and M16 fire erupted at the top of the ridge. The VC Rictor was watching sprang to his feet and started up the hill. Rictor's M16 rounds caught the VC between the shoulder blades. He was dead before he hit the ground. Rictor shifted his rifle to cover Olga who was sprinting toward the trucks. The Chinaman called out, "Hold your fire! We're coming out." Olga stopped in place, his rifle at the ready. Rictor was only mildly surprised to see the VC step into the clearing with his hands in the air. The Chinaman's shotgun was jammed against his back.

Rictor scrambled down the back side of the hill and took the point as they pulled back along the road to link up with Dave and Lockwood. When he reached the predetermined assembly area, Dave and Lockwood were nowhere in sight. He moved off the road and took up a security position. When Olga and the Chinaman arrived with the prisoner, Rictor saw that the VC was an old man with gaunt features. His sunken eyes were filled with confusion and fear. Figuring at the appropriate time it would be easy to learn anything the old man knew, Rictor asked the Chinaman, "Did you find any batteries?"

The Chinaman shook his head. "There's nothing usable down there." Reaching in his pocket he produced a set of scorched dog tags. "I thought you might want these." Rictor took the tags without comment.

Olga spat. "Why didn't you kill the fuckin' dink! All he's gonna do is slow us down."

The Chinaman studied Olga's face for a long moment. "Sergeant Rictor said he wanted a prisoner. I brought him one." Without taking his eyes off Olga, he continued, "If he don't want him, you can kill him."

Olga cursed.

The Chinaman grinned. "No sweat. I'll do it."

Realizing that he was being admonished, Olga snapped, "I'll do my own killing."

The sound of running footsteps announced the arrival of Dave and Lockwood. Dave came to a sliding halt next to Rictor and dropped to one knee to catch his breath. Rictor saw the radio strapped to his back and nodded approvingly. "Looks like you found Charlie's artillery observer. Have you got people behind you?"

Panting, Dave shook his head, "No. There were eight of the motherfuckers, and we got 'em all."

His face flushed with excitement, Lockwood chimed in. "Man, you should have been there. There was a goddamn mountain of supplies. The sons of bitches had been scavenging the knocked-out convoy and had collected enough equipment to outfit a fuckin' rifle company."

"We came down from above them," Dave added. "They were busy watching the Chinaman and had their backs to us. Like you figured, there was an artillery observer. He had a rifle squad for security and equipment collection. The goddamn stuff was stacked everywhere."

Rictor interrupted. "You sure you got all of them? If not, we'd better get moving."

Lockwood grinned. "They didn't get off a radio message, and we nailed every fuckin' one of them. It was like shooting fish in a barrel. We hit them with grenades and hosed them down with automatic fire. Their fuckin' asses were dead meat before they could get started. It was so sweet I nearly had a goddamn orgasm."

Dave reached in his pocket and produced a map. Holding it out to Rictor, he said, "I took this off the artillery officer. The radio was in one of the equipment piles. It's got squelch so the battery must be good. Lockwood has a couple of extra batteries in his rucksack."

Rictor said, "Give me one of the batteries, Lockwood." Turning to the Chinaman, he continued, "Soon as I get this battery changed, we're moving out. You take the point, cross the road and head south. Skirt wide around the ambush site and keep moving. I'll tell you when to hold up."

Dave said, "By the way, there was some C-4 explosives with the equipment. I set delay fuses. They should start going off anytime now. I don't think Charlie will salvage that goddamn stuff a second time."

Finished changing the battery, Rictor nodded to the Chinaman. "Move out." Glancing to Olga he said, "You bring the prisoner, and I want him alive. You understand?"

Olga cursed, but reached for the lead rope the Chinaman had fastened around the gagged VC's neck. Dave grinned at Olga. "What's the matter, sunshine? Can't I leave you alone ten minutes without you getting in trouble?"

Olga didn't answer. He yanked on the rope propelling the luckless prisoner forward. Dave laughed softly and fell in behind the prisoner.

A thousand yards south of the ambush site, Rictor checked the time and signaled a halt. With two maps to be studied and a prisoner to be interrogated, he wanted to take advantage of the remaining daylight. After sending Lockwood forward to provide early warning, he directed Dave back up the trail for rear security.

Still smarting from having been relegated to prisoner guard, Olga tossed the leash to Dave. "You watch this dink bastard. I'll cover our ass."

Rictor caught Dave's eye and nodded. "That's probably a better idea." Turning to Olga, he said, "Watch yourself. I've gotten used to having you around."

Olga nodded and headed up the trail. Turning back to Dave,

Rictor handed him the captured maps. "You go over these while the Chinaman and I talk to the prisoner."

Rictor took a closer look at the old man. His black pajamas were threadbare and torn. He was undernourished, barefoot and obviously terrified. When the Chinaman removed the gag, Rictor saw that he was also toothless.

Rictor's tone was soft as he addressed the Chinaman. "Tell him that his only chance to stay alive is to tell the truth, and he had better be quick about it." Casting a glance at the sinking sun, he continued, "We don't have much time. I want to know his unit's identification, where the unit is located and what his squad's orders were."

The Chinaman's tone was gentle but firm. After twenty minutes of questioning, it was obvious the old man knew very little about the VC commander's intent.

His squad, as a part of the Q762 Regiment, had participated in the attack on the capital and the subsequent relief force ambush. After the ambush, his squad had been detailed to salvage usable equipment and provide security for the artillery observer. The squad had completed its salvage mission and was waiting for a reinforced mortar squad which was to help transport the equipment to a linkup point with the main VC force. He had been told his squad would be moving out at dark, but he had no idea where the linkup was to take place.

Rictor guessed that the mortar squad they had knocked out near the river was at least a part of the carrying party. He surmised that small outlying units all over the area were moving to join the parent regiment. The only question was where.

Rictor said, "Ask him if the artillery observer was leaving the ambush site with the carrying party." The prisoner nodded and volunteered that the artillery observer had been in charge.

Speaking as much to himself as the others Rictor said, "Either the VC artillery is displacing, or the forward observer was moving to join his unit."

Dave had finished studying the maps and was listening. He spread the maps side by side on the ground. "Take a look at this, Rictor. It may shed some light on the location of the main force." He pointed to the map taken from the VC mortar squad leader. "See this symbol by the river? I think that was

261

the mortar firing position. As you can see it's in easy range of the capital." Dave moved his finger south along the road. "If you check your own map, I think you'll find this is the ambush site." Changing direction with his finger, he moved several hundred yards up the ridge line and tapped the map. "This is where Lockwood and I hit the artillery observer and security squad."

Rictor picked up the map taken from the VC artillery observer and studied it briefly. Noting a mark at the exact spot Dave was pointing to on the other map, Rictor nodded. "So the mortar squad we ambushed was the intended equipment-carrying party."

Dave said, "Look about four inches southwest. You'll find another mark which I can't make out. It's the same spot marked on this map."

Rictor grinned. "Unless they've moved I think you have just found the VC Q762 Regiment."

Dave flushed with excitement. "Holy shit! What do you make of that third symbol on your map? This one doesn't have it."

Rictor studied the mark. It was about eight hundred yards closer than the point he believed to be the *"Q"* regimental assembly area. Using his finger to measure the distance between the unidentified symbol and the relief force ambush site, he saw that both points were well within artillery range. He handed the map to Dave. "Are you certain this is the map taken from the artillery observer?"

Dave nodded. "I took it off his body myself."

Rictor smiled. "Old friend, I figure at worst we just located Charlie's artillery firing positions. At best we've found his artillery battalion assembly area."

"Christ, Rictor! If we've found a main force regiment and an artillery battalion, we're talking a big-time target. Maybe the biggest one so far in this whole fuckin' war!" exclaimed Dave.

Rictor grinned. "You want to have a look?"

Dave laughed. "Are you kidding! We've got a chance to waste more Charlies in one strike than we could ferret out with patrols in six months. Besides these bastards owe us, and it's time to collect."

Rictor nodded. "I figure the mortar squad and security force we knocked off were going to move tonight to join the main force. It's not likely a regimental-size unit would attempt to move in daylight. Even if the regiment breaks up into battalion- or company-size units, they'll be carrying wounded and probably won't move until tomorrow night."

Dave searched the sky through breaks in the thick overhead foliage. He finally located the Air Force spotter plane circling at fifteen hundred feet over the province capital. With his eye on the distant plane, Dave said, "If you're wrong, and they move tonight, we'll follow until we find them. With help from the Air Force we'll smoke their ass."

Rictor nodded. "I don't want to accidentally stumble into Charlie in the dark. You ease down the trail and brief Lockwood. Tell him to move back here when it gets dark. This is where we're spending the night. I'll brief Olga."

Dave indicated the prisoner with a nod. "What about the Charlie? We can't take him with us, and there's no way we can cut him loose."

Rictor said, "I'll work it out, go brief Lockwood."

The Chinaman had monitored the conversation but did not indicate he had been listening.

Rictor caught the Chinaman's eye and held it for a long moment. With the slightest nod of understanding he said, "I'm going to get Olga. I'll be back in ten minutes."

When Rictor returned with Olga, it was twilight. They found Dave busy putting out claymore mines for security.

The Chinaman sat on his rucksack eating cold rations. The prisoner was nowhere in sight.

Olga glanced around. "Where's the Charlie?"

Dave responded, "He tried to escape while Rictor and I were gone. The Chinaman had to kill him. Get over here and help me with these claymores."

Olga did as he was told but made it clear he was still smarting from the Chinaman's scolding. "I told the Chinaman when the time came I'd do my own killing."

Dave said, "Shut the fuck up and get busy!"

Rictor glanced at the Chinaman for a reaction to Olga's remark. Even in the fading light the Chinaman's brief grin was unmistakable.

The night dragged by. Each passing hour seemed longer than the one before. The patrol lay like spokes in a wheel with their feet forming the hub. It had rained most of the night. With the exception of the Chinaman, whose breathing was even and relaxed, the sleep of the patrol members was restless and intermittent.

Rictor had not slept at all. The increased throbbing in his leg and hand told him they were infected. He worked on a plan to confirm the location of the Viet Cong main force assembly areas and coordinate air support. Rictor checked the time and guessed it would be dawn in a half hour. Aware that first light was the most dangerous time for a patrol he reached out to his right and touched Dave's shoulder. Seconds later the Chinaman's light tap on Rictor's left side told him the signal had gone full circle. Without a spoken word the entire patrol was awake and alert.

Ten minutes after daylight, there was no indication of Viet Cong presence. Rictor sent the Chinaman to make a 360-degree close-in reconnaissance. He returned with a negative report. Rictor briefed Lockwood and Olga on his movement plan then sent them back to the security positions they had occupied the previous evening.

Twenty minutes later Rictor finished encoding a message to Major Strong which included a situation report, the patrol's location and a request for standby air support on a priority basis.

Dave had the radio working but was unable to contact the American compound. He adjusted the radio to the air to ground frequency and made contact with the FAC. Dave identified the patrol as Maverick. The FAC responded immediately, "Maverick, I was told to be on the lookout for you. Your Hotel Six (Major Strong) has ordered you to abort. I'm to arrange for an air extraction."

Dave cursed and handed the mike to Rictor. Rictor pushed the talk bar and spoke into the mike. "Bird dog, bird dog, this is Maverick. You're breaking up and garbled, but I've got you in sight. If you are receiving me, waggle your wings." Rictor released the talk bar and waited.

Dave moved ten yards to his right to get a better view through the jungle canopy. Seconds later he grinned. "He's flapping like a turkey."

Rictor pushed the talk bar. "Bird dog, I've got a message for Hotel Six, will you relay?"

The FAC responded, "Roger that. Send your message."

Dave laughed. "He's waggling like crazy."

It took what seemed like an eternity for Rictor to transmit the lengthy coded message phonetically. When he finished the coded message, he added a clear text transmission to the FAC. "If Charlie has any radio finding equipment, he probably has us fixed. So we'll be moving. Maybe we'll find a place where we can receive you better. In the meantime, we'll be on listening silence. Keep your ears open. If we need you, we'll holler."

Rictor turned to Dave. "Get Olga. We're moving." Strapping the radio on his back, he nodded to the Chinaman. "You're on point. I figure we're about five thousand yards northeast of the 'Q' Regiment." He took out his map and indicated the suspected artillery assembly area. "I want you to guide us to a point about midway between the two units. Keeping them to our west." He paused and made visual search of the Chinaman's cartridge belt. "You got a compass?" The Chinaman nodded and reached for his pocket. Rictor continued. "Good, when we pass by Lockwood's security position, leave the road and pick up a southwest heading." He paused. "You're our eyes and ears. Stay far enough out front for early warning, but don't lose visual contact. If we get hit en route, fall back to the road and haul ass for this position. It's our rally point." The Chinaman nodded and headed toward Lockwood's position. Rictor turned to Dave. "You and Olga bring up the rear and keep your eyes open for trackers. If you spot any, try and take them out without firing."

Rictor stepped out on the road. "If we get in a firefight between here and the targets, we'll abort and turn it over to the Air Force."

Dave nodded and winked at Olga. "Pick up the interval behind Rictor. I'll bring up the rear."

Three hours had passed without incident. Rictor figured they had moved about three thousand yards. The terrain had gradually become more steep. The trees were taller, but the undergrowth had thinned and Rictor was concerned about being spotted. Aware that the *"Q"* Regiment would be patrolling the area, he hoped their security would be oriented toward Binh Tien District, where the balance of the ARVN relief force was bogged down. He signaled a halt and reached for his map. Dave eased up next to Rictor. "How much farther?"

Pointing to a ridge line a thousand yards to the west, Rictor said, "If they haven't moved, they're in the valley beyond that ridge. See how the road winds across the south end of the valley? If I was Charlie, that's the way I'd get my artillery out."

Dave nodded. "And I'd have a lot of security up there on that ridge." He paused and let out a sigh. "My ass is dragging. You got any more pills?"

Rictor produced the bottle. "I've got three. We'll share."

Dave took one and popped it in his mouth. "We'd better wind this thing up today."

Rictor took the two remaining pills. "If we can get to the top of the ridge without being detected, that's where we'll set up shop. We'll recon down in the valley. But when the shit starts, I want us on that high ground."

Dave rose to one knee. "Well, let's get to it. If we stay here much longer, I won't be able to get up." Rictor pushed himself to his feet and signaled the Chinaman forward.

A hundred yards from the crest of the ridge Rictor checked his watch; it was 1230 hours. It had taken an hour and a half to move nine hundred yards. He signaled a halt and moved forward to a covered position next to the Chinaman.

For ten minutes they scanned the ridge. There were no signs of Viet Cong. Rictor tapped the Chinaman on the shoulder and pointed to a protected area under a rock overhang ten yards short of the crest. "Move up to the top of the ridge and check the other side as best you can without crossing over. I want you in sight at all times."

The Chinaman nodded and crept forward. Rictor signaled Lockwood to his side. "As soon as the Chinaman gives the all clear, we're going to move up to that overhang one at a time. Pass the word to Olga and Dave."

The Chinaman crawled the last twenty yards to the crest, flattened out next to a tree and lay motionless.

Rictor was impatient. Time dragged. Five minutes went by, then ten. Finally the Chinaman slid back from the crest and gave the all clear signal.

Cautiously Rictor moved forward. When he reached the protection of the overhang, he took up a firing position to cover Lockwood and motioned him forward.

When Lockwood was in position to cover Olga and Dave, Rictor moved from under the overhang. Crawling past the Chinaman, he eased up to the crest.

Studying the dense, double-canopied jungle that covered the valley from side to side, Rictor estimated that it was about eight hundred to a thousand yards wide. The ridge on the far side appeared to be about the same elevation and paralleled the one he was on. He searched for movement or any other signs of the Viet Cong, but the green canopy hid the ground like a mask.

After fifteen minutes of futile searching, he gave up and joined the others under the overhang. "No luck?" asked Dave.

Rictor shook his head. "Not even a woodcutter. The canopy is so goddamn thick, the whole fuckin' North Vietnamese Army could be hiding down there."

"On the other hand they might have already moved," Dave said.

Rictor nodded. "If they have, we're at least a day behind them and running out of steam." He shed his rucksack and strapped on the radio. "The Chinaman and I are going down into the valley and have a look." Indicating Dave's radio, he said, "Stay on the horn. If we get in trouble, we'll call you."

Dave began taking off his rucksack. "I'm going with you."

Rictor shook his head. "If we make contact, we can't run and direct the air attack. That'll be your job." Dave started to

protest. Rictor cut him off. "If you hear firing, call in the Air
Force. If we're not back in forty-five minutes, we won't be
coming back. Get yourself an air extraction."

Dave nodded. "Okay, you're the boss. But if you're not
back in forty-five minutes, we're coming into the valley and
kick ass till we find you."

Rictor checked the time. "It's 1315 hours. Remember what
I said about the extraction."

The Chinaman had shucked all his equipment except the
shotgun, a bandolier of shells and the machete. When Rictor
joined him at the crest the Chinaman grinned and crawled
over. Fifty yards down the hill, he stood up and moved forward. Five yards to his rear Rictor rose to his feet and followed.

Sparse vegetation offered little concealment, and their progress from tree to tree was a slow process. Less than three
hundred yards down the hill the Chinaman froze, then slowly
lowered himself to the ground. Rictor plastered himself
against a tree and waited. He neither saw nor heard movement. The Chinaman pointed to a thin screen of vegetation
thirty yards to the right. Rictor failed to detect movement but
the four barrels of a quad fifty anti-aircraft gun pointing skyward were unmistakable. He slowly let out his breath and
signaled the Chinaman to withdraw to the left.

They had moved less than a hundred yards when Rictor
detected movement to his right. He focused on a black pajama
clad VC squatting in a small clearing. The VC's back was to
Rictor, and his pants were down. He had obviously just finished defecating and was cleaning himself with a leaf.

Slowly unsheathing his machete, the Chinaman inched forward. Rictor stopped him with a head shake.

Finished adjusting his pants, the VC called out something
which Rictor did not understand. A chorus of laughter came
from an undetected group of Viet Cong near the quad fifty.
Rictor watched, motionless, as the VC moved to join his
comrades. When the VC was out of sight, he signaled for the
Chinaman to follow and inched forward. The Chinaman didn't
respond immediately. He was grinning from ear to ear and
obviously trying to suppress a laugh. Rictor failed to see any

humor in their situation. He cursed under his breath, scowled at the Chinaman and signaled again.

From a concealed vantage point fifty yards away, Rictor counted more than forty VC lounging around a second quad fifty and 75mm. howitzer. He checked the time and realized why he had been unable to pick up the normal movement noises made by troops and equipment. It was "Poc" time. The goddamn VC were taking their daily siesta. Silently cursing himself for a fool, Rictor signaled the Chinaman and headed back to the high ground.

From the top of the ridge Dave scanned the hillside for Rictor and the Chinaman. It was 1350 hours, and he was getting fidgety. Detecting movement forty yards down the hill he aimed his M16 and waited. A black pajama clad figure separated himself from a tree and moved forward. Dave saw the sawed-off shotgun and relaxed.

Under the protection of the rock overhang Rictor dropped to one knee. Dave and Lockwood were anxious. "Well?" Dave said.

Rictor grinned. "We found the artillery."

Dave's face showed his pleasure. "You can bet your ass the infantry regiment didn't move out leaving the big guns unprotected. They're still in the valley."

Rictor nodded. "I figure we've got at least fifteen hundred VC and a lot of artillery down there."

Dave's face lost its grin. "That's the good news, here's the bad. After you left, I sent Lockwood a hundred yards down the hill for rear security. About twenty minutes ago he spotted two trackers. They were a long way down the ridge, but we could have company anytime. I've got Olga putting out claymores."

"I guess Charlie checked on the artillery observer and carrying party." Turning to Lockwood he said, "You cover Olga. The Chinaman's watching the valley side of the ridge. Dave and I will work out the air strike plan. If you spot Charlie, blow the claymores and try to buy us some time. We need five minutes."

Dave was already studying the map. "When the strike starts, I don't see how Charlie can pull back to the north. That would put him against the river and in range of the capital artillery."

Rictor nodded agreement. "He's got to run south or come up over the ridges to get out of the beating zones."

Dave said, "He'll never get them heavy guns over the ridges under air attack."

Rictor studied the map. "It's pretty obvious why Charlie wanted to give the illusion he was still deployed around the capital." He pointed to the ridge line with his forefinger and traced it south. "Charlie's trapped in the fuckin' valley. If he runs south and crosses the main road, he'll be caught between the road and the river. That puts him in even worse shape. With this much daylight left, the Air Force would have a turkey shoot."

Dave grinned and began calling out the map coordinates of the VC troop and gun positions.

After recording the coordinates, Rictor dug an orange-colored signal panel out of his rucksack. Handing it to Dave, he said, "Keep your ass down and spread this in the clearing on top of the overhang. I'll move up to the crest with the Chinaman and give cover. When you get through, join us, and let's get this show on the road."

From the crest of the ridge, while keeping watch on Dave, Rictor saw the spotter aircraft circling the capital. When Dave was safely down from the overhang, Rictor pushed the talk bar on the radio mike. "Bird Dog, Bird Dog, this is Maverick, do you copy? Over."

The radio crackled, and the FAC's response was immediate. "Maverick, this is Bird Dog. I've got you loud and clear. How about me? Over."

Rictor said, "Bird Dog, I read you same. Have you got birds standing by? Over."

The FAC responded, "That's affirmative, Maverick."

Rictor said, "Roger that, Bird Dog. Stand by to copy target coordinates."

Rictor removed the pad from his pocket and transmitted the coordinates. "Bird Dog, when you're over the target area, you'll spot our orange identification panel. I suggest you napalm the north end of the valley and roll everything south. Put your gunships on the ridges. We'll spot for you but make goddamn sure the pilots know our location."

The FAC had already turned his ship southwest. "I'll have

birds on station in zero three minutes. I'm gonna take out the anti-aircraft guns first. Stand by."

Rictor watched the spotter plane approach. His adrenaline was high, and he felt a surge of energy. The FAC veered off to the west and positioned himself two thousand feet over the mouth of the valley.

Dave nudged Rictor. "If he gets much closer, he's going to hear from Charlie's quad fifties."

Rictor shook his head. "Charlie'd be crazy to expose his position by firing first."

Dave was unconvinced. "Maybe, but if they're monitoring the radio, they know what's happening."

The radio crackled and the FAC's voice was clear. "Maverick, this is Bird Dog. I've got you in sight. Get your heads down. You got action. Over."

One of Charlie's quad fifties fired at the spotter plane. Four strings of orange tracers arced across the sky, but they were off target. The FAC stood his ship on its nose and fired two white phospherous marking rockets. They exploded in the canopy a hundred yards short of the quad fifty and white smoke boiled up from the trees. Dave pointed to the northeast. His voice was heavy with anticipation and excitement. "Here come the jets!"

B-57 Canberras roared low over the valley. A second quad fifty fired. The lead ship shuddered under the impact of heavy rounds, but the napalm drop was on target. It struck just short of the marking smoke and skip splashed southwest. The overlapping drop from the second and third ships created a river of fire and turned the jungle into a burning hell.

Screams from the VC around the quad fifties were brief but agonizing. From Rictor's left he heard Dave whisper, "Burn, you motherfuckers. Burn!"

The stench of burning flesh drifted up from the valley. Rictor gritted his teeth and watched the jets scream in low. Anti-aircraft fire opened up from six hidden positions, and the sky was filled with tracers. One of the jets took a direct hit and exploded in fiery pieces. Heat from the napalm burned Rictor's face and singed his hair. He cursed and clenched his teeth tighter but kept his eyes glued to the action.

The northern half of the valley was engulfed in fire by the time the first flight of Canberras had made their run. They roared in again at eight hundred feet, dropping five-hundred-pounders. The valley floor erupted under the impact and debris from disintegrating trees filled the air.

Rictor watched as wounded and confused VC gathered in the small clearings made by the bombs. In an effort to escape the sea of napalm they stayed in the open only to be chewed up by relentless gun runs. The FAC had a flight of AIE Sky-raiders standing by at ten thousand feet. When the Q762 Regiment attempted to cross the main road at the south end of the valley, the FAC sent the World War II–vintage Skyraiders into action. Caught in the open, the VC were slaughtered by the hundreds. They attempted to retreat into the valley and ran headlong into a fire storm.

Survivors discarded their weapons and clawed their way up the ridges only to be chopped down by the helicopter gun-ships.

The air strikes moved farther south as the Air Force pressed the routed VC, and then Rictor's patrol was no longer in position to make strike adjustments. Convinced a move south along the ridge line would be suicidal, Rictor was considering requesting an air extraction when claymore mines began exploding to his rear. Small arms fire raked the ridge as Rictor and the Chinaman scrambled forward over the crest. Dave half-crawled and half-rolled down the hill to the overhang.

Small arms fire increased from the overhang side of the ridge. Rictor attempted to crawl back over the crest but was driven back by a hail of fire. From the heavy volume he knew the attacking force was at least a platoon and the sounds of exploding grenades told him the VC were close.

Pointing to the rock ledge over Dave's position, Rictor motioned for the Chinaman to follow. Once on the ledge, he crawled forward of the signal panel and peered over the edge. He was in an exposed position and immediately attracted small arms fire. Figuring if he stayed low and didn't get flanked, the angle was too great for the VC fire to be effective, he flattened out.

The Chinaman's shotgun spoke, and Rictor glanced to his

right in time to see a VC roll down the hill. Rictor cupped his hands and yelled for Dave at the top of his voice. The rattle of M16 fire from below the ledge was almost continuous. He yelled again. This time Dave responded, yelling, "Get us some air cover! There must be a hundred of the bastards, and they're just out of grenade range. If they assault, we've had the course."

The Chinaman's shotgun blasted three times in rapid succession, and small arms rounds ricocheted off the ledge.

Concerned about being flanked, Rictor shouted to Dave, "Put your radio on the emergency frequency and monitor. I'm going to get us some air cover and set up an extraction."

When radio contact was established, the FAC said he couldn't break off the strike. He advised Rictor to switch to the emergency frequency and contact the chopper gunships direct. He added that Hotel Six was airborne and directing the gunships.

Rictor switched frequencies and within seconds had Major Strong on the radio. Shortly after he briefed the major as to the situation, he saw three gunships farther south break off the attack, form up and head his way.

Rictor eased up to the lip of the overhang and peered down. A group of thirty or more VC had formed a skirmish line and were advancing. Supported by VC hidden in the trees, their fire was withering.

The fire from Dave's position was continuous and took its toll but the VC kept advancing. At a distance of thirty yards the VC ran into a dozen grenades thrown from under the ledge. The deadly shrapnel gouged holes in the skirmish line and half the VC went down. The survivors dragged themselves down the hill and regrouped.

Rictor had fired too long on full automatic and his rifle had overheated. The hand guard was smoking and threatened to catch on fire. As he jammed a fresh magazine into the rifle, small arms fire from the rear told him they had been flanked. The Chinaman's shotgun fired six times in rapid succession and the small arms rounds from the rear stopped. Rictor realized the shotgun was empty and glanced over his shoulder. The Chinaman was trying to reload but had taken a round in the shoulder and was having difficulty.

Rictor watched the gunships come in, followed closely by two slick transports. The radio came alive. "Maverick, this is Hotel Six, and we've got you in sight. Where do you want the hardware?"

Rictor spoke into the mike. "A hundred yards due east of the panel, and we need it now. They're regrouping for an assault."

The major said, "Roger that. Stand by."

The rocket runs were on target, and the VC caught in the beating zone were ground up like hamburger. From farther down the hill, the VC clear of the strike zone returned fire and hit one of the gunships. Trailing smoke, it broke off the attack and limped toward the capital.

Major Strong came on the radio. "Maverick, this is Hotel Six. We've used up all our rockets. We're going to continue to make gun runs on the VC farther down the hill, but there's a lot of them and I don't know how long we can hold them. Get your people up on the ledge. We're going to get you out."

Rictor saw the gunships turn to begin another run. There was a lull in the fire as the VC attempted to regroup. He yelled down to Dave, "When the gunships make their next run, set a delay charge, leave your equipment and try to make it up here. We're going out."

Dave shouted back, "It'll take some time. Lockwood's bad gut shot. I don't think he's gonna make it."

Rictor cursed. "We don't have much fuckin' time."

Dave's response was barely audible. "We'll have to carry him."

Rictor motioned the Chinaman to his side. Pointing to the shotgun, he said, "Can you still fire that thing?" The Chinaman nodded and moved forward.

Rictor shouted to Dave, "Get moving! Here come the gunships!"

When Dave and Olga, supporting the dying Lockwood, cleared the overhang, Rictor saw that Lockwood's intestines were dangling almost to his knees. He cursed and fired frantically.

Olga took a round in the right thigh, let go of Lockwood and fell to his knees.

274

Dave attempted to support Lockwood's weight, but he was too heavy. Both of them pitched backward and rolled head over heel down the hill. Dave hit a tree and came to an abrupt stop. Lockwood stopped five yards away.

The encouraged VC increased their fire and crept forward. Cursing with every breath Rictor crawled off the ledge to help Olga, who was crawling toward the crest. Glancing down the hill he saw Dave, dazed from impact with the tree and bleeding from a head wound, staggering toward Lockwood. Rictor saw what was about to happen. He opened his mouth to shout out in protest but choked it off and watched silently as Lockwood put the barrel of his 45 in his mouth and pulled the trigger.

Rictor cursed and grabbed Olga by the arm. "Come on, Olga. You're one fuckin' expendable that's getting outta here alive."

The gunships came in low with all guns blazing and flew tight circles over the VC concentration, firing continuously. When Rictor and Olga reached the ledge, one of the slick transport ships peeled off and came barreling in for the extraction. Rictor shouted encouragement to Dave who was struggling up the hill. Aware Dave would not make it in time, he charged down the slope to help him. Dragging Dave by the belt, he got back to the ledge as Olga was being dragged aboard the hovering ship.

Small arms fire from the valley side of the ridge raked the chopper. The crew chief took a hit in the chest and fell backward inside the chopper.

Rictor pushed Dave aboard and turned to help the Chinaman. The pilot revved the engine and began lifting off. Olga screamed for Rictor and the Chinaman to grab the landing strut and hold on.

Rictor grabbed hold and was immediately lifted off the ledge. Ten feet in the air he looked down and saw the Chinaman had been left behind. He released his grip and fell back to the rocky ledge. The impact was devastating, pain shot through his body like an explosion. The radio had partially broken his fall but was smashed in the process. Rictor discarded the useless radio, recovered his rifle and crawled back to the lip of the overhang.

The Chinaman eased up next to Rictor. "I tried to hold on but couldn't. You should not have come back."

Rictor studied the Chinaman's bleeding shoulder for a long moment. The bullet had passed all the way through. Shifting his eyes to the Chinaman's face, he held up his hand. The infected wound had burst open, and blood flowed freely. "What makes you think I came back? I've only got one working hand myself."

The Chinaman grinned. "Yeah, I know."

Rictor turned his attention to the gunships. They were still circling but had quit firing. He suspected they were running low on ammunition. Movement caught his eye as some of the more determined VC inched their way up the hill.

Rictor put the M16 fire selector on semi-automatic to conserve ammunition and took well-aimed shots.

The gunships buzzed the VC but didn't fire. Convinced the chopper guns were empty the VC left their covered positions and charged the overhang. They broke into the open, and Rictor cut down several easy targets. When his M16 clicked empty on the last magazine he dropped the rifle and yanked out his pistol.

The Chinaman fired his last shell, laid the shotgun aside, threw his remaining grenades and unsheathed his machete.

The screech of straining aircraft engines grew loud in Rictor's ears. He glanced to the south. Three Skyraiders in trail were barreling down the ridge at two hundred feet. Rictor flattened out and buried his face in the rocky dirt.

High-explosive rockets caught the VC in the open and cut them to ribbons. Body parts and flying debris rained down on the ledge. The third ship roared by, and Rictor raised his head. Peering over the ledge he saw several dazed and wounded VC dragging themselves toward the wood line, leaving behind their dead and dying comrades.

Rictor was watching the Skyraiders turn for another run and failed to see the slick coming in from the south. The Chinaman grabbed him by the shoulder and pointed. Thirty seconds later the slick was hovering over the ledge.

Rictor saw Major Strong leaning out the door. He shoved the Chinaman up to the major's waiting arms and went back to the lip of the overhang. Returning to the slick he tossed the Chinaman's shotgun aboard and scrambled in behind it.

Major Strong grabbed Rictor in a bear hug. He didn't speak, but Rictor was sure he spotted tears in the major's eyes.

As the chopper gained altitude, Rictor had a good view of the valley. It was on fire from one end to the other, and the Air Force was still hammering away. He looked at the major. "For a minute there, I thought we were going to have to walk back to the capital."

The major grinned. "We're not going to the capital. You're going to join Dave and Olga at the Navy Hospital in Saigon."

Rictor nodded and watched silently as the crew chief placed a pressure bandage on the Chinaman's shoulder. Satisfied that the bleeding was stopped, the crew chief lit a cigarette, extended the pack to Rictor and held out his lighter. Rictor took two cigarettes, lit both of them, reached over and stuck one in the Chinaman's mouth. Leaning close he asked, "When we were down there in the valley, what did that Charlie taking a shit say that was so damn funny?"

The Chinaman grinned briefly, then broke out laughing. "He called to his friends that he had just shit a giant American snake and needed help killing it."

Rictor rolled his eyes. "Amazing, utterly fuckin' amazing!" He lay down next to the Chinaman, and they laughed hysterically.

Glossary

"A" Detachment: Twelve-man U.S. Army Special Forces Operational Detachment

AR: 30-caliber automatic rifle

ARVN: Army of Republic of Vietnam

"B" Detachment: U.S. Army Special Forces Command and Control Detachment for "A" Detachments with Operational Capability

"C" Detachment: U.S. Army Special Forces Command and Control Detachment for "B" Detachments with Operational Capability

Charlie: Slang for Viet Cong.

CP: Command post

District: Geographical subdivision of a province (not unlike a county)

District Chief: Military commander and civilian administrator of a district

DMZ: Demilitarized Zone separating North and South Vietnam

DZ: Drop zone for receiving parachuted supply and/or personnel

FAC: Forward air controller

LZ: Landing zone for aircraft

MAC-V: (MACV) Military Advisory Command Vietnam

Maggit: A slur for MAC-V

II Corps: One of the four military regions of South Vietnam (Central Highlands)

Montagnards: Tribespeople who inhabit the Central Highlands of South Vietnam

Napalm: Jellied gasoline

Noung: Chinese ethnic mercenary

Province: Geographical subdivision of South Vietnam (not unlike a state)

Province Chief: Military commander and civilian administrator of a province

Recon: Reconnaissance Unit

RF: Regional Force (Vietnamese Provincial National Guard)

SF: American Special Forces

Slick: Lightly armed or unarmed transport helicopter

Skyraider: Single-Engine heavily armed World War II–vintage attack aircraft

Swedish-K: 9 mm. submachine gun made in Sweden

Uncle Ho: Ho Chi Minh (North Vietnamese leader)

USOM: United States Overseas Mission (administration for the dispersal of aid)

VC: Viet Cong

Viet Cong: Informal name for the guerrilla force that, with the support of the North Vietnamese Army, fought against South Vietnam and the Unites States.

Viet Minh: Guerrilla forces which fought the French in Vietnam

VNSF: Vietnamese Special Forces

Zipperhead: Ethnic slur for Vietnamese